THE OBSERVATIONS

JANE HARRIS

The Observations

faber and faber

First published in 2006
by Faber and Faber Limited
3 Queen Square London WC1N 3AU

Typeset by Faber and Faber Limited
Printed in England by Mackays of Chatham, plc

A CIP record for this book
is available from the British Library

ISBN 978-0-571-22335-0
ISBN 0-571-22335-4

2 4 6 8 10 9 7 5 3 1

For Tom – without whose opinions, encouragement and love this book might never have been written

My missus she often said to me, 'Now then Bessy, don't be calling me missus.' She said this especially when the minister was coming for his tea. My missus wanted me to call her 'marm' but I always forgot. At first I forgot by accident and then I forgot on purpose just to see the look on her face.

My missus was always after me for to write things down in a little book. She give me the book and pen and ink the day I arrived. 'Now then Bessy,' says she, 'I want you to write down your daily doings in this little book and I'll take a look at it from time to time.' This was after she found out I could read and write. When she found that out her face lit up like she'd lost a penny and found sixpence. 'Oh!' says she, 'and who taught you?' And I told her it was my poor dead mother, which was a lie for my mother was alive and most likely blind drunk down the Gallowgate as usual and even if she was sober she could barely have wrote her own name on a magistrates summons. But my mother never was sober if she was awake. And when she was asleep, she was unconscious.

But wait on. I am getting ahead of myself. Let me begin nearer the beginning.

PART ONE

1

I Find a New Place

I had reason to leave Glasgow, this would have been about three four years ago, and I had been on the Great Road about five hours when I seen a track to the left and a sign that said 'Castle Haivers'. Now there's a coincidence I thought to myself, because here was I on my way across Scratchland to have a look at the Edinburgh castle and perhaps get a job there and who knows marry a young nobleman or prince. I was only 15 with a head full of sugar and I had a notion to work in a grand establishment.

Not only that but this lad from the Highlands had fell into step with me the past hour, he would have been about my age and he had been to get a tooth pulled. He kept dragging his lip down to show me the hole. I was sick of this boy and his grin and his questions, fair are you going? fair do you live? fwot is your name? fwould you like to lie down with me? – all this. I had told him a whole clatter of lies hoping he would go away but he was stuck to me like horse dung on a road sweepers shoe. If I slowed down he slowed down, if I sped up he sped up, if I stopped to fix my shawl or shift my bundle, what did he do but stand with his hands in his pockets to watch. Once or twice he got a jack on him would have put your eye out, you could see it poking behind the trousers, and the feet on him were filthy.

I have to admit there was one added factor in my desire to leave the Great Road and that was the pair of polis that was coming towards us on horseback. Big buckers by the look of them. I had spotted them in the distance five minutes back, their top hats and big buttons, and ever since I had been looking for a way off the road, one that didn't involve me running across a field and getting mucked up to the oxters.

So I stopped walking and turned to the Jocky. 'This is where I go off,' I says, pointing at the sign to the castle.

'I fwhill be coming with you,' he says. 'Hand you can be making me dinner. Hand hafterwards fwhee can be making a baby.'

'What a good idea,' says I and when he stepped forward as if to kiss me I grabbed his danglers and give them a twist. 'Make your own babies,' I says. 'Now away and flip yourself.'

Off I went up the lane and when he followed me I gave him a shove and a few more flip offs and stamped on his bare foot and that was the last I seen of him, for a while anyway.

The lane to the castle wound up a slope between two beech hedges. It was September but uncommon warm and lucky for me as I had no coat. After I had been walking about a minute there was the faint thud of hoofs on dirt and I turned to look back at the Great Road. The two grunts trotted past on their way towards Glasgow. Did they even turn their heads, did they buckie. Hurrah, says I to myself and good flipping riddance. What I always say is if you can avoid the scrutiny of the law then why not.

With them out the way I thought I would have a quick skelly at the castle then find somewhere to sleep before it got dark. I had only 6 Parma violets and two shillings to my name and Gob only knew when I would get more, so I could ill afford a room. But I was hoping for a barn or a bothy where I could lay my head a few hours then press on to Edinburgh once it got light.

I had gone no more than two steps when what did I see but a red-haired country girl about my age come skittering round the corner. She wore a dark stuff frock and plaid shawl and she was dragging a box along the ground by means of a leather strap. Even though she was in a queer hurry, she was laughing away to herself like a woman possessed. The most notable thing about her was her skin, very rough and red it was like she had had a go at her phiz with a nutmeg grater. I stepped out her road and gave her good afternoon as she passed. But she just cackled in my face and carried on stumbling towards the Great Road, dragging her box behind her, there was not much would surprise me then nor now, but all the same you expect more manners from country folk.

The lane in front of me dipped right then left through fields, climbed again and after about ten minutes walking it passed the gate of a big mansion house in amongst a scutter of trees. I could see no castle but there was a woman running about the gravel drive and lawn. This way and that she went, waggling her hands in the air and every so often clapping. At first I thought she was gobaloon but then I looked over the wall and seen she was only chasing a pig. It looked like tremendous fun.

'Wait on, missus,' I says, 'I'll give you a hand.'

Did you ever try to catch a pig? It's not as easy as you think. That bucker had us running in circles. He shot round the back of the house to the yard and we followed. I nearly got him the once but he was a slippery old wretch he squirmed out my grasp like he was buttered. I would have dove after him but I did not want to ruin my good frock. Your woman kept shouting instructions to me, 'Quickly!' she goes and 'Watch out!' She was English, I realised. I had met English people before but never an English woman. At last the two of us cornered the pig by the hen run. We chased him along a fence then shooed him back into the sty and your woman slammed the gate shut.

I watched her as she stood there panting a moment or two. She would have been about 27 then. Her back was slender though it looked as though she didn't wear stays. And the colour was high in her cheeks with all the running but you could see by her forehead that her skin was pale as cream, there was not a freckle on her, she was alabaster. The frock she wore was silk, a watery shade, more blue than green, she struck me as being shockingly well dressed for running about after pigs.

In due course she got her breath back. 'Treacherous trollop,' she says through her teeth. For a minute I thought she was talking about the pig until she added, 'If I ever see her again, I'll take her and I'll –' She clenched her fists but did not finish the sentence.

The red-haired girl dragged her box through my minds eye. 'Did somebody do you wrong, missus?' I says.

Your woman looked at me startled, I think she had forgot I was there. 'No,' she says. 'The gate of the sty was left open. Probably an accident.' Then she frowned at me and says, 'What are you exactly?'

This threw me into confusion. 'What am I?' I says. 'Well, I was a – I suppose you could say I was a housekeeper for a –'

'No, no,' she says. 'What I mean is are you a Highlander?'

'Indeed not,' I says most indignant. 'I've never been near the Highlands.' She was still looking at me so I says, 'I was born Irish. But I'm more of the Scottish persuasion now.'

She seemed pleased enough about that. 'Irish,' she says. While we was chasing the pig two or three strands of her hair had fell down and now she gazed at me very thoughtful as she pinned them back up. You could have floated in her eyes they was that wide, and pale green like the sea over sand. At length she says, 'A housekeeper?'

'Yes, missus. For a Mr Levy of Hyndland, near Glasgow.'

'I don't think I ever saw a housekeeper in such bright clothes,' she says. Her mouth gave a twitch, like she might laugh, perhaps the sight of my frock cheered her up. It was a beauty, right enough, bright yellow with little blue buttons and white satin bows at the front, admittedly it was not as clean as when I had set out that morning. There was a smudge at the hem and the lace was ripped this was because the Highland boy had at one stage got me pinned to the ground, I had to near enough wrench his ear off before he let me up.

'I am between places,' I says. 'My Mr Levy he died on me and I am just now on my way to Edinburgh to find another situation.'

'I see,' says your woman. She folded her arms and took a turn around me, studying me from a few different angles. When she came back to face me, she looked doubtful. 'I don't suppose you've ever done any outdoors work?' she says.

'Well, as a matter of fact I have,' I says, and without a word of a lie too, for a good deal of my work was outdoors before I was taken in by my Mr Levy.

Your woman nodded. 'What about cows?' she says.

'What about them?'

'Can you milk a cow?'

'Oh certainly,' I says without hesitation. 'A cow, yes, I can milk a cow, that's no problem at all, I was born milking cows.'

'Good.' She indicated some buildings in the distance. 'We keep a farm over there, the Mains. You can have something to eat and drink and then let's see you milk a cow.'

'Ah well,' says I quick, 'it's a while since I done it now.'

But I don't think she heard me because she didn't reply, just led me across the yard to the pump and give me a tin cup that was hanging on a nail. 'Help yourself,' she says.

I drank two cupfuls. All the while she was watching me with those eyes. I says, 'I might be a bit out of practice with the cows now. I may have lost the knack, I don't know.'

'Are you hungry?' she says.

Gob was I and I tellt her as much. She pointed to a door in the house. 'There's bread in there on the table,' she says. 'Take a slice.'

'That's very kind of you, missus,' I says and did as I was bid.

The kitchen was a fair size but Jesus Murphy was it a shambles. A pail of milk had been overturned and there was lines of oats scattered on the floor and a smashed teapot laying against the skirting board. When I stepped in, a black cat was lapping at the spilled milk but as soon as it seen me it ran out another door with a yowl. I peered about me. The fire was out but there was a terrible scorched smell in the air. At first I wondered was it the runaway pig had made the mess. But when I looked more closely I seen that the oats had been scattered deliberately, in actual fact the lines of them formed four letters of the alphabet to spell a vulgar expression for a ladys private parts, I will not write it here but I thought to myself it would have to have been the very clever pig done that.

There was no sign of any cook or maid, so I cut myself a slice of oat bread from the loaf on the table and ate it and then I cut another one and I started to eat that and while I was eating I cut a 3rd slice and tucked it down my frock between my two titties. The bread lacked salt but I would have ate the snibs off the windows I was that hungry. As I threw the bread into me, I was wondering how difficult can it be to milk a cow. You grab the dangler bits and pull, for dear sake I had seen it done manys a time as I swanned about on market day only not close at hand. I was a city girl, milk came in a pail and went in your tea, I did not even like milk and now because of my own stupid pride I would have to squeeze it out a cow.

I cut another slice of bread and stashed that in my frock just in case then I went back outside, your woman was where I left her by the pump.

'There you are,' she says. 'I thought you were lost.'

'Oh, no missus, only it was such marvellous bread I didn't want to rush the slice.'

She didn't say anything about that, she just sniffed and turned on her heel. I hared after her. 'That's a tremendous place you have here,' I called out. 'By Jove it is.' But my words fell on deaf ears she did not even turn her head, I had no choice but to follow.

We walked away from the mansion house, up a back lane that led to the farm buildings and from there across a yard and into a big shed. The place was heaving with cows there was about twenty of them which is a lot of cows when you think about it and even when you don't. The stench in there would have knocked you down. There was two milkmaids stood talking up the far end, sisters by the looks of them, all dressed up in the cornthrasher duds they were, the boots and striped aprons. I near enough laughed out loud. To my mind they looked a right pair of bogtrotters but then I was only young and thought that anything in the country was to be looked down upon and mocked. Your woman went and spoke to them and then the two maids turned and stared down the length of the byre at me, their caps was comical but you would not have said their expressions was friendly. I gave them a smile and a wave, neither one of them waved back. The sour phiz on the pair of them, it is an unexplained miracle how the milk did not turn on a daily basis.

All this while, one of the cows was shoving her great behind up onto me until she near enough had me pinned against the wall. I had to juke out the way to save myself from being squashed. Your woman came back towards me holding a bucket.

'What a grand lot of cows you have, missus,' I says to her. She said nothing to that just handed me the bucket. I looked at it. Then I looked at the cows. Then I looked at your woman.

'What is your name?' she says.

'My name is Bessy,' I told her. 'Bessy Buckley.'

'Well then, Bessy, here you are,' she says and she give me a stool and pointed to one of the cows, the one had been squashing me. 'Go ahead.'

To my great relief she did not stay to watch, but went back to talk to the Curdle Twins who had sat themselves down and begun their own work. You could hear the milk firing into their pails like billy-o. I watched them, thinking to myself well gob that looks easy enough and so after a moment I settled on my own stool.

But could I get a drop of milk to appear? Could I flip. I sat there for what felt like an age with a bucket in one hand and a great pink tittie in the other. It wasn't my own tittie, it was the cows and it was that full it was touching the floor. I swear I squeezed till the fingers was dropping off me and the only thing that emerged from the cow came steaming out its hole and would near enough have ruined my good frock if I hadn't skipped out the way. At the end of about 20 minutes, the bucket was still empty.

Your woman came back this time with the Curdle Twins in her wake. She took one look in the bucket and says to me, 'Now then, Bessy, I thought you said you could milk a cow?'

'I lied,' I says, wishing I had never stopped to help with her flipping pig. The Curdle Twins was exchanging glances, very superior in the background, shock almighty, oh she said she could milk a cow but she can't oh she's a liar did you ever hear the like, and all this. My face felt hot. I shot up from the stool. It was my intention to say 'I'd better be off,' and then stride out with my head in the air but I must have got up too quick, and instead I said, 'Oh flip,' and keeled over in a dead faint. I would have fell in the cowpat if missus hadn't leapt forward and caught me.

How long I was out I haven't a notion but when I came to I had been carried out the byre. I was sat on a stool with my head between my legs and your woman had her hand in the back of my frock, she was loosing my corset. I had a good view down my bodice, there was a load of breadcrumbs in the cleft of my bosom, I had to fold my arms to stop them falling out.

'Keep still now,' your woman says, but kindly. 'You fainted. And no wonder with your stays laced so tight.'

After a while she let me sit up and brought me a tin cup of milk that she got from a bucket. She stood with her hands on her hips watching me. I was full of shame, I sipped at the milk just to please her and as soon as my head cleared I got to my feet. 'I best be going,' I says. 'Sorry, missus.'

She just nodded her head and waved her hand, I was dismissed.

I left the farmyard and went down the lane to the back of the big house. My bundle lay where I'd dropped it, near the hen run. I was about to pick it up when I seen your woman returning. A thought struck me and I called out to her. 'Missus, which way is the castle?'

'Castle?' she says. 'What castle?'

'Only the sign down the road there said there was a castle up this way and I wanted to have a look at it.'

'Ah,' she says and shook her head. 'There is no castle. Castle Haivers is the name of the estate.'

'Oh well,' I says and leaned down to pick up my bundle. 'Not to worry.'

'WAIT!' goes your woman, of a sudden.

Oh sugar, I thought, she's seen the bread in my bosom and I'm in for it. I straightened up. She was staring at me, her head cocked to one side. 'You didn't tell me you could read,' she says.

'Well you never asked,' I says.

'I just assumed. I thought – because –'

She did not say because why but I knew anyway it was me being only an Irish girl, everyone thought the same. Her eyes was gleaming now. 'But can you write?'

'Indeed I can,' I says. 'I write very good.'

'In English?'

I looked at her. 'What else?'

'Oh?' she says. 'And who taught you?'

I thought a second then I says, 'My mother, God rest her soul,' and I blessed myself.

Your woman tilted back a bit offended, I suppose it would have been the sign of the cross bothered her, even the English don't like it.

'Wait here,' she says, and hared away over to the big house.

I stood there looking about me. What next I was asking myself, perhaps she wants me to read something for her or write a letter. After a while she came back with a blotter in one hand and a pen in the other.

'Here you are,' she says. 'Now show me your writing.' She was not going to take me at my word not after the incident with the cow, who could blame her.

I took the pen, it was already dipped in ink. There was a stone base to the pump, I leaned the blotter on it and quickly wrote a few words I think they was *thank you for the bread missus sorry about the duplicity* or something like that. I remember I put *duplicity* because it was a word I had learned off my Mr Levy. I might not be able to milk a cow but I could spell and I was proud of it.

Your woman was watching over my shoulder. I would have wrote more but the ink run out. When I finished I handed her back the pen and blotter. 'Well, well,' she says, and laughs very gay. 'And how old are you, Bessy?'

'18 missus.' Which did not really count as a lie because I was always lying about my age. In any case there was some doubt about when I'd been born, my mother had not a very good memory for dates.

'18?' Your womans eyebrows shot up. Then she says, 'Well, no matter. I can pay you 4 shillings a week and you will have bed and all food provided. Would you like to work for me?'

'Oh dear,' I says. 'Oh no. I'm going to look for work in Edinburgh, missus.'

She laughed. 'But you don't have to go to Edinburgh now,' she says. 'You can stay here and I will look after you and give you 4 and 6 a week.'

'But – I can't really milk a cow, missus.'

'You have other skills,' she says. '5 shillings then, and I will look after you and give you a patch of garden to grow what you will.'

I tellt her she could forget about the patch of garden, the only thing I was interested in growing was rich. Of course there was little chance of that. 5 shillings was a pittance even in them days but I knew my prospects would be the same anywhere else and at least here I was out of the world, all there was in these parts was clodhoppers cows and a few coal pits. And there was something else made her words appealing. *I will look after you.*

I glanced over at the farmhouse. 'Do you have any books in there, missus? I mean story books.'

'Oh yes,' she says. 'Quite a number.'

'I have a fondness for reading,' I says. 'If I could have permission to read the books on occasion –'

'Hmm.' She sighed and walked about a bit and then at length seemed to come to some sort of *very reluctant* decision. 'Very well,' she says. 'Access to books. And 5 shillings a week.'

'Done,' I says, and I can honestly say I thought it a bargain.

She took me into the kitchen then and without making any comment about the smell of burning or the mess she kicked some of the oats about the place so you could no longer read the word they spelt. Then she sat me at the table to explain the full extent of my duties. Well, if you had wrote it down, the list would have been as long as your arm but it all seemed straight forward enough, there was nothing strange or startling in what she said. Most of the livestock was kept over on the farm and was looked after by farm servants but your woman said she liked to keep a few hens and a pig at the main house, more or less as pets, and I was to feed them. I was to keep the house clean and tidy, wash cook scrub sweep dust shake the mats and make tea. Every day, light all the fires and clean the range and keep it lit. Clean the boots empty the thunder mugs for her and the master. In addition, if they were short-handed, I might have to cart manure and pick stones out a field, then I might have to help put these same stones in holes in another field which, she said, was to make a drain. I'd have to help look after the vegetable garden and if I had any time left over I could always fill it by darning and mending. Generally, I had to do any chore you cared to mention since I was to be what they called the in and out girl, ½ the time I would be in and then the other ½ out. There were farm servants that lived on the farm and in bothies on the other side of the wood but I was the only domestic servant. The one thing she did not mention was the milking. I asked her about that.

'Oh,' she says. 'Don't worry about that for now. Jessie and Muriel will see to the cows. You would only have to help them out it in case of an emergency.'

That tickled me. Now what would be the emergency, I wondered. I got a picture in my head of everyone running around in a panic falling over each other to get the cows milked. Wash the pots, Bessy! Make a drain! I can't missus I have to milk the cows it's an emergency!

Your woman was looking at me. 'Don't tell me you are a daydreamer,' she says.

'Oh no, missus.'

'But perhaps you are lazy? Or bad-tempered?'

I shook my head. 'No indeed.'

She says, 'Are you, let me see – dishonest?'

She had me there, because of the cows. But I wasn't going to admit to it. 'No missus I am not,' I says. 'Not in the usual course of things.'

Your woman didn't look convinced. 'Now then, Bessy,' she says. 'Tell the truth and shame the Devil.'

My mother was forever telling me I wouldn't know the truth if it flew up my skirt and said 'How do you do.'

I says, 'Honest to Gob, missus, I'm not a liar.' And would have spat to swear my word except we was inside, so I just did three small pretend spits over my shoulder. Your woman looked appalled, I don't know why she was bothered, the place was a shambles.

'Bessy,' she says, 'I don't know what you have been taught, but don't *ever* do that in this house again.'

'Sorry, missus. But missus I only said that about the cows because I wanted you to think well of me.'

She sighed and then says very patient, 'Bessy dear, what did you call the lady where you last worked?'

'Nothing at all,' I says.

She looked at me.

'The reason being there was no missus, it was just my Mr Levy. He was an old bachelor gentleman and it was just me and one boy looked after him, missus.'

'Oh,' she says and frowned a moment. 'But I'm sure you called Mr Levy Master or Sir, did you not?'

'Well yes, I suppose I did.' I says that because it was what she wanted to hear. 'Master, that's what he liked to be called. Master this and Master that.'

'Bessy,' she says now very solemn. 'I would like you to call me *marm*.'

'Certainly I will. Whatever you like, marm.'

She smiled at me and nodded. 'That's better,' she says. She took a deep breath. 'Now Bessy,' she says. 'There is one other task that I want you to do for me.' And the way she made her eyes bulge out when she said it I knew it was the most important thing.

She crossed over to a tallboy and took an accompt book out the cupboard. Jesus Murphy, I thought, she wants me to do the accompts, she's got the wrong girl there for I might be able to write but I have never had a head for figures. But I was wrong.

'This book is yours,' she says and pressed it into my hands. 'Now Bessy, listen carefully. I will see to it that you are taught everything you need to know about the work about the house. But in return, every night, I want you to take the time to write down what you have done in this book, from the moment you get up until the moment you go to bed, leaving nothing out.'

I just looked at her. 'But what for missus?' I says, a bit nonplussed. 'Marm.'

She didn't even blink. 'Because it is what I wish,' she says. 'And be aware, it is the main condition of your employment. Don't think I would take you on if you couldn't write. It would not be worth my while to train you otherwise since it's clear you know nothing of this kind of work.'

Ever since I had scribbled those few words on the blotter she had seemed very excited. Even now there was a kind of a gleam in her eye and she was breathing heavy. I shivered, for the light was going and it was getting cold.

She says, 'I will take a look at what you have written from time to time. And when you have filled this book I will provide you with another. Is that understood?'

'Yes, miss – I mean marm.'

I stared at the book, it had a brown cover made of board and a lot of pages inside with lines on them where you could add up the totals of your purchases. I don't know how many pages perhaps a hundred in all. I could never imagine writing enough to fill it not in a million years. She handed me the pen I had used outside and then she says, 'You will need ink, just a moment,' and hurried out the room, the hem of her skirt trailing oats into the passage.

While she was gone, I glanced at the grate wondering did she ever in gobs name light the fire. It was then I seen the reason for the charred smell in the air. I don't know why but it made me shiver again. For laying among the ashes was an accompt book the exact same as the one I had been given. The only difference being that the book in the grate was burnt so bad that only the binding and a few pieces of its scorched cover remained. I took a candle and peered down at the hearth to have a better look. Up close I could see that all the pages had been ripped out and was now just wispy ashes in the grate. The cover was damp, as though someone had poured water on it to douse the flames. I flipped it open. Inside there was an inscription in a childs hand, the words was ½ scorched but you could still read 'belongs to Morag Sutherland' and a date in July but no year was given. Who was this child Morag, I wondered and why was her book burnt? I was about to lift it out the grate when I heard your woman coming back down the passage, so I stood up.

'Here we are!' she says, as she came back in. 'Now, hold out your hands, Bessy,' she says and I did as I was bid. Then she presented me with a bottle of ink and a spare pen, the way she done it with such ceremony for dear sake you would have thought she was giving you a prize.

And then, true to her word she did give me something to read, it was called *Bleak House*, I hoped it wasn't an omen. She showed me a label she had pasted inside, a black and white label, it had a picture of two ladies sat under a tree looking at an open book. Around the edge were the words EX~BIBLIOTHEC~CASTEL~HAIVERS. Every one of her books had that same label, she seemed to think it would stop them being stolen.

After that, she showed me where I was to sleep. She give me a candle and took one herself then led me out the kitchen into the hall. It was a drafty old house and the flickering light threw great shadows to dance against the walls, I had a glimpse of a hallstand and grandmother clock and then the banisters loomed as we turned up the stairs.

Up we went, along the main landing where all the doors was shut so you could not see into the rooms. I was a bit sad about that, I would have liked a look around. At the end of another narrower passageway we climbed a short flight of stairs to a little attic room with a sloping roof and skylight window. There was just enough space to fit a bed, a chair and a small cupboard, no more than that and certainly not two people which is why the missus stood outside, her candle held aloft for me to see my new domain. You could have took it in with one eye shut.

'This will be where you sleep,' she says.

'Very nice,' says I.

The bed was not even made and there was no curtain or cloth at the window. I was trying not to think of my own lovely room at Mr Levys in Crown House with the white marble mantelpiece, velvet drapes and all. That was the past, I would never see it again.

'For the time being I will eat my meals with you in the kitchen,' your woman says, like it were to be a great treat for the both of us. 'But of course,' she says, 'when my husband returns home, he and I will dine together and you will wait on us.'

'Oh of course,' I says. 'When will he be coming home, missus?'

But she didn't answer that, she just smiled at me and says, 'What time did you start work in your last place?'

I took a guess. '8 o'clock?'

'Ah,' she says, 'I'm afraid you will find us early risers here in the country. Tomorrow, you should have the fires lit and breakfast made by 6.'

So there I was with two pens, my two titties, Charles Dickens, two slice of bread and a blank book at the end of my first day in the middle of nowhere. Except as it turned out it wasn't quite the end.

Before I went to bed I had to clear up the kitchen, all except the hearth which your woman tellt me not to touch. She went up to her room and left me to it. The cleaning took forever because I was not used to such work and I did not get up the stairs until after 11 o'clock. I was too tired to unpack my things so I simply pulled my nightdress out my bundle and left the rest until such times as I had a moment. I wrapped the two piece of bread I had took from the kitchen in a clean shift and hid them in the cupboard, and I ate the 6 Parma violets that were in my pocket. Then I made up the bed and got into it. The mattress was hard but not lumpy and the blankets seemed clean enough. The clouds must have been thick that night for there was not a star in the sky. I lay there very alert for hours the reason being I would have to start my chores at 5 and I was terrified I would not get up in time. At length however I must have dozed off. I had been asleep what seemed only a few minutes when something made me wake with a start. My eyes snapped open. Your woman was standing over me with a candle, dressed in her nightclothes. She was raging, full of fury, her face so tight it looked like it might fly apart at any moment.

'Get up!' she hissed. 'Get up this instant!' She dragged back the blankets and hit the mattress a few times with her fist. 'I want to see you downstairs, girl,' she says. 'Two minutes. Don't get dressed, just come down immediately.'

And then she was gone.

Jesus Murphy my heart was going like the hammers of Hell, when I lit my candle I could see the thump of it behind the bodice of my nightdress. My first reaction was, I had slept in. I glanced out the window, it was still pitch black out there not even a hint of the dawn, it could have been ½ past 5 or 6 or even 8 for all I knew, I was not an early riser. My hands shook as I pulled on my shawl, I was not sure if it was the cold or the fright. In my bare feet I crept downstairs to the hall. Well the grandmother clock said it was 10 past two so I had not slept in. And then it came to me, why your woman was angry. She had examined the oat bread and seen that I had took more than one slice. I was thinking to myself, now you're in for it and you'll be back on the road in the morning with no job and not even a character and two boxed ears because you're a liar and a thief and you never milked a cow in your life.

It was with a heavy heart that I pushed open the kitchen door and stepped in. Your woman was sat at the table in the light of a lamp and two candles. She no longer seemed angry but she had a distant air about her, she didn't even look at me, just gazed at the wall. 'Come in please,' she says her voice kind of flat.

I shuffled forward a few steps. 'I'm sorry, marm.'

Her head shot round. 'Whatever for?'

'For the –' I hesitated, perhaps she hadn't noticed the bread after all and it was something else bothered her. So I says, 'For whatever I done that made you angry with me.'

'Angry?' she says. 'I am not angry.' She give me a big smile and then she turned her face to the wall and spoke again in the flat voice. 'There is cocoa on the shelf,' she says. 'And milk in that jug. I want you to make a cup of cocoa please.'

'C-cocoa, marm?'

'Yes thank you,' she says. 'I want you to make a cup of cocoa please.'

This change of mood and the please and thank you business and the flat voice was most perplexing. I wondered to myself was all mistresses like this, for I had nothing to compare her with except perhaps my mother. Right enough my mothers mood was changeable and she would think nothing of dragging you out of bed in the middle of the night but it wouldn't have been with the aim of getting you to make her a cup of cocoa that's for flipping sure, more about which I may write later.

'Very good, marm,' I says to your woman and I give her a curtsey, I don't know why for I was not in the habit of curtseying to anyone but it just happened that way, it seemed a maid-like thing to do. Then I took the jug from the table and started to warm the milk. Of course I did not know then what I was to find out in the weeks to come and so thought it strange that although she watched what I did she did not direct me once. Not a comment passed her lips, she only followed every move I made, her eyes gleaming in the lamplight like a cats. There was not much to do while the milk warmed but I got the impression she would not like me to sit down so I took a cloth and pretended to wipe the shelves.

After a bit, she took a breath and says, 'What did you do just then? A moment ago?'

'How do you mean miss – marm?'

She pointed to where I had been standing when I came into the room. 'You did something, while you were standing there.'

'A curtsey,' I says. 'Yes marm.' Oh flip, I was thinking to myself, perhaps you shouldn't have done a curtsey for dear sake can you do nothing right.

'Why did you do that?' she asked.

'I don't know, marm. It just came to me.'

'I see,' she says and blinked a few times, I honest to gob thought she was going to cry and then I realised she was looking like she might burst with joy. 'Carry on please,' she says eventually and waved her hand in the direction of the cocoa jar.

Well I turned around and took a cup off the shelf and mixed the cocoa with a little cold milk and then I poured the hot milk on top and give it a good stir. When it was done I took it over to the table and set it down in front of her with the sugar. Of a sudden she leaned forward and clasped my hands between the two of hers, for dear sake the smile she had on her it's a wonder her face didn't crack.

'Thank you, Bessy,' she says. 'You are an extremely good girl. Well done. *Well* done.'

'Don't mention it,' I says.

Her skin felt cool against my fingers, I went to pull away but she held onto me giving both me and the cup fond glances.

'This looks lovely,' she says. 'Absolutely *lovely*. It's perfect in every way and you made it so quickly and with such efficiency. I'm proud of you, Bessy, very proud of you. What a good girl you are! Thank you thank you *thank* you.'

Jesus Murphy it was only a cup of cocoa.

'Very good, marm.' I didn't know where to put myself. 'Will there be anything else?'

'Yes,' she says, suddenly grave. 'There is something.'

What next, I thought, she is mad as a cuckoo. And then she let go my hands which was a relief and surged to her feet.

'Sit down in my place, dear,' she told me, and I did as I was bid. Then she slid the cup of cocoa towards me.

'You have made such a good job of this,' she says. 'I want you to drink it.'

I looked at the cup. Then I looked at her.

'Me, marm?'

'Yes,' she says and then a bit concerned, 'You do like cocoa?'

'Well,' I says. 'I'm not overfond of milk but I don't *mind* cocoa.'

'Good,' she says. 'Now drink it up like a good girl and then get to bed, you'll want to be fresh for the morning.'

She reached out quick towards my face and I flinched, but she only smiled and give my cheek a little stroke with the back of her hand. Then she turned out the lamp, lifted one of the candles and left the room without another word. I was not at all sleepy. If I remember rightly it was a while before I went to bed. I think I sat there all alone for a long time with the cocoa in front of me, watching the steam rise up off it and get sucked towards the candle flame.

2

New Clothes and New People

Next morning I woke up and stared stupidly out the window for a few moments then lit out of bed with a yelp for the sun was high in the sky, there could be no doubt even I knew I had slept past 5. I tore into my clothes and skittered downstairs no wash nor nothing, fixing my hair as I went. The clock in the hall said it was after 9. Late by 4 hours Jesus Murphy that must have been some kind of record. I could have kicked myself. The night before as I was sat at the table, I had ½ made up my mind to move on and try my luck elsewhere for I wasn't sure I was cut out for this kind of work. But now that I might well be dismissed before I even started, I was having 2nd thoughts. And I don't often have them.

The missus was in the kitchen, putting milk in a saucer for the cat. She was wearing a plain grey dress and an apron. When I ran in she looked up. 'Ah Bessy,' she says. 'I take it you slept well.'

I thought this was her being satirical but I had my excuses lined up. 'Missus,' I says. 'I'm sorry, I –'

She raised a hand to stop me. 'Yes, yes,' she says. 'You had a late night. It's entirely my fault.'

Was she mocking me, it was impossible to tell. I says, 'Sorry marm, I wouldn't have slept so long only –'

'Hush, child,' says she. 'I decided to let you sleep this morning.'

'Oh.'

'After all, you have been travelling,' she says. 'You must be tired. And also upset what with your master – passing away and so on.'

I just nodded, at a loss.

'Well, Bessy,' she says. 'There are a few things I'd like you to do today but nothing too taxing. We can start properly tomorrow when you're rested. That is,' and at this point she gave me a close look, 'if you do intend to remain here?'

She was smiling fondly like a mother in a story book, her eyes was bright but you could see a trace of anxiety behind them. I hesitated but a second. Then I says, 'Yes marm, I certainly do.'

'Good,' she says, clearly much relieved. 'Now, you can have breakfast in a moment,' she says. 'But first things first. Are you wearing your corset?'

I blinked. 'No miss – marm,' I says. 'I had not time to put it on.'

'Excellent,' she says. 'Then you won't have to take it off.' And thereupon she produced a tape from her pocket and proceeded to take measurements of all my proportions, making notes on a scrap of paper as she went. I assumed at first that she was sizing me up for a set of maids clothes. I can remember as if it were yesterday what the dimensions were of my bosom and all the rest, modesty prevents me from writing them here, let's put it this way in those days I was very *well-formed*. Up close I could smell the scent she had on her, attar of roses, and underneath was her own fragrance, more earthy and warm. Once she was done with the *usual* measurements bosom waist and so on she also took the span of my neck and upper arm, I was not sure what to make of that only I thought perhaps she was very particular about collars and sleeves. Next she measured the palm of my hand and the length of all my fingers and thumbs. Gloves as well, I thought, by Jove this is the pigs whiskers. Then she put the tape round my head and wrote down *skull 21 and a ½ inches*, from which I surmised I was also getting a hat, I hoped it would be a good one and not just an old straw bonnet. After which she measured my mouth and the distance from my forehead to my chin and then between my two eyes and after that she took the length of my nose. Finally she measured the distance from my left nostril to my left earhole and my right nostril to my right earhole. To tell the truth I found it both confusing and disturbing but I was young and vain and when I squinted down at her paper I was only relieved to see that both sides of my face were 5 inch across for if the numbers had been lopsided I reckoned I might as well set off there and then to join Carneys Wonderland as a freak.

'All done,' she says, making a final note on her piece of paper.

'Please marm,' I says. 'What is –'

She waved a hand in the direction of a pot of porridge. 'It's over there,' she says. 'And after breakfast perhaps you would like to collect the hens eggs. There's a basket in the corner. By the way, where exactly did you say your master lived?'

'Hyndland, marm, Crown House,' I says and then I could have bit my tongue off since I hadn't tellt her exactly where he lived at all and only blurted it out because I was still perplexed about her measuring my face.

'Crown House,' she says, making a note.

'But of course,' I says quick, 'you can't write to him for my character because he's dead and the house is closed up,' and then I added, 'Unfortunately.'

She give me a hard look. 'Is it unfortunate that he is dead? Or that I can't write to him for a character?'

'Well – both, marm,' I says. 'But please marm. Excuse me but what for do you need all them measurements for?'

She smiled at me. 'What is your frock made of?' she says.

'Silk, marm.'

'Yes and what colour is it?'

I looked down at it. Then I says, 'It's red, marm.'

'And tell me, do you have any other dresses apart from this garment and the – thing you were wearing yesterday?'

I shook my head.

'I thought as much,' she says. 'Then you will need clothes will you not? Nothing you have is suitable.'

'Yes marm, of course,' I says. 'But what I mean is – the other measurements.'

She looked at me blankly. 'What other measurements?' she says, and then she turned her back on me and hurried out the room with her piece of paper.

Perhaps she intended to draw my portrait and wanted to get the proportions right or what have you. As I was stood there thinking, the missus climbed the stairs to her room. I wondered what she would do in there, all alone. There was the faint sound of a door closing and then silence except for in the distance the mournful hooting of a train and closer by my stomach grumbling with hunger.

I turned to pick up the porridge pot and as I did so happened to glance at the grate. I seen at once that the hearth had been swep clean and washed and that the ½ burnt book had disappeared altogether.

Before I collected the eggs, I had a quick skelly around the place. On one side of the house was the stables, on the other the vegetable gardens. Up the lane was the farm and byre where I'd been yesterday. The mansion itself must have been there donkeys years, the sandstone walls were dirty grey with age. For the most part it was two storeys high, with a few single storey wings built on. The chimneys were tall and from the layout of the roofs it looked as though there was a couple of other attics as well as the one that contained my little room. Here and there, the gables was notched to make them look like battlements. I dare say once upon a time it must have been grand enough but now everything looked run down. The window glass was cracked in several places, the paintwork was peeling and blistered and all the paths choked with weeds. Not that I knew much about it but either there wasn't enough money to maintain the place or they didn't keep enough staff.

Part of me was glad of the extra sleep I'd been allowed but funny enough I had an urge to throw myself into something, the dirtier and more difficult the task she give me the better. So I took a basket and went out to the hen run. Jesus Murphy you wouldn't think a few hens could stink so bad. The only way to do it was to go round with your breath held. Some of the eggs had hen skitters on them too, it near made me boke. But I got nine without breaking any then crawled out the run backwards gasping for breath. When I turned round who was stood in the yard staring at me with a big grin on his phizog and his hands in his pockets but the Highland Jocky from the day before. I near enough jumped out my skin.

'What the flip are you doing there?' I shouts at him. 'Are you flipping following me?'

I must explain that my language was only rough because he had put the heart across in me appearing out of nowhere and besides I was none too pleased to see him, he was a pest, not yet 16 year old but a more lecherous devil never put an arm in a coat.

'Keech,' he says, that being a foul word in his own language. 'Could hi not be hasking you the same?'

'Flip off and die,' I says. 'You great lump.'

'Hi'll giff you a lump,' he says with a grin then he put his hands on his hips so his fingers pointed to where his jack was pushing at his trousers, it was up and angry. Then he says, 'Fwhy don't you and me go hover to that barn hand lie down thegether like man and fwhife?'

He took a step forwards so I lobbed an egg, it caught him on the jaw and dripped down a yolky beard onto his scarf and waistcoat. It was so comical I could not help but chuckle. The boy swep his hand across his chin and wiped the mess on his trouser leg. Then he grinned like a madman and stepped towards me again. I was about to throw another egg when I seen the missus come hurrying towards us so instead I says to the boy, 'Now you are in for it when your woman sees you trespassing on her land.'

He glanced over his shoulder to see who was coming then slipped his hands in his pockets and stood there whistling and looking about him, for dear sake butter wouldn't melt.

'Missus,' I says. 'I mean marm. This boy is bothering me. He's followed me here and he's nought but a pest.'

The missus looked at the boy. 'Is this true, Hector?' she says.

Hector?

He give me a sly wink very pleased with himself so he was, the scut. Then he turned to the missus. 'Ach no, Mrs Reid,' he says. 'Not a tall. Hi fwhas chust hasking this brazen creature fwhat she fwas doing stealing your heggs – hand then she threw fwhun at me!'

He adopted a face of such innocence you would have swore he was a saint. Well I was fit to be tied. 'Liar!' I says and would have went on but missus interrupted me.

'Hector, this is Bessy,' she says. 'The new maid.'

'Och is that right now?' His eyes widened but he was not really surprised, I could tell a faker a mile off. 'A new maid?' he says. 'Fwhell, fwhell.' And he looks me up and down like I was a cow at auction.

'This is Hector,' says the missus to me. 'He helps us out on the estate. He's around here all the time for one reason or another.'

Needless to say I was not best pleased at this news. I looked *him* up and down like he was a big long streak of what you might find in a thunder mug of a morning.

'How is your tooth, Hector?' the missus asks him.

'Fwait till you see the hole,' he says and he stuck his dirty great finger in his mouth to pull back his lip just as he'd kept doing the day before. Missus hid her eyes behind her hand and who could blame her.

'I have no desire to see it,' she says. 'All I want to know is whether it was a successful operation.'

The boy plucked his finger from his mouth and wiped it on his sleeve.

'Hit fwas hindeed, marm,' he says. 'Hit came hout fwhith a great wrench, the sound hof it fwhas chust like huprooting potatoes.'

'Oh dear,' she says and made a face. 'Well you must get back to work.'

The boy give her a little bow and then give me a deeper satirical one and with another sly wink he was off and running out the yard, I don't know about uprooting potatoes but you could certainly have grown them between his toes.

The missus turned to me. '*Was* he bothering you?' she says.

'Only somewhat, marm,' I says. 'Nothing I can't deal with by myself.'

'Good for you,' she says. 'But do try and do it without throwing eggs.' She smiled at me. 'That was a pretty song you were singing earlier. I don't think I heard it before.'

'No, marm,' I says. 'It's one I made up in my own head.'

'Indeed?' she says. 'You are clever.' And then she reached out quickly and stroked my cheek. 'What are you thinking of, Bessy?' she says.

'Marm? Nothing marm. I wasn't thinking anything.'

In actual fact I was thinking how given ½ a chance I could split that Hectors head like a pea shod. But I didn't want to say that in case she thought wrong of me.

'I'm sure that's not the case,' says the missus. 'We are always thinking something, every one of us. Never mind. How many eggs did you get?'

'9 – well – 8,' I says.

'Good girl.' She smiled at me most kind, then turned and went back into the house. I watched her go.

What are you thinking of? What a thing to say. In my entire life, no-body had ever asked me such a question.

For the rest of the morning she showed me some of the things I had to do about the place then after lunch she sent me down to Snatter to buy scones. Snatter was the nearest village there, which to begin with made me laugh every time I heard it talked about for it sounded like a thing that came shooting out your nose. When it was time to go missus took me down behind the vegetable garden and pointed out the quickest way, down a track in a field called Cowburnhill and then along the lane to where the village lay at the crossroads with the Great Road.

'Don't be long,' she says to me. 'I need those scones this afternoon. Just get them and come straight back.'

'Yes yes,' I says to her. 'For dear sake woman don't fuss like a great lilty.'

No I didn't really. I just says, 'Certainly marm,' and took the pennies she give me. Then I made her a nice curtsey and off I went. She had been so lovely to me all morning, I had almost forgot how strange she had acted the night before.

Cowburnhill, I was not happy about Cowburnhill at all, there was cowpats up to your wishbone but luckily that day the cows themselves was all in the next field. The sky was the colour of the stirabout I had ate for breakfast but there was no wind and it wasn't too cold. As I walked along, I sang out loud the song I was making up, but it wasn't finished yet, I only had two verse and a chorus.

After a while the lane passed a small field in the middle of which was a man bent over looking at the soil. I stopped singing as soon as I seen him, I had no wish to draw attention to myself. But as I went past he straightened up and stared at me. He was short and slightly built and he spat constantly. I was later to learn that this was Biscuit Meek, one of the farm servants. By the outraged expression on his face and the way his hands clenched up into fists you would have thought I was old Nabs himself taking a dander down the lane. I give him a wave and a good afternoon, seeing as he might be my new neighbour. In response he hawked up a great oyster and gobbed it on the earth but by the looks of him that was only his next spit among what might be thousands that day so it would be unfair to say it was directed at me with malice.

Thank flip the lane soon took a curve and sloped down the hill behind a hedge. It was a relief to get out his sight. Before too long, I came into the village. In those days, before the new pits opened, it was a smaller place than now, inhabited mainly by miners and weavers, their dwellings clustered around the Cross and straggling for some distance along either side of the Great Road. I looked about me for a coffee house or other place of entertainment but was to be sore disappointed. Granted, there was a tavern at one end of the village called The Gushet and a small hotel just up the road from the Cross – the Swan Inn. But apart from that the only points of interest were an old smithy and the one shop that served as baker, grocer and post office combined. There was about ½ a dozen dirty children playing in the street, two mangy dogs and a few horses and carts and pony traps sitting here and there. Not even a theatre or a dance hall for a hooley, the only hall had a big sign up that showed it was reserved for the masonics, The Free Gardeners. I was most deflated. I seen in the shop window that there was a *Soiree* advertised but on closer inspection this proved to have taken place the previous month in another village called Smoller. Even though I could have murdered a few jars, I walked past both the tavern and the hotel without going in. My first day on the job it would be a disaster to roll up in a state of elevation. Besides, I had no wish to displease the missus, she had give me a fair start.

Inside the shop smelled of sweeties and tobacco and milk gone off and it was empty except for a bald-pated man behind the counter this was AP Henderson the grocer. What did he do when I give him good afternoon but fold his arms across his watch chain and stare up at the rafters, yawning. I had met his type before and knew just to ignore any snash, I got straight to the point.

'Have you any scones there, mister?' I says and just then I seen them in a glass case on the counter but before I could ask for them Henderson shook his head.

'No,' says he. 'Nae scones.'

I looked at him astounded then pointed at the case. 'What about those there?'

'These are reserved,' he says.

'Reserved?' I says. 'Reserved for who?'

'For the people of Snatter and this burgh.'

'Well in that case,' I says, 'you can give me 6 because I am bid to buy them for my mistress at Castle Haivers which I assume is in this burgh since it's only a mile or thereabouts up the road.'

This give him pause for thought. He examined me down the length of his nose. 'And who might you be?' he says eventually.

'I am the new maid at Castle Haivers,' I says. 'Engaged yesterday.'

At that he give a little sneering laugh. 'The new maid,' he says. 'Oh aye. And whit happened to the last one?'

I did not want to admit that I didn't know so I just says, 'She left.'

'Oh she did, did she?' he says then he says (and I thought this most strange), 'Did she go on the train?' and he started hooting with laughter. Hooting, so he was. I just stood there while he ruptured himself. It wasn't even funny, I thought he must be wanting. After several minutes he calmed down and wiped his eyes. 'Ah dearie me,' he says. 'Did she go on the train, Oh boy.' Then he leans over the counter and says confidentially, 'And how is the lovely Arabella?'

'Who?' I says, very haughty.

'Mrs Reid, your mistress,' he says. 'Or do you not even ken her name?'

'Oh yes,' I says. 'Arabella. I didn't hear you properly. She is very well thank you.'

'And what about himself?'

I guessed that by this he meant the master so I says, 'Himself is not at home just at the present moment.'

'Aye-aye,' says Henderson. 'Drumming up votes no doubt?'

'No doubt,' I says, of course not a *clue* what he was on about.

'Aye-aye?' he says again and raised an eyebrow. 'She's up there all on her own is she? Rattling aboot in that big hoose. She's probably in need of a bit company, eh?'

He licked the ends of his moustache hairs, no doubt who he was imagining in the role of companion. The very idea of him going anywhere *near* the missus filled me with revulsion.

'Not at all,' I says. 'Her house is full of guests.'

'Oh?'

'Yes, we have several people staying. Relatives of the missus, up from England. That is why we are needing more food, they have ate us out of house and home. Now if you please I'll just take 6 scones and be on my way. I'm expected.'

Well you could not have asked him for anything more troublesome, the way he sighed and dragged himself off his stool all the time shaking his head as if it was beyond him why anyone would want to buy scones, it was a desperate performance. Eventually he got the 6 scones in a bag and I laid out the money for him. He flicked it off the counter and caught it in his apron before throwing it in the till. The coins barely touched his lily-white mitts, make no mistake he did not wish to catch the germs off an Irish girl.

Arabella.

Arabella, Arabella, it was a lovely name. All the way up the road I kept thinking about a placard I had seen once outside the Theatre Royal with a picture of a ballerina on it, she had on a tremendous pale pink frock that stuck out all round and her skin was like milk, I don't know why, but that is what the sound of Arabella made me think of, something fine and delicate and beautiful.

Unlike Biscuit Meek. I was glad to see that he was no longer in the turnip field, no doubt he had went off to spit on somebody elses land.

When I got back to Castle Haivers, my missus was in the kitchen.

'You came back!' she says delighted, perhaps she'd expected me to make off with her tuppence. I give her the scones and straight away she showed me a pile of clothes that she had laid out for me on the table, there was aprons, petticoats, caps and two print cotton frocks, one striped, one dark grey both a little faded. I knew at once they was not new for she could not have got new clothes so quick. And being young and very particular about my appearance I was a bit disappointed at the thought of wearing cast-offs. Missus must have seen the look on my face.

'I think they will be about the right size, don't you?' she says and then, 'They are only temporary until we can get some made up.'

I picked up the striped frock and examined it. At least it seemed clean and it smelled like it had just been pressed.

'Put it on,' says the missus.

'Should I change here, marm?'

'Why not?' she says.

I took off my own frock and stepped into the striped one. It fastened up the front from the waist. My fingers was trembling for some reason and so the missus stepped forward and done it for me, every button, one after the other. When she had the frock all fastened, she stroked my hair and smiled and took a step back.

'Perfect,' she says.

'Are they your frocks, missus?'

'No, no,' she says. I looked at her and she went on. 'They belonged to a girl who was here some time ago. She – she left some things when she went. I put them in the attic, in case – in case she came back.'

Well, there was something queer about all this, the way she hesitated and avoided my gaze, you could have sensed it a mile off downwind with your eyes blindfold your nose blocked your ears stopped up and a cork in your hole. But before I could ask any more she clapped her hands together and laughed very gay.

'Now then, let's get started,' she says, as if she was inviting me to join her in a great old game. 'Put on a cap and one of the aprons. Reverend Pollock is coming to visit and I would very much like you to wait on us in the parlour.'

'Very good marm,' I says.

I had never met the Reverend Pollock but would have laid money that he was U.P. that is 'United Presbyterian'. I have to admit that I felt a little thrill of excitement at the notion of passing myself off as a maid to a Man Of The Cloth even if he was a member of what my mother always called The Opposition. Not that she was religious or Holy in fact to my knowledge the last time she'd went to Mass she was full and fell off the chair laughing and then was sick in her purse, but Blueskins or 'You Pees' I was acquainted with one or two of their number and they would have made a saint spit.

By 3 o'clock the transformation was complete, I was a maid good and proper. I had on me the striped frock, a white apron and a frilled cap, my hair combed flat over my ears and caught in a bun at the back very sober. I even had time for a wash. Whoever the runaway girl was she had no figure for my titties was squashed flat as fadge inside the frock but otherwise it did not pinch. Missus give me an inspection and pronounced me good and it was so.

She got me to lay a fire in the parlour and light it and then sent me back to the kitchen to butter the scones while she sat down with her sewing. At ½ past 3 there was a knock on the front door. I hurried into the hall and opened up there was the Reverend Pollock on the step, a well built man about fifty with side-whiskers and a handsome old phiz. He blinked in surprise when he seen me and give his curls a bewildered shake, I think he was expecting someone else.

'Well – gracious – hah!' he says in tones that was meant to be jolly but to my ears sounded awful forced. I made him a curtsey and give him 'Good afternoon sir,' then ushered him in all this, very fancy.

'Yes yes,' he says. 'Now then I haven't seen *you* before.' He said it like he was pretending to scold you and then he made this noise, not quite a chuckle and not quite a sigh but a sentimental sound somewhere in between, 'Aahh-hah!'

'No sir,' I says. 'I'm new.'

'Aahh-hah!' he goes again then set to nodding shrewdly and examining me out the corner of his eye while I took his hat and coat. The Reverend Pollock, as I came to realise, liked to think of himself as a wily fox, he hated anything to get past him. I noticed he had a strange smell wafting about his person of paraffin or somesuch and his boots creaked like an old galleon.

I hung up his coat and turned round. He was still nodding away shrewdly.

'Aahh-hah,' he goes another time. 'A new girl, eh.' He contemplated this notion fondly for several moments. At length he says, 'I imagine you have a charming name.'

'My name is Bessy, sir.'

'Oh,' he says. 'Well never mind. Names are not important . . . it is how a person is guided by God that counts. And also observation of the Sabbath . . . that goes without saying.'

'Yes sir.'

'Aye well,' he says. 'I'm sure you'll be *very* happy here . . . Yes, you have a *wonderful* mistress . . . Aye indeed . . . She and I are . . . very good friends . . .'

He had the air about him of a man that was preparing to launch into a long speech punctuated by great pauses so I butt in. 'If you would like to come this way, sir,' I says and hurried over to the parlour. But instead of following, he stayed where he was, smiling in a self-satisfied kind of way with his arms by his sides and his shoulders hunched up around his ears. Obviously he hadn't finished with me yet and I would lay good money we would still be there today if I hadn't just ignored him and went ahead and knocked on the parlour door.

'Come!' says the missus.

As I went in, she glanced up from where she was sat by the fire at her needlework. She had changed her gown again and dressed her hair lovely by Jove she was pretty as a picture, I could just see it hanging in a gallery, it would have been entitled 'The Fair Lady of the House'.

I was about to announce the Reverend when he thrust past me with a smug smile but he had a glint in his eye now he knew I would not be indulging him.

'The Reverend Bollock, marm,' I says.

Missus shot me a look as she rose to greet him, I think she was not sure if she had heard right or was it my accent but all his attention was on her as he moved across the room with one hand outstretched.

'Reverend Pollock,' she says. 'How good of you to visit.'

'Ah-hahh!' he goes.

This was my cue to boil the kettle.

I returned a while later with the tray and could hear their voices murmuring inside the parlour but when I knocked and went in they fell silent, it was as though they had been discussing something they did not wish me to hear.

They was sat either side of the fire, the Reverend had took possession of the big leather armchair, his feet splayed in the hearth. He looked to be quite at home.

'Ah, very good,' says the missus to me. She gestured to the table between them where I was to lay out the tea things. I began the process very slow, hoping they would resume their conversation. I set out one saucer – and then the next. And then I set out one cup – and then the next. One spoon – The Reverend cleared his throat.

'I don't know if I tellt you, Arabella,' he says. 'But I have had some rather – well, flattering news.'

I was a bit ticked off for this was clearly a change of subject.

'Oh?' says the missus. 'What is it?'

'Well,' he says, very pleased with himself. 'I have been prevailed upon to deliver a Monday Evening discourse in Glasgow.'

'Really?' says the missus. 'That is good news.'

'Aye indeed,' he says. 'At the Corporation Galleries or perhaps the Queens Rooms . . . it is not yet decided. In any case, it will not be until next year. However these affairs being so – important – it takes quite a long wee while to organise the publicity and what have you. I'm given to understand this lecture series is very well attended.'

'How wonderful!' says the missus. Dear knows she *sounded* impressed. I couldn't help but wonder how she put up with the old goat.

'Well I hope the committee have been right to put their faith in me,' he says. 'They did say that I had been highly recommended. People do tell me that I am one of the best speakers they have ever heard although I don't go along with that myself. And of course now I have to give some consideration to what I will have as my theme – perhaps you could contribute to my deliberations, Arabella. Of course, you know my Hobby Horse . . .'

Here he paused and waited for the missus to fill the gap.

'William of Orange,' she says with a nod.

'Aye,' says the Reverend. 'The old king is my strongest suit as it were. But I wonder whether I might not tackle something entirely new.'

Clearly this was going nowhere interesting so I swiftly doled the rest of the tea things off the tray and straightened up ready to leave.

The Reverend sat back and beamed at me with great indulgence. 'Aahh-hah!' he goes. 'I can tell you are going to be a very valuable asset to this house, Betty.'

'It's Bessy, sir,' I says.

'Oh?' he says. 'You told me your name was Betty.'

'Did I sir? I don't think so.'

'Indeed you did. When I arrived I distinctly remember you told me you were called Betty.' He smiled at missus and shook his head as if to say I was daft.

'Well, sir,' I says. 'In that case I must be mistaken about my *own name*.'

'That will be all, Bessy,' says the missus shortly. 'We can help ourselves to tea.'

I give her a curtsey and went out, leaving the door open a hair and then lingered a moment in the hall to see if they would pick up their previous conversation or talk about me but they didn't – at least not at first. The Bollix carried on bragging about his lecture and the missus promised to help him think of a suitable topic. She then made a few suggestions, the Electric Telegraph was one idea but he says 'Aahh-hah,' he was no expert on *that* subject and then she proposed he talk about farm servants, their religious and moral improvement or the like and he agreed that it was an interesting theme but perhaps a bit *narrow* for his taste.

Then there was a pause and he says, 'You may be right about her, you know.'

And she says, 'Well, it remains to be seen.'

At that point, very abruptly, they stopped talking. I froze for a second and listened hard but there was such an edge to the silence that I feared they had sensed my presence behind the door. I did not wait to find out, instead I flew down the hall on tippy toe, thank gob the new dress was of cotton and made not a whisper. I was back in the bowels of the kitchen in a trice and there I seized up a broom and began sweeping the floor even though it hardly needed it. There was no indication that anyone had heard or followed me but my heart did not stop leaping around in my chest for several minutes.

So I *had* been the subject under discussion when I arrived first of all with the tea tray! Of course in all likelihood their remarks was entirely innocent, referring only to my suitability for serving work or somesuch. But it was clear that the missus had been doing some conjecture and surmise about my person. Oh, I would have give my liver and lights to know what she thought of me or what she imagined to be the truth.

I sat in the kitchen playing with the cat until the missus rang for me to clear away the tea things and get Old Bollix his stinky coat. But could I get shot of the old scut, devil the bit of it. Even once he was in the blasted coat he stood there in the hall with his hat on smiling fondly, going 'Aah-haah!' and asking nosy questions. Right enough he was different to your usual You Pee, most of them was miserable as Sin, but he did not fool me for a second. I give him the old 'Yes sir no sir 3 bags full sir,' and at last, after what seemed like an Eternity I got him out the door and closed it firmly behind him.

So great was my relief at his departure that I found myself doing a little jig of victory up and down the hall. Unfortunately this was interrupted when I twirled round only to see the missus stood in the doorway of the parlour, observing me.

'You seem happy, Bessy,' she says in very even tones.

'Yes marm,' I gasps, a little out of breath and thinking quick I added, 'I am just so very glad to have this job.'

She studied me a moment, it was hard to tell what she was thinking. Then she says, 'Come through,' and turned on her heel.

Here we go, I thought, I am in for it, because of the dancing or because I had spoke sharp to Old Bollix earlier or even because she'd guessed that I had deliberately mucked up his name when I announced him, a whole catalogue of crimes there was and so I went after her with a certain amount of dread, dragging my heels, for all I knew she could dismiss me on the spot.

By the time I got into the parlour, she had settled again in her chair by the fire. I give her a deep curtsey and stared at the Turkey carpet. 'Marm,' says I, sick to my stomach.

There was a pause. Then she says, 'How have you enjoyed your first day at Castle Haivers?'

This question was, to my mind, designed to fill me with shame for cheeking the minister. I looked appropriately humbled.

'Well, marm,' I says. 'I have liked some aspects well enough.'

'Yes?' she says.

'But I do be thinking that in others it should be for the best if I tried harder.'

'Indeed?' she says. Something in her voice made me glance up, I thought I seen a twinkle in her eye but then she blinked and it disappeared or perhaps it was only my imagination.

She looked at me gravely. I thought here we go.

'On the whole,' she says, choosing her words carefully. 'I am of the opinion that you have done reasonably well today.'

I said nought to that, I was waiting for the tongue lashing.

'Just a few things to note,' she says. 'I think it might be as well, for example, when you speak to anyone, especially a lady or a gentleman, to make sure that you look at them straight in the face.'

'Very good, marm,' I says. 'In the face.'

'And perhaps when you are being addressed it would also be advisable to stand erect and perhaps not waggle your leg around *too* much.'

'Yes marm,' I says. 'Erect.'

'One other point,' she says. 'Just to bear in mind, when you speak to a lady or gentleman it would generally be better if you didn't have your finger in your mouth.'

'Oh!' I says a bit took aback, I was not aware I done that. 'Very good marm.'

'Generally speaking however I think it passed off quite well,' she says. 'But now – have you written anything in your little book yet?'

'Gob no, missus,' I says for she had caught me off guard. 'I mean no, marm.'

'In that case,' she says, 'you may go to your room for an hour. I suggest you take the opportunity to put some effort into your journal.'

I would rather have put some effort into a good long nap but I was that grateful that she hadn't tore a strip off me I practically threw myself at her feet.

'Very good, marm,' I says and made her another little curtsey. 'I'll do that right away, right away now.'

Oh how easy it is to fall into the habit of bowing and scraping. Dear knows if you had took my likeness at that moment you would have said I was a servant girl to my toe nails.

'I look forward to reading what you have done this evening,' says the missus. 'And perhaps later you can sing me your pretty song.' I thought that was me dismissed and was about to leave when of a sudden she carried on, 'D'you know, Bessy, that the Reverend Pollock is one of the busiest ministers in the land?'

As if I cared *the core of a cabbage* what he was. But I says, 'Oh? Is that right now?'

'I always think it a shame that he only manages to visit here about once a month.'

'Oh – dear,' I says.

'Sometimes he only manages every two months. Isn't that a *great* pity?'

I think I can safely says that this was my first experience of how a lady of the missus breeding has the natural ability to tell you one thing while meaning quite another. She did not like the Old Bollix either! She was looking at me straight and there was not a whisker of an edge to her voice, but somehow I knew she wanted me to understand the *exact* opposite of what she said. He was *terrible* company and the *less* he came to visit the better. I wanted to laugh out loud and embrace her, it was like a happy secret that we had together, her and me the both of us.

But that would not have been right so instead I just says, 'Yes marm, it is an awful pity,' and made her another curtsey and went out, smirking.

As for the little book, that soon wiped the smile off my face. Dear gob the cornuptions I went through with it to start with I do not care to recall (though I look at it now with some fondness as it lies here beside me on the table). The trouble was I knew how to spell words but joining them together to make correct sentences had me all in a pucker. Or perhaps it was not so much correct sentences that eluded me but sentences that I thought worthy for the missus to read. I may well have shed a tear or two over those first entries, for I can see the ink is blurred in places and also the pages are covered in blots since I had the pen constantly hovering over them, willing the words to come out. At the end of an hour, a single paltry line was all I had, however in my opinion that was plenty and I was glad to get back downstairs and throw myself into the simple task of making supper.

That evening missus elected to sit in the kitchen and read her *Bathgate Monthly Visitor* except she barely glanced at it, she seemed more interested in watching me clear away. I was beginning to think she had forgot about the little book altogether when she put down her *Monthly Visitor* and tellt me to bring her what I had wrote. I did so with heavy heart and even now am ashamed to copy down my first desperate effort.

thursday
got up done a few light chores for missus nothing else strange or startling

The missus glanced at it then looked up at me. 'Why did you stop there?' she says and I says to her I didn't know for sure but perhaps it was because my hand had got tired. 'After a single line?' she says and I told her that it was because I did not have the habit of writing a journal.

'Well, Bessy,' she says to me, 'a journal should be more specific. You must write down what the various chores are and say something else to give colour to the account. For instance, this morning what happened?'

I looked at her. My mind was a blank.

'The first thing that happened this morning?' she says.

I shrugged. 'I got up late?' I says.

'Well – yes,' she says. 'That is not what I was thinking of but it will do. Why not. Now, try again.' And she made me sit down at the kitchen table and have another go. What a shambles, I think it must have took about an hour to write.

thursday
got up late porridge for breakfast burnt roof of mouth on it collected eggs emptied poe for missus sheeps head broth for dinner went for scones served tea to missus and reverend other than that nothing strange or startling

'Well,' says the missus when she looked at it. 'That is better. But it still wants further elaboration and detail.'

So I says in jest Oh should I have elaborated what was in the pisspot, marm? (And then I could have kicked myself, for dear sake it was not the kind of pleasantry fit for a *lady*.) The missus just gives me a look and says no, but this account doesn't *speak* to me. I tellt her that I was truly sorry but I didn't know what else to write about. And she sighed and tellt me that the next day it would please her greatly if when I wrote in the little book I wasn't just to write what I *did*, the chores and all, I was to write down how I *felt* about what I did and what *thoughts* went through my head as I did it.

Jesus Murphy I thought to myself what *possible* interest could that be to any man jack and I may have said as much except not in those exact words and then the missus says if you do it I will give you another shilling so I thought well gob if it made her happy.

But I am being too pert. To tell the truth I did not care a ducks beak for the extra shilling. I just wanted to please my missus.

3

Friday

got up on time i was glad not to be late fire would not take i was happy when it did porridge too salty i was disappointed fed hens with missus fed pig on my own i like the hens but not sure about pig ripped a hole in my apron on the fence i was not at all pleased about that swep and dusted rooms and got dinner potatoes burnt but i was hungry and ate every pick missus showed me how to clean silver i was pleased then she showed me the garden vegetables i was interested and where the sheep got in to eat them last year i was shocked then i carted about a ton of manure across yard i was highly delighted when that was done while working i was thinking about my mother if only she was still alive and doing her good works especially with the poor men down on their luck just a smile from her and a kind word as she passed by on her way to worship brightened their day she was truly an angel sent from heaven

4

What I Did Not Write

That was what I wrote in the book. But that wasn't all what happened on the Friday, not by a long chalk. For instance when I went into the kitchen that morning the missus was already up, it seemed like she had been waiting on me for as I walked in she jumped to her feet.

'Ah, there you are,' she says, very excited.

Her face was pale and there was shadows under her eyes, she had the look of someone that had not slept overmuch. I give her good morning and went to light the fire but as I passed her by she reached out and gripped my arm.

'Let the fire wait,' she says. 'There's something I want to do first.'

She released my arm then stood aside and gestured to a straight-back chair in the middle of the floor, she must have moved it there before I came down.

'Sit,' she says.

When I had done as bid she started walking to and fro in front of me her hands clasped behind her. She had on a lovely charcoal coloured silk frock, the skirts whispered to me as she moved back and forth, the cut of the cloth showed off her slender frame. A real Aphrodite she was, only with arms. After a moment or two she stopped pacing and looked at me, straight in the face.

'Now Bessy,' she says very stern. 'Do you trust me?'

'Marm?' I says. 'In what sense?'

She hesitated, then she says, more kindly, 'I mean – do you think I would do you any harm?'

'No marm,' I says and was surprised to realise I meant it.

'So you do trust me,' she says.

'Well yes,' I says.

'Good,' she says. 'Now – be a good girl and close your eyes.'

'What – what for, marm?'

'Do you trust me, Bessy?'

'Yes, marm.'

'Then close your eyes.'

I closed them.

She walked about me a bit more like a big whisper and then she stopped nearby, somewhere to my left. I waited, not knowing what to expect. I ½ imagined that I might all of a sudden feel her touch somewhere, a stroke on the cheek maybe, her breath on my face or her fingers in my hair but she kept her distance and after a moment of silence she announced very loud in the flat voice, 'Stand!'

I got to my feet then waited to be told where to go but all she says, again in the flat voice was, 'Sit!' So I sat down and – thinking I had disappointed her in some way, began to open my eyes.

'Keep them shut!' she says quickly. And then she says again, 'Stand!' in the flat voice. And so I did. And then she says again, 'Sit!'

What she was up to I hadn't an inkling. She just kept on in the flat voice, Stand! Sit! Stand! Sit! I was up and down like a drabs drawers until about the 5th time of asking I could not bear any more to be told what to do whereupon I opened my eyes and says a bit sharp, 'Please missus I'm not going to do this any more so don't make me please.'

She was gazing at me, her eyes glazed over, she looked for all the world like she was in a Trance but when I spoke she nodded and muttered to herself, it sounded like, 'Of course. Of course she would.' Then she blinked and says out loud, 'Well done, Bessy. You may light the fire.'

Then off she goes, sailing out the room without a backward glance.

About ½ way through the morning a letter come for her. I had my ears pricked up for the postman partly because it would have been just nice to see another face but also on account of what he might be bringing, if indeed the missus had wrote to Crown House for my character, I was worried about the possibility of a reply.

This particular postman must have been the human equivalent of a badger for you never saw hide nor hair of him, only found his droppings on the mat, and this day was no exception. He was supposed to blow his horn to let you know he was on his way but despite the fact that I had my ears and eyes peeled and could have swore that nobody come up the drive there – like magic! – was the letter on the floor one time as I was passing through the hall. The heart went sideways in me for I thought it might be from Glasgow but on closer examination I seen that it was postmarked London so all was well. I thought it might be from the missus husband.

She had been closeted away in her room all morning and I was glad of an excuse to visit her so I took the letter upstairs immediately. I knocked the door and when I entered she was sat at her desk, she had a pen in her hand but oddly I could see no writing paper anywhere.

'This came for you, marm,' I says and give her the envelope.

She glanced at the handwriting on the front.

'It's from London,' I says.

She smiled. 'Yes, I see that.'

I waited for her to open it but she just put it on the desk and turned back to me expectantly. Up until that moment I didn't realise I had anything to say to her but then I blurted out, 'Marm, about this morning,' I says. 'I wanted to apologise.'

'Apologise? What for?'

'Marm for not doing what you wanted me to do. Stand up and sit down and all this. I don't know why. I just didn't want to do it. And I'm sorry.'

She shook her head. 'No matter, Bessy,' she says. 'You did very well.'

'Did I marm? Did I really?'

'Yes you did.'

'Do you want to try it again, missus – marm? That's to say – I don't mind, we could do it again now if you want. Downstairs – or here?'

'Perhaps not just this minute, Bessy,' she says. 'Perhaps on some other day.'

'You sure now, marm?'

'Yes, I think I'll read my letter now.'

'Oh certainly, go right ahead.' I waited for her to open it but she just sat there and smiled hard at me until I realised that of course she was expecting me to withdraw.

I left her to it, closing the door quietly behind me. I don't know what made me linger there on the landing. I expected to hear her slicing open the envelope but instead what I heard was a key turning in a lock and a drawer sliding open and shut, then there was a faint 'clink' I couldn't place and finally once again silence, so that I had to walk away on the very tips of my toes, and grab onto the wall for balance.

An hour later when I called her downstairs to eat I seen straight away that she had been crying. Her nose was red and her eyes was all swoll up and watery. Bless her she was putting a brave face on it, whatever it was, and I didn't want to pry so I kept my mouth shut until after we had ate. And then I says, very gentle, 'Forgive me asking marm but – did you have bad news?'

All at once, her eyes welled up. I'm afraid my imagination ran riot and I jumped to the worst and most Romantic conclusion.

'Whatever's the matter, marm?' I says, 'Is it blackmail?'

That kind of thing was always happening in The Peoples Journal.

The missus looked at me askance. 'Don't be silly,' she says. And then she stood up. 'It's nothing. I'm fine. Now, it's time you got on with your work.'

And with those words she marched out the room. At the time I thought it was something in her letter had upset her but looking back on it now, I'm not so sure.

*

By the evening, missus seemed to have recovered her composure. After I had cleared the table she tellt me to make Fridays entry in my book and then asked to see it straight away. I stood there very anxious while she read it over but she smiled when she finished and said it was a *great* improvement. Most of all she seemed to like the part about my mother and her good works which for dear sake was the bit I had invented! on account of I had forgot to remember what I was thinking about whilst I was working so I just made up the first thing that came into my head.

'This part about your mother,' says missus. 'Write more like this.'

'I'll do that marm,' I says, thinking well for dear sake if she can't tell the difference that's easy enough, I'll just make things up all the time.

Then she went and fetched a piece of paper she had wrote on herself. She laid it on the table beside my open book and said, 'Now Bessy, you spell very well but let's just have a look at these.' So the two of us stood there looking down at her writing and mine. I wasn't sure what I was supposed to be looking for, but I looked all the same. Her piece of paper was the first page of a letter she'd wrote to her father in the village of Wimbledon England. Hoo-rah! I thought to myself, secretly delighted to have the opportunity to read something private of hers but the first paragraph was only about the weather and then she started in about some book she had been reading dear gob it looked a very dull letter indeed with nothing very revealing at all but perhaps that was why she had chose it.

After a minute she turned to me and smiled.

'You see?' she says.

I thought about lying but I had a feeling that it wouldn't have done me much good. So I said no, I didn't see. Missus kept smiling.

She says, 'What is the difference between this piece of writing and that one?'

I says, 'This one is a letter to your father and that one is my book you give me.' A stupid answer I know but I was flustered and perhaps a bit cross for I hated to be put on the spot and made to look daft.

'Any other difference?' says the missus, still smiling.

I looked again. She leaned in and says quietly, 'Look at the spaces between the words.'

It was a clue. Well I looked hard at her 'Dear Father'. There was a space between the two words right enough. Then I looked at my 'got up'. There was a space there too. But the two spaces seemed much the same to me and one space plus another space is just a bigger space no matter how long you look at it.

The missus sighed and pointed at her page putting her finger next all the full stops. Then she pointed at mine. Not a full stop in sight. Then she showed me all the commas in her letter. And then she put her finger in my book. Not even a sniff of a comma there.

'I am very pleased that you are writing at greater length, Bessy,' she says. 'But do you see how what you have written is all one sentence from the top of the page to the bottom. You write as you speak without pausing for breath. Have you never heard of punctuation?'

Well I tellt her I knew all about punctuation it was just I was never sure where the flip I was supposed to put it.

That was when the missus decided she would be responsible for my education. She got quite excited about the notion, she sat me down and tellt me that when she was young she had it in mind to tread the streets of London town to gather up all the little ragamuffins who couldn't read and write and take them home to Wimbledon to teach them their ABC. I don't suppose her father would have been pleased about that, dirty wee beggars sitting on his chairs and mucking up his Turkey carpets but as it happened the furnishings was saved.

'In the end, Bessy,' she tells me. 'I didn't do it.'

She was smiling still but she wore a little frown and there was no mistaking the sadness that had crept in behind her eyes, she had fell once again into Melancholia.

'Why was that, marm?' I says very quiet. 'What happened?'

Now I was only chancing my arm, thinking she would more than likely change the subject or walk out like she'd done earlier. So you could have knocked me down with a feather when she leaned towards me, took my hand in hers and looked me deep in the eyes.

'Not many people know this, Bessy,' she says very earnest. 'Can I rely on you not to tell a soul?'

Well flip me I could have cheered. To be took into her confidence! But instead I pursed my lips put my head on one side and made my face very reliable. You could not have found a more reliable person in the whole of Scratchland. I was reliability itself.

'Indeed you can, marm,' I says. 'I would take it to my grave whatever it is.'

She nodded. 'Yes,' she says. 'I believe you would.'

And then she told me her story.

Of course I didn't write it down because it was tellt to me in confidence. And although as far as I knew she and I were the only ones to look in my book I was very aware of what might happen if it fell into the *wrong hands*. The missus wouldn't want her private business bandied about by the likes of Biscuit Meek or AP Henderson, the scuts, and neither would I, that was why I was always very careful what I wrote in there.

However.

Several years have passed since. I have thought long and hard about it and decided to write a brief version of what she told me here since it may be of use and I have been assured that this document is only for the PRIVATE perusal of one or two gentlemen.

This is what the missus said. Sure she herself hadn't known the first thing about cows either when she originally came to Scratchland, a young girl only a few years older than I was then, all the way up from London with her new husband, that is my master James as was. He had went down to that Great English City to spend a few weeks seeing the lions and attending concert parties, Promenades, Conversaziones and the like. Reading between the lines (not the lions) he was there to find a wife. And find one he did, in the delectable form of missus age 19. He tellt her he had trained in the law but that he did not practise any more what he done instead was dabble in a number of business interests he had inherited. After a few weeks courting he went down on his one knee in Wimbledon. 'Castle Haivers is yours, my dearie,' he'd said and that's what he tellt her father too though I don't expect he called him dearie and off they set after the wedding the new bride next her wealthy husband, her cheeks flushed and attar of roses in her hair, ready to greet the staff at her grand new home.

What master James neglected to mention, of course, was that Castle Haivers was just the name of the estate. Right enough, he had a queer few hundred acres and some tenant farmer buckos and he did not otherwise lack in wealth and business interests, but there was not a castle in sight only dirt land none of it too pretty and a crumbling old mansion and the Mains. Missus tellt me that on her first night in Castle Haivers she cried until she couldn't see out her eyes.

At that the both of us had a little weep thegether about her misfortune. Then she wiped her cheeks and wiped mine. I asked her why she hadn't ran away and she said Oh she had, the very day after they arrived. While master James was out talking to his foreman, she packed a little bag, ran down the road, got a ride on a cart, then jumped on the first train to London and threw herself on her fathers mercy back in Wimbledon which thinking about it now was a very brave thing for her to do.

'What happened?' I asked her.

She says everything was grand at first, her father said 'there there' and of course she didn't have to go back. But then he asked her about the nuptials.

'What about them, missus?' I says.

'Whether they had taken place,' she says and looked crestfallen. From which I gathered that they had and that she'd been daft enough to tell her father as much. Well my missus was back on the road north before her feet could touch the ground with her ears still ringing and her poor wee titties didn't stop bouncing till she was right back at Castle Haivers, missus didn't say that last bit, I did.

'And so you see I never did get to help the little ragamuffins,' she says.

'Och dear,' I says. 'Sure that's a terrible shame.'

My heart went out to her. In the back of my mind I was also thinking to myself that there's beggar children all over the place not just London and she could always have helped the ones in Glasgow or even them that passed through Snatter but I didn't want to spoil the moment when we was so cosy and she was telling me her secrets and all. By Jove I could have sat there holding her hand all night, it was lovely, more like being mother and daughter or very best friends than mistress and maid. A thought occurred to me now that we was so friendly, about that burnt accompt book I'd seen the day I arrived.

'Marm,' I says. 'Who is Morag?'

Well you would have thought I'd slapped her in the face. She pulled her hand away.

'What?' she says very suspicious. 'Who have you been talking to?'

'No-one, marm.'

'But where did you hear that name? Nora? Where did you hear it?'

'No marm, it was Morag,' I says. 'Morag. Not Nora.'

'Oh.'

At the time, I did not pay much heed to her mistake. It was only later I realised its significance. She seemed to relax a little but then she looked at me, through narrowed eyes.

'In that case where did you hear the name Morag?'

'I don't know,' I says, regretting ever having mentioned it. 'I – I think I might have seen it wrote down.'

She surged to her feet, her fists clenched. 'Written down where?'

'On a – on a piece of paper marm.'

'Where?' she says glancing at the ceiling as if it might be pasted up there. 'Where is this piece of paper?'

'I don't know marm – I – it was in my room – I – I threw it away.'

'What did it say?'

'Just – just the name, marm. Morag. Only that. I – I promise you.'

She held the lamp aloft and started peering about the place, frowning and making exasperated noises.

'I thought you said you cleaned this floor,' she says to me but when I jumped up to do it she says, 'Oh do it in the morning will you. But look here – the fire is nearly out.'

'I'll see to it marm,' I says.

'But don't take too long.'

By the time I had a good blaze going she was back at the table, studying my book. I went over and stood not too close and give her a little curtsey. She nodded without looking at me. Best friends no longer, we was mistress and maid once more.

'Sit down, Bessy,' she says. 'We have work to do. I think we should devote a part of every evening after supper to the improvement of your efforts.'

And then she took up a pen and dipped it in ink. 'Clink' went the pen against the ink jar and I realised that it was the same sound that I'd heard earlier that day, and then the missus began to teach me punctuation.

To tell the gobs honest truth I did not give a first-light fart for full stops and all the rest. I thought my page looked fine while her page looked like it was covered in goat droppings with all the wee dots and spots on it. But as my Mr Levy used to say, choices choices, life is full of choices. I thought to myself would you rather be up in your room where there is no fire and a draft coming through the window or would you rather be down here warming your titties by the coals and watching the lovely Arabella as she gives you a lecture on commas and capital letters and maybe from time to time holds your hand and takes you into her confidence?

I studied a lot of punctuation.

5

The Master Returns

Wednesday

Last night went to sleep with my fingers pressed into my cheeks to try and make dimples like the pretty ones missus has but sadly no luck there my cheeks are just the same and now I have one sore finger where I slept on it . Today we ran out of tea . missus loves a nice cup of tea so I went to buy more . it started raining on the way to Snatter , I was not pleased . I was looking about me smiling to see if I could see any of the folk that live there in the village but hardly a soul because of the heavy rain . I was disappointed . The man that runs the shop his name is Henderson, Mr Henderson to me, he tried to sell the tea ½ an oz short but when I pointed it out he pretended it was a mistake and give me a dark look . I asked him if he liked working in a shop but he told me he didn't work in it he owned it , there is a big difference he says , so I tellt him I used to work for Mr Levy of Glasgow , a very successful businessman who owned several shops selling furs , very wealthy he was with shops coming out his ears and such a nice pleasant man too , his success had not spoiled him one jot but of course he never stood behind the counter he had people done that for him . Henderson just looked at me . Then he said something about a bog . I just looked at him back . I think he is not too keen on an Irish girl . Missus says there was nearly a big fight a few years ago when a bunch of Irish fellows coming back from the harvest were menaced by some villagers, in the end nobody was hurt but hereabouts they don't like the Irish much. On the way up the road the rain stopped . A big country fellow with curly hair his trousers held up with a bit of rope and a short black pipe in his mouth came louping out a cottage and fell into step beside me . he had a big dusty face and he kept counting things on his fingers . You name it he counted it , hens , chimney pots , window panes , steps , washing on a line , legs on a horse , spokes on a cartwheel , fence posts , the stripes on my apron . always very serious , like his counting was the most important task in the world . I asked him some things like , what are you doing? But he just ignored me and carried on counting , clearly he is a lunatic . when I got home missus tellt me it was probably Sammy Sums that has been wrong in the mind since he was a boy . he scared me at first but missus says there is no harm in him so that put my mind at rest . people call him Sammy Sums because of the counting , he counts everything . Missus tellt me his busiest time is summer on account of the midgies , they are his lifes work . She did make me laugh . I tellt missus I would take up her offer of a patch of garden to grow things after all , I do not know what yet . I think flowers would be nice roses or sweet pea and then I could give a bunch to missus but she said I would be better planting cabbage and beans . I was all set to start throwing things in the ground straight away but she tellt me the soil has to be prepared , nothing is easy in the country . I made a start anyway in my hour off and tore a whole clatter of stones out the earth and then cleaned missus boots and my own and done some other chores nothing strange or startling . I have finished Bleak House and liked it so she give me another to read, it is about a boy called Pip . Tonight I read aloud to her first out the bible then out an old Monthly Visitor a story about two French cottagers called 'Darkness and Light' . Missus was kind and nice through the evening , I sang a song for her and she liked it and she said I did write very well now in my little book so I was pleased.

But the truth was, some days you just wouldn't know what to expect from missus. I got to realise this after a few weeks. One minute she was good as gold, you could not have asked for a more pleasant employer, the next she would fly into a rampage and yell at you. Then just when you got used to her acting the Mogul she would change again and go all distant. She'd talk to you in the flat voice asking you to do things that didn't seem *altogether* necessary like she'd tell you to take the pips out an apple and then leave it for you to eat, or make you draw some water and then just pour it away into the dirt. If you asked her what you had done wrong and why she was angry she would smile at you very kind and say she wasn't angry. And all the time she was watching watching watching you and afterwards she would scuttle up to her room and for a long time you would hear not a peep out her. About an hour later she would emerge looking much restored, I used to think she had been laying down for a nice nap.

I always did my best to please her. Once or twice more in that first month she bid me sit on the straight back chair and told me to close my eyes and then it was the old game of stand up sit down stand up sit down, flip me could I see the sense in it, could I chook but I went along with it as far as I was able. The 2nd time she asked me I went up and down 10 times but more than that I would not do. On the 3rd occasion, I got to 26 times but on the 27th something in me rebelled and like the broken horse, I went down but would not get up. She was always pleased with me though and said encouraging things like, 'Well done, Bessy, you are a good girl,' then tellt me to go back to my work.

Despite these fickle moods, I was enjoying my new life, for it was as much of an adventure and as exotic to me as if I had travelled to live in the jungle of South America. We was right as rain, me and missus, rubbing along on our own together with work in the day and then at night punctuation and I fair tore through the reading books she give me. *Bleak House*, *Great Expectations*, *Pilgrims Progress*, *Justified Sinner*, I went through them all and more besides. Missus usually went to church of a Sunday and sometimes a Wednesday, truth be told she was C. of E. but the only congregation in those parts was 'You Pee' and she only went for appearances sake. Needless to say I was not welcome, being R.C. and not one of the Chosen Ones, if I or any other 'Taig' had walked into the church service at Snatter GOB KNOWS what would have happened. I expect the roof would blow off, the place explode and old Scratch himself climb up into the ruins and show everybody his jack and jewels and make them smell his bottom. (That's probably what the locals thought anyway.)

On the rare occasions I had no other chore to do, I used to keep missus company by walking her down the lane to church. I'd wait outside until the service was over and then walk home with her. Which was fine and nice except for when Biscuit Meek would come out at the end of the service and give me filthy looks. I knew now that he looked after the plough and horses at Castle Haivers and drove the carriage and he was a fierce man for his worship. It was a shame that the Lord never saw fit to give Biscuit a chin seeing as how he was one of his staunchest. He had a mouth built straight into his neck and his lips was always frothy and wet and turned down at the corners like he had just took a swig of the buttermilk but really all that froth and wet was just a sign of *religious fervour*.

Apart from him, there was not too many farm servants. It didn't take long to work out that master James did not keep enough staff. In the house, they should have had a cook and probably a butler, a ladies maid and a housekeeper all this, but there was only me and I had so much to do, I hardly ever seen the other servants. I learned from missus that Alasdair the foreman ran the estate for master James. This Alasdair was married to Jessie the milkmaid and they lived in the farm up the back lane, along with her sister Muriel. Biscuit and Hector and any temporary workers that were hired stayed in the bothies beyond the woods. The only person I seen with any regularity was Hector when he came to the house to run errands. Once or twice I caught sight of the Curdle twins going up the lane or crossing the yard. But apart from that I was on my own. Or if I was lucky, with missus.

Mostly I worked like a man with 6 arms. My mother used to say hard graft was for fools but with the help of missus I began to see that this was not necessarily the case. For one thing there was always a purpose to the day and I found I liked that. I enjoyed working up an appetite especially when I could get out into the fresh air to look about me for missus said it put roses in my cheeks. It was not long before I had fine muscles forming in my arms from all the lifting and carrying, I tell you this I could have held a horse down in a gale. '*Parte pas les mains vides*' was one of missus favourite sayings and she taught me how it was said and spelt in French. It means 'Don't go empty handed' and it is a good motto in life for you will find there is always something to be carried from one place to another and if you are in the country it is usually manure. But I didn't mind that. The missus admired my muscles because she said that a servant girl *should* have strong arms, it was nothing to be *ashamed* of and she often asked to measure them to see how they were progressing.

I do believe there was times, even in amongst the shite (excuse me but no other word will do) when I was fillt with a kind of Glory, was it God himself had entered me or was it the missus? Or was it in fact just fresh air and exercise, who could say?

Most of all I began to think that if you could make someone happy with a good job well done, particularly someone as special as *my Arabella* (which was how I had already come to think of her – only never out loud!) then was that not worth something?

There was this one time, I found a horse chestnut in the yard it was a beauty about the size of a babys fist so I polished it up with butter and a cloth and give it to the missus and she said she liked it very well and would even display it on her dressing table.

Encouraged and delighted by this response, I spent the next two evenings secretly carving her name on a ½ of a raw potato, it looked quite good when it was done except the last 'L' and 'A' was squashed where I realised I was running out of spud. The missus liked this present very well too, she said I was clever and that you hardly noticed the squashed letters. Only she didn't think it was quite healthy to keep a potato in her bedroom so she put it on the kitchen shelf where we could *both* admire it while we ate our meals.

*

One afternoon, missus rang for me to come to her room. She was sat by the window gazing out at the darkening horizon, perhaps a little sad. But she brightened up when I come in.

'Look!' she says and gestured at the dressing table. Sure enough there was the horse chestnut I had give her proudly on display. I felt very pleased about that.

'Now, Bessy,' she says. 'Why don't you open up my press?'

I thought she might want me to brush down some of her clothes so I did as I was bid without thinking. I'd seen inside the press before, she had about ½ a dozen gowns on the shelves in there, all in soft shades of blue, grey, lilac and green.

'Which do you like the best?' the missus says to me.

'Oh I don't know,' I says. They was nice enough clothes all right but perhaps not *exactly* to my taste – in those days I was young and preferred brighter colours and satin and more trimmings.

'How about the aquamarine?' she says. 'I've heard you admire that before now.'

I looked at it – it was the one she had on the day I arrived and for that reason I did hold it in especial esteem.

'I suppose that *might* be my favourite, marm.'

'Try it on.'

I looked at her. 'Marm?'

She smiled and her dimples appeared, it made you long to bite her cheeks (though of course I would never have done it!)

'Bessy dear,' she says. 'You've been a good and a true friend to me and look what you have done, given me a lovely horse chestnut, so I must give you something in return.'

'And your potato,' I says.

'Yes, of course, my potato,' she says. 'All the more reason. So take off your frock and put on mine.'

Well what could I do but what I was bid. I found that her frock was a little tight for she was more slender than I was and not as big in the tit but it was not *too* bad.

Missus stood up and looked at me with her head on one side. 'My goodness, Bessy, one might almost take you for the mistress of the house!'

She watched me as I strutted about in front of the looking glass, admiring myself. Then she says, 'Bessy, there is something I have been meaning to ask you.'

'Yes marm?'

'You will be – discreet won't you, dear?'

'About what, marm?'

'About – certain things that have – certain things I have asked you to do.'

I thought a moment. 'You mean like my little book, marm?'

She says, 'Yes, that would be one thing. And also – other things.'

'You mean like getting me to stand up and sit down all the time? And letting me put on your frock?'

She blinked or maybe it was a wince. 'Yes,' she says. 'I think it would be for the best if you didn't mention any of that to anyone – anyone at all.'

'Och I will certainly be discreet, marm,' I says. 'You don't even need to mention it. I would have done it anyway.'

She took a deep breath and smiled. Clearly she was most relieved.

'Good girl,' she says.

'It's no bother to me at all, marm.' And then I blurted out, I can't remember the exact words but it was something like, 'I would do *anything* for you marm, *anything* at all, you only need to ask me. You've been awful good to me and – well a fair exchange is no robbery.'

The missus seemed took aback, or you might almost have said a bit alarmed.

'Well, that's – that's – good to hear,' she says and then she patted the empty shelf of the press and I took this as a sign that our dressing up game was over.

I didn't realise at the time that she was probably worried about her husbands return. Indeed, I'd almost forgot he existed. A few letters had come from London, where (apparently) he was on business. But missus kept no likeness of him and barely mentioned him. He was not part of our lives. The imaginative side of me occasionally wondered whether she might have done away with him. Sometimes, as I lay in bed at night I tried to guess where she'd put the body. Would she have buried him in the vegetable garden for instance? Or hid him in the attic? And would his blood drip through the ceiling and make a stain? And how long before he began to stink?

But as I found out ere long the master was alive and well and not at all stinky. The very next day after she let me try on her frock, missus lost her thimble and sent me down to the village to buy another. Reverend Pollock was emerging from the shop as I approached. There was no escape, since he stood in front of the door, blocking my way, hell roast him.

'Ah-haah' he goes. Then he fished a pamphlet out his pocket and pressed it into my hand. 'I have been saving this for you, girl,' he says.

I glanced down and seen that it was a tract, entitled, '*Dear Roman Catholic Friend.*' Before I had a moment to be irritated about that, he spoke again, waving a hand in the air.

'Read it at your leisure,' he says. 'I'll be happy to answer any questions you may have. Of course, you'll be rushed off your feet now your master is come home.'

'You are mistaken, sir,' I says. 'Master James is not at home.'

'Oh?' He raised an eyebrow and looked at me. 'I thought you would know all about the comings and goings at Castle Haivers. But perhaps your mistress does not much confide in you. I think you'll find that James arrived back today.'

He sauntered off, very pleased with himself. I crumpled up the tract and could have thrown it at his flipping head but had to content myself with waiting until he was out of sight and tossing it over a hedge.

Of course it was still possible that he was wrong but as soon as I got back to the house I seen a portmanteau stood in the hallway.

And the missus was shut in the parlour, talking with a man, in low voices. It was him, the master. Returned! The Old Bollix had been right. I have to admit I was a bit put out that my Arabella hadn't even *mentioned* to me that her husband was expected home, for I had the impression she told me everything. It was a little upsetting. It even occurred to me that she had sent me to the shop to get me out the way while she welcomed him home. But I convinced myself that she must have just forgot and tried to put it out my mind. Besides I was more than a little curious to get a look at this husband. So after a moments hesitation I knocked at the parlour door and waited for her to say 'Come!' as usual.

Instead there was a pause, then she opened the door a crack and peered out. I give her a nice low curtsey. She frowned at me. 'What is it now, Bessy?'

'I have your thimble for you, marm.' It was hard to see past her because she had only opened the door a few inches and she was stood right in the gap.

She held out her finger under my nose. 'Well?' she says after a moment.

'What?' I says.

'The *thimble*, please Bessy.'

I slipped it onto her finger.

'Thank you,' she says and started to close the door.

'Will you be needing anything else, marm?'

'No thank you,' she says firmly. 'We will ring soon and then you can bring us tea.'

We.

And then she shut the door in my face.

I did not have long to wait for about a ½ hour later the bell rang. Once the tea was ready I set everything on the tray and carried it through. This time when I knocked on the door the missus bid me 'Come!' and so in I went very careful not to drop the tray or spill anything or trip. A fine introduction that would be, me falling across the threshold, tea things flying whoops-a-daisy everything all over the place and me on the floor with my skirts up around my waist and the master staring at my drawers! That would never have done, I wanted the missus to be proud of me so I made sure not to rush and held onto the tray very tight.

The master was sat in the wing armchair opposite my Arabella. He flicked his eyes at me as I came in then glanced away again almost immediately. For dear sake he was a daddy longleg so he was! So tall and lean he barely fit the length of him in the chair. You would have put him older than missus but no more than 45 and just a shade off handsome on account of his phiz being on the lengthy side and he was not exactly going bald but lets just say his forehead was *high*. The hair he had was dark and shaggy and grew into louse ladders all up his cheeks. He still had his coat on but his hat was on the floor beside him, and now he was staring past his knees at it while he bit ferociously at his finger nails. The minute I seen him he put me in mind of a bird dog, there was something vigorous and high strung about him like he might bound away off at any moment to do something energetic.

'Bessy!' the missus says a bit sharp.

I looked round startled, I must have fell into a dwam. 'Yes, marm?' I says.

She give me a warning look so I knew I must have been staring. I made the both of them a low curtsey which is no mean feet when you're carrying a ½ a ton of tea tray.

'This is your master James,' says the missus.

'Pleased to meet you, sir,' I says and made him another curtsey. Being otherwise occupied with his 'manicure' he just nodded. I set the tray on the table and began to lay out the cups and saucers, you could hear every clink of the china and occasionally the sound of the masters teeth snapping together. Meanwhile the missus sat in her chair very still, her hands clasped. It was difficult to judge the atmosphere, it might have been that they were simply waiting for me to go or perhaps they had just had some kind of dispute, I couldn't tell. All the while even as he savaged his nails the master was casting sideways glances in my direction so I made sure I did everything just so. I began to think that I would leave the room with barely a word being spoke but of a sudden he sat back, put one hand in his pocket and spread the long bony fingers of the other across the front of his waistcoat. Then he proceeded to interrogate me.

It was a bit like a more amiable version of the Spanish Inquisition except that no matter how much he grilled you he never asked a single question, what he did was bombard you with *statements* which he then give you the opportunity to corroborate or otherwise. Perhaps it was his training in the law but I formed the impression that Master James thought questions were beneath him, that what he liked was to be a veritable *Font of Wisdom* and that for him every conversation was a way of proving that he was always – like Solomon – *in possession of all the facts*. He may even have thought he was being sociable but it was an unfortunate way of dealing with people. Combined with his beady-eye gaze and a clipped manner of speaking it was destined to put you on the offensive.

His first words to me was, 'You came with excellent references, I believe.'

Flipsake! Needless to say this filled me with great alarm. I shot a glance at missus but she had grabbed up the teapot and was staring at it fixedly while she poured, a high point of colour in her cheeks. What in gobs name had she told him? I had to think quick.

'Sir,' I says, with another curtsey. 'I have always gave good service in the past.' And not a word of a lie there too by Jove.

He nodded sagely. 'You have experience of the work.'

'I do, sir.' I says, (And did not add, a few weeks worth).

He seemed satisfied with that and nodded again. 'I'm told you can read.'

'Yes sir.'

'I know that you write also, quite well – bar a scant understanding of punctuation. But no doubt you learn quickly.'

'I hope so sir.'

It was interesting to listen to so extensive an account of your own character, especially from someone you had never even met before! I wondered what I would learn about myself next.

The master stretched back in his seat and splayed his legs out on the hearth. 'Well,' he says. 'You will have little need of reading and writing here.'

Gob I did not *dare* look at missus.

'Although perhaps you can read the newspaper to me of an evening. You would enjoy that I suspect.'

I nodded politely.

He says, 'Apparently, thus far you have proved to be quite indispensable. Very hard working and cheerful.'

'I do my best sir.'

At this point he leaned forward and fixed me with a very searching look. 'Towards the end of a morning,' he says, 'you are left with a heap of vegetable peelings.'

I just looked at him, quite bewildered by this change of subject.

'A pound or two,' he continues. 'Mixed peelings of potatoes turnips and the like.'

'Sir?'

'These peelings are a little dirty but not mouldered. Describe to me your subsequent course of action.'

'Excuse me sir?' I says.

Missus cleared her throat. 'What would you do with the peelings, Bessy?' she says quietly without looking at me.

'Oh!' says I as it dawned on me that this was some kind of test. I had no desire to let her down so racked my brains. 'Well I would put them – in – in the bucket for the pig?'

'Hah!' He slapped his knee and stared triumphantly at the missus. 'Wrong answer!'

She gazed back at him evenly. 'What would you have her do with them, James?'

'Why – rinse them and bile them up for broth!' he says.

'Oh James. Under my instruction she has been putting them in the pig swill.'

He tutted and turned back to me with his dark beady eyes. 'I sincerely hope,' he says. 'You are not a wasteful girl.'

'Oh no sir.'

'Nothing worse than a wasteful servant. We've had our fill of *them* in the past.'

He smiled over at missus, but she avoided his eye so he turned back to me and without further ado embarked upon another swift change of subject.

'Tell me about your parents. I know your mother is – departed.'

'Yes sir.'

'I presume your father is still alive somewhere.'

I looked appropriately mournful and mentioned that he was also 'gone'.

'I see.' He pursed his lips and frowned, then drummed his fingers against his chest, the nails was bit to nubbets. 'I'm very sorry to hear that. I imagine you will be wanting to visit their graves from time to time.'

'Sir? Oh no sir I –'

'A departed parent is a terrible thing, I take it you would not mind telling us the cause of their passing.'

'Sir, it was – the typhus sir.'

'Ah. Oh dear.' He nodded his head mournfully then looked across at missus. 'We would have no objection to letting her visit the graves on occasion, Arabella.'

'Oh?' says missus. 'No indeed.' I think she was as confused as I was by the turn the conversation had suddenly took. The master turned back to me.

'Unless of course they are buried in Ireland,' he says.

'No sir, Glasgow, but I –'

'Very well then. You have our permission.'

He then gazed at me expectantly. What he wanted was gratitude. I give it to him plus a curtsey, even though there was no graves and even had there been I don't know that I would have visited them.

'Thank you, sir. That's very kind of you.'

He frowned. 'You must miss your home country,' he says.

'Not really,' I says. 'I like it much better here. This is a fine country. It seems very beautiful – well parts of it anyway. And Glasgow is a great city – parts of it anyway – the suspension bridge and all the lights.'

He wasn't even listening. He only heard what he wanted to hear.

'Aye,' he says. 'It's a terrible thing to be far from home. You haven't told me how long you have been over here in Scotland.'

That was right, I hadn't. Gob it was remarkable how he needled you for information without ever seeming to be in ignorance! I wondered did he practise it.

'I been here two years now, sir.'

It was actually four so that was only ½ of a lie. I don't know why I hid the truth, there was no real purpose in it. Perhaps it was because the man was so keen to have what he thought was your Essence, it felt like he was stealing from you, and giving him the wrong information made me feel better.

'Two years, aye,' he says nodding, as if he knew that already but was just testing you. 'Well Bessy,' he says. 'We shall see how long you last here. You may go now.'

I give them both a curtsey and was about to leave the room when he called out. 'Just remind me. The name of the Register Office.'

'Register Office, sir?'

'The Office at which you registered for employment.'

'Oh,' I says. 'Yes, sir of course now it was – it was –'

'Lauders,' the missus said. 'On Hope Street.'

'That's right sir, it was Lauders sir.'

'I suppose that cost a fortune,' the master says but he wasn't talking to me it was my Arabella he was addressing. She dipped her head and smiled at him prettily.

'But I think we will find it will be worth it dear,' she says.

They held each others gaze and it was as though something invisible passed between them for after a moment the master seemed to relax and then he laughed fondly.

'Very well my dear,' he says. 'If you say so.'

Of a sudden I felt like an intruder and turned to creep out the room. It was at that moment that my gaze fell upon the missus sewing basket, I was surprised to see her old thimble sitting on top of it. She must have found it then, I thought, perhaps while I was at the shop. Or had she indeed just been trying to get rid of me? I turned to make some remark on the subject but before I could speak she addressed me.

'Oh by the way, Bessy,' she says. 'We are invited out this evening so you will not have to make any supper.'

'Out!?' I says.

'Yes,' she says and smiled evenly at her husband. 'Is that so unusual?'

'Oh – eh – no marm.'

But I was feeling confused. I was used to our evenings in together, somehow it had never entered my head that the missus would ever dine *out*.

'Close your mouth, girl!' the master says. 'Or you'll catch a fly.'

I looked at him. Then I looked back at the missus. 'Only I was wondering, marm,' I says. 'What about our punctuation lesson?'

'Not tonight, Bessy,' says the missus. 'We shall continue again tomorrow.'

The master give a yell of laughter. 'Oh dearie me!' he says. 'She doesn't like that!'

I made an effort to smile and give him a curtsey to show that he was wrong. He jutted his chin out at me.

'One last question, Bessy,' he says. 'About your father.'

I waited with great interest to see if he actually *would* ask a question but what he said was, 'I would like to know his trade.'

'He was a sailor, sir.'

And by all accounts that was more than likely true.

But I didn't really want any more enquiries on the subject, in the form of questions or otherwise so I curtseyed quickly and went out.

*

Oh there was a few things I could have tellt him about my parents. And I would have loved to see the look on his face if I had. Come to think of it, perhaps I should have tellt him. He might have dismissed me on the spot as unsuitable.

And then none of the rest of it might have happened.

6

I Make a Discovery

What happened next I am a little ashamed to recount. But since the rest of my tale depends upon it – indeed it is the very substance of my story – recount I must. With hindsight I have only one excuse and that is the natural curiosity of youth.

Missus and the master spent some time in their separate rooms before they went out for the evening. Hector was sent to tell Biscuit to bring round the carriage for 7 and at about ½ past 6, I went to see if the missus wanted any help with her clothes. But she didn't need me, she had got ready herself. She seemed very excited about the idea of dining out because it was some fellow what wrote songs and poems they were going to visit.

'I make up songs,' I says to her.

'I know you do,' she says. But she wasn't really listening she was inspecting her own reflection by the light of a candle, in the looking glass. 'Is this necklace too ornate?'

'No marm it's lovely,' I says. 'I wish I had one like it. Do you like to hear my songs, marm?'

'I do indeed,' she says. 'Now where are my gloves?'

'Here they are marm. Is there anything you want me to do while you're gone?'

'Not really.'

'I tell you what – I could do the standing up and sitting down if you like.'

She paused in the action of stretching her gloves and looked at me. 'What?' she says.

'Stand up sit down – I'll do it and tell you how many times when you get back.'

She frowned. 'No, Bessy,' she says. 'That is *not* how it works. And you will remember our little discussion, won't you?'

I looked at her.

'About being discreet?' she says.

'Oh, certainly marm.'

'Good girl,' she says. And then she give me a little kiss.

I think I must have flushed with pleasure and in my confusion stepped forward to return the kiss but she had already moved away and was pulling on her gloves. Where her cheek brushed mine she left behind the fragrance of roses, I could still smell it even after her and the master had climbed into the carriage and gone off together into the night. I wished it was me going.

Well – me and the missus, two ladies dressed in our finest frocks and off out for a night at gaming and cards. Now *that* would have been something to see. That would have been the pigs whiskers.

With the master and missus gone the house suddenly felt very big and empty. For a while I wandered about the downstairs rooms with a candle, realising that I had not really been there entirely on my own before. It felt very cold and lonely and my footsteps echoed on the boards and slates. Usually, the missus was always somewhere within shouting distance not that I ever shouted, she didn't like shouting, she said that was public house behaviour, you always had to go to her and address her quiet and nice if you wanted to ask something and not bawl it out the window or across the yard like a washer woman or somebody. At any rate after a while I grew restless and decided to go upstairs and have a look at the missus frocks while she was out. I think, in my girlish way, perhaps it was my intention to try to get into one or two more of them, I don't know. I did open her press but I only glanced at the frocks, didn't try them on or sniff them or anything. And then after that I thought I might have a peek in her desk. Well the drawer was locked as always. However it occurred to me that now she was out I had sufficient time to try and locate the key. It did take quite a while and I was on the point of giving up my little searches when it occurred to me that she might have left it in the frock she'd been wearing earlier. Sure enough, when I slipped my hand inside the pocket my fingers closed around a small key. I slid it into the lock of the desk and turned it, then opened the drawer.

There was a dead baby in there! And some jam! And a tin whistle!

No there wasn't really.

It was only a whole clatter of old notebooks and a big old ledger with a red leather binding. I took out the red book and opened it without much interest. There inside the cover was one of her black and white labels, EX~BIBLIOTHEC~CASTEL~HAIVERS. Now that I had seen the picture on the label in all the books she give me, I knew that it was not two *ladies* sitting under the tree at all, but one lady and her maid, in apron and mob cap. This particular label hadn't been stuck on very well. It was all puffed up like a blister and she'd used so much paste that it had turned lumpy. I turned to the first page of the book and was surprised to see that it was covered in the missus own handwriting in violet ink and I will transcribe some of what was wrote there.

Observations on the Habits and Nature of the Domestic Class in My Time

Had we an account of the nature, habits and training of the domestic class in my time and details of particular cases therein, no history could be more useful, but it strikes me that such matters are rarely heeded and that what knowledge we have remains within the realm of personal experience. It were to be wished that some good author would make his observations on the subject during his time so that the knowledge could be passed down, though it is only a man of great good sense could wish to do so with any success.

In the absence of such an author, I humbly offer the following theoretical discourse and case studies. Those servants I have lived to see myself I wish to remember and note down in these pages, both for my own use and for the elucidation of others. I am aware that being only in my twentieth year my experience is not yet extensive.

Nonetheless, as time goes on I will add to the account particulars of any servants who come to work here.

It should be noted that I may have to restrict myself to house servants since I am unable to observe farm servants with any depth or regularity as they are quartered elsewhere and, in any case, I gather that they are generally a sodden lot, much given to horse-play and obscene talk, receiving friends and drinking together in their 'bothy' to 'make night hideous with their revelry'. Am I now going to assert that the servant should toil ceaselessly, with no rest from his labours? Nothing could be further from my intention. Man is not a machine and used as one he is most imperfect. However, I venture to assert that the absence of food for the mind when labour is ended is a grievous cause of domestic ennui. We must teach our servants to read and write or, better still, endeavour to employ persons who already have the basic skills upon which some light and regular instruction can improve. Especial care should be taken with reading, above all that the girls read fluently. A mistress should ensure freely available access to texts including, for example, the Bible, Walter Scott, Mr Dickens, Richardson and so on.

However, my intention is not only to advocate the education of servants but also to examine how else we might get the best out of them. I cannot but acknowledge once again my inefficiency to discuss fully the many important bearings on the matter of the domestic class but it rejoices me exceedingly that in writing this book I am able to contribute my stock of information and if any single observation or suggestion of mine should tend to elucidate a difficulty or lead to any practical result such a prize is all I can expect. With all its imperfections, and I am aware that there may be many of them, I place this book before an indulgent public . . .

And so on. So this was it. This was why her fingers was sometimes stained with ink. The missus was writing her own book! She had been at it for years, indeed since not long after she arrived at Castle Haivers. *The Observations.*

You could have knocked me down with a feather.

I flicked through the next pages, they were a further introduction along the same lines about men of genius and how missus herself was barely worthy to look at a pen never mind pick one up which I thought at the time a terrible shame for in my opinion she wrote awful well with some lovely phrases and the punctuation was tremendous. In fact there was one or two sentences in there I thought were the most elegant I had *ever* read in *any* book.

In the next part, entitled 'Servants of My Experience Thus Far' missus started in observing about somebody named Freda. This Freda seemed to have worked for the missus father in Wimbledon. She was a foreign girl but she only got two pages of observations before she was sent packing back to Germany. Apparently she had behaved in a forward manner with a gentleman caller who came to tea then took his leave but was later found skulking in the basement after dark near this Fredas room. The gentleman himself was full of apologies when confronted and he was so charming about it all that it wasn't long before he was forgiven. Not so the bold Freda, she kicked up a powerful fuss and gave vent to some rude remarks before she was ejected onto the pavement.

Missus had summed it all up quite neatly.

> *This one example does not mean, however, that the Foreign domestic is not to be trusted. There are many cases that would prove the opposite. For instance, I did hear of one Frenchie that has proved to be meticulous in his duties as valet to a great man of importance who is of my father's acquaintance and it is well known in society that Mrs B— of M— goes nowhere without her coal-black Negress . . .*

Next missus observed at great length about Nanny P. – a paragon of a woman who I am surprised is not numbered among the saints judging from the missus account of her virtues. Nanny Ps death was a terrible blow to missus and a few lines here and there was smudged as though tears had fallen to christen the page.

After that there was a whole clatter of entries, none of them long and each headed up with a girls name. I got the impression that these were girls who had preceded me at Castle Haivers in the distant past and will transcribe some phrases to give the gist.

Margaret . . . sauce-box . . . refuse to record . . . impertinent . . . good riddance . . . Vhari . . . Highland girl . . . only five days . . . middle of the night . . . spoons missing . . . Shona . . . another Highlander . . . all of three weeks . . . somewhat wasteful . . . James displeased . . . bitter argument . . . marching orders . . . Peggy . . . rather pert . . . cow eyes at all and sundry . . . terrible cook . . . flounced back to wherever she came from . . .

And so it went, page after page of girls and misdemeanours. Then there was a few blank pages and another heading.

Some Notes on Physiognomy and Other Matters

Over the last few years I have begun to form in my own mind the belief that there may be some connection between the Physiognomy of a servant and his character. It has not escaped my attention that a skinny, ill-tempered looking girl will often prove to be just that, whereas a fat creature of amiable countenance will fail to surprise by behaving just as her appearance might suggest. For instance, from personal experience, my own Nanny P. could not have been a more lovely character and her good temper was well expressed in her rosy apple cheeks and plump homely figure. On a note not unrelated to the preceding, I am also intrigued by the notion that just as there is a 'type' of person that is naturally rebellious and naughty, there are also those that are born with the desire to serve – the inherently obedient. If such inherently obedient persons were found to have similar physical attributes – the same shape of face, for example, or ears set low on the head – how much easier then would be our task of hiring, since we could tell with one glance who would render good service and who would not!

As a preliminary measure, I will henceforth record descriptions of the physical attributes of each girl, including measurements of the proportions. By observation, I will also record the girl's general temperament and – specifically – her inclination to obedience. This information, once collated, can then be used as a basis for analysis . . .

One further area of interest to be explored is the notion that a servant will respond not only according to circumstances and background but also according to how he or she is treated by their master or mistress. I suspect all would become clear if only one could see directly into the mind of the domestic. To know how and what they think – surely then one would understand how to get the best out of them . . .

. . . Of course, readers may raise an eyebrow at the fact that we employ only one girl in the house, in addition to our farm servants. However, my husband believes that it is better to fully employ one servant than to waste money in keeping several idle. He also sees great benefit in my taking an active part in the running of the household and I quite agree, as how dull would life be if one had nothing to do! . . .

After this the entries became more detailed, they included the girls ages and a brief physical description. Then there would be a list of measurements of their bodies and faces, just like missus had done with me. And then some account of how they had acquitted themselves while in employment, if they could read, what books she had give them if so, when and if they had misbehaved and so on. None of it was particularly interesting to me so I flipped on through the book until I came across this more intriguing entry.

Tragic Loss of a Servant

All being well, a servant will remain with the household until such time as it is mutually agreeable for him or her to leave. Unfortunately, there are times when Fate steps in and removes a girl from the world before we are ready to let them go – and how then are we to deal with the loss? Of course, I am not suggesting for a moment that the death of a servant is of the same magnitude a tragedy as losing a family member or a friend or even an acquaintance of the same class. A servant is a servant and, in some cases, one would be hard pressed to remember their names a few days after they have gone on to work elsewhere (unless one keeps a record, as I do). However there are those among them who can – be it that they are particularly adept at work or pleasant in countenance or obedient to us – find a corner in our hearts. Should something befall one of these servants the loss can be harder to bear.

For example, it so happens that a girl of ours – Nora, the Irish girl previously mentioned in these pages – recently disappeared. The general opinion, in the first day of her absence, was that she had run away. Of course, anyone who knew her would realise that this girl would never do such a thing. She was reliable, trustworthy, loyal and amiable. I have found that Irish girls are much better tempered than their Highland counterparts and there is also not always the same language difficulty. Nora was amongst the finest of her kind, an extremely pleasant girl and all of these characteristics were evident in her engaging looks.

Sadly she met with a fatal accident. Apparently, a troupe of itinerants discovered some remains next to a line of the railway track and reported their find to the first person they saw, who happened to be our foreman. He immediately recognised Nora (despite extensive damage to her person there was no mistaking her identity). The local village does not have a policeman but with the arrival of the constable from Smoller, the itinerants were arrested, briefly, but were released when our Dr McGregor-Robertson examined the scene and pronounced that Nora's death was (of course!) caused not by her fellow countrymen but, without doubt, by a speeding train. This was confirmed a few days later when the rest of her body was discovered, further down the line, somewhere between here and the nearby town of Bathgate.

Our doctor informs me it is not known where exactly the collision took place, as her body could have been dragged any distance. No driver reported seeing anyone on the tracks. However, it seems clear that, at some point, the poor girl wandered onto the track and somehow failed to see a train approaching . . .

The funeral took place yesterday. I did not attend, being a little too upset and my husband did not think it wise. Of course, everyone is most shocked, myself especially since I was particularly fond of this girl. I felt that in Nora I had found (at last!) the ideal servant, always eager to please and well-liked by all who met her. Alas, she was with me for only six months . . .

Poor dear Nora! I fear I will never find another like her. In such cases, those who are not as close to the deceased have, of course, their own reactions to the death. For instance, my husband seems concerned in the main with potential scandal. He is horrified that such a tragedy should have happened on our land. I myself had the sorry task of packing up Nora's few belongings and putting them away in the attic. As far as we are aware there is no family but I shall keep her few things and her paltry pair of thin, faded frocks just in case anyone should come asking for them. I had thus far managed to remain in control of my emotions, but I must confess that, as I folded away Nora's clothing, I found myself shedding a tear or two.

At this point I paused in my reading of *The Observations* because an awful thought was forming in my mind. I stared down at the frock I had on. I must admit, I ½ expected to see it fall in rotting shreds from my body and crumble to yellow dust on the floor but it was just the same as always, grey and a bit faded and too tight in the tit. Could missus possibly have give me clothes belonging to a dead girl? For that was what the 'Great Tragedy' suggested. I could not countenance that my missus would do such a ghoulish thing but all the same it troubled me.

And then I remembered the words and hooting laughter of AP Henderson when he was asking about my predecessor. '*Did she go on the train?*'

So that was his joke – a very grisly one.
I flicked back several pages.

Nora

Age 22 years
Smaller than average height
Bust 32
Waist 28
Hip 36
Arm 10 and ½ inches
Neck 12 and ¼ inches
Skull 21 and ¼ inches
Mouth 2 and ¼ inches
Mouth to ear 5 and ¼ inches
Nose 1 and ¾ inches
Between the eyes 2 inches

By observation: brown hair, pleasant countenance, sparkling eyes, clear skin, one missing tooth (incisor), small frame, lively – darting – like a bird.

Nora has now been with us for five days and has proved to be most efficient and pleasant in carrying out her duties. She is Irish by origin and has been in this country for six years. Her mother having been a milkmaid, Nora knows her way around a dairy and has therefore thankfully been able – in addition to her other duties – to help with the cows in the absence of one of our girls who has gone to tend a sick mother. Nora's father was a ploughman and as a result she is thoroughly versed in the ways of the countryside. One could not ask for a better parentage in a country maid! She is also terribly pretty, and there is a definite match between her engaging looks and her demeanour, which is always amiable. True, I no longer adopt the position that a direct correspondence between looks and temperament is always inherent. Nonetheless the evidence in this case is convincing.

I am delighted to say that, in addition to her other talents, Nora is also a good cook. Best of all, she responds to my every request with consummate obedience. Some girls balk at having their dimensions recorded or at least put up a fuss if one should try to measure their face, but Nora uttered not a murmur. Indeed, although she looked slightly puzzled as I pressed the tape measure to her nose, she did not afterwards even question that I had done so! The nose in question is quite short and a little upturned (with, I venture to add, a charming dusting of light freckles!). I had thought a short upturned nose to be the sign of a liar, but now wonder whether this characteristic could be a key indicator of high obedience levels? . . .

At this point, I began flicking through the book, impatient to see if there was any mention of my own name and (hopefully!) similar praise of me, when something else caught my eye and I turned back a few pages. Here is what I read.

Morag

Aged about 15 (but doesn't know exact birth date). No measurements as she refused the tape measure point blank. By observation: teeth yellow and ridged but strong. Hair red (indicative of temper?). Skin very rough and ruddy (indicative of drink?).

This subject has been with us for two days, it having been necessary to acquire her with short notice at the hiring fair, since the girl who was supposed to replace Nora never arrived. (I believe on Mrs Lauder's authority that she has eloped with a footman!)

Morag does not seem afraid of hard work but on first impression she does perhaps have a capacity for stubbornness (see above remarks re: tape measure). She also has a startling way of cackling with laughter directly in one's face, which I fear may drive me to distraction ere long . . .

When I read this it occurred to me that Morag could only be the redhead lass that had cackled at me in the lane as I made my way towards Castle Haivers for the first time. The description sounded just like her. And surely then, it was her book that I'd found burnt in the fire? I remembered the night I'd asked about her, when missus misheard me and thought I wanted to know about that other girl, Nora.

I read on eagerly to find out about Morag.

I began with this girl by asking for the whole story of her life but she is taciturn and it was difficult even to persuade her to provide the simplest details. However despite her apparent lack of spark, I find that she can read and write, having received a few years of basic education from some enlightened soul in her home village. Her hand is childish but legible so that happily I can get her to keep a journal in the hope that it will reveal something of the inner workings of her mind. I am sensible that she may not write anything illuminating and it is even possible that she may use the book as a tool for deception – but that in itself will be interesting to observe.

I flicked forward a few pages and read several sections at random.

Morag has now been here a fortnight. She carries out 'normal' duties quite well (if rather sullenly) but refuses to take part in anything that does not pertain to what she regards as her proper area of work – in other words, any of my research! I have more or less given up the notion of carrying out any kind of experiments with her as she has proved to be uncooperative in the extreme . . .

. . . I have complained about Morag's sullen demeanour in a letter to my husband but his reply states that I was foolish to take her in the first place. It is his theory that the only purpose of hiring fairs is to give bad masters a better chance of getting servants and bad servants a better chance of getting masters. In my defence may I say that the only alternative girl on the day was so ragged and filthy and stank so badly, that in comparison this Morag seemed almost presentable . . .

. . . Relations with Morag have almost come to breaking point. We barely speak to each other. Yesterday she leaned forwards and regurgitated a mouthful of half-chewed sausage onto the table,

claiming the meat to be rank. I have now decided to take all my meals separately, as this grisly sight almost forced a reappearance of my own food . . .

. . . The very sight of Morag now turns my stomach. I am sure the poor girl cannot help being so ugly but I do wish that she would disappear so that my gaze would never have to alight upon her again. She is truly a wretch. I will be glad to see the back of her.

Here, I put down the book and went and looked out the window. There was nothing to be seen out there but the night sky, a few bluish clouds scudding across the face of the moon.

Such terrible things missus had said about that girl. I was having a premonition. And my premonition was this. That I should read no more of this book, *The Observations*, because I might find out some things that would upset me. I think I may even have spoke out loud to myself, 'Do not read on, my dear, do not read on.' At one point I even went over and closed the book and made to put it back in the drawer. But then I thought away to Hell out of this, you may not get another chance to see what she has wrote about you.

And so once again I opened *The Observations* and with trembling fingers turned the pages until I came across this title, *Bessy*.

And then I saw that it was worse than I feared for underneath – in different ink that had been added later – were these words, *The Most Particular Case of a Low Prostitute*.

But there I must stop for I have been writing for hours today, the hand is near enough dropping off me and they will be ringing the bell soon for supper.

PART TWO

7

A Most Particular Case

Introductory note. I beg it to be understood that what I transcribe here from Arabellas '*Observations*' is intended only for the eyes of those gentlemen that have asked me to give my account and that these extracts should *not* be reproduced by *anybody* in *any way shape or form whatsoever* without prior application to me.

I will transcribe only what I think relevant and leave out parts that have less bearing on this history for instance sections which itemise my measurements what have you, and the many detailed accounts of experiments where she notes how many stand/sits I performed or how I responded to her moods and strange requests &c. I ask the reader only this, to imagine the cold feeling of anguish that crept into my bones as I stood there in the missus bedroom and read what she did write about me.

Extracted from *The Observations*, by Arabella R.

Bessy
(*The Most Particular Case of a Low Prostitute*)

This subject came to us by chance, after the sudden departure of her predecessor. I employed Bessy in awareness that she had not much experience of domestic work, intending to 'train' her. Little did I know what dark secrets she had left behind her in Glasgow.

PREFATORY REMARKS

Age between 14 and 16 years (though claims to be 18!) Smaller than average height. The subject's hair is brown, a little wild and lacking in arrangement. She is rather broad in the face, with a short nose, startling blue eyes and an expression that occasionally has a shifty cast. From time to time, she becomes blank-eyed, as though stunned – although perhaps she is only daydreaming. The most pleasant feature is the mouth, which one might almost say was pretty, although she is much given to pouting and sucking on her fingers, which lends her an unfortunate sultry appearance. She sings little songs as she goes about the place, songs of her own devising it seems, but I suspect that a bad temper may lurk beneath her superficially 'sunny' nature. There is something about her – I cannot quite put my finger on it – but she seems rather 'deadened' and lacking in some element – perhaps emotion?

She claims to have most recently been employed as a housekeeper but I find this assertion, given her appearance and youth, unlikely. Initially, I presumed that she had wandered adrift from some kind of pageant or circus, because when she arrived here (en passant to Edinburgh) she was dressed in a brightly coloured satinet costume which was heavily adorned with bows and lace. However, I have since decided that she is not an acrobat or performer: she simply lacks discernment in attire. I have observed her over the past week and am now convinced that she is just a simple factory girl and her gaudy garments are what pass as 'Sunday best' clothes.

I doubt that she has ever worked in service because she appears to have little grasp of how to go about the most basic domestic task. For instance, yesterday I found her scrubbing at the pale yellow rug in the parlour with a crumpled up piece of newspaper – effectively rubbing newsprint into the fibres and staining them a dirty grey! When asked to explain her actions she told me that she had dropped a few shards of coal onto the floor while sweeping the hearth and she was just 'makin' it tidy'. In other words, not only was she rubbing newsprint into the rug, she was grinding pieces of coal into it in addition!

Such is the unpromising raw material with which I am presented: a coarse girl, with no domestic experience and very little common sense. Even Morag, despite her flaws, was familiar with housework.

Surely (I can hear the reader exclaim), this new subject is beyond even my powers to bring under control? Is it not the case that, faced with such a challenge, I must finally come to my senses and admit defeat? I am willing to give some thought to these objections and, having done so, find myself bound to reply forthwith and as follows: that, on the contrary, it is my intention to domesticate the girl, within a period of no longer than three months, to a standard that would be acceptable in any household!

I have written a letter to the address where she claims she used to work, explaining the situation and requesting of whoever receives it a character and any other information that they may have about her. Of course, she may just have invented the address, in which case there will be no reply.

INITIAL DISORIENTATION

With this subject, I began the process of experimentation on the very night she arrived by going to her as she slept. The air inside her room was unexpectedly warm and laced with an earthy, drowsy scent. I have smelt something like it before in the rooms of other maids. It is their personal aroma, issued forth in sleep, and very different it is from the scent emitted by those of more distinguished birth. I noted that this particular subject's odour is also tinged with a pleasant sweetness, as of Parma violets (am not sure what can be deduced from this, if anything. Does it indicate a sweetness of nature? Or is this too obvious an interpretation?)

By the light of my candle, I could see that she was sound asleep, breathing deeply, her dark hair spread across the pillow. I crept forwards for a better look. She looked so peaceful that I almost had a change of heart about waking her. But, coming to my senses, I decided to go ahead with my experiment as planned. I wanted to see how she would respond, after the disorientation of being awoken, to a range of different humours and I had settled for this occasion on 'anger' (the 'harsh' mistress); 'impartial remoteness' (the 'fair but distant' mistress) and then 'indulgence' (the 'kindly' mistress). In this way, as I believe I shall prove, the subject is made open to new influence and instruction.

Shamming annoyance, I woke her abruptly and ordered her to follow me downstairs. The girl was most apologetic when she finally appeared in the kitchen. From the anxious glances she kept directing towards the loaf on the table, I deduced that she thought I was angry with her for taking more than one slice earlier in the day, something that I had noticed but not commented upon. Keen to get on with testing the humours, I reassured her quickly and gave her a command in deliberately neutral tones.

It was at this juncture that something remarkable happened. Since she had arrived, the subject had shown no inclination to exhibit the due deference of a maid to a mistress. Indeed, something in the way she pronounces the word 'missis' (her favoured nomenclature for myself) makes it almost more of an insult than a courtesy and she has to be gently and often reminded to employ the term 'ma'am'. Of curtsies and other tokens of respect, there had been no sign. Perhaps this is only to be expected. In a factory, I doubt that one rarely, if ever, encounters a person of any breeding. However – she now proceeded to make me a curtsey! So very happy was I with this turn of events that it took little effort to adopt the next of my humours, that of extreme indulgence. Predictably, the girl is – like most of her kind – unsettled by such behaviour in a person of superior status. She gave every sign of being uncomfortable and her relief, when I announced my intention to retire, was palpable.

Clearly, the disorientation had produced in her some (albeit deeply-buried) trait of servility – but I began to wonder whether the mere fact of having been awoken from sleep caused this or whether it was provoked by one of the humours that I had displayed, and if so was it anger or indifference? I was even tempted to wake her for a second time and try the experiment again and it was only with great difficulty that I refrained from doing so.

I have heard tell of distinguished and learned gentlemen who spend all night in their laboratories, mixing chemicals in vials and scrupulously recording the results of their experiments. Of course, I could not compare myself to a true Scientist, being only a Dabbler, but even I have lost sleep, so preoccupied have I become with my little 'hobby-horse'. Nevertheless, no matter how great the urge to press on with my enquiries, I must be careful not to disturb the subject's rest too much. After all, she is not a vial of Sulphuric Acid that can be lifted and peered at and shaken, no matter what the hour of day or night. Sulphuric Acid needs no sleep and does not hand in its notice, whereas maidservants can and do.

CLOTHES MAKETH THE MAID

I am still strongly of the opinion that, in order to make a subject truly obedient, she must be appropriately dressed. Neither of the frocks that Bessy arrived with is in the least maid-like. Perhaps that sort of apparel goes un-remarked in Glasgow among the factory crowd, but here in the Shires, ordinary folk dress more simply and I suspect that (particularly given our dairymaids' scandalised attitude to her) eyebrows would be raised at the sight of satinet and scarlet silk.

Not only must the subject feel like a maid, all who see her must be able to identify her as what she is, in order that they respond to her appropriately. Thus any faux pas can be avoided. I have heard tell of a lady's maid who, in best clothes and on her day off, took a shortcut through the drawing room, and was there engaged in conversation by a gentleman who had mistaken her for a fellow house-guest. The girl was inexperienced enough (or perhaps the more cynical among us might say sly enough) to talk to him as an equal and it seems that quite a budding romance was underway when, just in time, the mistress of the house appeared. One can only imagine this lady's mortification, under the circumstances. I do not know what happened to the maid in question, but there can be no doubt that she was severely chastised. Of course, a servant need not have a uniform – and indeed in all but the very best households uniformed staff can strike a vulgar and aspirational note. However, to avoid embarrass-

ment, a maid should always be dressed simply and plainly, in her proper clothes.

To this end, I sent our new girl off on an errand yesterday while I had a look through my own wardrobe for something for her to wear amongst my old everyday clothes. I found nothing suitable but then remembered that in the attic I had stored the belongings of Nora, the very excellent and devoted maid whose death is recorded elsewhere in these pages. It occurred to me that it might be eminently practical to get some use out of her things. They are doing no good to anyone, hidden in a box, and it seems unlikely now that someone will turn up to claim them. Indeed, the more I thought about it, the more I considered it to be a sheer act of extravagance to leave them up there, mouldering, when here was a girl under my roof in desperate need of decent attire!

The clothes were in need only of a little pressing, which task I accomplished in a matter of moments. The girl returned from her errand soon thereafter (to my great relief – I had begun to worry that the call of the open road, her natural Gypsy instincts and the money in her pocket might seduce her, after all, into wandering off to Edinburgh). Anxious to see what she would look like in the clothes – in other words, that they would be the right size and that she would look appropriately maid-like – I persuaded her to try them on. They are a little tight in the here and there but the fit is adequate. I must say, she was quite transformed. Of course, I certainly did not want this subject to dwell morbidly on the origins of these frocks. Girls of her sort, especially the Roman Catholics, are ruled by a complex set of superstitions, and so I gave her a plausible explanation for the sudden appearance of the clothes.

The afternoon brought a gentleman caller. Subject served us tea and although Nora's clothes and a little instruction had made her more maid-like in rehearsal, when faced with a real guest some aspects of her performance were disheartening. It seemed she took a dislike to this guest (all too evident in her dealings with him) and in general, her demeanour lacked an appropriate level of civility. A maid should never betray her own feelings, no matter how deeply they run or how much she absolutely detests and despises a particular character. Unfortunately, we do not always have a say in who enters our home, in who must be entertained and given refreshment. But we have to be polite nonetheless.

Following his departure, I happened to catch the girl dancing a little jig in the hall and I suddenly had a glimpse of her as a 'person'. For a moment, I almost envied her the freedom she has – the lack of responsibility and care, only simple duties to carry out, no need to deal with irksome society, her brain untrammelled by the kind of anxieties and worries that plague her superiors and so on. Of course, one could not imagine changing places with such a person – and nor would one wish it! Nonetheless, I suddenly viewed her in a slightly different light.

I also felt a rather mournful regret for dear Nora. If only it were she, dancing in the hall and not this new girl! I may not have mentioned it before, because it is of no importance, but there is a slight resemblance between the subject and Nora. This Bessy has a little more flesh on her and is younger and under scrutiny, of course, it is clear that she is not dear Nora (with her charming habit of calling me 'm'lady'!). Nonetheless, Bessy is of Irish origin, of similar height, and the hair is a comparable shade – though Nora's was, of course, always tidy. Even the shape of face and length of the nose are similar. Of course, anyone might have remarked upon Nora's prettiness, whereas this girl is not so much pretty as – perhaps, one might say – voluptuous, but now that she was wearing Nora's clothes, the similarity was more pronounced. I mention it only in passing, as it is of absolutely no importance. All the wishing in the world will not bring Nora back and no-one can replace her since she was in many respects, the perfect servant.

OBEDIENCE TESTING AND 'PURPOSE'

I have already documented the use of the 'stand/sit' test for gauging a subject's tendency to obedience (a less hazardous and more easily controlled version of the 'walk' test). Without question, I have shown that the stand/sit test is initially an excellent indication of whether or not a subject is naturally inclined to obey. Readers may not fully appreciate, however, that thereafter, it can be used to measure how well a subject is progressing in terms of aptitude for servility. I had hoped to illustrate this with Morag, Bessy's predecessor, but her refusal to co-operate in anything but what she saw as 'regular' duties meant that we were often in conflict. She refused the stand/sit test point blank, no matter how many times I tried to persuade her. I admit that I was at a loss to know how to proceed. In the end (and with some misgivings) I trapped her in the pantry one morning, having first ensured that it contained some food, a jug of water, a chamber pot, a cushion to sit on and her preferred reading material. I told her (through the door) that I would let her out only as and when she agreed to submit to my test. Morag remained in the pantry for four and a half hours (the length of time I believe it took her to read 'The Courant' and take a short nap), after which she seemed to realise that my will was stronger than her own and she agreed to co-operate if I would only set her free. Upon release, she refused to speak to me, and glared rather a lot, but when asked she did perform the stand/sit test for the first time, achieving a rather poor six repetitions. Despite this, I congratulated her and gave her gifts of a shilling and the rest of the day off. It seems, however, that she was only shamming co-operation in order to achieve her freedom, as – within the hour – she was gone forever from this house. I will pass over the exact manner of her departure. Suffice to say, it was plain that she had very much taken against me and had no intention of returning. (Luckily, that was the day that the new subject wandered onto our land.)

Of course, Bessy lacks the kind of natural obedience that was present in dear Nora, but at least she is certainly more compliant than Morag. However her early results with the stand/sit test were also a little disappointing. Of course, one must bear in mind that she is not used to service and is therefore perhaps not accustomed to responding, daily and unthinkingly, to what a mistress might ask of her. Unlike those that have been more in the world than myself, I have no real knowledge of how a factory operates, but I imagine that once the labourer has mastered his small task – the pulling of a lever here, or the turning of a cog there – he is left to get on with his work unsupervised, and if this (as I strongly suspect) is the girl's habitual environment, she will be unused to taking repeated commands.

When asked later why she did not co-operate fully with the experiment, Bessy stated that she did not understand the 'porpoise' of what she was being asked to do. Of course, a truly obedient mind would not question purpose but carry out instructions as commanded, without stopping to analyse why or how. This and certain other of the subject's peculiarities add weight to my suspicion that she is not innately obedient.

In an attempt to draw more evidence from the subject, I found occasion to ask about her so-called previous employer. The girl has clearly invented this character – 'Mr Levy' – in order to fit in with her story about having served as a housekeeper. Having created this invention, however, she appears to have been taken in by it. She talks incessantly – and always in glowing terms – about her 'Mr Levy'. One would think that the man was a saint. I find myself disliking him intensely – and yet I realise that he is only a figment of her imagination! (Needless to say, there has been no reply to the letter that I sent to the address she provided.)

Playing along with her Phantasy, I put this to her: had she always known the purpose of what 'Mr Levy' – (this great Paragon!) – had commanded her to do? She thought for a moment and then said that she had understood the porpoise of most things he had wanted, without even having to ask him, but that some of the things he made her do had indeed left her a little baffled. However, as she seemed unable (or unwilling) to be specific about or to describe what these particular duties were, we had to drop the subject. (Mr Levy, apparently, did not mind if she used newspaper to wipe coal off the carpet.)

Hell roast her, I thought. Calling my Mr Levy a figment! It seemed she had got no reply to her letter, which made me a bit hopeful. But what she had said in the title about a 'most particular case' still had me worried and so I read on.

COAXING PHASE

Alongside the element of disorientation I have introduced, by degrees, the 'coaxing' or 'bonding' process, whereby the disoriented subject is encouraged to form a closer, trusting relationship with the mistress. As a means of spending more time with the subject when our daily labours had ended, I instigated punctuation lessons. (Perhaps dear Nora did not have this girl's vocabulary, but she certainly knew what to do with a full stop!) The evening lesson gives us a chance to be seated side by side, in quiet and intimate circumstances, and I believe that Bessy would already (secretly) rather that we were friends than mistress and maid. She has a tendency, unless instructed otherwise, to seek out my company at every opportunity, for instance, walking me to and from church. If I retire to my room, it is only a matter of time before she will come knocking, often with little excuse. She is also keen to get me to divulge information about myself and my husband and often asks questions that are a little 'off colour'. Rather than discourage this, I have been (very subtly) encouraging it, in the interests of gaining her trust. From time to time, I tell her a little about myself, giving her something of my history with one or two mild embellishments. Rest assured, I reveal nothing too personal, but simply give her enough to make her feel that I am confiding in her. I do believe that she is quite ensnared by me. (By the by, she will also now perform 40 sit/stand repetitions, without question or complaint. However, here we seem to have stalled – if only I could get her to 50 it would feel like real progress!)

By this time I was sick to my stomach and I had the sweats. But that was nothing compared to how I began to feel when I came across the title of her next entry, whereupon I was filled with dread.

AN INTRIGUING LETTER FROM A JEWISH GENTLEMAN

This morning, I was most surprised to receive a short communication from a Mr Samuel Levy of Candleriggs, Glasgow. It seems that he is the brother of 'Mr Benjamin Levy' of Hyndland, the gentleman (now indeed deceased) whom Bessy claims was her former employer. Mr Samuel Levy says that he found my letter at Crown House when he went there to supervise the clearing of the premises, which has been shut up for several weeks, ever since his brother's funeral.

According to Samuel Levy, there was an Irish girl who did indeed spend a number of months in his brother's house. However, he says that this girl's name was not Bessy Buckley, and he requests that I send a description of the girl that I have engaged, so that (in the first instance) he can establish whether or not we are speaking of the same person.

I must admit I am now rather intrigued, and have responded by return of post. I strongly suspect that my description will not match that of the ex-servant. It is my opinion that Bessy, in a moment of panic, gave me the address of one of her female acquaintances, perhaps a maidservant that she met one day while out walking in the park. Bessy may even have visited this girl at her place of work and had a glimpse of the master (which, no doubt, is where she will have gleaned her impression of the famous 'Mr Levy'). The maid may also have spoken of her master's death, hence Bessy's story as told to me.

It remains to be seen whether I should confront her with her lies or not, and what course of action I should take. However, in the meantime, and until I hear from Mr Levy (brother), I intend to continue with my research.

STARTLING NEWS CONCERNING BESSY

I have just, this very morning, received a reply from Mr Samuel Levy. To my great surprise, it seems that my description of Bessy matches perfectly that of the girl who used to live at Crown House. Mr Levy says that there is no mistaking her, despite the difference in names. He claims that although the girl was ostensibly employed as his elderly brother's housekeeper she was, in fact, kept there under IMMORAL CIRCUMSTANCES, the specifics of which he does not enter into but which can be guessed at, even by someone like myself who has not been much in the world.

This girl's name, he writes, is not Bessy but DAISY (!). No surname is known. The brothers Levy were apparently estranged for many years, a family argument having caused them, in earlier times, to set up in competition as rival furriers and although Benjamin was retired, the feud continued until his death (aged 62). Subsequently, Samuel came to know what went on in his brother's house and upon learning full details from the neighbours he closed up the premises and ordered the girl to leave.

Could it be possible that he is mistaken? This girl is so young – I find it hard to believe that she can have been involved in anything of the sort. Nonetheless, he does mention brightly coloured clothes and a habit of sucking her fingers – and apparently her parting words as he put her out on the street were that she didn't care 'a farthing dip' anyway because she already had a position lined up at the Edinburgh Castle (which sounds very like Bessy!).

Despite this, I am strongly inclined to think that what he has been told about the girl is simply malicious gossip, spread by another servant who may have her own reasons for wishing to slander her rival's name. This kind of thing is not uncommon, I believe, especially in town, where the servants live in close proximity to each other and are in the habit of forming jealousies and alliances.

I have replied to Samuel Levy's letter by return of post with a number of questions which I beg him to answer.

In the meantime, it would be a terrible mistake to jump to any conclusions. I must admit that, upon reading Levy's letter, I did become slightly anxious that I was harbouring a degenerate. Suddenly fearing what she might be up to, I tracked the girl down to the kitchen, from behind the closed door of which emerged a loud and repetitive rasping sound, accompanied by heavy breathing. Now that doubt had been cast over her history, I was perfectly prepared upon entering for an offensive or licentious sight to greet my eyes, and I pounced through the door at once – only to discover her in the act of scouring the table, an occupation both innocuous and useful. May I venture to assert that one should be careful not to judge too quickly, even when dealing with the lowliest of persons.

THE MAID WITH A SHADOWY PAST

I believe I can say without fear of contradiction that we know too little about our servants. All the evidence we have about them is written on a single piece of paper, by a former employer, who – for all we know – may be glad to be rid of them and to this end invents an immaculate character for them instead of giving us the lamentable truth. Occasionally, depending upon circumstance, we may not even have a written character for them. Why then should we blame ourselves if something comes to light about a servant's past which surprises us? Clearly, it would be a mistake to chastise oneself, if this were the case. Even if a servant arrives with excellent testimonials, we take on him or her as a matter of trust. How are we to know what has really gone on in their lives before they come to us? And (some might say) is it really our concern, provided that they perform their duties punctually and well?

My own experiences of recent days bear this out. I have received another communication from Mr Samuel Levy. In reply to my questions he assures me that there is no mistake about what went on in his brother's house. It is some relief to learn that Crown House was not, in fact, a public brothel for use by all and sundry, but a 'respectable' private residence, and that Benjamin Levy, who was apparently besotted with the girl, kept her there exclusively, as his sole concubine. This is small comfort, but at least we can be sure that the girl was not wandering the streets like an animal to ply her trade and that she has been sullied by only one 'satyr'. Samuel Levy says that he cannot tell me where the girl came from (because he does not know) but says that she was reputedly sold into his brother's care by an elder sister, who in return collected a weekly payment from Benjamin Levy's solicitor (this payment has now been stopped, at Samuel's command).

One is forced to wonder what kind of person would sell her younger sibling for immoral purposes. Such a person can be no less than a monster. Of course, the family would have been in financial straits after the death of both parents, but surely there are other means of living before resorting to such depravity?

However, one must also consider that – if she didn't like it – the girl could always have run away from this man. Clearly she did like it, as apparently she remained there for almost a year. According to Samuel Levy, the neighbour's servants claim that she was hardly ever dressed, and spent most of her time (when not engaged with Mr Benjamin Levy), reclining on a chaise beneath a chenille rug, eating lollipops and reading novels.

Of course, many of the characteristics that the girl displays – characteristics that I have previously remarked upon in these pages – do fit well with this new information about her. For example, her sultry looks and the unsettling mix she has of innocence and worldliness: these qualities are, I am sure, to be found in girls of her sort around the globe. It is now easy to understand her overwhelming attachment to her 'dear' Mr Levy and why she chatters about him in such glowing terms: she was none other than his mistress!

What on earth is the householder to do upon learning such a disturbing set of circumstances? I must admit that I have become somewhat disheartened since receiving this letter, and have even harboured some doubts about the likelihood of fully domesticating this girl. How can it be possible, given what I now know? Despite some progress in other areas, we are still stuck at 40 stand/sit repetitions and I begin to despair of coaxing more out of her.

I have even begun to find her presence a little unsettling, although I try not to show it. At one point yesterday, as we worked, I had reason to be standing next to her and – quite by accident – my sleeve happened to touch hers. The shock of brushing so close against her was overwhelming. It was as though a spark had leapt up my arm and shot into my heart. I hardly know how I managed to stop myself from crying out. I simply gasped and clutched at my chest, but managed to pass off this state of agitation as a mild digestive disorder. The girl expressed concern for my welfare and begged me to rest while she made me a drink. She busied herself with the teapot, apparently very happy to have me present in the kitchen while she saw to my needs. Indeed, she seemed almost elated to be tending to me. I must say that, despite everything, she does seem a sympathetic little soul, but I do wish that she would not fuss over people quite so much, with quite so much familiarity. It is unnerving to have her so near at hand, rubbing one's back and tucking a rug over one's knees.

Of course, there are some people – lovers of scandal and the like – who might derive a thrill or base excitement from proximity to a person of her sort, but I need hardly say that I am not one of them. It is true, I have always been interested in those less fortunate than myself (as evidenced by my youthful preoccupation with the poor), but my curiosity is always scientific in origin and owes nothing to the emotions.

A MOMENT OF TRIUMPH

It is with great pleasure that I record an unprecedented 55 repetitions of the stand/sit test, as performed by Bessy this morning. Recently, as the preceding pages will confirm, I had been very disheartened about her progress and, in fact, had almost made up my mind to get rid of her, fearing that she was beyond my help. In this spirit, I made a small, rather desperate wager with myself: if I could get her beyond her usual 40 repetitions then I would retain her services; if not, I would give her notice.

In truth, I did not expect her to perform and so it was with great excitement that I saw her hesitate for a second as she sat on her 40th repetition, before bobbing up swiftly into a hitherto unheard of 41st! I caught my breath and believe I must have held it through a subsequent 14 repeats as, when she finally desisted and requested permis-

sion to get on with her work, I almost fell to the ground in a dead faint! When asked what had caused her to have made such an advancement she simply shrugged and said that she didn't know for sure, only that she thought it might give me 'pleshur'. Pleshur indeed!

Given this remarkable breakthrough, I have elected to keep her here. The poor wretch should be given a second chance in the world! Otherwise she might end up once again at the hands of an exploiter or debaucher. Good sense also proclaims that it would be a waste of time and effort to dismiss her now that she knows how things are run. She is clearly capable of concealing the details of her history from anyone she encounters. I have tested this ability by (amongst other things) asking her supposedly 'innocent' questions about her stint at Mr Levy's residence and she did not betray herself with so much as a blush. Indeed, she has the ability to talk around a subject in a way that makes the listener forget what they asked in the first place. Of course, there is the small consideration of the inconvenience to my research, were she to leave, but this is of secondary importance. What really matters is allowing this subject a new start and helping her to make the most of a decent life in service. She will never be as perfect as dear Nora, but I will use her to demonstrate that a decent servant can be made from even the lowliest of prostitutes (and I have altered the title of this section accordingly). I now have no qualms about retaining her and am very interested to see what can be achieved.

This admission may perhaps have excited in the reader feelings of horror and outrage, who might have expected me to dismiss the girl without question upon learning about her shadowy past and I am prepared, briefly, to look into these attitudes to discover whether they are justifiable. I find that there is no cause for revulsion. It is possible for a householder to turn a blind eye to a servant's past, as long as said householder is vigilant and does not take advantage of the situation.

For the past week or so, I have been anxious that the subject may have formed too great an attachment to me and I am sorry to recount that my fears have not been without foundation. This has become inescapable over the last few days. Yesterday, while we happened to be tidying my press in preparation for my husband's return, the girl blurted out something that seems to go beyond the bounds of what might be viewed as appropriate, professing a love for me and stating that she would do anything for me, including laying down her own life to ensure my happiness. Needless to say, I had to bring our little rendezvous to an abrupt end and have tried to avoid her company ever since.

Then today, I had to send her on an errand to the village. As I was describing the purchase I required, I noticed that she had leaned towards me and seemed to be actually sniffing me, in the area of the neck. I do not think I was mistaken. So unnerved was I by this that I recoiled and, anxious to get away from her, I muttered something and fled to my room. Moments later, I remembered that in my hurry to escape, I had neglected to tell her about my husband's arrival. (It had been my intention to call something out to her about it as she left. In this way, I would not have to explain too much, or deal with any of the sulks that were sure to be forthcoming when she learned that our little idyll was to be disrupted.)

Readers might be forgiven for thinking that I have been misguided in (perhaps) cultivating her affection a little too much. However, I do not believe that to be the case. Such coaxing is a perfectly acceptable means of managing a young girl. If a servant becomes too engaged then it is hardly the fault of the mistress. The girl should have been more in control of herself.

I have come to the conclusion that I must now disengage from her. This is easily enough done: henceforth, I will simply avoid her as much as possible and, by whatever means, attempt to distance myself from her. This must be done carefully, so as to avoid making her feel rejected. I can imagine that she might make things very awkward for me, were she to be offended.

Here was where the entries in *The Observations* ended. After that, it was nought but blank pages, waiting to be wrote upon.

I have to admit that despite all evidence to the contrary – and right up to the last – I did hold out a glimmer of hope that Arabella was making up all what she'd wrote. That there was no such person as Nora and that missus did not really mean the rotten things she said in there about me. Or perhaps she wasn't writing about me, only about another girl called Bessy.

Of course deep down I knew the truth. It was a desperate blow to learn that she had found out some aspects of my past, let's just say I would have preferred her not to know. But what was worse was how she thought of me. Hells teeth, how can I explain the wretched despair I felt, except to say that my heart was banjaxed. I was no more than a 'thing' to Arabella, a thing that might be experimented upon, toyed with and cast aside at a whim when it had outgrown its use.

Bad cess on her.

I closed up the ledger and put it back in the drawer, just as I had found it. Then I locked the drawer and returned the key to her pocket. After that I went upstairs to the room she had give me, curled up on the mattress and pulled the blankets over my head. I wanted to die. I felt rotted right down to my socks. Of course, you get over these things in time, but the fact is that I was still a child and easy hurt and all the scutting bedding in the world could never have hid me from my shame and humiliation.

8

Depression

Is it not always the way that when you get a shock to the system your body retreats into illness? So it was with me back then at Castle Haivers. That very night I was struck down with a terrible gut-ache and fever and for the next few days I remained in bed unable even to lift my head except to boke off into a bowl. This was desperate inconvenient for the missus so it was. Not particularly the boking but me being abed, especially now that the husband was home, but there was flip all could be done about it, even if I had wanted to work I could not have. Not a word of a lie I sweated so much that my hair curled! And I succumbed, in my fevered state, to a series of godawful nightmares. In one I was a witch with crooked wee fingers. And when I awoke, still ensnared by my dream, I threw back the sheet raging for it was white in colour and I was convinced that now I was a witch I loved only black things. In another, a great boil appeared on my thigh and when I squeezed it all this stinking guff oozed out and kept oozing for it seemed that my body was filled with a foul clay. And in a 3rd nightmare, I stole into the missus room and found a book she was writing in which it was plain that she did not care to be my friend and did not like me except as a thing to be experimented upon. Moreover she had snooped into my past and to top it all I learned that I would never measure up to her perfect darling Nora not in a month of Sundays, Oh no I do apologise, I am mistaken, that was not a dream at all that was *the simple facts of the matter*.

Missus came to my room on the first morning wanting to know why I hadn't come down for work. I knew she was there, stood in the doorway asking me what was wrong, but I couldn't bring myself to answer or even look at her, I just turned my face to the wall and lay there shivering. Later on, other people loomed up beside me like visions. One was Jessie the milkmaid, sent by missus (as Jessie made very plain she would not have come on my account alone). She gave me water to drink and a cold cloth for my head, these acts of kindness somewhat diminished by the resentful look on her phiz. I fell asleep again until I was awoken by a noise and opened my eyes Jesus Murphy there was a beak-nosed man in a dark suit peering under my bed. Then he took my wrist and held it, which was a comfort right enough but it seemed to me that he was late for an appointment for he kept staring at his watch and sure after about a minute did he not go away again, all this without ever once having looked me in the face or spoke to me. I fell asleep, hoping he was not just some mad bucko that had wandered in off the road. (As it turned out he was in fact the doctor, McGregor-Robertson, summoned by missus.)

Over the course of the next few days missus herself came and went from my room, she brought me broth, she cut my hair, she slathered cool cloths on my head, but would I speak to her, would I chook. I kept my potato trap shut and my eyes closed, I did not even want the sight of her. A few times, I heard her voice below in the yard as she spoke to someone, Hector or a Curdle twin. And at night there was the creak of the stairs as she and the husband climbed to their separate chambers. Every time I thought of what she had wrote in that blasted book the pain grabbed my heart and squeezed it tight, leaving me dizzy and short of breath.

On the afternoon of the 3rd day I felt a little better (although I now suspect I was only delirious). It occurred to me that I would leave Castle Haivers, forget about wages and what I was due, just walk out let her struggle on without me, slap it into her. I even began to pack my duds, but was interrupted in this task by the sound of somebody on the stairs. Thinking it might be *HER*, I stuffed my bundle in the cupboard and lit back into bed. But it was only Jessie, bringing more broth and not at all happy as she had been instructed to empty my poe. (It contained nought of substance but of course she made a right Holy Show about keeping it at arms length as she put it out the door.) Then she turned to me, hands on hips.

'Her majesty wants tae know have you goat all what ye need.'

'Where is she?' I asked. 'What's she doing?'

Jessie gave me the dead-eye. Then she says, with imperial scorn, 'She's downstairs wi' her skirts up, sitting on a jelly.'

Now an ample sufficiency of strange things had happened since I arrived at Castle Haivers, but I did not think for one minute that this was true about missus, it was only Jessies way of letting me know that she held neither missus nor me in any great esteem and that by the same token, she had no intention of answering my every silly question.

Once Jessie had went hurpling off I found I had no strength to finish packing. So I shoved my bundle back in the cupboard and crawled shivering between the sheets.

Over and over, I kept picturing the missus lowering herself onto a jelly. Except in my head it was not a deliberate undertaking (as Jessie had implied) but an accident, in which the frock that missus was wearing – a lovely white one – got ruined by stains of red jelly, the whole thing witnessed by a gathering of local nobs, to her great mortification. I am sorry to say that I found comfort in this daydream.

Now I am not going to pretend that during this period of laying there in bed I did not think about my past. Since I had got to Castle Haivers I had mostly tried to forget about it. But reading all what missus had wrote about me in her book brought it back and I was hankering after the old days with Mr Levy. I am not exactly champing at the bit to tell about it. But I suppose now is as good a time as any because unless I do, some of what follows will not make sense.

So here goes.

Oh for dear sake just get on with it.

My Mr Levy was a modest man and I know he would not like me to be saying 'Mr Levy this' and 'Mr Levy that' all over the place in a document which may be read by others but if he is looking down from wherever he might be and can see the page I hope that he will be secretly pleased. What can I say about the months I spent with him at Crown House in Hyndland except that for me, they were a time of solace, and I hope for poor Mr Levy too. I say poor Mr Levy because (I'm sure he won't mind me saying) he was old and before he died he suffered terrible from a constriction of his bowel and most days I had to rub his belly until the hand was dropping off me, it helped him go. But it was a small chore and I was happy to do it. In fact I had never been happier! Crown House was a very grand villa with four floors. I had my own room with a white marble mantelpiece and a fire in it every day, and I washed in hot water and could take whatever I fancied from the pantry no need to ask permission, cakes, chicken, wine, pies, gingerbread, you name it, I had never seen a cupboard with so much food. Mr Levy even gave me a watch to tell the time. He was a private man, weary of society and did not like everyone to know his business. And although he was rich, he hated the place to be crawling with servants and had over the years let them all go except one boy Jim that had been there a few months when I arrived.

This Jim was about my age with dark red hair and watchful eyes beneath fair brows and I soon saw that he would not let me interfere much with the running of the house. To tell the truth, Mr Levys eyesight was none too good and as a result his standards of housekeeping and so on was a little lax. Jim knew a good thing when he seen one. He had an easy life in Crown House and was worried that I might take his place, if he got dismissed as well. But, as time went by and it became clear that Jim was needed and would not get his notice, we even grew to be friends. And as I pointed out one afternoon (we was playing chucky stones against the back area wall, which was our habit while Mr Levy took his nap) everybody had his purpose in life. I did things for Mr Levy that Jim could not do, Jim fetched whatever was needed by us, and Mr Levy paid for it all. Simple.

Now my Mr Levy was a bit like missus, he was an educator and wanted me to know my ABC. Every day of the week he would sit me down for a lesson. First of all he taught me the alphabet by using the first letters of all the foul words he could think of and he even taught me several I'd never even heard of before. (In actual fact I think he made some of them up, but he always claimed they was genuine curses in one language or another.) Next we put these letters together to make words and after that there was no stopping me, Mr Levy said I was sharp as a tack. We had soon graduated to long difficult words like 'duplicity' 'reticule' and 'sententious' (now that I come to think of it I don't actually know what that last one means but I believe I can *spell* it right).

And once my lesson was over, we would go to Mr Levys study together and look at his fossils – he had a great old collection – and in the evening we would sit by the fire and sing songs and sometimes when we sang a sad song it brought a tear to my Mr Levys eye. I think he may have been a lonely man, I don't know. He had no wife or children, nor never had either and no other family, as far as I knew. I was his hearts companion.

'Oh Nuzzler,' he would say.

I forgot to mention, that was his pet name for me, and while he was taking his pleasure he liked me to smack him and tell him that he was a bad old donkey. 'Donkey you have been bad,' I had to say, 'But Nuzzler loves you just the same.' But there was no harm in it, for I never did smack him with any force.

(I apologise if I have put that bluntly. I thought it better to get it over with.)

Where was I?

'Oh Nuzzler,' he would say. 'What will become of us?' And then he would make me promise not to leave the house much in case of the gossipmongers, his neighbours. Which I was happy to do. In 8 months I stepped out only a handful of times, and always discreetly by the back door. And I never went near the Gallowgate either, where I used to live, the furthest I got across town was Miss Doigs of

West George Street, *Modiste*, at which establishment I was fitted for a new frock at Mr Levys expense (the satin one with blue bows and lace). I made no other visits and received no visitors. And any time I was out I kept my eyes peeled but I never seen anybody that I knew.

However. All good things come to an end.

I am trying to think of a polite way of putting it but perhaps blunt is best. My Mr Levy died on the pisspot. I think it was the strain that killed him, his heart gave out, from too much pushing. God bless him, all he forced out was a leathery pellet the size of a hazelnut. It was the first thing I seen that morning when I found him keeled over in his room. There it was, in the bottom of the poe. I had knocked on his door for ages but there was not a peep out him, so in I went. The poor old soul was laying on the Turkey rug, all twisted and buck naked he was, the two bones of his arse pointing at me.

'Mr Levy, sir,' I says but there was no reply.

I walked round to look at him. His eyes were open and he had this ½ surprised expression on his face like he'd just remembered something. Not something important like 'GOD SAVE US! I FORGOT TO GET MARRIED AND HAVE BABIES!' but a small thing like 'Ah! So that's where I left my tobacco.' Who can say what really was the last thought crossed his mind. I hope it was a good one.

I put my hand to his mouth just to see if he was breathing, but he wasn't. Then I touched his face with the backs of my two fingers. He was still warm. I tried to rouse him, thinking he might come back to life, but it was no good. So I put my bare foot next to his, to see the difference in size. Then I lifted his arm and had a look at his oxter. The hairs in there weren't even white. If all you could see was his oxter you might almost have mistook him for a younger man. I lay down and put my face in there. He smelled like soup, with just a hint of vinegar. I lay like that for I don't know how long. I didn't cry but I think I might have fell into a Trance, for I had a premonition that my days at Crown House, Hyndland was over. And then I got up and covered him with a sheet for I didn't want them to find him naked.

One last thing before I sent for the doctor, I made sure to preserve Mr Levys last act. I found a small velvet pouch in a drawer and went over to the pisspot. I took his pellet between my finger and thumb and dropped it into the pouch. Then I put the pouch in my pocket and shoved the poe back under the bed.

I don't know why I did that apart from I didn't want anyone to be staring at his last act, because it was his private matter and nobody's business but his own.

Then I called downstairs to Jim to fetch the doctor.

Such a gull was I that I believed it might be possible to live on there in the house but as it turned out, Mr Levy did have some family after all, a brother that lived at Candleriggs, him that had wrote to missus. This brother Samuel didn't need a hearts companion. He had a wife and children and servants of his own. He and Mr Levy hadn't spoke for years but it was him that inherited Mr Levys wealth, in the absence of a will. The brother came to Crown House the day after the funeral, at the crack of dawn, and spent a long time talking to the neighbours and their servants. Jim had made great claims for me as the housekeeper but once it was established that I wasn't really a housekeeper as such (Mr Levy was right – they were gossipmongers), both me and Jim was turned out into the street, not even a sniff of a wage or a character between us. Poor Jim was obliged to go back to his mothers in Govan, and after we parted on Byres Road I took my bundle (the scutting brother would not even believe that the smart new box Mr Levy had bought me was mine) and went and sat in the West End Park, staring into space. All I had in the world was my clothes, my watch, two shillings I had found in an old coat under the stairs, six Parma violets and a pellet of human waste in a velvet pouch. But I never held my circumstances against my Mr Levy, and still don't. It wasn't his fault. He couldn't have known he was going to die and leave me without a penny.

As the day went on, I realised I had nowhere else to go except back to the Gallowgate. I left the park and hoofed it all the way along Dumbarton Road and Argyle Street. Never have so few miles been walked so reluctantly. I dragged my heels and it was mid-morning by the time I reached the Cross. It was Wednesday, the place was going like a fair because of market. This was the very spot where Mr Levy had first found me all those months previous.

You see he had started off the same as anybody else – that is to say as a paying customer. And before our first time he'd sat me down and tellt me he was a Jewish man and did I mind? I said it didn't matter if he was a Hindoo or an Eskimaux, as long as he paid what he owed. Then I told him I was Irish and did he mind that? Which made him laugh. And so it was that a couple of nights a week he took to strolling by my patch and off we would go together to a room above a wobble and do what had to be done. Afterwards, he liked me to sit on his knee while I rolled cigarettes for him and sometimes he fed me chocolate drops and once he even brought a pineapple which I had never tasted before but took a great liking to. Oh, he had his foibles but what man does not? All in all, he was a good gentleman with a kind heart.

One evening, after this had been going on several weeks, Mr Levy tellt me he needed a housekeeper. But more than that, he said, what he really wanted was a 'hearts companion' for his dotage. And he had chose me for the job!

Now, by this time I will admit I was heartily sick of life which is a terrible thing to say at the age of 13 or thereabouts. Having to go with every man jack no matter how foul or drunk or mad they was and making only a few bob here and there and then having to hand over the lions share. I didn't have to think very hard. I tellt Mr Levy straight away that I would be delighted to be his hearts companion.

But of course, it was not up to me to decide.

'I will speak with your sister,' Mr Levy says. And so away he toddled to her usual haunt, a rats arse of a wobble known as 'Dobbies'.

Well, when Bridget came home, she was fit to be tied.

'Away to flip out of it and rot!' she tellt me. 'What am I supposed to do while you're lying around some auld scuts mansion? Leave me and see what happens, I'll flipping CRUCIFY you!'

I was crestfallen to say the least. I spent the rest of the night sulking. But in the end, she let me go for my Mr Levy came back next day and persuaded her. He gave her a purse of money up front and agreed that his lawyer would provide a weekly sum (I don't know how much but it must have been a good deal more than I would have made in the normal run of things).

After he left, Bridget sat staring out the window, stroking the purse. She had a thick smile on her face and her eyes were glazed over, I think she was trying to calculate how many pints of Dutch gin she could now afford to buy.

Not much of a sister, you might think. And you would be right. But that is hardly the worst of it. For you see, Bridget was not really my sister. Not my sister at all. As it happens, the truth of it is, *she was my mother*.

But perhaps now that I am at it I should say something more of my early life, what I know of it. Till this day, my fathers identity remains something of a mystery. According to my mother and a few that knew her from the old days back across the water, he was a sailor from the north that went by the name Whacker McPartland, not his real name of course, that was Dan, but apparently he *preferred* to be called Whacker.

According to my mother there was never a couple so devoted as herself and himself, Bridget O'Toole and Whacker, they were 'loves young dream'. Whacker was as handsome as the day is long and a marvellous dancer to boot, the jig his favourite and he only had eyes for my mother so he did and guarded her most jealously. Indeed on one occasion that my mother would often proudly recount, Whacker having drunk too much at a penny reel was overcome with nausea in the middle of a dance but would not leave the hall to vomit as that would have meant abandoning her to be spun around by RIVALS so instead what did he do but cleverly boke up his own sleeve, button the cuff and continue the jig, only thereafter with one arm held casually aloft.

If you listened to my mother, this man my father wanted but two things in life. One to be dancing and two to have her pinned to the wall by his jack upon which organ by her account you could have slung a packsaddle. Strange to say, as soon as old Whacker discovered that 'the love of his life' was carrying a child, away off he jigged out of town taking his jack with him, never to be seen nor heard again, well I don't suppose his jack made a sound. Mind you perhaps it nickered.

As for my mother Bridget, due to a fondness for Dutch gin and various knocks to the head, her recollection of the past was shocking and in her time she claimed variously that I was born on a Tuesday or perhaps a Thursday in April or more likely May. It was the middle of the night, or just before teatime, this was in the year '47, '48 or '49 and the birth took place in *either* Dundalk or Drogheda, or possibly somewhere else altogether. 'How am *I* supposed to remember all that!' my mother would cry if ever I asked about the circumstances. 'I was in PAIN! I was GIVING *BIRTH!!* It began with a 'D'! D something! Was it Donaghadee?'

But wherever we were and whenever it was, she was ABSOLUTELY CERTAIN of one detail and that was that she was in the middle of a fight when I came out. In her melancholy cups, when I was only small, she'd fix me with a watery gaze and declare, 'Look at you! You were born with wigs on the green!' a notion that caused me a certain amount of confusion at the time.

One other thing she does remember is that while she was carrying me she took a powerful notion to smoke a pipe. Any time I asked about my birth it was this first pipe that my mother went on about claiming that it was only the very *final* puff of the very *last* little ember in the bowl that gave her *any* pleasure whatsoever. Jesus Murphy the pounds of tobacco she had to smoke her way through with dogged determination in order every time to get down to that final glowing little coal. 'It was a wonder,' she used to say, 'that when I came to term I had a child at all and not a flipping fall of soot.'

*

My first memory is of light, pretty dappled patches of light playing across the dusty floorboards of a strange house where my mother had took me, this was back in Ireland. A gentleman lived in the house, he had straw-coloured moustachios and blue eyes like chips of sky. My mother had went into the next room with him and they had closed the door, telling me to stay put and amuse myself with a wooden clothes peg. I soon got bored and so drank off the dregs of the strange mans glass (my mother had left none) and went to listen at the door. It seemed that my mother and he were dancing in there, at any rate they was out of breath and I could hear the creak of the boards, which stopped when the man made a terrible sound like his throat had been cut and moments later my mother hurried out the room counting coins then bundled me from the house and up the road. She has killt him and took his purse! I thought, until we saw the very same gent the very next day, not a mark on him! He was in the street, walking arm-in-arm with a fine lady. I was most glad he was alive and my mother not a murderer (though I did not doubt she was capable of it, she was forever threatening to kill *me*).

I waved to the gent and gave him good afternoon, for he had been kind and chucked my chin and made me a present of the clothes peg, but he just frowned and steered his lady away across the square and then sure did my mother not practically yank the arm off me as she dragged me up an alley. Christ the Night I had put her in a foul temper, you knew that because of the way her eyes flashed and her nostrils flared. When you got her in a rage you were never sure exactly what she would do but you knew she was bound to lash out. This time she spat at me through her teeth, 'DON'T-YOU-EVER-DO-THAT-AGAIN!' each word accompanied by a blow to my head or backside. 'Else I'll THROTTLE YOU!'

From that day forth I never in public acknowledged a man I recognised unless he had greeted me first, and I did this even if a man was a frequent visitor to our home and even if the last time I seen him my mother had – let's say for instance – been sat on his knee and letting him like a big baby suck on her titty, excuse me but such is an example of how I viewed the confusing and disturbing scenes I witnessed from an early age.

My mother always used to claim she worked in a shop that sold umbrellas, a notion I never questioned until I got a bit older and then could not understand why the umbrella shop was open only at night instead of like other shops in the daytime. When I asked my mother about this she told me don't be daft she didn't sell the umbrellas, not at all, what she did, she had to be up all night fabricating them for to be sold the next morning. Fabricating them. Her very words. It took me a long time to realise that whatever she was fabricating it was not umbrellas.

By the time I was 8 or 9 (or 10, she didn't know), we had settled in Dublin and lodged next door to a pie shop, in a room at the very top of a dark narrow stair. More often than not I would wake up in the morning and my mother would be back from 'work' and there would be some man or other dossed down in the bed recess or on occasion just crumpled in a heap in the middle of the floor as if overnight he had fell from the ceiling. All shapes and sizes and sorts of men were to be discovered in the mornings, sometimes two or 3 of them were laid out on the floor and snoring in a row. The smell of drink would knock you down and when my mother woke up she would glare at whoever was there like she hated them and demonstrate shocking bad form until they gave her the money they owed her for the lodging and went away. Whereupon she would take her sore head straight back to bed.

Unless of course they was a young handsome man and she was in love with them, in which case it was a different story altogether, Jesus Murphy she would be fastened onto their coat tails and trying to drag them back between the sheets if they even so much as glanced at the door. There was always this one or that one that she made a fool of herself over, chief I remember among these was a piece of work named Joe Dimpsey and a more slippery article never pulled on an elastic sided boot. It was said that Joe Dimpsey came originally from good stock and had rich relations over in Scratchland and that he had even attended the Queens college for a while before he had to sell his textbooks to pay off a debt. Thereafter things didn't go too well for Joe and by the time my mother met him he was working odd jobs at the racetrack but he soon gave up that profession in order to lay about our hearth ½ clad, his main tasks seemed to be to flex his muscles while flicking through the racing pages until the early hours when my mother would return from the so-called umbrella shop with more money or another bottle.

Right enough, Joe Dimpsey was very good-looking, he had dark curls and an insolent grin and when he thought that nobody was listening he would stand in front of the glass and tell himself, 'Flip me but you are one handsome scut.'

My mother would not hear a bad word said about Joe Dimpsey, as far as she was concerned he was the Angel Gabriel and had a great future ahead of him as a learned Man of Science just as soon as he took it into his head to resume his studies. After some months, when he showed no signs of taking anything into his head apart from liquor (indeed it was his party trick to suck a measure of gin up his nose), my mother bought him the necessary textbooks herself but he barely opened them and preferred instead to while away the time when she was not at home by catching the gas of his farts in his hand and trying to make you smell them, that was the nearest thing to Science that passed in our house while Joe Dimpsey was in residence.

One afternoon, Joe came back from the track looking very down in the mouth and early next morning away out he went with the textbooks under his arm. He returned an hour later, empty-handed and looking rather shifty. Even I could guess that he must have sold the books. I watched him from my little tick on the floor as he tried gently to wake my mother, never an easy proposition, you might as well have danced a jig at a milestone. Finally, he gave her a shake. She opened one eye a crack and looked at him crossly.

'I'm going,' he told her and jerked a thumb at the wall, behind which lay nought but the attic of the pie shop, I did not know much but I didn't think that was where he was headed.

'What?' says my mother, a bit groggy and also probably ½ drunk, she still had her frock on if I remember right. 'Where to?'

Joe glanced over his shoulder, out the little window and after a pause he said, 'Over the water. I've bought the ticket. I'm away today.'

My mother leapt out the bed recess and grabbed his arm. 'What?' she squawked. 'You can't! You can't leave me here on my own! On my ownnn!!!'

It seemed, not for the first time, that she had forgot she had a child, even though I was sat on the floor, right in front of her! sucking on my breakfast, a lollipop. Joe shrugged her off. 'I have to,' he says. 'It's that or stay here and decide which arm gets broke, the right or the left and I can't decide, so I'm going before they come to get me.'

My mother wept and pleaded as she dipped slyly into his pockets, looking to pinch the boat ticket and destroy it but Dimpsey had been with us long enough to have her measure and I reckon the ticket was tucked well down his boot or hid in some other private orifice, at any rate she didn't find it. She tellt him she'd pay what he owed but no matter how much she begged he would neither change his mind nor reveal his destination – which was, he claimed, 'for her own safety' in case excuse me 'the bastards' came after her. At this, my mother prostrated herself on the bed, calling him some names and when he tried to pat her shoulder she screamed at him, 'Flip off you SCUT!' and lashed out a series of vicious kicks at his tallywags.

I think Joe seen this as reason enough to leave. My mother clung to his legs and screamed at me to help restrain him but I knew better than to get involved in disagreements between Bridget and her men, I had done so once before and got a bruise on my arse the size of Canada for my trouble. So I stayed where I was and took only the twin precautions of removing my lollipop from my mouth (as in those days you were always hearing of terrible accidents involving lollipops) and of lifting aside a glass of ale I had found and planned to drink later. Just in time, for Joe dragged my mother by the hair right over the spot where the glass had been, then threw her on the bed like a sack of coal. Before she could sit up he'd slipped out the room and turned the key in the lock from the outside.

It took an hour before any scut responded to our cries for help but at last we attracted the attention of the pieman who had stepped out the back of his shop in order to relieve himself into a drain as was his habit. He had to bust the lock, for Joe had took the key with him. As the door came in my mother turned to me and said, 'You stay put until I come back or I'll skin you alive.' And with that she flew down the stairs and out into the street. I was fond of my skin and had no wish to be parted from it so I did not budge.

My mother returned in the late afternoon, long-lippit and alone. I was highly delighted to see that Joe was not with her but knew better than to show it so I sat on my smile and kept quiet. That night, before she went to work she seemed very thoughtful, chewing the stem of her pipe as she stared at the cinders in the grate and every so often throwing me a dirty look. I had no idea what I had done wrong. This set of circumstances was not uncommon but in hindsight I believe I know exactly what was going on in her mind. After numerous scowls and sighs and shakings of her head she seemed to cheer up and come to some kind of decision.

'You'll be all right now, won't you?' she said.

I did not like the sound of this, not one bit, and so was cautious in my reply.

'. . . When?' I says, eventually.

'When I go away with Joe,' she says. 'You'll be all right here on your own for a few years until you grow up, will you not?'

I jumped out my seat in a panic. 'YOU WOULDN'T!!' I cried.

My mother grinned, showing the space between her front teeth, a gap so wide you could have slotted a shilling through it. Clearly she was glad to see the fear evoked by her suggestion of abandonment, I could have kicked myself. I sat down again quick.

'You're lying,' I tellt her. 'Joe's gone. He's left.'

She was still smiling, with one eyebrow raised. She seemed very confident. What did she know that I didn't?

'Well that's funny,' she says. 'Very flipping funny.'

I said nothing, didn't even bother to look at her, only out the corner of my eye. 'Oh yes, very amusing,' she says, but I didn't rise to the bait. 'That amuses me greatly,' she says and when I still made no response she pointed her finger at me and continued, 'And I'll tell you for why. Because who did I see down at the dock.'

I gasped and whipped round to face her. 'You did not.'

'I'm not going to argue with you. I seen Joe and we made up. He was very nice to me, very apologetic. All over me, so he was.'

My heart sank. It was just possible that this was true. My mother and Joe was forever having fights and then making up.

'The long and short of it is,' says my mother. 'He wants me to go away with him.'

And seeing as how I wasn't included in this plan she took the opportunity to gaze at me with great pity.

'Where – where to?' I says.

'Across the water, to Scratchland. But the passage costs a flipping fortune and Joe says we can't afford to take you. But sure you'll be all right if we leave you here on your own, won't you?'

I just stared at her.

She shifted her pipe from one side of her mouth to the other and gazed into the hearth. 'You'll probably have to beg for food,' she says, 'but if you ask very nicely you might get the odd scrap off the pieman.'

I am sorry to say that at this point I began to cry.

My mother laughed. 'Och,' she says. 'Don't be such a big baby. You can look after yourself for a change. And sure if you get thrown out of here you could always sleep on McSweens doorstep.'

At this prospect, I fell wailing at her feet. She let me weep many hot and bitter tears into her lap, while she stroked my hair and told me to 'Shhh'.

'Don't – leave – me – mammy!' I sobbed. 'Please – don't – go – away!'

'Well now,' she says. 'I wonder.' She tutted and sighed and shifted in her seat and when, a moment later, I looked up into her face she was scratching her head and looking thoughtful. 'There might just be one way that you could come with us.'

I grabbed her hand in both of mine. 'Oh mammy, please. Please let me.'

'Och, I don't know,' she says. 'You would have to do everything I tell you.'

'I will, I will, I'll be good.'

She pointed a finger at me. 'You'll only get one chance,' she says. 'And if you muck it up, that's it. We'll have to leave you.'

'I won't muck it up, I promise, mammy, please?'

'Well, we'll just have to see.'

And then she sat me by the light of a candle and proceeded to paint my face. Oh it was a great game at first. I was very excited to have all her attention for a change, I wished she would always sit with me and stroke my hair and tell me I was a good girl and pretty as a picture. However. As much as I liked the thought that I was old enough now to wear paint, I soon began to dislike like the feel of it on my skin. But when I tried to rub it off my mother smacked my hand.

'Stop that!' she says.

'I want to take it off,' says I.

She snorted. 'You will not!' she says. 'What's the use of a shop without a sign?'

At the time I don't think I understood her comment. I believe I confused the shop she mentioned with the umbrella shop – for she herself always put paint on her face before she went out to work there. And so I arrived at the conclusion that – finally! – I was going to get to see where she worked, and I was even to be allowed to help her. That was how we were going to make the money for my ticket, I was to become a fabricator of umbrellas!

Of course I don't have to even tell you, that was not at all what my mother had in mind.

*

But perhaps that is enough of my past for now. Much of what went on in those days is a source of great shame for me. It is difficult to write about and I am sure not a very pleasant read! Indeed it makes me feel queasy to remember some of the terrible things that followed and I dread writing about it. For the moment, I have said all I can but I will return to this subject later since I have been told to leave nothing out and I want to be helpful. The incidents I lay down here are not Creations of the Brain, but the Truth. As events occurred so they will be given. I am confident that should my words remain in private hands they will not be lightly read since those distinguished gentlemen that have encouraged me in my efforts at authorship are gentlemen every inch of them, gentlemen to their backbones, to their very TOE NAILS.

But now to return to Castle Haivers, where I was still laid up with the bokes.

For three days in all, I didn't budge from my little attic room. Then on the 4th day I woke to find that I was well enough to return to work. I did consider shamming illness and remaining in bed but curiosity got the better of me and so I roused myself and dressed in one of dear darling Noras blasted frocks. In fact, I had not yet dismissed the possibility of vacating the premises, the notion of stalking out in high dudgeon if missus put one foot wrong held some appeal and so I left my bundle in the cupboard, ready to grab at a moments notice. But I couldn't bring myself to leave just yet. For I couldn't believe, in my heart of hearts, that she would truly disengage from me.

I spent some time making sure my hair was tidy then presented myself downstairs. There in the kitchen was missus, her back to me, transferring eggs from a basket to a bowl. She didn't hear me come in. I could have went up behind her and done anything, put the heart across in her by shouting 'Boo!' or I could have bashed her on the head with the rolling pin or I could have slipped my arms round her and kissed her throat or any scutting thing I wanted. But as a matter of fact I hadn't a baldy notion what I wanted, so I just stood in the doorway and watched her put the last egg in the bowl and then turn around.

'Oh!' she goes, startled when she seen me. The bowl near dropped out her hand but she caught it. Which at the time I thought a powerful shame.

'Bessy!' she goes. 'You gave me a fright!'

'Crumbs and Christopher!' says I. 'Did you think I was somebody else?'

'Hmm?' she says and then she frowned. 'No, I just didn't hear you come in. You look much better. Are you feeling better?'

'Indeed so,' says I.

'Oh well, that is good news,' says she and set down the bowl of eggs. 'In that case I shall let you get on with it. When Hector appears be so good as to tell him to tell Jessie I won't be needing her today.'

And with those words she left the kitchen. I stood there a moment, blinking, and then followed her. She was heading upstairs no doubt to write something in her flipping book. The back of her skirts were clean, no hint of jelly there.

'D'you not want a breakfast, missus?' I calls up after her. 'What about the master? Will he be wanting some?'

She turned, ½ way up the stairs. 'Now think, Bessy dear,' she says. 'Do you want a breakfast . . .?' And here, she paused and looked at me with her eyebrows raised.

'I'll have some in a minute,' I says, deliberately misunderstanding her.

She sighed. 'Ma'am,' she says. 'Do you want a breakfast, ma'am? Now are you sure you're well enough to work, Bessy? I don't want you exhausting yourself.'

'Yes, marm,' I says.

What a fake! Her I'm talking about, not me.

And yet when she turned again and made her way up the stairs I stood rooted to the spot, watching her as she retreated, the lovely sway of her back.

*

The master was up and away already, looking over his policies with his foreman. He was absent all morning and the missus might as well have been for all I seen of her. For some reason the kitchen seemed a gloomier place than I remembered. I kept noticing dirt everywhere, in the cracks in the table and down the sides of things and in all the little corners it was hard to reach. Had it got so filthy in the space of just 3 days? Or had it always been like that? And if so why had nobody noticed?

Nothing seemed to go right that morning. I stood in the saucer and spilled the cats milk. The broom handle broke in two as soon as I looked at it and so I had to work bent over like a ½ shut knife. Then the crumbs and dirt just didn't want to be swep up, they kept escaping from the bristles. And when I finally did manage to fill the dustpan, what did I do but step on it so that all the muck went skiting across the floor again. Making broth was no better. The carrots was wormy and the turnip was like an old sponge, slicing them up seemed to take forever. I used to like looking out the window whilst I prepared the food but on that day the view gave me no relief, so foul and foreboding was the weather. A rainstorm was brewing in the distance and the sky was that dark and menacing the gulls appeared bright white against it, soaring across the black clouds like slips of ghosts.

I had only been awake a few hours and already I was flipping banjaxed. Of course, the real problem was that there was too much work for one person. This had never really bothered me before. But now it struck me as a great injustice. And now I felt betrayed by the missus, everything was laid bare before me and I saw the place for what it really was, more like I'd thought of it when I first arrived – a crumbling, drafty old wreck in a dismal landscape scarred by pits and with the stink of cows trapped under a leaden sky.

Oh how I longed for Crown House! To be tucked up under a rug by the fire, eating hot buttered crumpets and playing Cassino with my Mr Levy!

*

Much as missus was not in my favour, I found myself longing for her to put in an appearance as the day went on. But she seemed inclined to avoid me, as stated in her book. I only caught a few glimpses of her, once as she hurried out to speak to Muriel and once as she swep past me on the stairs, on her way to sort through the linen chest. She greeted me both times with a smile, but I could tell she was really giving me the bony shoulder.

That afternoon the master returned to the house about 4 o'clock and ½ an hour later called me to his study with a ring of the bell. When I went in he was stood at the window, watching the rain drip down the glass.

'Excellent,' he says when he seen me, although in my current mood I did not feel that I excelled in any way shape or form whatsoever. I give him a curtsey and he indicated an old nursing chair upon which lay the folded newspaper.

'Sit yourself down,' he says, 'and please read me the notices in the left hand column on the first page.'

'Just the left hand column, sir?' I says and he replied that the left hand column would suffice for the present.

I sat down, unfolded the newspaper and began to read aloud. Normally, I might have been soiling myself about this whole procedure, but I was so sunk in my gloom that nothing seemed to matter. It was a Glasgow newspaper, I don't remember the exact wordings but the gist of the first notice was as follows. '*The Gentleman who took the Wrong HAT from the U.P. Church, North Portland Street, last Sabbath afternoon, will greatly oblige the Owner by returning the same to him at Mrs Grahams, 57 South Portland Street.*'

Master James appeared to find this very amusing. 'Heh-heh-heh!' he goes with great glee. 'Fellow lost his hat! But before we go on, I suspect there is something the matter with you, girl. Your face is that long you may trip on your chin. I fear you are still unwell.'

'No sir. I am quite recovered thank you.'

'I see,' he says. 'Well – try to sound less like a funeral orator. Next one. Speak out.'

It was a great effort but I raised my voice. '*STOLEN or STRAYED, on Wednesday or Thursday, an English TUP belonging to Robert Kerr, Milngavie. A Suitable Reward will be given to any person giving such information as will lead to recovery.*'

Master James chuckled. 'Wonderful,' he says. 'Imagine what kind of mentality could lose a tup. No doubt the animal was sharper than its master. It did not care for Milngavie or Robert Kerr. Aye, it has moved to Dumbarton and become a procurator fiscal. But you do not seem to find it amusing, girl.'

'Oh I do sir,' I says, very mournful.

'Well then,' he says. 'Continue please, with greater levity.'

I did try to render the next notice more cheerful but the content of it was so sad that I grew increasingly depressed as I read and by the end of it I was near enough in tears. '*LEFT HER HOME on last Saturday and has not been seen or heard of since, MRS AGNES FAULDS or CRAWFORD. She is about the ordinary height, thin, pale complexion, brown hair. Had on grey shawl, wincey polka, dark petticoat. She is about 27 years of age and is a little wrong in the mind. Any information will be thankfully received by her Husband, T. Crawford, 42 King Street, Calton.*'

'Och dearie me!' says master James, pacing up and down. 'This time at least you are right to look sad. Aye, a real tragedy. But mark you,' he raised a finger and addressed me like as if I were a member of a jury, 'no compensation is offered. You see that one man will give a reward for the recovery of his tup, while another will give only thanks for the rescue of his wife. I suggest to you that one need not read the articles in the newspaper at all, for here – in the humble notices – all humanity is laid bare. Aye indeed. Next one.'

And so it went. I read the notices, he commented on them. All the while, I strained to hear every sound from the rest of the house, worrying that missus might, in my absence, go into the kitchen. The longer I stayed in the study, the more likely I was to miss her. So it was with great relief, as I turned the page of the newspaper, that I heard master James clear his throat and begin to shuffle papers. He had picked up a catalogue from his desk. There was a drawing on the front of an ornate metal structure.

'No, that will do, Bessy,' he says. 'You may get on with your own work. Well done.'

'Thank you, sir.'

He narrowed his eyes and gave me a canny look.

'I suspect that there is a young man behind all these melancholy sighs and faces,' he says. 'But remember, Bessy, these things are never as bad as they seem. I guarantee you that you will wake up one morning and think to yourself – how foolish I have been.'

'Indeed sir,' I says. 'You seem to know me better than I know myself.'

And I left the room quickly, biting my tongue in case I said anything worse.

Earlier, I had closed the kitchen door behind me but now it lay open and despite myself I felt my heart soar. I slowed my pace and sauntered into the room, glancing from side to side in a relaxed and natural fashion, ready to sham surprise at seeing missus there. Perhaps I might persuade her into conversation. She might even sit with me while I made the dinner. I could write something quick in my little book to show her. But the kitchen was empty. Instead, awaiting me on the table was a note. Although it bore no signature, the handwriting was unmistakable.

Dear Bessy, Dinner for two to be served in dining room at six o'clock please. Soup, then mutton (follow Actons recipe – DO NOT make it up). Serve with potatoes. No dessert. Please lay up plates in kitchen and bring them upstairs. Once plates are on table, leave room and do not return until rung for. Thank you. Please excuse note but I have headache and must lie down.

So this was what we were reduced to, communicating in writing (I did not believe her about the flipping headache). I crumpled up the note and threw it into the swill bucket in a temper and must add that my mood was not improved by later having to fish it out because I had forgot at what o'clock she wanted the dinner to be served.

That evening, as requested, I took them their meal in the dining room. This was to be the first time I had ever waited on missus and her husband together and it should at least have been an occasion for curiosity. But the novelty of the arrangement was lost on me, as throughout proceedings I felt as drear and brown and lumpish as the gravy on their meat (I *had* followed the recipe but unfortunately it had not turned out quite as expected). Master James nodded at me as I set down his plates but for her part the missus did not look at me once, indeed she seemed at pains to avoid my eye. Any time I was in the room she strained to keep the conversation going with her husband, firing questions at him one after the other as you might bat at a ball to keep it in the air and it seemed to me that this was mainly in order to prevent me from making any remarks of my own (as if I would!).

Nobody rang for me again that night and I went to bed at 10 o'clock, weary and dispirited. The following day I awoke better rested and with a sliver of hope in my breast but this was dashed when missus told me that she and her husband were going out for the day and when later, upon their return, she claimed to be too tired for a punctuation lesson. She was all smiles and politeness and calling you 'dear' but I knew fine well she couldn't get away from me fast enough.

All that week it felt to me like the two of us sashayed around each other, the rules of the dance was never to be in the same place at the same time, for if ever I waltzed into a room it would only be a matter of moments before missus went reeling out of it.

The masters presence in our midst also gave life at Castle Haivers a new character. His routine did not vary much. Off he'd go to meet his foreman in the morning and that would be the last you seen of him and his louse ladders until late afternoon. About 4 o'clock, if he'd got hold of a newspaper from Glasgow or Edinburgh I had to read him the notices, after which he would attend to his paperwork.

He was a busy man right enough for as well as the estate to run and his business interests in Glasgow, it seemed that master James had political ambitions which is one reason why he had been in London. Mr Weir-Paterson, the local Member of Parliament, was known to be not only of advanced age but in poor health and fond of a glass of port to boot. And although it was never spoke aloud, it was commonly thought that his constituency might become available at any time. James Reid had his eye on that seat, his step was quick, his buttocks limber, given ½ a chance and the indulgence of the public his arse would be in it before you could say 'Gout'. Even though Weir-Paterson was not yet dead, master James electioneering had already begun in earnest, with good works and society. His good work was a plan to install a public fountain in Snatter, fed from a new source (since the water supply thereabouts was of notorious poor quality). As for society he was always out to dine with this one and that one in the neighbourhood, only them that had the vote, of course. Sometimes missus went with him on these visits and sometimes he took his friend McGregor-Robertson. If the master dined at home, missus ate with him but if he went out and left her behind she avoided me by keeping to her room.

I don't know much about politics. But I do know one thing.

No I don't. I knew one thing a minute ago but now I forget what it was. I'll tell you this instead. I watched them. When the two of them were together and when it were possible I watched them close as a dipper studies his mark. The ways of married ladies and gentlemen were not familiar to me. I watched them, and it seemed to me that there was something amiss between this pair, the missus and her husband, and not just the fact that they did not share a bed. For one thing, his treatment of her was puzzling. Mostly, he was gracious to a fault with her but in a manner that was over-polite and assiduous (now there's a word for you!), as you might be with a person you just met or an invalid rather than with your young wife. At other times, however, his patience seemed to snap for no good reason. He became brusque with her, interrupting or ignoring her, or contradicting what she said. As for missus, no matter how he acted, she was pleasant to him and dutiful and all the things a wife is meant to be. Except, of course, for one minor detail.

She was lying through her teeth to him the whole time.

I had already guessed that her husband was unaware she was writing a book. It did not take long to work out that he didn't know about what she got up to with the servants either. Proof of this was that – from the moment he arrived at the farm – the experiments ceased altogether. No more strange moods, no outlandish requests, no more sit, stand, sit. It was as though none of it had ever happened. I realised that when she had went on about me being discreet, there was one person in particular she wanted me to be discreet with – and that was her husband. Well I had a good mind to tell him all about what she got up to when he wasn't there, so I did. Make her laugh on the other side of her mouth.

But it was not long before I was to discover another, more entertaining, way to take my revenge.

9

An Important Dinner

Two things happened at about this time. Master James decided to give an Important Dinner. And a little later, I thought of how I would get my own back on missus. Let's have dinner first. On the day the invitations went out the master and missus were that excited Jesus Murphy it were a shame only a handful of guests was invited because with all their nervous agitation the pair of them was lit up like a couple of candelabras and could have illuminated a ballroom. In comparison, my own mood was shabby, my spirits low, my hostility for missus at a peak. The Reverend Pollock was to be among the guests (I need not tell you the jig of joy I danced at *that* news) as was McGregor-Robertson, the doctor. Mr Davy Flemyng was also invited. He was only a tenant of master James, but a cut above the rest by virtue of his growing repute as a poet. (It was with him that they'd dined on the night of the masters return.) The other guests were strangers to me, according to missus they were 'people of influence'. There was Mr Mungo Rankin who owned adjacent farmland but was now turning his fields over to coal pits. He was to be accompanied by his lady wife. And most important of those invited was Mr Duncan Pollock, *Member of Parliament*, no less. This bucko was the Reverend Pollocks younger brother and apparently 'a leading light of the Liberals'.

It was really for him that the dinner was being held, the rest of them could have drowned in the mulligatawny for all master James cared. It was only Duncan Pollock *Member of Parliament* that he wanted to impress since the fellow had much sway over the local party and would be able (if so inclined) to support master James when he went up for the elections. Not only that but every so often

Duncan Pollock held a *Soiree* in Edinburgh, which old Lord Pummystone himself was said to have attended! Lord save us all!

Of course, these distinguished guests would have to be waited upon. My one previous attempt at silver service had not been a great success, I will not go into too much detail but gravy was involved as was the masters neck and despite my *genuine* best efforts the two became accidentally conjoined in a way that is not usually acceptable in polite society. Ever since then I had plated up the food in the kitchen. But now there was to be a dinner, missus put me in training with the silver and drilled me until I could have served a single pea off a platter to the Pope himself. It seemed that I was not to be alone in my endeavours on the great night, for Hector and one of the Curdle Twins were to be recruited to assist at table and behind the scenes. In the absence of a cook, missus took charge of the menu and supervised the preparations.

By the time that the day of the dinner arrived the lady of the house had reached a peak of luminescence. If beforehand she had been a candelabra she was now a blazing chandelier. From midday onwards, the kitchen was a Frenzy of activity lit up by her majesty presiding and me a mere wick smouldering low and resentful beside her. For once it seemed that no expense was spared. We made soup and pies, we roasted pheasants and a forequarter of lamb, we boiled beef and carrots.

At some point Hector arrived, with dead chickens he had to pluck, which he did in due course, having paused only to carry out a horrified examination of the birds private parts. Once the plucking was finished I believe he would have happily slipped away but missus gave him more work, he had to polish the silver and wash the potatoes, chore upon chore she gave him and in all the confusion it is a wonder that he didn't end up washing the silver and polishing the potatoes. Normally I felt little kinship with Hector but that day I warmed to him somewhat for whenever the missus made some new pronouncement he would wait until her back was turned and then he'd stroke his chin like a wise man while puffing, straight-faced, on an imaginary pipe and this mockery did afford me some private amusement.

Muriel, or Curdle Features the 2nd as I called her, presented herself in the late afternoon once milking was done. Her task was to keep the kitchen clean and later to assist me in serving at table. She was all prinked up, her cap was off and she had put ribbons in her hair but you might as well have stuck primroses in a cowpat. While missus was in view, she was keen to appear a hard worker. She bustled round the kitchen pretending to be out of breath and swiping at things with a cloth. But if ever missus left the room it was not long before C. Features ceased to bustle. She was that lazy I bet she lay down to fart. Not once did she open her beak to me apart from this time she came up behind me and put her mouth to my ear. I thought she might be going to whisper me a secret but all she says was, 'Ma waist is ½ the size of yours,' and then she skipped away, giggling. This endeared her to me no end, apart from anything it wasn't true.

I do believe that missus was suffering from a last-minute attack of nervosity, because she decided that only the mulligatawny was to be dished out at table. The remaining courses we was to lay up in the kitchen, to save accidents.

At ½ past 7 exactly Hector was stationed at the kitchen table, commanded never to desist from washing plates. C. Features and I had donned fresh aprons, ready to make our first entry to the dining room. We were unable, however, to decide who should carry the soup and who should serve it, both of us were inclined to serve, as it seemed the better job not least because the tureen was flipping scalding. Quite the old tug-of-war developed over the ladle and only the intervention of missus prevented it from being bent completely out of shape. She settled the argument in my favour and then returned to her guests. Moments later, Muriel and I followed and never did a more shambling and ill-tempered little procession enter a dining room.

For once there were candles in all the sconces and in holders on the table and the place was lit up and going like Argyle Street. Never once in my experience had the house seen so many people. Several polite conversations were going on all at once, missus at one end of the table next a fair-headed young man with eyeglasses that I took to be Mr Flemyng. Mrs Rankin (as the only other lady present I presumed it was she) was at the far end, to the right of master James and she had to be served first according to missus instructions so I prodded C. Features in that direction with the ladle and used it to steer her around the table. She would take only one baby step at a time for fear of spilling the soup and as a result we advanced at a desperate slow pace. I was not sorry, however, for this afforded me the opportunity to eavesdrop at leisure.

'Surely that can be of no interest?' I heard Mr Flemyng murmur in reply to something that missus had asked him.

'On the contrary,' she says. 'I would be fascinated to know.'

'Very well,' he says. 'I do it in the evening. After the days work is done. And I stop when my hand is tired or when the candle burns out, whichever is first.'

Missus gave the appearance of hanging on his every word but I knew for certain that she'd caught a glimpse of us out the corner of her eye and was watching our progress (or lack of it) with some alarm. She made a wafting motion with her hand below the level of the table but she had not let slip a gastric *faux pas*, she just wanted us to hurry up. I poked Muriel harder with the ladle and missus applied herself once more to Mr Flemyng.

'And do you favour any particular colour of ink?'

'Any that I can get my hands on. I'm not superstitious – and ink is expensive. But what about your good self, Mrs Reid? You were talking of writing a poem.'

'Oh dear no,' says missus. 'As I said, I do not write. But please,' and here she put her hand on his wrist, 'do call me Arabella.'

We crept along behind Reverend Pollock, who was sandwiched between Mrs Rankin and Flemyng, a situation which placed him as far as possible from both missus and master James (but of course this could have been accidental rather than strategic). Mrs Rankin was a lean woman with a head like a skull and a phiz to frighten the horses. She was grinning at the Reverend with all her many prominent teeth.

'Might I ask, Mrs Rankin,' Pollock was saying, 'are you familiar at all with the Queens Rooms? The Queens Rooms in Glasgow?'

'I don't believe I am, Reverend,' says she her voice all breathless and girlish, quite at odds with her ageing appearance. 'Are they something to be seen?'

'Ah-haah,' says the Old Bollix. 'Dearie me no, they are not an attraction to visit as such. It is just that I am to give a lecture there next year and I am not familiar with the building. I do believe that it is an important venue. Apparently, a number of prestigious speakers have graced the very stage upon which I am to deliver my own humble oration.'

This news near enough fetched Mrs Rankin off. She squeaked and panted. 'Oh gracious me,' she says. 'How dreadfully clever of you.'

At long last C. Features had reached the end of the table, I jabbed her with the ladle to make her stop and then prodded her forwards into a better position, it is as well we were in company for the look she gave me, I don't know what class of thing she might have said or done otherwise. Here's how much I cared. *The rind of a cheese.* Ignoring her, I removed the lid from the tureen and set it on the sideboard as instructed by missus (and *not* on the *carpet* as I had so foolishly done before my training). Then I began ladling soup.

There was 3 gentlemen occupied the opposite side of the table. I surmised that Mr Duncan Pollock as guest of honour would be the suave looking cove with the neat brown-and-ginger moustache, seated on the missus right. He was talking to McGregor-Robertson while master James was in conversation with Rankin, who was a portly fellow with a whiskey face on him. He wore a wig and a high neck cloth and seemed to have little control over his fleshy lips which slobbered something fierce as he spoke, distributing a spray of spittle before him, by Jove he would have made a fine French polisher.

'Not for an instant have I regretted it, mark you,' he was saying. 'In fact, it is my intention tae turn over the rest of what I have tae the very same purpose.'

'I see,' says master James, mildly. He had leaned well back in his chair, giving the impression that he preferred to remain aloof from this discussion or perhaps it was just the slobbers he was keen to avoid, who can say.

'Aye indeed,' Rankin says. 'We begin further exploratory work in the spring. I also have it in mind tae build a brick and tile works over at Tuppethill. And there is a fellow wants tae put a chemical works at Mossburn if I'll let him. But it's the mines is where the money is. Farming is a thing of the past, believe you me.'

This last comment was addressed to the company in general since – during the course of his speech – his voice had grown so loud as to drown out other conversations and one by one all heads had turned in his direction. Even missus and Flemyng had wrenched themselves from their little confabulation and were spectating, the missus with a beatific smile on her face hell roast her.

Confident that he had the attention of everyone present Rankin had turned his attention once again to master James.

'Here's a question for ye. Which pit do ye think gives me my highest yield?'

Master James expressed (very dryly) his regret that he'd never seen the need to become an expert in matters of coalmining – ho ho, he was a wag all right. After pausing to acknowledge the polite laughter prompted by this remark he confirmed that – Alas! – he did not know which pit gave the highest yield.

'Well, let me tell ye,' says Mr Rankin. 'The highest yield comes frae the one pit I have that borders your land. And ye know what that means.'

Master James allowed that he was not in fact in possession of that information. But he was sure Mr Rankin would be good enough to tell him.

'It means that you might be very lucky indeed,' Rankin says.

'Should ye take ma advice and give up farming and start sinking pits, or you could lease the land out to them that will dae it for you.'

Duncan Pollock, *Member of Parliament*, was holding up his glass to the light, which gave him the appearance of one who was not listening. But he had the air about him of a man who doesn't miss a trick. Master James flicked a glance down the table at him. Then he nodded at Rankin and affected a certain weariness.

'I take your point, Mungo,' he says. 'However, my ambitions lie elsewhere.'

Rankin scoffed. 'Politics? Ach, ye'll soon tire of that.'

Master James chuckled. 'Well, that remains to be –'

'Hoot-toot-toot! Wheesht man wheesht! If ye don't get into mining, James, ye're passing up a golden opportunity. What have you got here – some tenants, some cows, a bit land – a piece of nonsense, that's what the farming business is and you're short-sighted if you don't realise it.'

Master James was clearly irritated but seemed unable to come back with a response. He took a breath but before he could speak, missus addressed Rankin, apparently with great affection.

'Dear Mungo,' she says. 'And I presume, that when all the farms in the land have been turned over to pits, as you would like, you would have us eating coal and ironstone instead of bread and meat.'

At this, Flemyng snorted so hard that he blew out the candle in front of him. Master James sensed a point well made (albeit by his wife). He joined in with the chortles and glanced in triumph around the table. Reverend P. remarked that it was admirably put. Mrs Rankin squeaked. There were general murmurs of assent, yes yes, she has a point, you're not wrong there, well done, all this.

Missus smiled graciously at Rankin, to show him that she had simply been teasing. I noticed that Duncan Pollock MP gave her a long and admiring glance, the man was that oily he'd float on water.

By this time, Muriel and I had accomplished a circuit of the table and all the guests had been served with soup. Since C. Features was no longer required I elbowed her out the room and shut the door in her bake. Then I took the bottle of claret from the sideboard and began to circle the table, filling the tiny glasses. As instructed, I served Mrs Rankin first but forgot that missus should get hers next and had already poured for master James before I realised my mistake. However nobody seemed to have noticed and so I just continued around the table clockwise.

Now he had it between the old gnashers, Rankin wouldn't drop his bone. He wondered aloud whether his host would like to conjecture just *how much* money he had made from turning his land over to mining. Master James very graciously said that he would not presume. And when Rankin tried to goad him into hazarding a simple guess at the matter, master James attempted to change the subject. But Rankin interrupted and named two sums, one large the other astronomical and asked master James if he'd care to choose which was nearer to the amount of money brought in by the pits.

Substantial though it may have been it seemed unlikely that Rankin would brag about the smaller sum. You could tell master James had sensed defeat. With all eyes upon him and with great reluctance he named the larger. Rankin gave a shout of laughter, then brought both his fat fists down on the table, making the cutlery rattle.

'Not bad, for a wee laddie frae Linlithgow, eh?' he demanded of the company and jabbed his finger at his own chest just in case anybody was in any doubt about the identity of the wee laddie. 'Eh? What aboot that, eh?'

And then everyone did what was required which was to laugh and be gay and murmur congratulations. Except that is for two people, these were Duncan Pollock MP, who was quietly watching the proceedings from his end of the table, and master James who appeared uncomfortable in the extreme, as though he sensed that he'd been played like a puppet. He cast a distressed gaze around the assembled guests but no-one met his eye except missus. Without hesitation, she addressed Mrs Rankin down the length of the table.

'You must be terribly proud of your Mungo,' she says, not a hint of an edge to her voice. 'He has done so well for himself, has he not?'

And then in a seamless move she shifted the focus of attention by turning to Flemyng. 'You should write a poem about him, Davy,' she says. 'A eulogy.'

Flemyng looked up from his soup, a little startled, I suspect that writing eulogies to Mr Rankin did not count among his primary ambitions. However, missus had already swivelled around to fix her gaze upon Mr Pollock MP.

'Did you know, sir, that our Mr Flemyng here is gaining quite a reputation in literary circles? His poems really are rather wonderful. Our very own Rabbie Burns.'

'Och, foof! Too kind, no, no!' protested Flemyng. But nobody paid him a blind bit of notice, he was only a tenant farmer after all. Missus was still turned towards Duncan Pollock, who seemed unable to take his eyes off her.

'I understand you are a poetry lover, sir?' she says.

'Indeed I am,' he says. 'But I must admit that my real love is Song. Fine words are all very well, but I prefer them to come with a tune to gladden the heart.'

Here was a man that spoke in the slow, measured tones of someone who is used to being attended to and although what he said was not all that profound it might as well have been Great Philosophy such was the admiration expressed by the others. Heads were nodded, agreement was murmured, and a few of them chuckled even though what he'd said was not particularly funny. McGregor-Robertson the doctor piped up.

'Do you prefer Haydn sir? Or Mozart? Or Boyce?'

Duncan Pollock twitched his whiskers. 'As a matter of fact,' he says, 'my taste is for humbler music. Plain songs, the ballads of ordinary folk.'

'Ah-haah!' says the Reverend his brother with a wink at nobody in particular. 'Dear Duncan is obsessed with traditional melodies, the simpler the better, the sort of thing you might hear sung in the street in Glasgow, by ragamuffins, I can't imagine why.'

At that instant, I was about to pour claret for missus but she grabbed my wrist as I reached out to move her glass. 'In that case,' she says to Pollock, 'I think we have someone here that might interest you.'

My left hand was fast in hers and I was trapped. Panic rose in my breast, for it struck me that she was about to blurt out something about me that I wouldn't like.

'Please, marm?' I murmured, Jesus Murphy she's lucky I didn't crown her with the wine bottle but she didn't seem to hear me, she was talking to Pollock.

'Bessy here concocts songs in her head and goes about the place singing. I am not a musical person but you, sir, might make something of them. She is a lovely singer.' She turned to me and gave me one of her most irresistible smiles. 'Bessy, dear,' she says. 'Do Mr Pollock and the rest of us a great honour by singing one of your marvellous songs?'

She turned in appeal to the rest of the table. They were all looking at me now, their soup bowls empty and their faces shining in the candlelight.

'Ah-haah, yes indeed, Bessy!' goes the Old Bollix fondly. As though he knew and loved all my songs – when he'd never heard a single flipping one of them!

Sensing my hesitation, missus tightened her grip on my wrist. 'Do please sing, Bessy,' she says gently. 'Mr Flemyng is a noted collector of songs. Perhaps he will collect one of yours? I am sure they would be perfect for him. We *must* hear one. Even just a single verse and a chorus.'

Master James called up the table. 'Come on, Bessy!' he goes, his face flushed. 'Give us a song!' He began to clap and encouraged the others to do likewise, until they were all clapping and staring at me. And I hadn't even sung anything yet! Sometimes, it is nice to be asked to sing. However, nobody likes to be treated like a performing monkey. Missus didn't care two flips for me. She just wanted to impress their honoured guest. Smiling away at me, so she was, in encouragement. No doubt later on she'd chalk it all down in her blasted book, how 'the subject' responded to being asked to perform. Well, I'd give her a performance, by hicky I would.

I set down the bottle and stepped away from the table. Then I faced my audience.

'This is called "The Wind that Blows down Barrack Street", I says and then I launched into the song. The title has a romantic cast. However, it was one of my bawdier efforts, about a man who is afflicted by a severe case of intestinal gas and who is prone to fart in inappropriate places. I will give you a flavour of it here.

There's a pieman lives on Barrack Street
His shop's next the urinal
There's a pieman lives on Barrack Street
With a problem intestinal

He can't take beans nor beer nor prunes
Nor apples pears nor whisky
Not cabbages nor cauliflower
And even bread is risky

There's a wind that blows down Barrack Street
A wind to make you fearful
There's a spicy gale on Barrack Street
If you go there please be careful

On market day, he bakes away
The pieshop it is jumping
You can smell his wares as far as Cowlairs
His windward passage pumping

When for a wake, he has to bake
For friends of the departed
Then all that goes must hold their nose
In case the pieman farted

There's a wind that blows down Barrack Street
A wind to make you fearful

There's a spicy gale on Barrack Street
If you go there please be careful

(And so it goes for a few more verses, with the pieman disrupting a wedding and blowing a hole in his breeks &c.)

Upon hearing the song title, missus had looked delighted but her smile had glazed over somewhat by the end of the first verse and as the chorus progressed both she and her husband began to look quite ill. They threw glances of alarm in the direction of their distinguished guest. Nobody made a sound to begin with. And then at the end of the first chorus, Mr Duncan Pollock MP began to chuckle and his chuckles grew until he was hooting with laughter. Seeing that he was enjoying himself, missus and master James started to laugh too, in fact master James became almost hysterical. The rest of the guests took their lead and joined in the merriment. Except for the Reverend Mr Pollock, who sat with a puzzled expression on his phiz from which I gathered that *Presbyterians do not fart*. When I'd finished, his brother Duncan applauded like his hands were on fire. He clapped me and then he clapped missus, I'm not quite sure why he clapped *her*, perhaps because she was clever enough to have me as a maid.

I made them all a curtsey then looked at missus. 'Shall I sing another, marm?'

She laughed very gay and fanned herself with her napkin, indeed she did look hot. 'It was a most amusing song Bessy,' she says. 'But perhaps that's enough for one evening. Besides, we must give our guests some more food.' Then she turned to Flemyng. 'What do you think, Davy? Given that example, would you be interested in collecting Bessys songs?'

Flemyng, who had just taken a swift gulp of claret, almost choked.

'Yes indeed,' he says, when he had finished coughing. 'I'm always interested in transcribing songs I haven't heard before. How clever of you to suggest it.'

Missus nodded. 'That is decided then,' she says. 'I will send her to you and you can transcribe to your hearts content.' Then she turned, with an air of finality, to address Mr Pollock MP.

'James and I are great believers in the preservation of traditional tales and songs and the like,' she says. (The liar!) 'We must move forward, of course, but we should not forget our past,' this with a nod at Mr Rankin, 'in our hurry to meet the future.'

Mr Duncan Pollock smiled, the way he looked at her you thought he might want to eat her (or at the very least give her a nibble). 'I couldn't agree more, Arabella,' he says and raised his glass. 'To our wise and most venerable hostess. And, of course, to her husband.'

And with varying degrees of enthusiasm the company toasted missus and master James. The most zealous were McGregor-Robertson and Flemyng who hoisted their glasses high and echoed 'To our hostess.' Reverend Pollock beamed at her without drinking while Rankin craftily lifted his wine straight to his lips with devil the bit of the toast in between, and Mrs Rankin held up her glass, a smile plastered on her face, but she too did not drink and there was not a squeak out of her for missus had surely put her in the shade.

While they were eating, I cogged a bottle of claret and drank it in the pantry as the evening progressed so that by the time the guests were away and the kitchen was cleared, I was in a state of elevation. I had a real head on me to have a proper drink and got it in mind to mooch off and investigate one of the local taprooms. And so when Hector and C. Features had left and the missus and master away to bed, I snuck out the house.

The shortest route to Snatter was over the fields but I wasn't convinced that I could negotiate my way in the dark and so as precaution took the longer route down the lane and along the Great Road. Chancy for me there was a ½ moon and not much cloud, else I'd not have been able to see my foot in front of my face. After about a mile on the Great Road, the first cottages of Snatter appeared dark against the night sky. The place was deserted no doubt because of the late hour. I went straight to The Gushet, it was one of the first houses on the left.

Even though the door to the porch was pulled almost shut I could make out the sound of laughter within. Here at the threshold, I hesitated. It was a good wee while since I'd visited such a place and I was still a stranger in those parts. Also, it suddenly occurred to me that missus wouldn't approve of me being in an alehouse, not in the least.

But what was I on about? Damn the fears of me doing what she wanted! I gave myself a shake. For dear sake catch yourself on, I thought. I whipped open the door and stepped inside only to find myself inside a long porch, the off-licence part of the premises. The hole in the wall was shut but just then a fresh burst of laughter came from behind it. I rapped on the hatch. Instantly, the laughter stopped. There was a brief silence followed by some agitated whispers and then scraping sounds as of chairs being pushed across a slate floor. I perceived yet more whispers and some unidentifiable rustling. Then silence. After a pause the hatch slid open and a whippet-faced woman with dark hair looked out. This had to be Janet Murray, the proprietor. I had heard missus mention her.

'Aye?' she says. 'What can I dae for you?'

At first glance she appeared to be alone but some telltale signs suggested otherwise. Several candles burned in the little taproom behind her and I could see a table around which a number of stools were gathered, now pushed back as though recently vacated by persons unknown. Tobacco smoke hung in the air. The table surface was marked with wet rings as might have been left behind by assorted overflowing glasses and here and there playing cards lay in disordered piles. But not a soul to be seen.

Janet was peering into the darkness behind me. She talked through her nose.

'What are you wanting?'

'Just a drink,' I says. 'I know it's late but I'll stay here in the porch.' And I set a coin on the sill of the hatch.

The woman picked it up and studied it. Then she put it in her pocket and fetched me a glass of ale. She watched me take the first sip, then leaned forwards and spoke quietly.

'I hope you dinna mind my saying,' she says. 'But I've got a few friends here at the moment.' She jerked a thumb towards a curtain in the corner of the room. 'We are just celebrating some good news. All at my expense, of course! They havnae put their hands in their pockets once! But now you dinna just mind if they just carry on celebrating, dae you?'

She indicated the empty table behind her with a sweep of her hand.

'No,' says I. 'Not at all. Go right ahead.'

At these words, Janet leaned back from the hatch and gave a low whistle whereupon the curtain in the corner was pulled aside by an unseen hand and several reprobates filed into the room, each bearing a glass or mug, Sammy Sums was among them. It seemed they had all been standing in a very small recess and were pleased to be out for they shook themselves and stretched their limbs as they appeared. Then they took up their places at the table one after the other, giving me a glance or nod as they sat. Sammy Sums settled in the corner and began counting the spots on dominoes. Last to emerge was Biscuit Meek. He sneered when he seen me and looked utterly disgusted, a girl in a public house, look at the big titties on her, the disgrace, all this. Hypocrite! And when he took his place at the table, he deliberately chose a stool that meant he could turn his back. Various pipes were lit and the card game resumed.

'You see,' Janet says. 'They've no *paid* for their drinks, not a penny, but I realise how it might look tae an outsider, no?'

I knew fine rightly what she was up to. It was after midnight, the early hours of the Sabbath and she probably should not have been serving drink at all. But I cared not a pigs pizzle what she did.

'And yourself, dear?' she says. 'Where are you on your way to this night?'

'Nowhere,' I says. 'I work nearby is all and I came out for a budge.'

'Is that so now?' She looked me up and down with greater interest. 'And where is it you work at? I have no seen you afore.'

'Castle Haivers,' I says. 'I am the in-and-out girl up there.'

Well. The look she gave me, you would think I had said that I worked the bellows for Old Nick himself. 'Castle Haivers?' she says. 'Well now, indeed. The replacement.'

'The what?'

'You know. You replaced the girl that was there afore you?'

I gave her my empty glass and a coin. The ale was not a patch on the knock-me-down we usually drank in Glasgow, but it was not too bad. She poured me another, this time studying me as though I was a specimen. There was a sign on the wall, 'Rooms Available' and directly underneath it said 'No Vacancy'. I couldn't work it out. Was there rooms or wasn't there?

Janet says, 'Morag – the girl that worked there afore you – she was a regular here. Near enough every night she came doon. We had a right laugh thegether, so we did.' She picked up her own glass and raised it to me. 'Not that I care for gossip,' she says. 'But if you dinnae mind my asking, how does Mrs Reid treat you?'

'All right,' I says.

'She doesnae lock you in a cupboard, leave you to starve for days on end?'

'No.'

Janet looked doubtful. 'Have you got any wages oot them yet?'

In fact, I had not been paid what I was owed. The missus tended to give me bits of money here and there, but my full salary had never yet transpired. However, this was nobodys business but my own so I just says, 'I have had wages, yes.'

'Well you're lucky,' says Janet. 'That James Reid would touch a man in a shroud for a penny. Just the one wee lassie tae dae all the work aboot the place – would you credit it? In-and-out girl, indeed! In a big hoose like that? It's a piece of nonsense. They should hae a hoosekeeper and two lassies, at least, and your missus should hae a ladies maid all her ane. But Oh no! Not for that yin – he's too much of a skin flint. Do you know what I am going to tell you?'

'No,' I says. 'I don't.' (By this time I had her down as an old clash-bag.)

She pulled her shawl up closer around her neck. 'Well,' she says. 'Your James Reid would not keep a decent staff in his hoose – but he has nine chamber pots stashed under his bed, each one of them filled to the brim – wi' solid gold.'

I just looked at her. I tellt her that there was but one pot under the masters bed, that I emptied it every morning and that she could rest assured that what was in it was not gold.

Janet widened her eyes. 'Nine pots,' she goes. 'Brim full. How is your beer?'

'The beer I'm not displeased with,' I says. 'But I'm less happy with the ant.' For there was such a creature drowning in my glass, he sank to the depths as I watched, frantically waving his little arms and legs. Janet took a look at him.

'He was probably just in the glass,' she says. 'Not the beer.'

Well that bathed me with relief. I tossed out what ale remained and handed my glass back to her. 'Thank you,' I says. 'I have to be going now.'

She looked at me of a sudden with great pity. 'Och, you're just a wee bairn. I dinnae like tae think of you going back to that dreadful place all on yer ane. You know there's girls have died up there.'

She could keep her gossip right enough – but these last words did give me pause. 'Girls?' I says. 'What do you mean? How many girls?'

'Well,' says Janet. 'Just one *confirmed* death. But there's plenty disappeared.'

I looked at her.

'Oh aye,' she says. 'One minute they are there and then next morning all trace of them has vanished.'

I laughed. 'That's just girls have decided they don't like hard work and cleared out in the night. Is it not?'

Janet glanced over at Sammy Sums like she might consult him on the matter but he was licking a domino and did not give the appearance of being an authority on any subject. The rest of the men (Biscuit Meek included) was engaged in drink and play and business with pipes, they had no interest in the clack of womens tongues. Janet turned back to me.

'What does Mrs Reid say aboot that girl Nora, the one that died?'

'She never talks about her,' I says, which was true enough (although it did not take into account the screeds missus had wrote about Nora in *The Observations*).

Janet widened her eyes at me and nodded, several times, as though I had proved something beyond doubt.

'What?' I says.

'She *wouldnae* talk aboot her, would she?' says Janet. 'Nora was drunk and fell in front of a train, that's the official story. But do you know what I am going to tell you?'

'No.'

'I'd be willing to bet that Nora didnae just *fall* on that railway line.'

I looked at her blankly. 'What are you on about?'

Janet folded her arms and pursed her lips. 'You want tae ask your Mrs Reid how that Nora died,' she says. 'See what kind of answer you get.'

'Well I might just do that,' I says.

At the time, I didn't pay her any heed. I was drunk and thought she was just a gossip, with her 9 pisspots full of gold and all this nonsense about Nora and missus and pressing me for information. So I kept my trap shut. In fact I was ready for my bed, so I gave her goodnight and left.

It was not until much later that I began to wonder about what Janet had said and to have 2nd thoughts. And as I believe I have already pointed out, I don't often have them.

10

I Have an Idea

The day after his Important Dinner, master James was in the best of form chuntering away over his porridge so he was, chunter chunter chunter. The meal had been a great success because before Duncan Pollock MP had quit the house he'd invited the Reids (with especial entreaties that missus should attend) to his next Edinburgh *Soiree*. You should have seen master James, strutting like a crow in the gutter he was. For dear sake! He would never have got within a hounds *howl* of the *Soiree*, if it hadn't been for his flaming wife.

It was bucketing down all that day. In the afternoon, missus rang for me and when I made an appearance in the parlour she was all smiles and flummery about how wonderful my singing had been the night before. Marvellous, wonderful Bessy, she goes. Superb, marvellous, all this. I was a precious prize, a real find, a rare creature, so on and so forth.

Well I'll tell you this. So flipping rare and precious was I that she sent me out in the pouring rain! To hoof it all the way over to Thrashburn Farm and sing for Mr Flemyng. No doubt they wanted to boast to Duncan Pollock when next they seen him that they were 'preserving traditional songs' and the like. My eye! She was just using me to impress their flipping friends. It would have served her right if I'd just walked out and kept on walking and never gone back. I might even have done so, but for the rain.

Thrashburn was about twenty minutes north of Castle Haivers, away up the lane and over a railway bridge. Missus had already sent Hector over with a note, warning Flemyng to expect me. I walked fast but by the time I got there I was drookit, the water running down my back. This I must say, Thrashburn was a right shambles. One gatepost was near falling down and everything about the place was overgrown with blackened weeds and grass. The farm building was only a single storey cottage with a small barn beside. A few sorry looking hens scattered as I walked across the yard.

Flemyng himself opened the door to my knock and without a word he turned and showed me into the room. A fire burned in the grate and a lamp was already lit against the gloom. I glanced around, it seemed to me that every surface was hid by sheets of manuscript, crumpled parchment and stacks of books, which also stood in piles upon the floor. All the papers were covered in lines of writing and most of them had many scorings out. Flemyng looked different somehow and it took me a moment to realise that he was not wearing his spectacles. He paced about in the gaps between the book towers, scratching his head, while I took off my coat and shawl. At the time, I thought he was searching for something but on reflection I believe he was avoiding my eye out of shyness.

As for me, an unfamiliar gentleman held few fears. 'I never met a poet before,' I says. 'Tell a lie, I did meet a peddler fellow once, he had the most godawful pockmarks all over his face and he showed me a ballad he had wrote on a filthy old piece of paper. Would that be the kind of thing?'

Flemyng stopped pacing and for just a second a scowl crossed his face. I don't think he much liked my talk of peddlers and filthy paper.

He says, 'I have been known to *collect* peddler ballads, yes. But as I'm sure you are aware, my own poetry is something quite separate from that. A different order of verse, concerned with meter, rhythm, rhyme, scansion and – of course – meaning.'

'Oh, of course,' I says. I hadn't a baldy *what* he was on about.

'Not cheap and tawdry sentiment,' he says. 'Not that.'

I don't know why, but I felt vaguely insulted – but only in a very *nice* way.

He gestured at a bottle on the sideboard. 'Can I offer you a glass?' he says.

His hand was trembling and I noticed that the wine bottle was ½ empty. I wondered had he had a few knocks already to fortify himself.

'No thank you, sir,' I says, though in truth I could have murdered a drink, I had a bad head after all the claret and ale of the night before.

Flemyng lifted some papers off an armchair and placed them on the table. 'Please do sit,' he says, indicating the chair. Once I was seated, he crouched down beside me and spoke in a coaxing voice like as if he was talking to a baby.

'Now then, Bessy,' he says. 'These songs of yours. Am I to believe that you have made them up all by yourself?'

'Yes sir.'

'Excellent. That's wonderful. So they are not something that you have picked up, for example, from the likes of this peddler chappie you were speaking about?'

'No sir. I do *know* songs like that, ones I've heard about the place, "Anything for a Crust", "Jessie O' the Dell", all them ones, sure everybody does. But I don't confuse them with my own songs.'

'Well that's good,' he says. 'I am most grateful to your dear mistress for sending you to me. What a wonderful lady she is. Terribly clever, I think, and kind. And of course her beauty goes without saying.'

Yes yes you fartcatcher, I thought to myself. It was on the tip of my tongue to say something. If only you knew what nasty things she writes in her book. Something like that. But I kept 'stumm', as my Mr Levy would say.

Flemyng smiled at me, then stood up and threw more coals on the fire after which he turned to face into the room. He had his hands clasped behind his back and what with the sparks and smoke flying up behind him and the Holy look on his face he was the very glass and image of a Martyr burning at the stake. It made me want to giggle. To distract myself, I asked a question.

'What will you do with my songs, sir?'

He frowned. 'I'm not quite sure, Bessy,' he says. 'If they are of any quality then the important thing is to have them committed to the page. Then they will not disappear. I may send them to my publisher, see what he makes of them. But alas! He is most importantly waiting for more of my own poems and I must finish the one I am writing.'

'What's it about, sir? If you don't mind my asking.'

'About? Oh! All manner of things, Bessy. All manner of things. At its simplest level, it is about the ghosts that are said to haunt parts of Edinburgh. The story goes that a few hundred years ago when plague was rife the City fathers walled off certain closes and left the residents and livestock to perish of the disease. And later, they hacked up the rotting bodies and carted them away. And ever since then, folk have seen and heard strange things. Shuffling noises. Creaking ceilings. Severed limbs. Disembodied heads with terrible eyes. Ghostly children with weeping sores on their faces. And deformed horrifying phantom beasts creeping about.'

'Oh dear,' I says. I had thought he'd be writing a poem about a wee flower. Or a summers day. But here he was making my flesh creep and it was getting dark outside.

'Do you – do you think there really are such ghosts, sir?'

'What?' he says. 'No, no. It's all just superstition. But of course, I am only using it as a metaphor.' He glanced at his watch. 'In any case, *tempus fugit*, we must get on.'

He struck a listening pose, hand on hip, head tilted forward, staring at the floor. 'When you are ready, please begin. Perhaps *not* the song you sang last night.'

I cleared my throat, trying not to think about deformed ghosts and weeping sores. 'This is a song,' I says, 'about the time when we was coming over to Scotland on the –'

Without even lifting his head, Flemyng held up his hand to interrupt me. 'Please,' he says. 'No lengthy explanations. A good song speaks for itself.'

'Oh,' I says. 'Right you are. Well – d'you want to know the title, sir?'

'Very well,' he says. 'What is it called?'

'"Ailsa Craig",' I told him. 'It is called "Ailsa Craig".'

I was proud of this song, for it contained something of my own past, though in disguise. Here it is.

All you who mean to tramping go, and cross the foaming sea
A while draw near and you shall hear what happened late to me
O Mary Cleary is my name, I'm twelve years old and pretty
And when my father passed away we had to leave our country
My mother took me in her arms, said do not cry my darling
In Scotland we will try our luck, we're leaving in the morning

(Chorus)

She said Scotland she is rare and sweet
Scotland she is pretty
All Scottish towns are green and neat
And none beats Glasgow city

We sailed that morning right enough, that truth I'm not denying
But when I spotted land draw near, I thought my mother lying
For Scotland she was just a rock, a-sticking out the sea
An old worn tooth or caved-in skull, with stone of dirty grey
No pretty towns nor parks of green, just cliffs and seabirds shrieking
A lonelier place I'd never seen, the sight soon had me weeping

(Repeat Chorus)

What ails you dear my mother said, why look so broken hearted?
I told her why I shed a tear and this she then imparted
Fear not my love that island stump is not our destination
That's Ailsa Craig, the Fairy Rock, a landmark for our nation
For that old Milestone marks the spot 1/2 way between our lands
We'll soon be docked at Broomielaw and shaking Scottish hands

(Repeat Chorus)

Now here we are in Gallowgate where the closes they are spacious
The tenements in good repair, the landlords not rapacious

There is no dirt upon the streets, no factory smoke is choking
Our fortune's made, we're filthy rich. Perhaps you've guessed I'm joking.
My mother lied in what she said, for Glasgow is no haven
Now Ailsa Craig looks not so bad, to one who can't be leaving

(Repeat Final Chorus)

When the last note was sung, I made him a curtsey and waited for his response. He showed his appreciation by patting the tips of his fingers thegether, several times, it was a bit like clapping, but without making a sound.

'Not bad,' he says. 'Of course, I might change a phrase or two, here and there. But on the whole, it is a fair example of its kind.'

Uncertain whether this was a compliment or not, I decided to take it as one. 'Thank you, sir,' I says. 'Would you be wanting to write it down then?'

'Yes, why not,' he says. 'Let me just . . .'

He turned to the table behind him and lifted piles of paper until he had unearthed a pen and some ink and – finally – his eyeglasses, the last of which he fastened onto his face.

'Now then,' he says. 'Fire away, Bessy.'

In all I sang four songs for him that day. He wrote them down and put symbols by the words and when I asked him what they meant he told me that they showed the tune, at least they did to those that knew how to read symbols, to me they were gibberish and I still cannot tell a semi-quaver from a crotch.

When it came time to leave I went skyting up the road with the 7 league boots on, for it was dark by this time and Flemyng had fair give me the wild squirts with all his talk of Phantoms. It was a great relief to be back in the kitchen at Castle Haivers. And once I was safe I began to feel a bit pleased with myself, that a poet might send my songs to his publisher. I couldn't wait to see the look on missus face, knowing how much she longed to make a book of her *Observations*. But I decided to wait and see what happened before I tellt her, just in case he didn't send them after all and I was left looking like a great ninny.

As for Janets blethers the night before, I knew fine well there were no pots of gold about the place. But I did begin to wonder what she might have meant to imply about missus and Nora. As far as I could tell missus practically worshipped the girl. But I had no idea what Nora might have thought of missus. Perhaps she hated her. It occurred to me that I didn't know much at all about MY RIVAL. And then I remembered what it said in *The Observations* about missus putting Noras things away in her trunk in the attic. What would there be in that trunk, I wondered? Surely, if missus made me keep a journal, Nora would have kept one too? There was no telling what she might have wrote in there about missus. Even if she did disguise her true feelings it might be possible to read between the lines. And I was curious to know more about her, this perfect flipping maid.

I wasted no time in finding out. That very night I waited until missus and master James had went to bed and then sneaked out my room and down to the landing on tippy-toe. Behind a small door at the end of the passage was a set of wooden stairs that led up to the main attic. I'd never went up there before, never had reason to and besides I once had a quick skelly through the crack of the door and Jesus Murphy it would give you the creeps it was that dark and drafty.

Now I opened the little door and crept up the stairs. Five steps and then a balustrade and above that a great dark space opening up like a cavern. As I emerged into the attic the icy air hit my face, it was a damp musty chill that bit into your lungs. I cannot say that I was not anxious. But I kept telling myself not to be hen-hearted and get on with it.

Life at Castle Haivers did not create much that was surplus to requirements and a quick hoist of my candle showed that there was not a lot stored up there. Some old dining chairs piled in a corner, a few empty portmanteaus, a broken fire screen, a music case with a cracked glass door, that was about the size of it. And then I seen what

I was looking for. It was set apart from the rest of the things against the wall and near the stairs. A servant trunk, canvas-covered. Although none of the luggage was expensive you could tell that this box was cheap and shoddy in comparison to the rest.

I lifted the lid and peered inside. It was hard to see clearly in the shadows and candlelight. The first items that rose to my view were a pair of lace-up boots, well-polished and hardly worn, no doubt Noras Sunday best. I lifted one boot and held the sole against my own. Not much difference there, though I admit that perhaps her foot was a *little* smaller. Next the boots was a Bible and a whole pile of religious tracts. For dear sake could you not have guessed that she would be Holy? Next, an old-fashioned workbox, the lid painted with a picture of a girl in white playing with a hoop. Next a cloth doll in cap and apron. What a big fat baby she must have been, to have a doll! Beside that was a metal hair clasp painted with 3 flowers, like blue daisies, and a bottle of scent, which proved on opening to be Honeysuckle. Digging deeper, I found a folding knife with a horn handle, and right at the bottom a small bundle of linen, mostly undergarments and stockings, worn and darned but clean. The knife was a good one and might come in useful so I slipped it in my pocket. Under the linen I found a comb with a clump of dark hairs still clinging to the teeth. Dead girls hairs. That fair made my skin crawl.

What with all those tracts and the dolly, I could just imagine her, so I could. Little Miss Perfect. One of those articles that's happy as Larry all the time, no matter what. If you tellt her, 'Away and chop down an acre of trees and carry the logs to Coatbridge on your back,' she'd jump for joy. If you said, 'Nora, we believe you have the typhoid,' she'd just tell you it was her hearts desire to go to heaven and meet her Lord. If you said, 'Nora, the leg has to come off and what's worse you have the leprosy,' no doubt she'd have some flipping cheerful answer for you.

But no sign of any journal whatsoever. So I was none the wiser as to what she thought of missus.

Could I sleep that night. Could I chook. I lay there plotting how I'd take revenge on missus for ill-using me. Her boots might mysteriously develop holes in the sole. The hem of her frock could come down unexpectedly. Some of her linen could find its way back into the drawer unwashed. The sugar bowl might accidentally get filled with salt. A mouse might crawl under her bed to die. Little things that I couldn't be blamed for. But everything I thought of seemed too trifling and silly.

And then, the following morning, missus herself provided me with the means of revenge when she came to find me in the kitchen. She looked ill-slept.

'Bessy dear,' she says. 'There are cobwebs on the hall ceiling. I want them brushed away, please. You will need to use the ladders.'

'Yes marm,' I says. 'I'll do it directly after breakfast.'

I expected her to leave then, but she just walked about the kitchen with her arms folded. Perhaps she had some other command to give me. I waited but none was forthcoming. She picked up a nutmeg grater, examined it, set it down again. And then she says, almost as an afterthought, 'By the way, last night there were some – sounds – in the attic. Noises. Were you – did you happen to go up there? For any reason?'

'The attic?' I shook my head. 'No marm. Why would I go up there?'

'I have no idea,' she says. 'But I definitely heard noises.' She fixed me with a hard look. 'Are you *sure* it wasn't you?'

'Hand on heart, marm,' I says. And if you say that, it means you can't tell a lie or you will go straight to Hades in a handcart except of course if you have the fingers of your other hand crossed behind your back, any fool knows that old trick.

The missus frowned. 'Well,' she says. 'I'll take your word for it. But did you not *hear* anything in the night?'

'No marm. I must have been asleep. What d'you think it was, marm? Was it a gnawing sound?' I opened my eyes wide. 'Could it have been a rat?'

She shuddered. 'No,' she says. 'I don't think so. The ceiling in my room was creaking, as though someone was – pacing around, in heavy shoes. And I am convinced that I heard a deep cough.'

'That must be some rat,' I says. (Clearly, I'd not been as quiet up there as I'd thought!) 'Do you want me to have a look for you, marm, put your mind at rest?'

I stepped towards the door but her hand shot out to detain me. 'No!' she says. 'That won't be necessary. I shall simply get Hector to set a trap.'

'As you like, marm.'

I went back to stirring the porridge, thinking about the creaking ceiling. Something Flemyng had mentioned the day before came into my head, about the poem he was writing, the ghostly children with weeping sores and phantom beasties &c.

'You don't think, marm – no, never mind.'

'What?'

I knew at once from the look on her phiz that the thought had already occurred to her. 'Well – you don't believe in evil spirits, do you marm?'

'Of course not!' she says, but immediately began chewing her lip and frowning, the very glass and image of anxiety.

She was scared of ghosts, I realised. And in that moment the idea formed in my mind, a way to get my own back. It was only a childish prank. How could I ever have foretold the terrible consequences of what I was about to do?

11

Both Strange and Startling

Extracted from Bessys journal

Monday 30th November
It seems the past few nights missus has heard noises in the attic I do hope she doesn't worry about it too much. Any person of sense will tell you there is no such thing as ghosts although I have heard a tale or two would make your nosehair stand on end. Of course there are those that might say missus is quite correct to be anxious after all there is a particular atmosphere about Castle Haivers you might call it spooky. But that is easy explained, it is only because we are so remote here and the sky seems low and the wind whistles through the trees at night. Well in that case what about the inexplicable happenings? For Pete sake what are you talking about? Well if you give me a minute I will tell you, I'm talking about those times that you set something down and two seconds later when you go back to look for it has the thing not moved apparently of its own accord. That happens ALL THE TIME at Castle Haivers so it does. But again there is usually a simple explanation often you will find that some person has moved the thing whilst you were not looking. Or conversely it will transpire that you have disremembered where you set the thing down in the first place. It would be entirely wrong to jump to the conclusion that there is an evil or malevolent spirit about the place come to torment us. That is what I say.

Tuesday 1st December
I am beginning to wonder whether missus might not be right about those there noises in the attic for last night I do believe I did hear something myself. Just as I was about to fall asleep after writing in

my journal I think I heard a few creaks and some shuffling steps. I suppose it did sound a little like someone walking about up there but more likely as I told missus, there is a rational explanation. A few slates have came off the roof and the wind has got in. Or it is just vermin. Not phantom beasts or dismembered limbs. Anyway Hector went up there this morning with traps &c. so we shall see what gets caught. I would put money on a rat or a pigeon. It might even be the cat. When Hector came back down I had to laugh he says to me in all seriousness 'I do love nature' and this with a bag of rat poison under his arm and the tails of 3 squirrels stuffed in the band of his hat.

Wednesday 2nd December
Nothing strange or startling.

Thursday 3rd December
Hector checked the traps in the attic this afternoon. All are empty as yet. But it can only be a matter of time. Apart from that nothing strange or startling, I do believe that we have been getting worked up into a froth over nothing.

Sunday 6th December
After a few quiet days last night about midnight I was laying abed when I heard noises coming from the attic. Right, says I to myself, once and for all I am going to find out what all this is about. And so I got myself dressed and snuck up there with a candle. I was not happy about going up there of course but also determined to find out what is upsetting missus. I had a quick skelly about the place but could find nothing and was on the verge of heading back down when I seen somebody coming towards me up the stairs! Crumbs and Christopher it scared the behicky out me. Thank goodness, it was only the missus herself (she too had heard noises and this time bravely ventured forth to investigate) but she startled me so much I screamed and dropped my candle. I don't know which of us got the bigger fright me or missus for her hand was shaking so bad that her

own candle was in danger of going out. She asked me what I was doing and I tellt her that I had heard noises and come up to investigate same as herself. I tellt her that I had already searched the place and found nothing. Just to be sure we relit my candle with hers and had another look around but there were nothing out the ordinary we then compared what we had heard. Missus thought she had perceived someone walking back and forth. I told her that I had the same impression but I also thought there were sounds of someone crying or whimpering as well. At this news missus grabbed me by the shoulder all this. Who was crying? she says. And when I tellt her I didn't know she says, Was it female? After some thought I tellt her it did sound more like a woman than a man. Then she wanted to know was it a young woman and I said yes it sounded more like a young one than old. Well when she heard this her face took on such a look of anguish, I was quite scared for her. Her eyes was practically out on stalks. Then she says to me in a whisper, Was it an Irish girl? and I had to say I didn't know since I didn't hear her speak but that for all I knew it might well have been. Well missus clutched her head and looked so strange after that I insisted we go downstairs and I put her back to bed. I do be thinking she was very brave to go up to the attic if I were a lady like her I am sure I wouldn't dare have done so for fear of what horrible thing I might have found. Of course master James slept right through everything, you could fire a brace of cannon over him and he wouldn't wake, it is only me and missus that are subject to these night terrors. I tellt missus that if she heard noises again she should just pull the covers over her head and try to sleep and not go wandering about in her nightgown, she will only catch her death.

Tuesday 8th December

Sunday night both me and missus was alert in our beds for noises in the attic but neither one of us heard a sound. I thought that might be the end of it. However. Last night something happened that gave me the quivers again I am sure there is a rational explanation only I have not yet been able to think of it. What happened was this, I was the last to bed and had gone through the rooms checking that the fire screens were in place and the candles and lamps all out. It so happened that one candle was still burning on the side table in the parlour and so I snuffed it and left the room. A while later as I went back through the hall on my way to bed I seen a flicker of light under the parlour door. That is strange, I thunk to myself. And when I went in was greatly surprised and not a little worried to see the same candle on the side table. Burning brightly as before!

The only thing I can think of is that I had not snuffed the wick well enough first time and that the flame had rekindled without my noticing the more I think about it now, the more I am convinced that this is surely what happened.

Wednesday 9th December
Now something else strange has happened. Earlier today when the missus came back from church she called me to her room and when I went in she was stood by the bed. I seen straight away that she was desperate pale in the face and worried looking. Have you been in this room while I was out? she says and I tellt her no marm I had been down in the kitchen ever since she had left, washing the walls as she had commanded me. Then missus stepped to one side and showed me a pair of pale yellow gloves laid out on the bed. Did you put these out for me? she says. Tell the truth Bessy and shame the devil I promise I will not be angry with you, she says. Well I wish I could have said otherwise but I had to tell her that hand on heart I had not touched the gloves. We both stood there staring at them, the missus transfixed and trembling like she might run from the room or scream at any moment. After a few seconds, I pulled myself together. I stepped forward very matter of fact picked up the gloves and put them back in her glove drawer. There, I says. You probably put them out yourself marm and changed your mind at the last minute (for she had wore her grey gloves to church). And indeed this is probably what happened. But missus just shook her head at me and then she

turned and went downstairs. When I followed her down I seen her out in the yard sweeping (in her good frock!) and it was an hour before I could persuade her to come back in, she was foundered and shivering and I had to warm her up at the kitchen fire. She made me promise that from that moment on I would report to her anything out the ordinary no matter how small or inconsequential it might seem and I agreed. Even though I dare say she is letting her imagination run away with her like what master James says.

Sunday 13th December
Well the strangest thing this morning. I was not witness to it myself so can only report 2nd hand. It seems that missus had another restless night she has been troubled by further noises either that or she can't get to sleep for wondering whether or not she is going to hear things. Anyway. Apparently she gave up trying to sleep after some hours and went downstairs to start the day around ½ past 4 o'clock. Everyone myself included was of course still abed. Imagine the surprise of the missus upon entering the parlour to find that the fire had already been cleared, laid and not only that but lit! A little blaze burning merrily in the grate. (Almost like as if the room had been made ready for her! – that is what I says after missus tellt me about it when I got up a few hours later.) The minute I appeared downstairs Missus pulled me into the parlour and pointed at the hearth. And what is your rational explanation for that? she says to me. I have to admit I didn't have one. My only thought was that perhaps master James had stoked up the fire and whaled on more coals before he went to bed and that somehow these coals had lasted all night. But when master James got up he claimed he had done no such thing. And when missus and me exchanged a startled look he put up his hands and waggled them and made a scary wailing noise. Then strolled away laughing to himself about women. Master James does not believe this balderdash about ghosts and is too busy to give it consideration he is up to his oxters with plans and preparations for his fountain in Snatter. Only a few days ago I might have been as

sceptical myself but even I am beginning to wonder. Poor missus is quite beyond herself I think the fire this morning gave her a fright. She will not thank me for this but despite all evidence to the contrary I still hope that we might find a rational explanation.

Thursday 17th December
The last few nights have been quiet neither missus nor I have heard any noises. However, a few more strange things have happened in the daytime. The first might simply be due to my forgetfulness. I swear that when I came down on Tuesday morning I have no memory of filling the kettle and putting it on the fire, but when I turned around next minute there it was full of water. Steaming away, for all the world like someone knew my job and was doing it for me! I did not want to worry missus by telling her this but after some consideration I decided it was better to do so as she had asked me to report anything unusual. I did stress to missus that I may well have filled the kettle ½ asleep and put it on the fire without even remarking upon it, as we often do habitual things in a mechanical way. But she did not seem too convinced by my explanation. One thing should be borne in mind. As I said to missus. If it is a ghost that is doing these things it is a very helpful and considerate ghost, you might almost say an eminently practical ghost (so far at any rate). You would almost think it wanted to give service.

One further strange occurrence. Missus called me to her room this afternoon, she was sat in her chair and when I came in she pointed at a pair of shoes on the floor. Missus has several pairs of shoes and I recognised these as one of her everyday pair she wears around the place. She continued pointing at them while looking at me and saying not a word. There appeared to be nothing out the ordinary about the shoes and so I wondered why she was drawing my attention to them. Eventually she spoke. Did you clean these Bessy, in the last day or two? she says. Think carefully, she says. I looked at the shoes. They were very clean right enough, the shine would have reflected your threepenny bit. Much as I would have liked to lay claim to such expertise in shoe polishing, I could not. No marm, I says. Take your time, says missus. You might have cleaned them and forgotten about it. No marm, says I again. Sure I would have remembered giving them such a polish as that. Missus seemed strangely satisfied at that and yet somehow panicstruck. And then she tellt me I could go. I am a little worried about her. There was a faint smile on her lips when I left the room but her eyes was blazing like she had a fever. I do hope she is getting enough rest.

Tuesday 22nd December

A few nights ago master James near ate the head off missus because she was yattering on about her shoes being mysteriously polished, like as if the ghost had done it. He shouted at her that she was being foolish and that he didn't want to hear another word on the subject OR ELSE! And so she has not talked about it in front of him ever since.

Having said that, these past few days have been very quiet and once more I was beginning to believe that we were returning to normal at Castle Haivers when something happened today to make me think otherwise. The morning started ordinary enough with me going about my chores as usual and missus sorting through the linen upstairs. About ½ past 10 down she came to the parlour to get on with her sewing and I took her in some tea at about 11, it was as I was setting down the tea tray that I noticed something under the bureau. Look, marm, I says. Something has fell here. I reached down beneath the bureau and pulled out the object it turned out to be a metal hair clasp painted with blue flowers like daisies. How did that get here? I says and turned to look at missus. Well I have never seen the colour drain from a face so quickly. Whatever is the matter, marm? I says. Is it your clasp? And I held it towards her. She shrank back moaning and covering her eyes. Take it away take it away, get it out my sight! she goes. But what shall I do with it? I cried. I don't care, wails missus. Just get rid of it. So I ran out the room with the clasp and made sure to put it in a place that missus will not see. It is a mystery to me why a hair clasp should cause any-one to be so upset but it is none of my business. In any case I trust that missus has good reason as she is not one to get upset over noth-ing. We were not to have a special bird for Christmas as master James does not want too much fuss on the day. But lucky enough a fox ripped the wing right off a goose over on the farm and it has been killt and will go on the festive table, I do hope there is some left for me.

Friday 25th December
Christmas Day is here and we have had a quiet time of it as missus has not been feeling quite her usual self. She hardly ate one pick of her goose at dinner. It is not a good meat to serve cold because of the fat but we will have to make do with it for the next while or give it to the cat. Missus smelt lovely of honeysuckle perfume, it must be a Christmas gift from the master. Tomorrow is Saint Stephens, I am hopeful.

Saturday 26th December
Missus gave me a book for my gift it is about a servant girl what is kidnapped by her master because he has took a fancy to her, I do be thinking the girl is feeble, she keeps writing letters to everybody about her predicament which is as much use as a sick headache what she should do is beat the lard out him. Master James told me that they do not really believe in giving gifts just for the sake of it but that after some consideration he had decided to give me a handker-chief (plain). I cannot express how grateful I am at his generosity. Such a useful present! For everyone always needs a snoot cloot. From now on every time I blow my nose I will think of him.

I was also surprised to receive a gift from Hector a bag of Parma violets, he said he remembered I was eating them the first day he met me walking along the Great Road and so he knew I liked them. It was a kind thought and I felt bad I had not got him anything. He has been better behaved of late, he is only young what can you expect.

Later in the day, missus called me into the parlour and asked me if I had took to wearing scent. No marm, I tellt her. For it is a fact I do not have any perfumes, only my natural odour! Missus came up and sniffed my neck and wrist, but she did not smell anything she seemed most perturbed. Then she started walking about the room, sniffing the air. Can you not smell it? she goes to me. I did as I was bid and sniffed but could smell nought. No marm, I says. What is it you can smell? Honeysuckle, she says. I looked at her. Marm, I says. Did master James not give you a honeysuckle perfume for Christmas. No, she says. He gave me no perfume. Well that is strange, I says. For I thought I smelt you wearing honeysuckle perfume yesterday and I noted it. Because normally you wear your Roses. Yes, she goes, my Attar of Roses. I do not wear honeysuckle. And then she looked very strange and says, But I know someone who did.

Who was that, marm? I asked her, but she just shook her head.

Let me know if you ever smell honeysuckle about the place, she says. And fetch me immediately. Then she left the room sniffing the air like a hound dog, I note it down here so that I am sure to remember to tell her if I ever smell the honeysuckle again.

Thursday 31st December

After more unexplained noises last night I ventured to make a suggestion to missus this morning. My suggestion was this. That we should in the daylight hours go up to the attic and make an inspection of it from top to bottom. To put our minds at rest that there is nothing up there. At night you imagine all sorts of horrors because of the dark. But who knows in daylight we might even find the nest of whatever vermin is causing these disturbances or perhaps the hole where they are getting in. Master James would only pour scorn on our activities he says he will not countenance any more claptrap about ghosts and so we waited until he had left for the day before arming ourselves with two lamps to illuminate dark corners and then we climbed the stairs. Missus began at one end of the attic and

I took the other and we scoured the place from top to bottom. Neither one of us discovered anything out the ordinary. Though I did find an old canvas trunk that seemed to merit further investigation but when I drew missus attention to it she told me just to leave it be. After about ten minutes or so we met in the middle of the attic beneath the skylight and confirmed to each other that we had found nothing.

It was then that I happened to glance upwards towards the light and noticed that some person had traced something in the dirt on the window pane. Look here, I says to missus. Someone has wrote on the window. We both strained upwards on tiptoe to see more clearly. What does it say? says missus. I can't see, she says. I peered hard and read it out to her. It says, something something My Lady. Wait a moment, yes I see now, it says Help Me My Lady.

And that was when missus fell to the floor in a dead faint she just crumpled at the knees and dropped like a flower scythed at the stem. I tried to revive her and shouted for help but nobody came and so it was on my own that I had to carry her downstairs and put her to bed. Which is where she has been ever since.

PART THREE

12

I Get Another Shock

And that was when missus fell to the floor in a dead faint.

Well that is what I wrote in my journal. Because I thought she would probably read it later as she always did and there were certain things I did not want her to know.

But wait till I tell you, what really happened that morning was a flip sight worse, even now remembering it all these years later, the skin on me crawls. I can shut my eyes and in a moment put myself right back there in the attic with her along side of me.

There she is. Flushed from the exertions of our search, her head tilted back as she peers upwards. A strand of hair is come adrift, it hangs at the side of her face next her dimple. My hair is also falling down – for what am I after doing but walking slap bang into a flipping cobweb. I just about leapt out my skin and then had to spend ten minutes shaking out my hair in case the spider was on me. I am still a little breathless from this encounter. Both me and missus have put down our lamps. Rain pitter-patters against the glass as we strain on tiptoe to see the window more clearly. The light is not good and missus leans against me to get a better view.

'What does it say?' she goes. 'I can't see.'

I let on I can't make it out. 'It says something something, My Lady,' I tell her. 'Wait a moment. Yes, I see now. It says Help Me My Lady.'

At this point, missus gasps so she does and clutches my arm, just above the elbow. 'Thus do lambs nuzzle the slaughtermans hands.' (Nobody said that, it was more of a thought in my head). Clutch away, madam, is what I am also thinking, for I suppose she has simply took fright and caught a hold of me for support. As for me, I am still acting my arse off pretending to peer at the 'ghostly' writing. Then the noises start to bubble up in her throat. The first no more than a cough, a clearing of the passages. But then she begins to gag. Much as if she has swallowed a spider or fly and is trying to hawk it back up. I turn to look at her and the sight that greets me draws chills down my back. She is staring at the skylight, but her phiz shows not the mild alarm that I have been expecting, instead it is as though something has took ahold of her, as though she is in some kind of horrific Trance.

'Missus?' I says.

Her mouth flaps but not a word emerges. Then as I watch, her head hangs to one side. Her tongue juts out and moves in spasms, the gagging sound in her throat now has the threat of boke behind it Jesus Murphy she is in convulsions. Her fingers grip my arm but she no longer seems aware of my presence. Her shoulders jerk back and forth as the low gargle begins to rise in pitch and volume higher and higher until she is screaming, screaming at the top of her lungs, it makes my ears buzz. Her mouth froths, her eyeballs roll back in their sockets and at the highest note of the scream her eyes snap wide open. She stares straight at me her mouth agape, her wild gaze locked onto my horrified one. And still she screams. The sound travels right through me, my whole body prickles, it is as though she is Electrified. Yet can I prise her fingers off my arm, can I buckie. If only I could break away from her grasp then she might stop. Yet how? I consider giving her a skelp but this does not seem forceful enough and so instead (may God forgive me) I punch her as hard as I can, a good old biff square in the jaw.

Her head snaps back, her fingers lose their grip, she staggers away from me. Then she crumples at the knees and drops, drops like a flower scythed at the stem. She tumbles sideways, there is a thud as her head hits the floor. Dust rises, floating to the rafters, and all around her spread the soft petals of her skirts. For a minute I stand there petrified, my fist still raised. Missus has landed on her side, one arm outstretched the fingers curled. Blood trickles from her lips.

Apart from that her face is drained of colour. Her eyes are shut her mouth sags, tugged down at the corner like somebody dead. She looks completely lifeless.

I do be thinking that I might be in a spot of bother.

Not least, I might lose my job. Either for punching her or if it is discovered that the haunting has been my doing.

At worst she is killt and I am a murderer, bound straight for Everlasting Flames.

I do believe I panicked. It is my impression that I lifted her up and got her downstairs, that I laid her on the bed and ran outside for help, that I found Hector nearby (he was malletting stakes to repair a fence) and that I sent him haring off to Snatter for the doctor. All these I realised later but not at the time from anything I felt or knew. In my distress, I was aware of nothing at all until I was back in the chamber and seen her laying there and the sight of her insensible form and whey face cut me to the heart.

Cobwebs clung to her skirts. I started to brush them away and then thought catch yourself on for who cared about cobwebs when she might not even be alive. Would I be able to wake her and what if I couldn't and what the flip would I say to master James and Oh Jesus Murphy would I really go to Hell? And if I am honest, there was another thought in the back of my mind, one that I pushed aside – what would I do without her?

Drops of blood from her mouth had trickled down her neck onto the bolster-cover, they made a crimson stain the size of a plum. And still she had not come out her Trance. Hoping to feel the warmth of her breath on my cheek I bent down so that my face was next hers, but felt nothing. I leaned in closer until her lips were almost touching mine. No breath came from them.

So it was true – I had killed her!

In my minds eye I seen my own form swinging from the gallows, my mother in the crowd leading the cheers.

And in that same moment, in a flash, missus opened her eyes and grabbed my arm. I near lit out my skin and shrieked and made to pull away but she held me fast and close.

'It's you,' she says, very quiet and slow. 'I knew it was you.'

Oh Jesus Murphy, I thought. She has found me out.

'Right from the start,' she says. 'I knew.'

Tears began to spill out her eyes and wet her cheeks. Ate up as I was with anguish and guilt, I supposed that I had disappointed her, and that she was sorry to have to dismiss me, yet I could not help but notice that she was staring at me strangely. It was as though she was waiting for me to say something, perhaps to make an excuse or attempt a lie. But I couldn't. Couldn't do it.

'Please forgive me, marm,' I says.

'Forgive?' She blinked, as though astounded. 'What is there to forgive?'

I took this as her being satirical, like as not she was even angrier with me than I had thought. But then she says something else.

'Dear girl, it is *you* who must forgive *me*.'

I just looked at her. More tears welled up in her eyes.

'It was *my* fault,' she says.

What in Gods name was she on about?

'I should never have –' Here, she sobbed and moaned. 'Oh Nora dear, it was all my fault. And now you are dead and gone. I'm sorry, Nora. I'm so sorry, dear.' Whereupon, she broke down and wept in my arms.

I stood there, hunched over, embracing her. It was a most uncomfortable position but I dared not, could not move. I stroked her back and shoulders. Beneath the taffeta, she was burning with fever.

What in the name of God had I done? She was out of her mind!

'Shhh,' I tellt her. 'It's all right, Arabella. Everything is going to be all right.'

After a short while she fell insensible again and when I set her down she did not lie still, but thrashed around like a fish on the shore. Somehow I undressed her and got a clean nightgown on her and lifted her into the bed. She weighed no more than a bolster. (Even though I was after carrying her down from the attic I'd been in such a panic that I'd failed to notice how thin and frail she had become.) I wiped the blood and tears from her face and then sank down into a squat wicker chair to watch over her until the doctor came, my legs weak and my mind racing.

Of course to begin with I had simply wanted to scare the mullacky out her. And why not, I ask you? Why not indeed, you reply. Well I'll tell you why not. She had misled me and betrayed me and took advantage of me and poked around into my past, moreover she had said some rotten things about me in her scutting book, about my appearance and how I followed her round like a Tantony pig, all this. It seemed to me that a small fright or two here and there was not overmuch to ask in the way of retribution. It was only a cod so it was. And boys oh dear, was it not a lark to see her looking so thrilled and nervy! Every door that banged she leapt about 6 foot in the air. And if ever I happened to emerge suddenly from a place she wasn't expecting, she would shriek and clutch at her chest.

'Oh Bessy!' she'd say. 'What a fright you gave me! Feel this.'

Then she'd take my hand and press it to the place where her heart throbbed beneath her bodice. Well that happened a few times, I daresay I was not averse to it. And it was a laugh that she had got stuck on the notion that the ghost was Nora. I made the most of that with the gloves and hair clasp and honeysuckle and what have you.

But nothing prepared me for her reaction to the writing in the window. I had put 'My Lady' because according to *The Observations* that is what Nora called missus. But now – what if my Arabella remained deluded? What if (God forbid) she were to die?

How long I sat there watching over her and cursing myself for being a terrible person I know not, it seemed as if my care for life was all gone. I tried to soften it for myself by saying I was brought up wicked and didn't know any better, so it wasn't really my fault I couldn't help what I done. But a voice inside me kept raising objections. Saying things like, 'You could have gone to Mass when you was at Mr Levys, for he would have let you go if you wanted. But Oh no, what did you do instead of a Sunday? Lay stinking in bed and then go and eat hokey-pokeys in the Park.' And it said, 'You could have forgive missus and turned the other cheek, she is a lady after all.' And it said, 'Brought up wicked or not, you know what is right from what is wrong.'

To punish myself I resolved to bite off my own thumb at the root. I did *begin* to do so and might even have achieved my aim but that the task proved much too painful and so instead I bit at the flesh of my arm very hard indeed, so you could still see the teeth-marks two days later. And although I never was much of a one for prayers it is an indication of how desperate I was that I got down on my knees and put my hands together for missus. I begged over and over again that she would please get well. After which I prayed that I could be made into a better sort of girl than I was and not be sent to Hell. And then I ran out of things to say about that and got to praying that the doctor would just hurry up and come. He took forever – but eventually I heard a pony trap rattle up the lane.

I hurried over to the bed and peered down at missus. She was fire-faced now, covered in sweat and her breathing came in fits and starts. Even in this state she seemed to know that I had done her harm for when I touched her hand she moaned and pulled away. With a final glance at her lovely face, I left the room and flew up to the attic.

There was the dirty skylight – and traced upon it the message of which I had previously been so proud.

HELP ME
MY LADY

I had so many reasons to get rid of that writing, not least my own shame. God knows I didn't want the chance of missus seeing it again. For look what it had done to her the first time. And I daresay

I did not want master James to find it. I had a feeling that if he *did* happen to turn his steely gaze upon it not much time would pass before the same gaze were turned upon *me*.

I cast around for a rag to wipe away my crime but found none. Instead, I stood on tiptoe and rubbed the filthy glass with my sleeve until every trace of the writing had disappeared. If it were necessary, I would have licked the scut clean.

As I left the attic, I heard the sound of hurried footsteps in the hall down below. And when I reached the landing I was shocked to see master James coming upstairs with McGregor-Robertson hot on his heels. This (the master) I was not prepared for. I stood with my mouth open as the pair of them dashed towards me, two men. A dark blur of limbs shoulders elbows clarty boots and the doctors bag and coat tails.

Master James gave me a scowl as they barged past. 'I'll be wanting a word with you later,' he says. 'Get downstairs now and wait.'

'Sir!' I says. 'The missus –'

But before I could continue they had disappeared into her room and slammed the door in my face leaving behind them only a stale whiff of cigar smoke.

Back in the kitchen I just sat there feeling helpless staring into the fire. I couldn't seem to shift myself to work. What did I care about a few crumbs and a speck of dust? Not a fartleberry. I got to wondering whether I should run away. But that was the cowards way out. I couldn't do it, especially since missus might think wrong of me. Then after a while I had an idea. I *would* take French leave but not without a word. What I'd do was compose a private note for missus, a full confession and apology. That way she'd know I'd done wrong, but I'd have owned up and said I was sorry. And as time went by she might find it in her heart to forgive me.

Feeling somewhat better already I got a piece of paper and a pencil and wrote.

Dear Madam, You know you thought there was a ghost in the house well it were me all along that done the haunting, I put your gloves on the bed and wrote the message in the window and all the other things like walking in the attic I done them as well. I don't know why I done it, except I thought you did not like me any more. But that is no excuse and I hope you can believe me when I say I am TRULY SORRY. I am sure you will understand that I can stay no longer at Castle Haivers. I hope that my departure does not inconvenience you too much. You will find someone else and they had better know what a lucky girl they are. I hope that the hurt I done you will heal and that you are feeling better. A thousand apologies please FORGIVE ME I am not really DUPLICITOUS

Your very devoted servant
Bessy

PS I punched you in the face as well when you took your fit in the attic but it was only because I wanted you to come out of it. I would never have hit you otherwise. I just wanted you to know that in case you remembered and thought wrong of me.

PPS Also I went in your drawers a while back and read what you wrote about me in your book. It was a shock to see some of those things you said and I was hurt but as I sit here and stew over this letter I do be thinking what a truly wonderful lady you must be for you have known all this time about what I was before and you have never mentioned it once to me nor tret me any different (because of that anyway) nor dismissed me and there is not many would have done the same. So I am grateful.

PPPS May the next one be a better girl than I was, I hope your book goes well, it is awful well done.

My spirits rose upon finishing this letter, at least I had done the right thing and confessed. Perhaps I was good after all. In fact it is a wonder I did not float out the window I was feeling that saintly. I was tempted to walk out the kitchen door there and then but just as I was about to depart I heard footsteps running downstairs and the master calling out.

'Bessy! Bessy!'

Like that, my heart flew up into my head and beat its wings between my ears. In my minds eye I seen missus laid out in white, surrounded by golden angels. Then I seen a vision of her with hair all wild and matted, chained up in an asylum, screaming 'Nora! Nora!' Next she appeared, smartly dressed, all this, but looking stern as she stood in the doorway of the house, pointing me (sorry-faced) in the direction of the Great Road. Then a final vision, this time a return to the gallows, where my mother hove into view, throwing back her head and cackling as my body swung to and fro.

All these visions took no more than a few seconds. I glanced towards the kitchen door, I could have stepped out and vanished into the trees before anyone noticed. Instead what I done was steady myself for a second by leaning against the table. Then I put the letter in my apron pocket and went along the passage into the hall to face the master. All very noble yes, yes. But I near had a dose of the scutters if you want the truth of it, or maybe you don't.

The two gentlemen were stood outside the study talking in low voices. When I approached master James motioned me to wait where I stood, at some little distance from them. He and the doctor exchanged another few hushed words then shook hands. The master stepped into his study and – without giving me another glance – closed the door. What to make of that I knew not, but it didn't look good.

In the same moment, the doctor turned towards me. It was impossible to tell anything from his phiz he was not an animated man at the best of times, I've seen more expression on a ham bone. Today was no exception. What made it worse, he never looked you in the eye. He was forever glancing off to the side and if he did ever face you he was one of those condescending articles that talks to you with their eyes shut as though they do not care to include you in their field of vision.

'Sir, can I do anything? Is she all right, sir? Should I go up and see her?'

Without replying, McGregor-Robertson set down his bag by the hallstand. Then he removed his gloves from his pocket and began to pull them on, finger by finger. I stood in silence, awaiting my fate. Was I to fetch the undertaker? Or was missus gone moony?

Once the gloves were pulled on to his satisfaction, the doctor addressed the banister sternly. 'Aye, your mistress has suffered a wee collapse. Do you know how it happened?'

My confession was for missus not for the likes of him and so I felt only a twinge of guilt in replying, 'No I don't, sir. But is she going to be all right?'

'That depends,' he says. 'I fear her symptoms are much more complicated than a simple fainting fit. Her condition is grave. She may be very unwell.'

His words rained down on me like blows. Very unwell. More complicated. Grave. That depends. Oh if only I could exchange places with her! I'd have done it in a second, so I would. I would have peeled the skin off my own face with a blunt paring knife, if it would have helped her. But the doctor was still speaking. 'Aye, for the time being,' he says. 'She is not in a lucid state. She has spoke only a few words.'

'What did she say?'

He shook his head. 'It does not bear repeating, for none of it makes one whit of sense.'

'What – what about the blood at her mouth, sir? Is she hurt bad?'

'Her mouth? Oh aye – she must have bit her lip when she fell. No, that's a minor cut, nothing to worry about. What is of concern to me is her fever and the state of her nerves. This next day or two are crucial. She'll need care, somebody to watch over her through the night, somebody who will keep her temperature down and send for me if her condition gets any worse. Are you capable of it, lassie? Or do you want me to send a woman up from the village or the farm?'

These words he had addressed to the hallstand. In the whole conversation he had not looked at me once. Was it shyness or condescension, it was hard to tell but it gave the impression that his opinion of you was none too high.

'I'll do whatever's needed, sir,' I says. 'There's no need to send for anybody. I am quite capable of looking after my missus.'

He glanced at me for the first time. 'Are you crying, girl?'

'No, sir,' I says. 'Not at all. Now will you please tell me what it is that I have to do to make missus better?'

All this while, not a peep from master James. The door to the study remained resolutely shut. Once I'd shown the doctor out I legged it to the kitchen and began to gather the things I would need. I found Hector in the yard and charged him with feeding the animals and a few other tasks and then I went upstairs. For the time being, I put the thought of taking flight out of my mind – that could wait until missus was better. I resolved to restore her to health and then creep away only afterwards, leaving behind my note as explanation. All I could hope was that she would recover. I would burst my hole to make it happen.

I found her asleep but restless. Jesus Murphy she was hotter than a roasted apple and so I draped a few cool cloths on her brow and throat as the doctor had instructed and then I laid the fire. Once that was lit I dragged the wicker chair to the bedside and began rotation of the cloths in and out cold water and onto the missus skin.

About an hour passed in this fashion. It had grown quite dark since I first sat down and I had not yet lit a candle, the only light came from the fire. From time to time missus moaned and her eyelids fluttered. I must have been powerful absorbed in my task because I was startled when the chamber door swung open and I turned to see a figure standing just inside the room. Master James. He closed the door but did not approach the bed.

'Tell me how the patient fares,' he says. His eyes were gleaming in the firelight, the rest of his face in shadow.

I busied myself wringing out a set of cloths, glad to have something to do. 'Much the same, sir. She still has the fever.' I was trying to make my voice sound normal but it shook, thank God the room was gloomy and my face ½ hid.

'The doctor tells me this was a collapse due to nerves or somesuch.'

'Yes, sir.'

Master James came to the foot of the bed. He glanced at the prostrate form beneath the covers and then looked at me. What he saw seemed to displease him. 'Your bun is loose,' he says.

He was right, so it was. I had not thought of it since I had shook out my hair in the attic. I reached up and began to tidy some loose strands.

'Never mind that now,' he says. 'For the moment, I would be interested to hear from you in your own words what happened today.' He put his head to one side and with one hand in his pocket, he lay in wait for me.

'Well, sir,' says I, careful. 'There's not much to tell. She collapsed, sir, but I'm sure she'll soon be back to her old self. The doctor tellt me how to look after her and I'll do it sir every bit of it, you needn't lift a finger. I'm going to make her better just you see if I don't. And I'll get you some dinner in a minute as well. Now would you like lamb chops sir or there's herring? A fishwife came by this morning.'

The corners of his lips curled upwards but it was a mirthless smile not so much a grin as a grimace, at any moment he was bound to pounce. 'Be so good as to tell me,' he says. 'What brought on this collapse.'

'I am not a doctor, sir.'

'Come come, Bessy,' he says. 'You must have some thoughts on the subject. I suspect you do.'

'Me sir? No thoughts at all, sir, there isn't a thought in my head. Hand on heart, sir.' (At that precise moment my hands were submerged in a bowl of cold water.)

Master James leaned down to stir the fire. Then he replaced the poker on its hook and watched it swing to and fro for a moment.

'Of course,' he says, very casual. 'I don't suppose all this has anything to do with *ghosts*.'

Now there was a pounce, if ever I heard one. I assumed my most innocent face.

'Ghosts, sir?'

'It would be inconceivable,' he says (gesturing with his hands as though making a speech), 'that ghosts or Phantoms or spirits or whatever you want to call them were involved in this collapse. You would take issue with anyone who suggested as much.'

Here he paused and I realised he was expecting some kind of response. But at that moment missus moaned and shifted, causing the cloths on her head to slip off. I discarded them and took fresh ones from the bowl then spent some time arranging these across her brow. When I glanced up again master James was staring at me expectantly.

'What was the question sir?'

He sighed and fixed me with his beady eye. 'For the past few weeks my wife has been getting agitated. She seems to believe that the house is haunted. Now today we see her collapsed in a fit of nerves. And you are telling me that in your opinion her collapse and all this nonsense in her head about ghosts are in no way connected.'

'I suppose I am, sir.'

'You have no idea what happened to make my wife collapse.'

'No, sir.'

'In that case, I take it you were not with her at the time.'

'I wasn't, sir.'

'Tell the truth, Bessy, and shame the Devil.'

Flip the scutting Devil, it was *me* felt ashamed! Cornered as I was into giving out a whole clatter of lies, just when I was after turning over a new leaf! For my own sake, I was beyond caring, I had my confession wrote down for missus. But I didn't want to get *her* into trouble with her husband and I knew he would be furious if I tellt him we'd been hunting for a ghost in the attic.

'Sir,' I says, 'I don't know what more you want me to say.'

For a moment his eyes glittered in the firelight as he continued to study me. Then he appeared to let the subject drop. He sniffed and pinched the end of his nose, rubbed it ferociously, then took out his snoot cloot and trumpeted into it several times.

'Very well,' says he, when he'd tucked away his trumpet. 'However, it would interest me to know whether there have been any other similar occurrences of late. Any other dizzy spells, for instance.'

'No sir. None at all.'

'I take it you believe your mistress to be in good health.'

'I do sir. Well, I did, sir, until today.'

'Fair enough,' he says. 'Chops.'

'I beg your pardon?'

'You wanted to know what I would like to eat. I was expressing my preference.'

'Oh *chops*!' I says. 'I thought for a minute there you were calling me a name.'

I don't think he heard me, he was staring at his wife with a glum expression on his face. He seemed both mournful and a little irritated. After a moment, he turned and walked out the room, without another word.

Missus fought her fever all through that evening and on into the night. Once only her condition got worse and I near sent for the doctor but it seemed that application of the cool cloths brought her temperature down and made her less restless. Master James poked his neb round the door once again before he went to bed but when he seen that his wife was still insensible he crept away. Midnight came and went. The new year! But there was no celebration for us. About one o'clock, a gale blew up and swirled around the house. It rattled the windows and gusted in the chimney, sending smoke billowing out into the room. Soot fairies floated down onto me and missus, I had to wipe them off her lovely face. So beautiful she was! But nothing seemed to wake her, she slept on through it all like a baby.

I tellt myself I'd make her some broth in the morning if she was well enough to drink it. Lucky it wasn't my mother looking after her. Bridget would never have thought of making broth and she didn't cook if she could help it. And Joe Dimpsey was no better, he always had the same piece of advice for anyone with an ailment. 'A pint of whisky and a good bang, you'll be right as rain,' he used to say.

I didn't think I'd be recommending *that* particular cure to missus.

At one point, I lay down next to her on the coverlet and cradled her in my arms. I meant no disrespect by it, I only wanted to comfort her. At least she had somebody to look after her. Even if it were only me – a bad girl that was trying to turn over a new leaf. I kept making excuses for myself about being wicked. Normally I am not one to dwell on things but once again I could not help getting long-lippit about the way I was brought up. 'If only' this and 'If only' that. If only my mother had not been what she was &c. As I lay there next to missus I was reminded of the old days when Bridget and me often used to pig together in the same bed in Dublin. That is, before Joe arrived. After that I was on a tick on the floor. That very same tick I had sat upon while my mother painted my face for the first time. And I remembered that once she had finished with my face she painted her own, then led me out of our room and down stairs. Out in the street, she paused to examine her reflection in a windowpane and then she smiled down at me.

'Who am I?' she says.

No, she had not took leave of her senses. This was something she often asked me and I was well-schooled in the required response.

'You're my big sister,' I says.

'Exactly right,' says Bridget.

This was a little vanity of hers. She did not like people to think she had a child so I always had to say we were sisters and that is how we were known wherever we went.

She took me to a wide and busy street and stood me under a lamppost beside a row of cabmen, several of whom were asleep sat on the doorsteps of their vehicles.

'Smile, dear,' my mother says. 'And keep smiling.'

Two of her cronies were there in all their finery, Kate and Eliza Rosa, they stood under another lamppost waiting for somebody (or so I thought). My mother went and spoke to them and all 3 turned and looked at me. Eliza Rosa looked distressed at the sight of me for some reason but Kate called over very cheerful, 'If anything starts to droop love, come and find me I'll loan you some starch!'

I did not understand this comment or why it made her laugh so raucously, but decided it was most likely something particular to the umbrella trade. Neither Eliza Rosa nor my mother appeared to agree with Kate's advice for Eliza gave her a shove and my mother scowled at her and came back to stand with me.

When a gentleman in evening clothes approached us, I supposed he was the owner of the umbrella shop. He looked to be the jolly sort that would run such a place. His cheeks was pink the ends of his moustachios waxed. He wore a rose in his buttonhole and a brightly coloured scarf. My mother walked with him, a little way up the street. I couldn't hear what they were talking about but there was no doubt that I was the subject under discussion for they both flicked glances in my direction and once or twice when the gent wasn't looking my mother flashed her eyes at me and bared her teeth like a wild jackanapes which at first I thought strange until I realised she was reminding me to smile.

The man gave her something and then she came over and knelt down to look me in the face. 'Listen here to me,' she says. 'I want you to go along with this gentleman and do as you're bid and be polite and correct. And if you do it all right and mind your manners then me and Joe will let you come with us. D'you hear me?'

How could I fail to, she was right slap in front of me?

I went with the man, like she had tellt me. We walked away from the busy streets. Any time he happened to glance sideways at me, I made sure to smile. Presently (I'll always remember this), he cleared his throat and says, in quite a scolding fashion, 'Were it the case that you were an inhabitant of the continent of Africa, you would in all probability be married by now to a dark brown native with a bone in his nose.'

Not having been much in society and not quite knowing how best to respond politely to this remark, I decided to say nothing. A full minute passed in contemplation. Eventually the gentleman says, 'I see you would like that.'

'What, sir? Excuse me?'

'You would *like* to be married to a native with a bone in his nose.'

I shook my head. 'Oh no sir, I – I don't think I would like it at all.'

'Then why are you smiling so?'

'I don't know, sir.'

This amused him greatly for he barked with laughter, but then fell suddenly silent and frowned at me. 'Perhaps you are a simpleton,' he says shortly. He began to peer at me more closely as we walked on, examining my face for signs of idiocy.

'Away to flip!' I cried, then remembered I was supposed to be polite. 'Sir, excuse me, I'm not simple. I'm quick to pick things up. And I'll do exactly what I'm told.'

'I'm glad to hear it,' he says. 'At least you have stopped grinning like a loon.'

Indeed I had, for I suddenly felt like crying. All this strange talk of brown men and loonies. I wished my mother would come and get me and we could go home. But then I remembered that she and Joe were going to Scratchland and I had to go with this man and do as I was bid, else I would be left behind to eat scraps and sleep on the grocers step.

After some time of walking, the man led me down an alley at the side of a theatre. I had never been to the theatre before. Once or twice, I had heard some of my mothers cronies talk about a time they had snuck in by a back door and got a look at the stage, upon which the inimitable John Drew himself happened to be performing. I think perhaps I imagined that this gentleman also knew some secret way in and was taking me to see the end of the play before we went on to work. And so, I went with him quite willingly.

About ½ way down the alley, he drew me into a gloomy alcove. There was indeed an entrance there, but the door was barred and locked with a heavy chain. Upon discovering this, I felt a moment's disappointment that we might not get to see the show after all, but this was quickly replaced by panic as the gentleman bent down and put his tongue in my ear. I struggled to escape his grasp but there was nowhere I could go as he was backing me into the corner. I was dimly aware of certain things happening, his hat falling to the ground and rolling away, some urgent un-fastenings in the region of his trouser, a sensation of lifting as he hoisted me against the wall. I did not know much in those days but I had seen enough to realise what was about to occur, and I wasn't certain whether I liked it or not. Surely, I thought, this was not what my mother had in mind.

'Excuse me, sir,' I says. 'But what about the umbrellas?'

The alcove was dark and I couldn't really see his face, but he hesitated. 'Umbrellas?' he says, not unkindly. 'What d'you mean?'

'Sir, is this what I am *meant* to do?'

He stroked my head and sighed. 'Yes, dear. And you are doing it very well. Just keep still and – let me –' He made some minor adjustment to my undergarments. 'That's better. Are you all right?'

I nodded, hoping that he could not see that my eyes had filled with tears. It was quite clear to me what was going to happen.

'Now then,' he says. 'All being well and as advertised, this should cause you a small amount of discomfort.'

When it came to it, I could not bear the thought of his dirty great jack anywhere near me and so I imagined in its place nothing more sinister than an umbrella (indeed it might as well have been an umbrella for the pain it caused me), a gentlemans umbrella, silky and unfurled, just like the one I might have made at the shop, had we ever gone there and had the shop even existed, which – it was finally beginning to dawn on me – had never been the case.

I was a virgin on five more occasions that week, each time with a different man and by Saturday we had enough to pay our passage to

Scratchland. To begin with my mother claimed that Joe would be travelling with us on the same boat. And then, as the date of our departure drew near she said he had gone on ahead and we was to meet up with him in Glasgow. When pressed to be more specific about when and where, the best my mother could come up with was, 'Never you mind.'

I think it was at around this point that I began to suspect that her story about the emotional reconciliation down at the docks might not be true. But I kept my trap shut and tried not to dwell on it, I could never have put it into words back then but I suppose the implications was too painful even to consider.

After Dublin, Glasgow seemed to me to be huge, noisy and full of mad people. Within the first minute of disembarkation I seen a grown woman on her hands and knees barking like a dog, a man who played a fiddle that was made of a horses skull strung with strings, and a boy who twirled a mackerel around his head until its glossy guts flew out like streamers. Hanging above us all as we swarmed along the dock was a terrible sky lit up with fire and black smoke that looked to be from the very Jaws of Hell but in fact came from Dixons iron works across the river. And was the bold Joe Dimpsey, spoony man, awaiting us on the quay, all smiles and hearty welcomes? Was he buckie.

My mother took a room off Stockwell Street near the ropeworks and spent the first few days looking for Joe. She went to every race track, every wobble, every den and dance hall, and when that didn't root him out she put a notice in the *Herald*, offering a reward for information about his whereabouts. But no news came.

After about a week, when the money ran out, she put me to work. She was in semi-retirement, she says. She had wore herself out for years putting food on the table for me and clothes on my back. Now I was broke in, it was my turn to fetch the coin on a daily basis, and she would join me only whenever she felt like it.

From that day forth, it was as though all my thoughts and feelings was trapped in my chest, crammed together, taking up all the room there and making it difficult to breathe. But I knew no other way of life and so I pushed any doubts to the back of my head and did as I was told. Besides, I was very frightened of my mother.

As time went by she schooled me in some of the more sophisticated Arts of the trade (which I am sure I will be forgiven for not describing here) and before too long she had contrived to place entries for us both in a privately circulated catalogue entitled 'Sporting Ladies of Glasgow', in which I was listed as 'Rosebud, a fair and fresh young Sap' (I suspect that she may have meant 'sapling') 'who despite her tender years is fond of playing the silent flute and can perform all the stops very well'. My mother had described herself as 'Buxom beauty Helena Troy, whose outstanding Good Points cannot be rivalled on this World or in the next'.

Before too long we was just as much fixtures on the streets as the local girls, most of them it transpired were originally from across the water anyway and so there was a bond there in common. Saturday and Monday were good nights, because of Sunday being 'dry' and everybody drinking more on either side to compensate. But all us girls were competing with each other for work and unless you were a knockout beauty or you offered some particular 'service' or other, it was hard to make a living. Especially the way my mother drank. Before too long we got thrown out Stockwell Street for non-payment of rent and ended up in a basement room off the Gallowgate. Not shared, thank Gob, but the air was chill, both winter and summer, and your clothes got mildewed if you laid them down for even a second. The only way to keep warm, my mother said, was to have another budge.

After the move to the Gallowgate, she seemed to forget all about Joe Dimpsey. She found herself a new set of cronies and inevitably took up with a succession of men. The thing about my mother, she never was happy unless she had some piece of goods in tow but she couldn't just take up with any old fellow, they had to have some talent that marked them out from the ordinary. Take my so-called father Whacker McPartland. It was his gigantic jack and his talent for dancing that she liked to brag about. And Joe Dimpsey was of course notably handsome, but what she especially liked everyone to know about was his so-called wild genius and the possibility, however slim, that he might one day take it to university to be tamed. She was forever hitching her wagon to a star.

The first man she took up with in Glasgow was a night porter at the Tontine Hotel. Nothing too special about that you may say and you would be right but this cove was an Italian by the name of Marco that she had met at Parrys theatre. Marco the night porter had a face like a sick camel. He was known about the place as Macaroni because people were stupid and that was the only Italian they knew. Marco was slippery as they come, his stories was always changing. One minute he was from Rome, the next from Verona. Sometimes he claimed to be in exile. Exile my fat aunt Fanny. If they threw him out his country it can only have been because they were sick fed up to the back teeth of him, the lying thieving scut. Other times, when he'd had a few, he went around telling people he was of noble birth, which because of his accent often gave rise to great hilarity, especially when he was specific about his rank. 'I am a curnt,' he would tell you, and there was not many would argue with him on that score. Thank gob, my mother soon tired of him. In the end, she threw him out for drinking the last drop of her budge while she was asleep. She still kept him in tow as one of her cronies, but when he wasn't there she would go on at great length about his flaws and tell you how she felt dreadful sorry for him, he was only to be pitied, which was a way she had of putting herself above people.

After that, she went through a few other types each no better than the last. My memory of that time is hazy as I soon, like my mother, resorted to a dram to keep my spirits up. In those early days were I going out without a budge I might as well not go, I wouldn't make a ½ penny for I could not speak to a single man. Of course I grew less timid with the passing months and in the end was as 'gallus' as the next girl, but by that time I was too much in the habit to pass up my morning drop and any that followed thereafter.

And so in this way two or 3 years passed. I cannot say that I was either happy or sad. I felt nothing much of anything. I do believe that somewhere deep inside, I knew that what I was doing was wrong. One gentleman I met gave me two shillings just to talk to him about my life. He was an English man and a member of some kind of Society and he was at pains to point out where I was at fault in the life I had chosen. I had no answer for him. I was only fascinated that when he spoke he called you 'thee' and 'thou', which I found most quaint, having never heard the like. For a shilling more he asked to see where I slept and I thought to myself, now we have it, he will be pressing his diddle agin me before we get through the door. But after a glance at our room away he went and the only thing he pressed on me was a tract that he bestowed on parting. I hadn't a notion what it said because at the time I could not read, besides my mother used it to light the fire when she came home. Tell the truth, she could read and write a bit, having had a few years schooling when she was a girl, but she had passed none of what she learned on to me. All she had taught me was how to please a man.

It was about this time I began to have nightmares. Instead of two or 3 drinks, I was having many. I don't know how many. Just to forget what I had done. The terrible things I had done, that my mother made me do, to 'keep the gentlemen interested'.

Thank God for my Mr Levy, for he saved me. Poor Mr Levy! Gone to Kingdom Come, or wherever a Jewish man might go. It broke my heart when he died. And I dreaded going back to my mother. I remembered that morning, after I had been thrown out of Crown House and tramped back to the Gallowgate, scouring the market for her and looking in at our rooms, but in the end I found her at 'Dobbies', already on the gin. Marco the night porter was sat next to her, slumped across the table.

'Christ almighty!' my mother shouted when she seen me pushing towards her through the throng. 'What's the aul' scut feeding you? You're awful fat in the face!'

Then she laughed her head off. Here I was, back home less than a minute and already there were so many things annoying me it was hard to know where to start. Marco peered up at me through bleary eyes.

'I am a flipping exile, if you like to know!' he says. 'You are not worthy of lick my boots.' Then he slumped down again.

Meanwhile, my mother was waving at someone behind me, over by the bar. 'Yoo-hoo!' she shrieked. 'Come away over and see who's here!'

I turned, and just about fainted. There, propped against the wall in deep discussion with another man (and true to form, ignoring my mother) was none other than the bold Joe Dimpsey himself. Leaner in the face he was, and with a new moustache but there was no mistaking him.

'Flip sakes *JOE*!!' my mother shrieked. This time, he looked round, swaying slightly. My mother pointed at me. Joe grinned and tipped me his hat (also new) then turned back to continue his conversation.

'That's Joe,' my mother said, delighted.

'So I see,' I says.

'He's going to be starting up the university soon, going to be a doctor. He can do it over here just as well. They all think he's brilliant up there. They asked him a whole pannopoly of questions. Said they'd never known a brain like it. He'll be starting soon, next week it is, once he's bought his books. There's no stopping him. He's like a tiger.'

At that moment Joe was swaying from side to side, close to passing out, a tiger would not be the first description that came to mind. I turned back to my mother.

'So to what do we owe the pleasure of this visit?' she says. And then her gaze fell for the first time on my bundle. 'What have you got there?'

'Nothing,' I says. 'Just clothes.'

I sat down, shrugging off my coat. My mind was leaping from one thought to the next. I could see that everything was the same here, and would ever be so. What had I been thinking? I should never have come back anywhere near her.

'They're for you,' I says. 'Mr Levy bought them for me but –'

'How is the aul' bastard?'

'He's very well,' I says. 'In the pink.'

'He's a man of his word,' says my mother, lifting her glass. 'I'll give you that.'

I nodded. 'Like I was saying, these frocks don't fit me now so I thought I'd bring them over for you.'

'Really?' says my mother. 'That's decent of you.'

Her expression did not change a whit but I could tell she was suspicious at this unaccustomed generosity, in the past I had learnt to hoard my few possessions from her.

I laughed. 'Away and take a carrot,' I says. 'As if I'd give them to you. No, I'm going to sell them. Can I just leave them up in the room for now while I get a drink?'

My mother shrugged. 'If you want.' She flapped her hand. 'You could just put them under the table here.'

I looked at Marco. 'And get them pinched?' I shook my head. 'I'd just forget them anyway. I don't mind telling you, I have the day off and I'm here to get mortal.'

'Good for you!' my mother says. 'Glad to see you in good form for a change.'

'I'm going to get swacked,' I says.

'Hurrah!' says my mother.

'Tanked! Lit to the gills!'

'Yippee!'

'I'm paying!' I says.

'Then I'll join you,' says my mother.

'Wait now and I'll just stash these clothes up in the room,' I says. 'I'll be back in a minute. Get me a budge in to start with.'

Bridget gave me a slow wink. She was drunker than I had thought.

I put the bundle on my shoulder and made my way slowly

through the crowd. At the doorway I paused to wave at my mother but she was too busy staring across the room at Joe, like a lovesick cow. I stepped outside the inn and the minute my foot hit the ground I started running. Too late I realised I had left my coat. Well, I wasn't about to turn back. I did not stop running until I had passed Janefield and was well on the road to Edinburgh and a young prince. Or, as it turned out, to Castle Haivers and missus.

It wasn't only the prospect of going back on the streets that scared the behicky out me. There was another thing, something a flip sight worse, something that I knew my mother would inveigle me into doing. The 'special' service that she had dreamed up, that she had made me do before I went to live with Mr Levy.

Jesus Murphy I didn't want to think about it.

I jumped up from the bed to give myself a shake. The motion must have disturbed missus, for of a sudden she opened her eyes and gazed at me, a little bewildered. Then she give me a weak smile.

'Bessy,' she says. 'Have I been asleep?'

'No marm. You are not well. You are to stay in bed and rest.'

'Not well? Oh yes. I remember.' Her voice was hoarse, almost a whisper.

I sat down on the bed and with trembling hands took the cloths from her forehead and throat. The wind had dropped and dawn light was creeping in at the window. Missus face was pale as the bolster-cover. It was as though the light bleached her skin. As I leaned over her, she looked at me, a little surprised.

'But – you are upset!' she says. 'Whatever is the matter?'

'Nothing, marm. I am just happy that you seem a little better. Would you say my name again, marm?'

She looked puzzled. 'You mean – Bessy?'

'Yes, that's it,' I says. 'That's right. I am happy now.'

For though she was pale and weak it seemed that the worst of her illness, whatever it was, had passed. At any rate, she recognised me.

'Tell me, marm, what do you remember?' I says. 'We were up in the attic.'

Missus frowned. 'Let me see,' she says. 'We saw the writing in the window. Four words.' She looked pained, before continuing. 'A cry for help.'

'And then what?'

She thought a moment. 'I must have fainted,' she says. 'That is all I can recollect.'

'You don't remember falling? Or what happened just before you fell?'

'No. I can see the words in the window and I hear your voice saying them, but then it all goes dark, as though a lantern has been turned out.' She clutched my hand. 'Why?' she says. 'Did something happen? Did you see someone? Or something? What was it?'

'No marm,' I says. 'Nothing like that. Marm, you woke up and spoke to me. Do you remember?'

'No,' she croaked. 'What did I say?'

I considered telling her the truth, then thought better of it. 'Nothing. You just said my name and then you – fell asleep again.'

'All I remember is that message.' She looked at me eagerly. 'You know I've been expecting something like this. I told you as much, didn't I?'

She wanted some sign of encouragement but I gave her none. 'Marm,' I says. 'We need to decide what to tell master James. Do you want him to know we were on a ghost hunt in the attic?'

Her eyes widened in alarm. 'No!' she says. 'What have you told him?'

'Not a thing,' I says. 'I believe he might have suspected something about ghosts or the like but I think I put him off the scent. We'll be all right if we tell the same story and stick to it. Now, I've thought of what we can say. We'll pretend you were writing a letter in your room and you stood up too quickly, and that's the last thing you remember.'

She closed her eyes. She stayed like that for so long I began to wonder if she'd fell asleep again.

Then, of a sudden, her eyes opened. She looked at me intently. 'I could feel a presence up there,' she says. 'It was so cold. Couldn't you feel it?'

'Attics are always cold,' I tellt her. 'Except in summer.'

'No, there was something there, I'm sure of it. It can only be a matter of time before something happens – something more extreme. An apparition, perhaps. Someone is reaching out to us, Bessy. Someone needs our help.'

Her eyes were that wide and she seemed so earnest and anxious it would have been funny – if only it didn't make you feel guilty and sad. I nodded, slowly, and appeared to consider her statement. 'You might be right about that. But I wouldn't be at all surprised if what happened yesterday was the end of it altogether. I suspect we may have seen the last of that ghost.'

Weak though she was, she gave a wry smile. 'What's this – your rational explanation again?'

'No marm,' I says. 'I just have a very strong feeling.'

I simply had to get her off this train of thought. Very off-hand, I says, 'Did you ever go up to the attic, marm? Before you started to hear all the noises and everything?'

'Not really,' she says, eventually. 'I can only think of – one occasion.'

That would have been when she put Noras box up there, I knew as much from *The Observations*. But the box wasn't what concerned me. I began to move around the bed, needlessly tucking in the covers.

'Did you happen to look at the skylight, marm, when you were up there?'

'I don't think so,' she says. (As this was the best possible response she could have give me, I felt a thrill of excitement.) 'Why do you ask?'

I took a deep breath. Here goes. 'Was there never someone in this house marm, that did call you "My Lady"?'

She gave a little gasp and her eyes widened. You would have thought I'd yanked up her smock for a peek at her parsley. She stared at me for a moment, her breath coming quick and shallow.

Then she says, 'There was a girl, yes. A few months before you arrived.'

My heart was going like the hoofs of Hell. But I knew I had to continue.

'And – marm – might this girl not have wanted your help at some stage?' I says. 'Could she not have been in the attic one day, for some reason, perhaps she was a little sad, I don't know, and couldn't she – might she not have wrote those words up there in the skylight, in an absent-minded way?'

Missus was staring straight ahead. No words came from her lips, but her eyes were like windows, I could see a dozen thoughts flit through the rooms of her mind.

'Is that not possible?' I says. 'That this maid wrote those words *months* ago, but that we only just noticed them the other day, and *mistook* them for the words of a ghost?'

It wasn't a certainty, perhaps it was even a long stretch – but it was just possible.

'But, you see,' says missus. 'You don't understand. This girl – actually is dead.'

'Oh dear,' says me. (What a performance! I was acting my arse off.) 'I'm sorry to hear that, marm. What was her name?'

Missus licked her lips. 'Nora,' she says, faintly. 'Nora Hughes.'

'Well forgive me marm, this Nora Hughes might be dead *now*, but presumably she was alive when she was working for you.' I flashed her the ivories but she made no reply. 'Don't you see? She was here but a few months ago. She might easily have gone up to the attic without you knowing and wrote that silly message in the window.'

For a moment or two, missus continued to stare into space. Then she took a shuddering breath and let it out again. 'Yes,' she says. 'I had not thought of it like that. But you might be right. It could have been written – before.'

I laughed. 'There now, marm, you see? We have the explanation. The message wasn't left by anybody dead at all. It was done months ago, by a real live maid.' Here, I paused a moment to give her time to fully absorb my suggestion. Then I says, lightly, 'It seems so obvious, marm, I almost wonder why we did not think of it at once.'

How had I expected her to react? I suppose I had imagined that she would be relieved, even pleased to learn that there was a rational explanation for everything. Nonetheless, at that moment, her face showed neither relief nor pleasure. In fact she seemed disappointed, I might even go so far as to say that she gave every appearance of being bereft.

'What's the matter, marm?'

She gave a start, as though she had forgot I was there. And then she fixed me with an odd look I couldn't quite fathom. Partly devious, as though she felt she had outwitted me in some way and at the same time distrustful, as though she suspected that I might try to outwit her in future. This was my impression for it only lasted a second or two and I might have been mistaken. Then she smiled and gave herself a shake.

'Nothing!' she says with a little laugh. 'Aren't you clever, Bessy, working all that out? I believe you may well have solved our little mystery. Isn't that marvellous?'

I would happily have stayed on talking to her for donkeys years but she made it clear that I should leave, by telling me that she wanted to sleep and then turning on her side and so I was left to creep out the room and quietly close the door.

Back in the kitchen, I put my hand in my pocket and my fingers closed around my letter to missus. I took it out and looked at it. Only hours had passed since I had wrote it but it felt like days. Thank gob, none of the worst things that I had feared had come true. Missus was neither dead nor gone mad. She didn't remember that I had punched her. And if we both stuck to the same story about what happened then master James would be none the wiser.

How silly I was to have worried so much. Indeed (I tellt myself), revealing the truth now would only do more harm than good. Missus was in a delicate state. She needed calm and quiet. Knowing that I had made a fool of her would only upset her and possibly make her ill again. Just when she was on the path to recovery. Really, when you thought about it, there was no reason to run away or to confess anything at all.

Anyway, for dear sake, where would I go?

What a relief I had not give her the letter already!

And just to make sure that she never learned what I'd done, I destroyed it. There was no fire lit yet in the kitchen so it took several matches and a lot of blowing, I think the paper must have been a bit damp. But I persevered, lighting match after match until eventually my confession was no more than a little heap of ashes in the grate.

13

A Trip, a Tea Party and a Mysterious Object

It was that gloomy time of year so it was when each day seems too short, as though the sun has bare crept across the sill of the world before it has to shrink once more into the shadows. I burned extra candles by the bed to cheer missus and hunted for things to brighten the chamber and distract her from thoughts of ghosts. There was no flowers to be found outside but in spare moments I searched the hedgerows and collected sprigs of holly and rosehips and evergreen leaves these I wrought into little displays for the chimneypiece. Each night I invented a few riddles, I wrote them on paper and gave them to her with breakfast so that she had something to occupy her while I went about my work. I was careful to write up my journal and show it to her at the end of every day that she might check exactly what chores I had done and what had gone through my mind as I worked. (It is my belief that she was too weak to write up her *Observations* for I never once seen ink on her fingers in this period.) To pass time in the evenings, we played at cards. Most often she chose *Humbug* which I had taught her though I told her it was called *Doubles* as that seemed a more agreeable name. Sometimes I read to her from novels. Only excerpts that I thought she would find striking or amusing. And instead of sleeping in my own room, I elected to doze in the chair beside her bed, just in case she should want something or get sick in the night and be too weak to ring for me. In short I done everything I could to make life easier and more pleasant for her.

One morning, she wanted me to read her out the Bible, I opened it at random, Isaiah 24. It was all about the Lord making the earth waste and turning it upside down, curses desolation treachery and everybody being thrown into a pit. Yes that would do her good to hear. Not really! I decided to give her Christ feedeth the four thousand instead, because everybody likes a nice miracle, I was just trying to find the page when I glanced up to see her laying there with a fearful look on her face. I jumped up at once and knelt beside her.

'Whatever is the matter, marm?'

She took my hand and squeezed it.

'Oh Bessy,' she says. 'I just have to get better. You must help me. Will you do that, Bessy? Will you help me to get well?'

More than anything I wanted to take her in my arms and hold her. Yet I didn't do it. I wanted to say, 'I would do anything for you, marm, anything.' But I kept my potato trap shut. You see, I knew better now than to frighten her off by gushing or pestering her, she didn't care for that kind of behaviour as I had discovered to my shame when I read her *Observations*. Perhaps I had allowed my feelings to run away with me. And being a kind person, missus tolerated me for a while, but she wouldn't have welcomed it, some wee skullion clinging to her petticoats like a bad fart. In the end wasn't she *quite right* to have put me at bay?

When you got to know her (like I had) you seen that she was delicate as a butterfly, and like a butterfly would flutter away if pursued. The only way to catch her was to sit stock still so that she might venture closer. And after a while (if you were lucky) she might even settle, quivering, on your thumb. No doubt about it, I'd have to keep myself in check and be careful not to frighten her away. No fool me! This time I would be more prudent.

So I didn't embrace her or any of that tripe. All I says was, 'Of course I'll help you get better, marm.' And left it at that.

To master James we maintained the fiction that missus had got up too quick after writing a letter. The man was no gull but he seemed to swallow our story. Needless to say there were no more noises from the attic no strange occurrences about the house, not a bit of it. Missus gained strength with each day that passed until one morning she seemed so much better that I allowed her to get up. She sat in her chair for an hour staring out the window and later (since she appeared none the worse for the experience), we went for a short walk, arm in arm, around the vegetable garden.

The day was crisp and cold but I made sure that she was well wrapped up in her cloak and mittens. The garden was a shambles so it was. Apart from the cabbages and onions, the autumn vegetables were tramped down and withered or blackened by frost. The pea and bean nets had collapsed and the ground was covered with slimy brown leaves that had blown down from the woods. The few remaining cauliflowers had rotted where they grew. 'Cauliflower soup,' I says to missus and feeble jest though this was it made her laugh. I could feel the heat of her hand through the mitten. Her nose and cheeks were pink from the cold and the breath rose from her in gusts, like steam. All around was death and devastation yet she seemed alive and for the first time I began to believe she was going to be all right. The relief of it washed through me like a swig of Godfreys.

Later I stole a few moments from preparing dinner and sought out master James in the study to let him know that – at last – it looked like his wife might be getting better. He had been standing behind his desk when I entered, thumbing through a small book and now he glanced up from its pages.

'That is good news,' he says. 'If it is indeed the case.'

'Oh it is, sir. I think she'll be right as rain in a week or so.'

The book in his hand snapped shut, he tossed it down on the desk between us, like a challenge. 'In that case,' he says. 'She will – in your opinion – be fully recovered in ten days time. By next Thursday.'

'Well I couldn't be so precise as to say *exactly* –'

'I'm afraid I need you to be precise, Bessy.' He had spoke sharply but then he paused and stroked his whiskers and seemed to soften a little. 'Perhaps I should explain. We have been invited to a *Soiree* next Thursday evening, in Edinburgh. A rather important function, hosted by our Reverends brother, Mr Pollock. The fountain I am purchasing for Snatter will probably come from his foundry in Glasgow and I have some plans that I need to discuss with him. This would be the ideal opportunity. And he is very keen that my wife accompany me. I had it in mind to take her away for a few days, in any case, for a change of scene. It's not good for her being shut away from the world. I suspect her isolation here has contributed to this – this collapse, whatever it is. So I intend to take her to town. And, while we are there, it would be – convenient – for us both to attend this *Soiree* on Thursday. Now, if I am not mistaken, you are suggesting that she will indeed be fully recovered by then.'

'Well, sir, I *think* she might but I don't–'

'*Think* is not good enough, Bessy. I need you to *ensure* that she is well.'

The way he stared at you it made you want to look away, but I held my ground.

'Sir, if missus is not recovered by next Thursday then might I suggest that she stays at home and you go to the important dinner yourself.'

He smiled smoothly. 'I'm afraid it's not quite that simple, Bessy. As my wife, she is invited and expected. Now I will be very busy for the next few days, and I want you to keep a close eye on her and make sure that she is well enough to accompany me. I hope you understand what I mean.'

I was not sure that I did and tellt him as much.

'I mean – let me put it plainly to you.' He planted his fists on the desk and leaned towards me. 'She is to be kept calm and quiet and she must be discouraged from entertaining any notions about this house being haunted. It has upset her. You are not to let her talk about it and you are not to become involved in these – wild imaginings and – and – flights of fancy of hers. It will only make her worse.'

It was on the tip of my tongue to protest that this was *exactly* what I was trying to do but instead, I found myself leaping to her defence.

'She *has* heard noises, sir. And strange things *have* happened that can't be explained. If I were her, in her position, I would be thinking the same thing, sir.'

He raised an eyebrow. 'So you *have* been encouraging her to believe this nonsense.'

'On the contrary, sir, I have been doing everything in my power to convince her otherwise.'

'Well then.' He sniffed. 'Fresh air is what she needs. Take her out tomorrow.'

'But–'

He waved away my objections. 'I have just spoken to her about it and she is agreed it would be a good idea,' he says. 'Go to church, or Bathgate. Look in at shop windows. Amuse yourselves. Call in at the railway station and regulate your watches.'

'But sir–'

'That will be all, Bessy.'

He picked up his book and, opening its pages, began to read.

Go to church, look in at shop windows, regulate your watches – now you're talking! Now there's a flipping Jamboree and a ½!

Next morning, Biscuit Meek brought the carriage round. It was a drafty old ramshackle affair that went out with The Ark. Perhaps it had been grand once but now it had bits hanging off here and there and all the fabric inside had worn away. The windows were cracked and the stuffing was coming out the seats. There was even a hole in the floor you could have put your leg through and if you glanced down unexpectedly you got quite giddy to see the road rushing away beneath your feet.

Missus did not seem to remark upon any of these details or find them unusual, she simply stepped over the hole in the floor and sat very quiet in the corner on the way to town, fingering her purse and gazing out the window. I took the place opposite her, to catch her in case the horses should stop suddenly (although the likelihood of them doing *anything* suddenly was slim, they were that ancient). At first, I tried to engage her in conversation about what we might do in Bathgate (she had talked about looking at materials for a dress) but as she did not reply with anything other than a distracted 'Yes' or

'No' I soon gave up and stared out the window myself. There was buck all to see except cows and sheep and the odd coal pit. This was the first such journey missus and I had undertook together, indeed I had not been further than Snatter since my arrival at Castle Haivers. In different circumstances I might have enjoyed the trip, going in the carriage with her, all this. But my over-riding mood was one of anxiety. I could only hope that she was well enough to be out and that the day would not be a strain on her nerves.

It looked like Bathgate was still under construction, everywhere you turned there were ½ raised buildings and men digging foundations and carts carrying stone and mortar. Biscuit Meek set us down outside a hotel on one of the main streets. Dear joy the place was going like a fair. No sooner had we alighted than missus bought a pot of yellow crocus from a flower stall then set off walking at a great lick. Since I hadn't a baldy where we were, I had to skitter away after her. Compared to the great cities Bathgate is a rats-arse of a place but it was such a long time since I had been in a town of any size and we led such a quiet life at Castle Haivers that it all seemed hectic to me. To think I used to stroll about Glasgow where the streets were twice as wide and fifty times as busy without turning a hair! And now my heart was racing at this modest bustle of people, carriages, handcarts, livestock and horses. Passers by seemed to throw themselves into my path deliberately. To add to my confusion, snow began to fall, it whirled and gusted in icy flakes, enough to blind you.

Missus might as well have put wheels under herself she moved along that quick, it seemed a remarkable recovery of strength. Before too long we had left the well-built streets for the narrow, crooked lanes of the old town, where it was much gloomier. After a few moments, she turned a corner and juked into an old-fashioned drapers. In goes yours truly after her and gladly so for my bake was fair froze.

The atmosphere in the shop was close and cosy, there was several people waiting to be served. 4 or 5 ladies stood talking in the middle of the room and two others were seated in chairs beside the counter. I went and stood next the fire at the back. Out the corner of my eye, I watched missus. Pot of crocus in hand, she was moving along the shelves, gazing at materials. The heat from the coals and the murmur of the ladies chatter soon lulled me into a little day-dream. I watched a man lay a bolt of grey worsted on the counter. Framed by the large window, he began to cut the cloth with shears, in the background snowflakes tumbled out the sky in pucks, as though the angels were emptying sacks. Behind me, the bell tinkled and the shop door opened and closed as some other customer came in. One of the ladies at the counter was taking forever with her order. Every time you thought she'd finished, she started wittering on again. I looked round, to check that missus was not getting impatient. She was no longer stood at the shelves where I'd last seen her and so I turned to the counter – but she wasn't there either. Remembering the tinkle of the bell, I peered around to see who had come in but nobody had come in at all. With a dull thud in the pit of my gut I realised that when the door had opened and closed it was missus that had slipped out.

I lashed over to the entrance and stepped outside. At first I could see only strangers but then I recognised missus. She had raised the hood on her cloak and was heading uphill. I called out a few times, but she didn't look around. Then she turned a corner and disappeared from view.

Since I hadn't a notion where we were, I had no choice but to go after her, my feet slithering on the slushy ground. Upon turning the corner, I glimpsed her in the distance and called out again, but she gave no sign that she'd heard me. Instead, she crossed a little square and began walking even faster up a broad street. I charged after her. As far as I could tell, we seemed to be heading back towards the new town. Snow continued to tip out the sky in blinding flurries. I paused for a moment to wipe a few flakes off my eyelashes and when I looked up again missus had disappeared. In panic, I ran along the pavement, glancing in at doorways and shop windows. On the other side of the street, set back behind a burial ground, was an old white-washed church. A movement there caught my eye. Glancing over the churchyard wall I seen her, a dark grey shape in a cloak flitting between the gravestones. What in the name of flip was she up to?

I found the gate and went in. The churchyard was overgrown, narrow paths led between crowded rows of stones that jutted in all directions like snaggle-teeth. Now that I was inside, it was hard to get my bearings. I began walking towards where I *thought* I had last seen missus but the track led me in a direction I had not expected and so I turned back and chose another route. The snow eased off, then of a sudden ceased to fall. As I advanced, I peered this way and that around the ivy-clad headstones, but saw no sign of missus or any other soul. I had just begun to lose faith in this 2nd route when I glanced over at the adjacent footpath and saw the pot of crocus laying on the ground beside one of the graves. What was the go here? I scrambled between two headstones and emerged dishevelled on the other side. However, missus was nowhere to be seen.

This part of the churchyard seemed newer than the rest. I realised that the crocus pot had been set down beside the grave, rather than dropped in haste as I first thought. The headstone beside it was of white marble and the letters of the inscription were delicate and curved. My gaze was drawn towards the top of the stone, perhaps because the name carved there had lately been at the forefront of my own thoughts.

Nora Hughes.

For dear sake! It was as though I had both read her name and thought of it in the same moment. I was shocked and yet not surprised at all. In a way, I realised I had been thinking of Nora so much that it was almost like stumbling across my *own* name writ large upon a gravestone. No sooner had I thought *that* than someone touched my shoulder. I leapt about 6 foot in the air. Only to find missus standing next to me, with a trowel in her hand, she used it to point at the stone.

'You see?' she says. 'This is where she is.'

With that, she knelt down and began to clear the snow from a small patch of ground at the foot of the grave.

'This corner is marked out for Roman Catholics,' she says. 'It was lucky that we got her in here, otherwise I don't know where she would have been put. Space is short in this graveyard, but James managed to arrange it.'

She stabbed at the frozen earth with the trowel. I was forced to wonder where this implement had come from. Had she brought it with her, concealed about her person? Up the sleeve of her cloak perhaps or in some other private place? Had she planned this graveyard trip all along?

The ground was hard as a monks mickey and the trowel made little impression on it. Missus glanced up at me. 'D'you think it is too cold to plant these?'

'I don't know, marm,' I says. 'Where did you get the trowel?'

She glanced at it. 'From the sexton,' she says. 'He gave it to me but only grudgingly. He thinks it too cold to plant anything.'

'Perhaps he's right, marm. Why did you run away from the shop?'

She made an impatient, tutting sound. 'Oh it was going to take hours,' she says. 'With that dreadful woman. I got tired waiting.'

'But you left without saying anything, marm.'

She raised an eyebrow. 'Well, I knew you would be right behind me!' She banged the trowel impatiently on the ground. 'Blast this weather!'

She looked so pathetic and frustrated, I forgave her for running off.

'You could leave the flower in the pot for now,' I says. 'And then we can come back when the weather is warmer, and plant the bulbs.'

'I suppose so,' she says. With a reluctant sigh, she gazed at the grave. 'I did so want to get something into the ground today.' She glanced up at me again, a little anxious. 'Do you think Nora will know that I came? If I don't plant the crocus, I mean. If we just leave it here, by the headstone, will she know it?'

It was not often that she deferred to me on any matter but I supposed it might be something to do with me and Nora being Irish and so I nodded.

'Oh yes,' I says. 'I'm sure she will. I mean – Nora will know up in heaven. It's not her *ghost* that will know, because there is no ghost, is there? It's her angel self. Else why would people leave flowers on graves? And they do that all the time.'

That seemed to put her mind at rest. She spent a moment or two positioning the plant pot at the end of the grave. Then she began scraping the snow off the headstone. I watched her in silence.

After a moment, I hazarded a question. 'Were you here at the burial, marm?'

'No,' she says, regretfully. 'James thought it would be for the best if I didn't attend.'

She took out her handkerchief and unfolded it. In preparation for tears I thought, but then she used it to wipe the remaining snow off the headstone.

'You are wondering something, Bessy,' she says, without either looking up or pausing in her labours. 'What is it?'

'Nothing, marm,' I says but then curiosity overcame me. 'Well – only perhaps, what happened to Nora. I did hear that she was killed by a train on the railway.'

For a moment missus stood nodding, as though politely thinking this over. And then she began to speak.

'Nobody is quite sure – how it happened,' she says. 'There was – a celebration – a party of some sort, in one of the bothies. It was summer. We always take on more hands in spring and summer to cope with the extra work. The bothies were full, I believe, and it was a holiday, the day of the Free Gardeners Parade. I don't quite know what Nora was doing in the bothy. She didn't normally mix with the farm servants. As you know yourself there is not much time or opportunity to do so. But anyway that night, I'm told, Nora had gone to join the celebration after her work was done. At some point, late in the evening, she left the bothy. Nobody saw her go, she must have slipped out, unnoticed. A lot of drink had been consumed by the farm servants, and so all the stories are rather vague and unhelpful. I don't expect Nora was drunk. She was not that kind of person. At any rate, I was surprised the following morning when she did not appear for work. And then, when I went to her room to look for her, I saw that her bed had not been slept in.'

'Oh dear,' I says.

'Yes,' says missus. 'That was my thought. I hoped, perhaps, that she might turn up during the course of the day but when there was no sign of her by nightfall, we raised the alarm. There was a search of the immediate area but they found nothing for the first few days. And then a group of itinerants came across – part of her body – at the side of a railway track. The rest of her was found later, further along the line.'

She flapped her handkerchief a few times to shake the snow from it and then returned it to her pocket. We both stood a while, gazing at the ground in front of us. I thought of Nora buried deep under there in an earth bath, all in pieces in a box.

'But why was she on the track, marm? Did she lose her way home or what?'

Missus tilted her head. 'That is what is commonly believed, yes, that she lost her way in the dark. I am told that there are a number of cases, very similar, all across the country. Every year it happens. People simply wander onto these lines by mistake and are killed by railway trains. It is just something that occurs in this modern age. It was a complete accident. A terrible shock to us all.'

She was putting a brave face on it, I could tell. But I had a feeling that deep down she somehow blamed herself for all what had happened. I thought of the day she'd collapsed, the words she'd said. 'It's all my fault.' She must be feeling guilty – perhaps for not having kept a close enough eye on Nora. I did so wish she wouldn't!

I had thought missus was going to say more, but instead she bent down of a sudden and picked up the trowel. 'We must return this,' she says and with one last glance at Noras grave, she set off down the path towards the church.

Upon our return to Castle Haivers I was able to inform master James that all had passed off remarkable well. Of course I didn't mention that missus had gone haring out the draper's shop or that she had visited the grave of her dead servant, I chose to dwell only on the more optimistic aspects of our day out. Like I told him missus had inspected some epaulettes but decided against their purchase and instead bought some braid with which to trim a jacket. Master James was anxious to know how much braid cost – I told him a few pence. He seemed reassured if a little weary. I then mentioned that we had seen a dancing bear outside in the street while we were in the coffee house. 'Coffee!' he exclaimed. 'Dear God!!' and then he wanted to know how much it cost and whether the gypsies had come round with a hat for the bear – I told him that I didn't know as we'd only watched for a few moments and then gone to the Upper Station to adjust our watches.

'Ah!' says master James with evident pleasure like as if the notion of watch regulation was as gratifying as that of a bang-up meal. 'Very good, Bessy,' he says. 'You have done well.'

'Thank you, sir.'

'Now,' he says. 'Just to ensure that your mistress will be able to cope with a trip to Edinburgh and all that will entail, we will be hosting a tea party tomorrow afternoon at 3 o'clock. I have sent Hector out with the invitations. You can expect the Reverend Pollock and Mr Flemyng, myself of course and your mistress. She managed a trip to town without much trouble – but let us just see how she fares in company.'

Missus never minded Flemyng of course. But later on, I happened to overhear her talking with her husband and noted that she was less than thrilled about the inclusion in the party of the other guest. As I listened, she put up a number of objections. Not enough notice had been given, she says, and the Reverend would not be able to come. On the contrary, said master James, the man had already replied in the affirmative. In that case it was selfish, says missus, to keep the minister from his more important business about the parish, he did not want to be frittering his time away with tea parties.

Nonsense, says master James, he was delighted to come, wild horses could not keep him away. After a pause, missus expressed some doubts about whether the tea service had seen its best days. Would it not be far better, she proposed, to postpone until a smarter set had been acquired? Balderdash, goes master James, there was bog all wrong with the china.

Eventually, after a much longer pause, missus sighed and admitted that – perhaps – she wasn't as yet feeling quite well enough to play hostess and was it *inconceivable* that she might keep to her room while master James held the tea party in her absence?

'Foof!' went master James. As it happens circumstances prevented me from hearing the rest of his response but the mark of her success in avoiding the tea party lay in the fact that on the following afternoon at 5 to 3 missus was at her place in the parlour, ready and waiting. She was white of face and stony of aspect, it was perfectly clear to me that she was not looking forward to the afternoons events, not one iota. I wished master James had listened to her for I feared she would have a relapse. But she seemed resigned to playing her part for the course of the next few hours.

Mr Flemyng was first to arrive having walked over from Thrashburn. I opened the door to him. He said he had not yet heard from his publisher but that as a gift to me he had wrote out a neat copy of one of my songs complete with musical notes. However he had forgot to bring it. He was most apologetic, calling himself all classes of fool and insisting that he go home to fetch it. This, of course, I could not allow as it would have made him late for the tea party which might then be construed as my fault. Therefore I protested that he do no such thing. Flemyng kept making as though to step out of the porch and I had to keep pleading with him and plucking at his sleeve in an attempt to prevent him from leaving. It was while we were thus engaged that the Reverend Pollock appeared.

'Ah-haah!' he goes. 'Here we are! Ah-haah!'

I had not heard him approach and wondered how this was possible unless he had levitated across the flipping gravel. At any rate, from the delighted look on his face, he was under the impression that he had disturbed some sort of illicit liaison.

'Reverend Pollock, good afternoon,' says Flemyng with a nod of his head. Then he turned to me and sighed most regretfully. 'It seems, Bessy, that the other guests are arriving,' he says. 'Perhaps there won't, after all, be time for me to return to Thrashburn.'

'I should think not, sir,' I says. 'Don't worry, I can see that thing any time.'

'Of course,' says Flemyng. 'I was a fool to forget it.'

Reverend Pollock was listening to this exchange with a great deal of interest. Smiling and nodding away, the old nosy scut. I decided that the best thing was to deliver the both of them into the parlour without further delay. This was not possible however as the Reverend was in no hurry. He and Flemyng exchanged a few pleasantries on the step until I insisted they step inside out the cold then the Reverend turned in the open doorway and stood there for several moments gazing out with great admiration at the drive and shrubbery as though they were amongst the 7 Wonders of the World. It took a good deal of manoeuvring on my part to put myself between him and the door and to close it behind him. Once he was in, the usual struggle to get him out his coat and hat ensued. From some pocket he produced one of his tracts and this he attempted to push into my hands. I demurred and pushed it back at him. Eventually after a little chivvying from me the paraffin-scented coat came off. Then the hat. And finally, with great relief, I showed the two men into the parlour.

Missus was on her own as master James had not yet deigned to come out his study. She ½ rose from her chair to greet the guests. She looked frail and a little nervous. I would have stayed to make sure she was all right but she gave me a couple of warning looks and finally she says, 'That will be all, Bessy,' so I had no choice but to step outside and close the door.

On my way to the kitchen I noticed the Reverends tract on the hallstand, he must have snuck it there while I was hanging up his coat. This time it was not *Dear Roman Catholic Friend* but *The Evil Effects of Modern Dancing*, I had a good laugh over that in the kitchen. Apparently dancing damaged the health of all who engaged in the pursuit. The waltz came in for particular disparagement since invariably it resulted in the violation of the 7th commandment, generally speaking there was no valid excuse could be offered in favour of dancing since 'even a stupid African or monkey might be taught to excel in the art'.

Flip me if I didn't waltz over to the fire and drop the tract onto the dancing flames.

When I returned to the parlour with the tea tray, master James had just joined the company, they were discussing the progress of his plans to install a fountain in the village. Personally speaking I do not think master James cared the core of a kidney whether the villagers had clean drinking water easily obtainable or not, it was just another way of currying favour. Especially with Duncan Pollock MP since he owned the foundry that made the fountains. Master James had received from him a manufacturers catalogue, he brought it out now to show his guests, as proud as a dog with two jacks. As I began to set up the tea table, he opened the catalogue at the relevant page and passed it to the Reverend.

'Here it is,' he says. 'This one. Perhaps you know it, sir. Number thirty-three. It has four columns as you can see and a canopy.'

Reverend Pollock settled back in his chair and began, slowly and carefully, to read aloud what was printed on the page, in a way that forced everyone to attend to him.

'"*Pagoda-shaped drinking fountain nine feet six inches tall. On two of the sides provision is made for receiving inscription." Ah-haah! "Whilst on the other two sides is the useful monition 'Keep the pavement dry'.*" Ah-haah! Very good, James, very good. But what will your other inscription say I wonder? Something pertinent, no doubt. I have it, the very thing.' He adopted a tone that was not only loud but threatening and doleful, I assumed it was his pulpit voice. '"Whoever drinketh of this water shall thirst again!"'

Master James took a breath and leaned forwards as though to speak, but the Reverend raised a finger for silence, he was not yet finished.

'"But whosoever drinketh of the water that *I* shall give him shall *never* thirst but the water that I shall give him shall be in him a well of water springing up into everlasting life!"' He turned, smiling, to missus and with a little bow of his head, concluded, 'John, chapter four, verse 25. Ah-hah! New Testament perhaps but pertinent nonetheless.'

Master James screwed up his eyes as though considering the Reverends suggestion though if you ask me he looked more like he was in pain. 'I fear,' he says, 'apt and admirable though that sentiment may be it would prove too discursive.'

'Oh?' says the Reverend. 'Discursive?'

'It would not fit on the inscription plate,' says master James shortly.

'Ah-haah!' says Bollix. 'Something pithy is required then. In that case, let us go to Psalms number 42.' Again, the doleful pulpit voice. '"As the hart panteth after the water brooks, so panteth my soul after thee, oh God!"'

'Yes,' says master James. 'That is more concise. However, unfortunately, I have in fact already commissioned the inscription.'

'I see,' says the Reverend. 'Pray tell, what did you choose?'

'Yes dear,' says missus. 'What does your inscription say?'

Up to this point she had been silent and anxious-looking and I had begun to worry about her but now I could see a twinkle in her eye as she regarded her husband.

Master James cleared his throat. 'It says simply, "Donated by James Reid".'

The Reverend raised a disapproving eyebrow. 'Pithy indeed,' he says and went back to reading the catalogue, this time muttering the words under his breath. For a moment or two nobody else spoke. But master James seemed to feel the need to explain himself, he turned to Flemyng.

'You see, every letter is charged extra. I felt that after outlaying such a substantial sum on the fountain itself, it would be more thrifty to keep the inscription to a minimum.'

'Of course,' says Flemyng. 'Quite right, sir, quite right. May I be so bold as to enquire how much such a splendid installation might cost?'

Master James blew a gust of air from between his lips and shook his head. 'One can pay 50 or a hundred pounds, depending on the–'

'I believe this type costs 18 pounds,' the Reverend interjected, with a crafty smile. 'I know it from the factory. It is one of the most basic models. The exact price should be noted here, let me see . . .' He began flipping the pages of the catalogue.

Master James scowled at him and turned back to address Flemyng. 'Some of them are overly ornate in my opinion. All those fanciful Moorish designs and griffins and strange beasties. Far better to have simplicity of line, less curlicues.' He spoke with what sounded like authority but this was undermined by the fact that as soon as he fell silent he began biting his nails.

'Indeed,' says Flemyng. 'I quite agree. And where will you put the fountain, sir?'

Master James didn't seem to hear this question, the way he was scowling at the Reverend Pollock you would almost think he'd have liked to be savaging the clerical gentleman instead of his own nails.

Missus reached out and gently took her husbands hand away from his mouth. 'James dear,' she says. 'Davy would like to know where the fountain will be put.'

But just then the Reverend let out a cry. 'Here we are!' he says. 'Price list!' He began running his finger down the page.

Missus leaned forwards and spoke to him. 'I wonder, Reverend, would you mind showing me the picture of the fountain, I have not yet seen it.'

This was a cod to distract him from the price list, master James cast a grateful glance in her direction but the Bollix would not be swayed.

'Yes, Arabella, just a moment,' he says without looking up. The briefest scowl crossed her face and for a second only you could see how much she disliked him. 'Now where was I?' he goes. 'Number 33 – yes – that would be, as I thought, 18 pounds and 10 shillings precisely.' He sat back in his chair and beamed around at the company.

'Well,' says Flemyng. 'What a remarkable bargain. I am sure the folk of Snatter will be tremendously grateful to you, James, both now and in perpetuity. It is most generous. I take my hat off to you, sir. You are an example to us. And if you ever chance to do a fart I would be most delighted and honoured to catch it.'

Matter of fact he didn't say that last bit, I did.

'How kind of you, Davy,' says missus. 'But you are absolutely right.' She turned to her husband. 'I am proud of you, James, for providing such a thoughtful and useful amenity. We could have a little opening ceremony to celebrate, what do you think?'

The Bollix was in danger of falling into a sulk, since his revelation about the price had not had quite the discomfiting effect he desired. Noticing this, missus appealed to him.

'I wonder, Reverend,' she says, 'if we might impose upon your generosity to say a few words in honour of the occasion? I know you are busy, but I don't think a ceremony would be complete without an inaugural speech from your good self.'

Straight-faced, as though she really meant it! You had to admire her, she was wonderful.

Needless to say the Bollix was not immune to such flattery. 'Ach well,' he says. 'I may be able to do some wee thing.'

'I do hope it,' says missus. 'I have of course read your pamphlet on William of Orange many times but have never heard it spoken aloud. Perhaps, at the fountain ceremony you would do us the great honour of reciting it for us?'

'That is one option,' says master James hastily. 'Or perhaps the Reverend could be persuaded to write something more suited to the occasion.'

Just then, missus glanced up and caught my eye, I suppose I had been stood there for some time watching them having long since finished arranging the tea things.

'Is tea ready, Bessy?' she says and when I nodded she says brightly, 'Very good then. Thank you.'

I curtseyed and left the room, pausing on the way to shoo out the cat that had crept in through the open door. As I left, they were all on their feet in a general movement towards the tea table. Missus had took the Reverends arm and was listening politely as he deliberated over what form his speech might take. While Master James, confidence restored, had assumed a magisterial pose (one foot propped upon a chair and arms akimbow) and was explaining that over 200 feet of pipe would be laid to service the fountain, information which was greeted by Flemyng with such astonishment and admiration by Jove you would have thought it an unprecedented feat of engineering.

About 5 o'clock the guests left, apparently satisfied with their tea. All in all missus had acquitted herself well, you might say better than her husband. I myself was greatly relieved. Despite a shaky start she had been gracious and charming, almost her old self. Not only had she been effortlessly diplomatic with the Old Bollix but she had more or less saved her husband from embarrassment. If she could do all that, then surely she must be well?

And yet before the week was out something happened that caused me to doubt this conclusion. It was a few nights before they were due to leave for Edinburgh. I had gone to bed at the usual time and spent a while writing my doings in my little book to show missus the next morning. But when I blew out the candle I found I was unable to sleep perhaps the thought of being parted from her for a few days was troubling me. As I lay there fidgeting like a dog with fleas I became increasingly aware of the silence in the house. I was not frightened for I knew that missus and master James were in their chambers on the floor below. But it did make me think of a few days hence at which time they would be in Edinburgh and I would be entirely alone. How silent would the house seem then?

It was as I was wondering about this and perhaps feeling a mite anxious in anticipation that I became aware of a noise on the landing. A rustling, flapping sound, followed by the faint creak of a floorboard after which there was a period of silence and then the rustling resumed – then faded. To my ears, it was as though someone was walking stealthily along the landing. At once I thought of intruders. Although there was not much to steal at Castle Haivers missus did have a little jewellery that had belonged to her mother, these trinkets she kept in a box in her room. I imagined an intruder staring down at missus as she slept and it was this thought that made me lit out of bed. In my haste I took no candle and had to feel my way down the stairs as quick as I could.

Upon reaching the landing, I noticed that the door to missus chamber was open and that a light burned in her room. I tiptoed forwards, not a breath in my body, but to my relief I seen that the room was empty. The blankets on the bed had been thrown back as though missus had lain there a while and then got up. Concluding that she must have went down to the kitchen perhaps for something to eat I stepped onto the landing and was about to return to my own room when a faint noise from overhead alerted my attention. It was the sound of a creaking board.

I glanced along the corridor towards the main attic staircase and just as I turned missus hove into view, coming down the stairs in a pool of light. At first all I could see were her velvet slippers and the hem of her nightgown as she descended. She was stepping carefully and lightly. The upper part of the staircase wall blocked her view of the landing, hence she had not yet seen me and so I ducked out of sight behind the linen press, I suppose I didn't want her to think that I was creeping about spying on her. In one hand, she held a lamp. And there was something tucked under her arm. A small, dark squarish object that I couldn't quite make out.

These things I gathered just before she stepped onto the landing. I drew back into the shadows and held my breath, thankfully she was so intent on reaching her room quietly that she only looked at the floor directly ahead of her and didn't see me. She kept the object close to her side and I only caught a glimpse of something dangling before she disappeared into her room and closed the door. Whatever it was had been tied up with a length of pale red ribbon.

What could it be this mysterious item? Something she wanted to take with her to Edinburgh perhaps? Or something that she had got out Noras box in the attic? And why had she waited until all hours of the night to go up there?

14

Missing Pages

Of course, I tellt myself that there was most likely a perfectly ordinary explanation for missus sneaking about after dark. But my worry was this. That somehow it was all connected to her recent collapse. And just when she'd seemed to be doing so well!

Next morning when I went into her chamber I glanced around me but was there any sign of a mysterious object. No. The one ½ decent hiding place in that room was the desk where she kept her *Observations* and it occurred to me that she must have stashed whatever it was in there. The key was in the lock and I was sore tempted to have a quick skelly in the drawer. But although I found ample reasons to visit the room that morning missus was always present so that put the kybosh on my plans. One time I went up with more coal she was darning by the fire and when I came in she gave me a narrow look, I thought she might have been going to say for dear sake what the Hell do you want now for I had been in and out of there since the skrakes of dawn I don't know how many times, about a hundred and forty-six.

But it wasn't that at all. As I soon found out.

'I happened to notice,' she says 'while I was up in the attic this morning, that someone has wiped that message from the window.'

'Oh?' says I. 'What were you doing up in the attic, marm?' All this as casual as I could muster, for some reason she was fibbing about *when* she had went up there.

She indicated something at the foot of her bed. A portmanteau which I had not until that moment noticed. Of course she'd need a bag to take to Edinburgh and right enough the portmanteaus were kept in the attic. So perhaps she *had* went up earlier that morning. But this article was certainly *not* what she'd been holding the previous night, not a bit of it.

'I was fetching this down,' she says. 'And I saw that the window has been wiped.'

'Yes, marm,' I admitted. 'That was me, the day you collapsed.'

She clucked her tongue. 'Oh that *is* a pity,' she says. 'I want to examine the hand.'

'The hand, marm?'

'The writing. I might have recognised the style you see.'

By Jove was I ever glad that I'd wiped that skylight! Right enough I'd disguised my own hand by using capital letters, I was not entirely stupid. But to be honest at the time I traced the message in the window I hadn't even considered Noras handwriting for I hadn't a notion how she wrote and besides who could say what a ghosts style was like and whether they'd write the same as they had done when they were alive?

Missus was looking at me expectantly.

'I am terrible sorry about that, marm,' I lied. 'I just thought I should get rid of it. Would you be wanting anything else now?'

'No thank you, Bessy. However, if you do see any more handwriting like that or any messages please be sure *not* to wipe them away and come and fetch me immediately.'

I just looked at her, flabbergasted. We were going round in circles.

'But – marm – did we not agree that there'd be no more writing, because there is no ghost? That the message was most likely left there by this girl Nora *before* she died?'

Missus blinked several times as though trying to remember something. 'Oh yes,' she says. 'Of course. I only meant that perhaps the girl might have written *other* messages in other places. Hence I meant when she was alive.'

Hence my fat aunt Fanny!

She smiled, and lifted up another stocking to peer at it but her eyes were glassy. 'I hardly think this one worth saving do you?' she says. 'It's so very full of holes. Ah well, needs must.' And with a shrug, she continued darning.

This little episode fair gave me the scutters for there could be no doubt that missus was acting a bit airy. I had no desire for her to fall ill again. And so it was that I decided to investigate her drawer once they had left for Edinburgh.

They set off the following day as planned. Master James had not yet travelled in an easterly direction on the railway line but he wanted the experience and so they were to take the train from Westerfaulds to Bathgate and from there through to Edinburgh. The ride had been ordered for 11 o'clock but Biscuit Meek arrived 10 minutes late. Hector, hell mend him, was nowhere to be seen and so I grabbed the bags and whaled them outside myself. Master James (who had been hopping about the hall like a hen on a hot griddle) rushed out behind me and leapt into the carriage with such vigour I am surprised it did not collapse around about his ears. Biscuit set the portmanteaus inside without a word and then climbed back up to his perch, though 'climb' is not quite the word. If in fact it is possible to climb and slouch at the same time, then that is what he did.

I waited on the steps for missus to emerge. The rain had stopped at last and the sun come out but everything all around was drookit. The steps, the gravel, the big bare trees, the moss, the dripping shrubbery, everything to my eyes looked slick and greasy. The sound of Biscuit gobbing away like an old geyser grated on my ears and it seemed to me that his horses were equally spiteful for they pissed and shat to beat the devil, more than was called for anyway. Tell the truth I was not in best form. I don't know why exactly. Perhaps I was worried about missus. And also, if I am honest, I was not looking forward to spending two days without her.

Master James was clearly itching to be gone for he kept peering up at the doorway and making exasperated noises and after a while when there was still no sign of missus he charged back inside the house. There was the sound of him bellowing something up the stairs, a moment or two passed then missus finally scuttled out wearing a dove grey gown under a black cloak. I could tell at once she was distressed from the agitated way she was biting her lip. She came to me and grabbed my hands. The kid leather of her gloves felt hot and dry in my fingers.

'Bessy,' she says. 'Have you seen the key that opens my desk drawer?'

'No, marm.'

I looked her right in the eye when I said it. She frowned and her gaze drifted away. 'But I can't find it anywhere,' she says, as though to herself. 'It must be lost.'

Master James barged out behind us. 'Come along! Come along!' he says making several sweeping movements with his hands as if to brush the pair of us off the stairs and I was forced to skip out the way. He grabbed missus by the arm and propelled her down to the carriage.

'Goodbye,' I says. 'Enjoy your trip, marm.'

Master James handed her inside, then sat next her and shut the door. Biscuit flicked his whip and shook the harness. The horses tottered across the gravel. I waved to missus but I don't think she could see me since her husband was in the way.

As the carriage sped down the drive, I slipped my hand into the pocket of my apron and wrapped my fingers around the cold metal shaft of the key, which article I had managed to filch while she was out at the necessary.

I watched until the carriage was out of sight then stepped back inside and shot the bolts. The house felt very different with nobody at home so it did. Too big, too cold, too dark and apart from the ticking of the grandmother clock silent as the grave. The very air itself seemed poised as though it were waiting. My footsteps echoed in the hallway and various items of furniture at which I had often flicked a rag – the clock, the hallstand, the letter table – suddenly looked unfamiliar. I realised all this might be due to my imagination since I was not used to being left alone for more than a few hours. Nonetheless I hurried back to the kitchen which at least had the benefit of greater familiarity.

Just in case they should return for some forgotten belonging, I intended to give missus and the master an hour grace before embarking upon any illicit activity. Earlier in the day I had gathered all the coalscuttles, these I now cleaned inside and out. Heavy work though that was it killt only ½ an hour but I was so black at the end of it that it took another 20 minutes to wash myself and find a clean apron. After that I hurried upstairs.

Arabella was gone from her chamber but numerous traces of her remained. A shift and two stockings discarded on the Turkey rug. The scent of roses in the air by the bed. A few strands of her hair on the bolster-cover. And on the toilet table, some drops of water from when she had washed herself that morning.

My feet made no sound as I stepped over to her desk. The key turned easy and the drawer sighed as I drew it out.

To my surprise there before me lay *The Observations* – wide open. At a page headed up with the title 'Nora Continues to Excel'. That cleg Nora again! Drat and blast her! Missus must have been reading about her. I had a good mind to turf the book out the window. But wouldn't you know it, like a tongue that returns to probe a rotten tooth I was drawn to find out more about my rival and so I cast an eye over the page.

EXTRACTED FROM *The Observations*
(SEE RESTRICTIONS AS PREVIOUS)

Work in the area of obedience testing continues apace. Indeed, it seems I have unintentionally created a pun in that 'apace' since recently I have concentrated on developing the 'Walk' experiment with Nora. Readers may remember that in the early days of her employment she would walk forwards when commanded to do so until met with an obstacle, at which point she would swivel, turn and continue walking. This action she performed unbidden from the start. Personally, I had expected her to come to a complete standstill when met with an obstacle and it was a delightful surprise to see her pause and then veer off in another direction, rather like a clockwork toy. However, this changing of path when met with an obstacle meant that her movements were always restricted to a small area – as she paced around the room we happened to be in, or the back yard, if circumstances had allowed us to work outside. In order to expand the scope of the experiment, I suggested that henceforth she should not change direction when confronted with obstacles. Instead, she should overcome them. In other words, she should go around, or over, or through, or (if necessary) under any obstruction she came across.

The effect of this was extremely interesting. On the first day I positioned her at the front of the house and told her to 'Walk', whereupon she set off across the gravel, skirted around a tree, clambered through the shrubbery and would have climbed over the wall and continued across the road had I not called out to her to desist – whereupon she jumped down and meekly returned to my side. I rewarded her good work with fulsome praise and, next day, took her to a field at the back of the house where I once again commanded her to walk. This time I had faced her in an easterly direction. Off she set across the field and when met by a fence at the far side, she scrambled over and continued on her way until I called her back. This experiment was repeated over a period of days, always with satisfactory results and each time I allowed her to venture further. Rather than having to run alongside her, I have purchased a whistle and trained her to retrace her steps when she hears me blow three times. She claims to enjoy this experiment more than any we have attempted so far, especially (she says) because she can see it pleases me very much. And she is right, it does please me, perhaps because, in essence, it is a completely pointless task – and yet she always does it for me without question or complaint.

Not once had missus shown any interest in getting *me* to walk for her, neither inside the house nor out of it. I was fit to be tied. Boys oh dear, was I raging! I grabbed *The Observations* and threw them on the floor. And there – beneath them in the drawer, atop all the maid journals – I seen another book, this one bound with a length of pale red ribbon.

I reached in and pulled it out, it was nought but a cheap accompt book just like the one missus had give me. The ribbon around it fell away with one tug. I flicked open the cover. Inside, someone had wrote in copperplate letters the name 'Nora Hughes'. The pages were full of dated entries in the same hand. It was Noras journal. So here it was, the mysterious object. The words of the blessed Saint.

Of a sudden I realised what missus had been doing in the attic. She kept all her maids journals here in the drawer, probably including this one of Noras which she must have took upstairs with her in order to compare the handwriting with that in the skylight – only to find that the message on the glass had gone.

I turned the pages and read a few entries just to see what Nora wrote like. Her spelling was fair and by gob she knew where to put a punctuation mark (something I myself aspire to but even though I have improved since those days I am still not always quite sure where all the little goat droppings should go). Her letters were neat as a bees toe yet despite these merits in presentation I failed to see how what Nora had wrote was any better than my efforts. There was no spark to the content or anything of interest. Suffice to say for the most part she just noted down what she did about the place. Sometimes she wrote about the experiments, what she had to do, how many repetitions &c. And sometimes (no doubt on instruction from the missus) she would tell about her thoughts and what went through her mind. Each entry much the same as the last. The book was about ¼ full. I read a dozen or so pages and then flicked to the end to see what her last entry said. I cannot remember the exact wording but write here an approximation.

Walked without stopping for my lady across country today, after work was done. Encountered no obstacles bar a few fences, which were climbed over. Easterly direction was kept, according to my lady's instructions. It was a beautiful day and the walk gave me a chance to think. Find that I am very reflective just now, and was lost in daydreaming until a terrible sight became visible not far from the path – a magpie tearing apart a small animal or bird that was still alive. The dreadful ear-splitting shrieks and cries of this dying creature were most tormenting. Wanted to stop the brutal killing but dared not – and of course, had to keep walking without pause if to follow my lady's instructions. Reasoned that – even if the magpie was chased away – the little animal was bound to die of its fatal injuries. Also knew that the courage to kill it is not in me. As result, never found out exactly what kind of creature it was – perhaps a mouse or newborn rabbit or fledgling bird of some sort. Eyes were averted and tears were shed until I heard my lady's whistle, then dried my eyes and turned back to Castle Haivers – a slightly longer route was taken that meant the tragic scene of death could be avoided.

My lady says that in a day or two, with God's grace and weather permitting, another walk to be undertaken, only this time I must keep heading north from the stile in our top field, a direction not taken before now. My lady has hinted that this time she might not whistle for me to return and that I am to keep walking until my conscience dictates me to stop. She did not explain but I believe she wants to know how far I will go to do her bidding. She should know by now that of course there is nothing I would not do for her and there is no distance I would not travel, even if the boots were walked off my feet.

Perhaps am in too sensitive a frame of mind these days but have decided that I hate magpies. They are the most horrible of birds, worse even than crows.

Here the last entry ended, a lot of balderdash about birds and wee beasties. But I was intrigued and irritated by the references to walking. '*Walked without stopping for my lady*' and '*Another walk to be undertaken, only this time I must keep heading north*' &c.

This walking caper. You would think it something special that only certain people was good enough to do. My heart throbbed, it was a pang of jealousy. That missus was independent of me, that I did not have control over her thoughts and feelings, that she could actually *like* another girl more than me, think her a better servant or entrust her with special experiments – all these were sources of great frustration. Most vexatious of all was that I could do nothing about it Christ the night I hated this Nora. And I hadn't even met her! I was sick to the back teeth of her perfect flipping ways. What did she have that I did not to make missus so fond of her? After all, she was nothing but a pile of rotting bones.

I was about to close the notebook and shove it back in the drawer when I noticed some thin paper shreds caught in the stitching and – upon examining the crease of the spine more closely – I realised that several pages had been removed. Not ripped out, as that would have left frayed edges and those I would have noticed straight away. But cut very close to the binding, quite deliberately and with something very sharp.

Now given the dates and what was described in the rest of the book it seemed a fair bet that what was in the missing pages was an account of Noras last days at Castle Haivers, perhaps including this walk north that she'd mentioned in her last entry. But why would she have wrote things down and then cut them out? Had she decided to hide her doings from missus? Perhaps when she went on the walk she got in a fight. Or was she being diddled by a secret sweetheart? I tell you what, I was highly delighted to have discovered something that might blacken Noras character for once. Sicken her, the mimsey mouse. Well if she could do a walk for missus, then so could I, fine rightly. Not that I'd be able to *tell* Arabella about it because that would mean revealing that I'd been snooping about the place, in her drawers and all. But I was most curious to walk in the footsteps of *MY RIVAL*!

I put wheels under myself to get through my chores and by ½ past 3 o'clock I was heading up the top field with a coat on my back and a hat on my head. The coat was one missus had give me, an old one of hers made of grey worsted. The hat I was none too happy about, I'd found it in the cloakroom, it was an old-fangled poke bonnet that a granny might have wore, it kept my lugs warm – although a few months previous I would not have placed it on my head even had you paid me *one hundred* pounds.

At the highest point of the field was a wall with a slate stile set into it, this I climbed and then stood for a moment on the top step. Behind me in a hollow lay the woods and Castle Haivers. I was about to go on when I was startled by the faint but distinct slam of a door. The granny bonnet restricted my view and so I had to turn my whole entire head in the direction of the noise, which had come from somewhere to the left of the woods where the bothies lay. I was surprised to see how close I had passed to these for I could look down on them like they were a set of dolls houses. A wisp of smoke rose from one of the little chimneys. Then a movement caught my eye and I saw a miniature Hector scuttle away from the buildings towards the trees, perhaps he was headed for the house well he was too late the scut, there was nobody home, he should have been there in the morning to help with the flipping bags so he should. I considered whistling and giving him a wave but then remembered my daft bonnet and changed my mind, I'd never hear the end of it.

Stretched out before me was another field of grass, sloping downhill. Beyond this, the land levelled out though the distant horizon was invisible because of mist. I jumped down and carried on walking. Behind me, Castle Haivers disappeared below the brow of the hill. On I went, keeping to the hedgerows until I came to a narrow dirt road where the pasture seemed to end. Straight ahead lay an area of scrubland, blotted here and there with great heaps of coal. The track I'd been following continued across this expanse and so I pressed on, for I knew that if I kept heading away from the Great Road I would stay roughly northward bound.

This was now a bleak, scarred landscape that I walked through. Against the wintry sky a few bare trees showed black and scrawny, bent from the prevailing wind. To my mind they looked like giants lifting their arms and fleeing in shock from some great terror. Not a bird sang in that place and nothing of beauty grew, it was all rusty bracken, moss and weeds. The air grew colder as the light began to fade. Mist rolled along the ground like smoke and a scent of burning hung on the air. I gave up trying to keep my skirts clean for in places the path was only muck and glour. My face was numb with cold and my eyes watered.

But for flipsake. It was only walking! *Anybody* could walk. And I was fairly sure that I was doing it just as well as old Miss Perfect. And under worse circumstances what was more! For had she not been doing it in summer whereas now it was cold enough to freeze your fartleberries. I found myself wondering whether she had indeed trod this same path or crossed this burn or stared at that tall works chimney visible to the north-east, the black smoke rising from it to mingle with the mist and clouds. What was on her mind as she trotted along with her neb stuck in the air? I doubt she would have liked getting her skirts dirty. Probably she was plotting how to worm herself further into Arabellas ear, the cleg. And she was that Holy it wouldn't have surprised me if she'd tripped along saying her prayers. As for whether something had happened on the walk that she might have wanted to keep secret, well as for that I was mystified for there was nought about here to speak of. Nowhere to get drunk or in a fight. And certainly this was no lovers lane, not at all the kind of place you would go to join giblets with somebody.

So lost was I in my own thoughts about Nora that I failed to notice the ground directly before me, which dipped away sharp of a sudden. I stepped into mid-air and lost my footing then tumbled down a slope. I only just managed to stop myself from slithering further by grabbing handfuls of coarse grass.

Stunned I was and lay there stock still for a moment to catch my breath. My ankle throbbed, but I was not hurt bad. In the process of saving myself, I had twisted round to face the way I'd come. My first thought was I had fell into some kind of sunk fence for at the moment of tripping I had glimpsed another grassy slope opposite and I'd heard tell of these hazards and the folk that stepped into them by accident to the great amusement of their companions. But then I turned my head and seen that I was wrong. For at the base of the hollow or cutting formed by the two slopes (and stretching out to either side where they disappeared eventually into the mist) were wooden sleepers and gleaming metal rails.

I was on the point of getting up when I became aware of a faint whispering close at hand. The air seemed to shimmer as the whisper increased to a roar and then all at once there was a shriek as a great black train hurtled out the mist and passed before me in a Pandemonium of fire and steam and smoke, with a wail and the clang of a bell and the many lit windows flashing by so near that Jesus Murphy you could have reached out and touched them.

I had to run most of the way back to beat the dark. All the way I was thinking about Nora and the railway line. Right enough I couldn't help but wonder about Janet Murray and all those hints she'd dropped that night when I'd been at The Gushet, about missus being involved in Noras death. But I was trying not to jump to conclusions. Certainly it was not *impossible* that Nora had been hit by a train whilst out walking for missus. But surely it was unlikely. *The Observations* did go on about how loyal and obedient Nora was, all this. But I doubted that her obedience included stepping into the path of a moving train just because missus told her to keep walking without stopping, that was not so much dutiful as plain daft. Of course it might have been an accident, after all had I not near tripped onto the line myself. But she'd have had to fall down at the exact moment a train was passing. Either that or banged her head and been knocked out cold. Otherwise she could just have picked herself up and gone on her way.

Or had Janet been implying something worse? The most dreadful thing I could think of was that missus had followed Nora to this desolate place and then pushed her under a train. But that was just ridiculous. Missus held Nora in great esteem. (Why, I don't know. But she did.) It just was not possible that she could have done her harm.

Besides which. Catch yourself on! I didn't even know if this was the right line. Sure were there not railway tracks all over the countryside that Nora might have stumbled onto by accident, all by herself. Matter of fact master James had a map on the study wall upon which, if I recollected right, the position of all the local railways was indicated.

Don't get me wrong. I wasn't too worried about missus being to blame, not a bit of it. But I just thought that I might take a look at that map, if only to prove Janet wrong.

When I got back the house was cold as the grave. I headed straight for the study where I lit several candles and their light cheered me a little. Then with lamp in hand I peered at the maps on the wall. Most were of the Empire but I soon found the one that depicted the local area. It was smaller than the rest and framed in dark varnished wood. I lifted it off the hook and set it on the desk amongst the candles. Then I leaned over it to take a look.

There was Snatter at the crossroads, a cluster of buildings straggling along either side of the Great Road. I found Castle Haivers nearby marked next a group of tiny fir trees. On the far side of the wood, the bothies were shown as four little squares. To the west, Flemyngs farm, the Thrash Burn itself and its tributaries spreading out across the map like thread veins. And there sure enough was a railway, a black and white line that curved across the country towards Bathgate. But a little further to the east another similar line swep up and entered the same town. And to the south and west there were yet more lines, thinner than these two, but with rails marked across them, I reckoned they must have been branch lines that served coalpits or works of some sort.

There you go. Railways all over the place so there were and Nora could have met her fate on any one of them. I have to admit to being a little relieved. I was just about to lift the map and put it back on the wall when something made me glance up. Perhaps I had sensed or heard movement outside, I don't know. But there at the study window, though horribly distorted by condensation and darkness, was the unmistakable shape of a face, close to the glass and staring straight in at me.

All this happened in seconds. I do believe I screamed and jumped to my feet, in the process knocking over a candle, which was instantly snuffed out. My first impulse was to hide from view. How I negotiated the desk I can't remember, I may well have vaulted it since I all but fell from the room. Once I was stood in the hall I felt a little more safe because out there the only window glass was etched and impossible to see through. In the darkness, I fumbled my way to the front door. Both bolts were still fastened and I knew the kitchen door was also secure for I was after bolting it behind me when I came in. I retreated a few paces and stood there, trembling and panting, every fibre of my being alert.

At first I could hear nothing. The lamp in the study spilled a faint glimmer into the hallway and as my eyes adjusted to the gloom I peered around for a potential weapon but all I could make out was an old gamp in the umbrella stand. Then I remembered Noras knife in my pocket. I had been carrying it around with me ever since I'd found it in her box.

I took it out, unfolded the blade and extended it in front of me, my ears, eyes and mind alike strained by dread. After a moment, I detected the crunch of gravel, someone was approaching from around the side of the house. They reached the portico and climbed the steps. Then silence fell. I waited for something to happen, for the handle to turn or for hammering blows to ring out. Instead, a pair of glinting eyes appeared in the postage slit. Someone was staring directly at me! I shrank back into the shadows. And then the intruder spoke my name.

'Bessy? Fwhere are you? Bessy! Hit's me.'

Jesus Murphy, Hector! I could have knocked the bark off him. Given how alarmed I was you will forgive me that I neglected my manners and discharged in the direction of the posting slit an explosion of oaths like so much cannon fire, I'll skip the worst and come to my closing remarks. 'You scut what the flip are you doing staring in at the flipping windows!'

'Now chust a minute!' says Hector from the other side of the door, he sounded most offended. 'I fwhas not staring hin, not a tall, not a tall.'

I tellt him I doubted his word and mentioned an impolite act in which I suggested he'd been engaged whilst looking through the window. Hector protested this allegation most hotly. Something about the careful way he pronounced his words made me realise that he was in his altitudes. I invited him to depart without delay.

'Listen now,' he says. 'I seen the light on hin the rhoom and I looked in – I did – but I swear I was chust habout to tap on the glass fwhen you saw me and then you chumped up and started screaming like a lunatic. I honly came to see hif you fwhanted to come and haf a dance with me? Fwhee are haffing a ceilidh.'

Shaken though I was I had little desire to present myself at the bothies with Hector for I could not bear the thought that Muriel and the rest would think he and I were courting or anything like it and I suspected that Hector would do all he could to convey that very impression, false though it was.

'Hy am a ferry good dancer,' he says and as further enticement he averted his face from the door and belched.

'That's kind of you for inviting me,' I says. 'But no thank you.'

'Ach, go on! Don't fwhorry. None of us fwhill feel you up or nothing.'

I tellt him he was a smooth talker and that he knew how to tempt a girl but that I was too tired for dancing. Then I crouched down beside the posting slit.

'Listen d'you remember a girl used to work here, Nora was her name?'

His face appeared in the slot, the drink had filled him up it was brimming out his eyes, they were silvered like mercury. The fumes would have knocked you down.

He says, in a low voice, 'Fwhill you be fwhanting me to come in for company?'

'No!' I says. That put his wick at a peep. Without reply, he stood up abruptly and stumbled away down the steps. I peered out after him. 'Wait!' I shouted and he turned round, swaying. 'Which line was it Nora died on?' I asked him.

He pointed vaguely over the roof of the house. 'The fwun hup there.'

'Past the top field?'

'That's de fwun,' he says.

'Oh,' I says, deflated. 'Well – was she deaf or blind or something?'

'Fwhat?' he says. 'No! There fwas nothing wrong fwith her.'

'So what happened to her then?'

Hector shrugged. 'She used to be doing your chob. Then one night she fwalked in front hof a train.' He paused, then – 'Fwhoosh!' he went, smashing his hands thegether and rubbing them against each other until Nora was just smithereens that he shook from his fingertips. 'Now, hif you fwhill forgif me I haf lost good drinking time.' He made a low bow. 'Farewell Scary-bunnet,' he says.

Then he staggered away across the gravel and was gone.

I got to my feet and wandered across the hall in a dwam. Well then fair enough she *had* died on that line. But that didn't mean to say it was the fault of missus for having sent her on a walk. The stupid girl could have stepped in front of a train at any time. In fact, hadn't Hector said it happened 'one night'? And now I thought about it, according to missus had it not happened after a hooley? If that was the case (which surely it was since missus was no liar) then it certainly followed that Nora was not engaged in any experiment at the time of her death and that missus had nought to do with it.

Besides. It suddenly occurred to me (of course!) that Nora must have returned from the walk experiment alive – otherwise how would she have wrote in her journal and then later cut out the pages?

It did cross my mind that perhaps it wasn't Nora herself had done so but I dismissed this notion almost as soon as I'd thought of it for as far as I could see there was no earthly reason why anyone else would deface her journal.

But what was it Nora had wrote that she wanted to hide? I would have loved to find that out so I would, especially if it showed her in a bad light.

I wandered awhile from room to room and then went upstairs, wishing that the shadows thrown by my lamp did not jerk and shudder so. It was like an icehouse in missus chamber because after airing the room I had forgot to close the window. I pulled it shut then noticed that the *The Observations* still lay on the floor where I had thrown them.

A thought occurred. And the thought was this. That I hadn't checked on what missus had wrote about *me* of late. I opened the book just to take a peek and was sore disappointed to see that she had added not a single word about me since her husbands return. The entries ended with her remarks about withdrawing her affections, as had upset me before. I flicked through the rest and found nothing but blank pages. That is, until the very last leaf where the following phrases appeared scrawled in large and jagged letters.

IT IS HER
I KNOW IT IS HER
SHE HAS COME BACK
MAY GOD FORGIVE ME FOR WHAT I HAVE DONE

At first glance I just about died, it looked as though the words were wrote in blood. But on closer inspection I came to the conclusion that missus had used a brown ink instead of her usual violet (at least I hoped that was the case). Even so, the hairs at the back of my neck were up on their hind legs. Jesus Murphy! It seemed certain that missus had wrote this about Nora at some point (though when exactly she had done so was impossible to tell).

Here she was again, begging forgiveness. The more I thought about it the more it seemed likely that she was under the same misapprehension that had (briefly) bothered me, in other words she thought that Nora had died whilst carrying out her instructions. Would that not explain why she blamed herself and felt so guilty? And why in the graveyard she'd sounded as though she were trying to convince herself (as well as me) that Noras death was an accident?

If only I could persuade her otherwise. Poor dear missus! She was such an angel.

I shoved the book back in the desk just the way I had found it, open at the page about Nora. Of a sudden I realised I was banjaxed. It would do no harm, I thought, just to have a little lie down on the bed. I whipped off the coat and bonnet and laid them on a chair. Then I slid off my boots and climbed between the sheets. It was not done out of disrespect, I just wanted to warm up a little and to rest. The lamp was shining in my eyes and so I extinguished the flame.

I only meant to lie there for a minute before going to my own room but I must have fell asleep for next thing I knew it was some time later and I was waking up (or at least I *thought* I was waking up), convinced that somebody was standing over me. My head was filled with a strange buzzing sensation and my teeth felt like they were vibrating in my skull. I had not yet opened my eyes, nonetheless I knew that somebody was there, standing right beside the bed. And even without looking I knew that the person was my mother. I could picture her, she was stood there with a lantern in her hand, glaring down at me with a great leer on her face and I knew that she had come to get me and kill me.

And then all at once it came to me – of course, it was only a dream! What a relief! In order to make my mother go away all I had to do was to wake myself up and look directly at her and then she would disappear.

And so that is what I did (at least, that is what I *thought* I did). I convinced myself that I woke up and turned to face her. But when I opened my eyes, standing over me was not my mother at all but a girl, a girl I had never seen before, and yet I knew her instantly to be Nora. She was dressed in nightclothes, her hair loose about her shoulders. It was *she* that held the lantern, and *she* that leered straight down at me. I got such a fright I am surprised my heart did not leap out my chest. The most striking thing about her was her eyes, her wild staring eyes. She was insane, you could tell by just looking at her. And although I believed myself to be awake, *I could not make her disappear*. I stared at her and kept on staring but she just glared back at me with this dreadful look on her face. I was convinced that she wanted to murder me and that if what she held in her hand had been a knife instead of a lantern she would have plunged it straight into my heart.

Fear pinned me to the mattress. I don't know how long I lay there in a cold sweat. Perhaps it was minutes, perhaps only seconds. What I do know is that, eventually, after what seemed like the course of ages, I was able to move my hand and drag the bedclothes up over my head. Nora did not seem to notice she simply kept staring down at me as before. I managed to pull the covers all the way over my head without attracting her attention. Strange to say, but this felt like it would protect me from the Spectre at the bedside. For I quite believed she was a Spectre. She was there and not there. She saw me and yet she didn't see me. She and I were in the same place and yet I had the sense that somehow we were separated by time. I was there now, but she was there in the past.

And if that was the case who was it she thought was lying beneath her in the bed? Was it me she was looking at with that murderous intent on her phiz? Or was it missus?

PART FOUR

15

An Apparition

Eventually it felt like I fell into a stupor and I awoke some time later only to realise that it was morning. With great trepidation I poked my head out from beneath the covers. The room was empty. I slid out the bed and got down on my knees to examine the spot where Nora had stood. Not a mark not a speck, just the fibres of the rug smooth and undisturbed almost as though they had never been walked upon. Nothing to suggest that anyone had been there though as far as I knew ghosts left no trace. But was it a ghost or was it a dream? I hadn't a baldy.

As the day proceeded and I went about my work, I tried to forget about what had happened but the house felt desperate spooky to me and so in the afternoon I went outside to clear up the vegetable garden. As I worked, pulling weeds and raking leaves, I kept on picturing Nora, looming over the missus bed. To kill her? But why would she want revenge on missus? What had missus done to her? Once again the railway line came to mind. I imagined missus, sneaking up behind Nora, her hands outstretched, ready to push – but no. It was all daft. I did not, could not believe that missus would harm Nora. About 3 o'clock I decided to go in for a cup of tea to warm me up. Due to lack of sleep I was in a bit of a dwam so I was, barely aware of putting one foot in front of the other. I could have passed bodily through the back door for all the notice I took of it as I lifted the latch and stepped inside. It was only when I entered the kitchen itself that I was brought sharply to my senses by the unexpected sight of a figure in the room.

A woman in a dark cloak rushing towards me. Jesus Murphy my heart all but stopped. But it was only missus. Missus! Back a day early. She grabbed my hand, apparently too excited to notice my shock at seeing her. Her eyes were shining.

'Come and see!' she says, and began to drag me towards the table.

I tried to remember whether I had locked the drawer of her desk and put everything back in place. Was her bed made? And what had I done with the blasted key? And why were they back early? Meanwhile missus had opened a box that sat on the table and took out a number of cards in shades of black and grey.

'Look Bessy look!' she says. 'What do you think?'

She laid out several likenesses of her and master James. One photograph showed them stood in front of a rustic backcloth of trees with a potted fern at their feet, which gave the impression that they had paused for a moment in a woodland glade. Master James rested his elbow on a fence and stared into the distance while missus, in a strange and unnatural pose, had placed both hands on his shoulder as though she needed to lean on him for support. There was a small dog in the foreground propped up on his back legs all frisky like he was leaping. But if you looked closely you could see that the poor bucker was stuffed and mounted on a pole. On another card master James sat in a chair with his hat on, one big boot outstretched, a great long whip dangling between his legs. Then there was a picture of missus stood alone at a table, which bore a vase of flowers. She held a straw bonnet in her hand and it was all so artfully done you could have sworn that it was summer and that she had just wandered in from the garden.

In the remaining portraits the couple had been dressed in extravagant costumes. Here was master James for instance in pirate togs with a cocked hat on his head and a sabre in his hand. Here was missus hardly recognisable as a dark-skinned princess of the Orient, draped in a robe with a sash at her waist and a pitcher balanced on her hip. And in the final portrait the couple appeared together. Master James looked very regal, stood behind a draped lectern his robes trimmed with fur and hung with golden chains. And missus was crouched at his feet dressed up as an old-fashioned maid in apron and mob cap, her sleeves rolled up and her head bowed as she offered a goblet of wine to her master.

I believe it was this last photograph that most caught my attention, perhaps because it was strange to see missus all tricked out in maids duds and acting the servant.

'We went to Henderson, on Princes Street,' missus was saying. 'He has done them well, has he not? Have you ever had your likeness taken, Bessy?'

'No, marm,' says I. (Not strictly true, I had been took once or twice in what might be called 'classical' poses at least that's what the man said they were.)

'Next time I go to Edinburgh,' says missus, 'you must come with me and we shall go back to this shop. I should like him to take you in your working clothes. That would make a lovely portrait.'

She continued to arrange the pictures on the table, pointing out details here and there to bring them to my attention. Apparently she'd had to rub a yellow paste on her face in order to look dark for the Oriental portrait. The goblet was not real but made of painted card. And although the fur-trimmed robes looked impressive they had stunk of camphor.

While she prattled on I caught up with my own thoughts. I was fairly sure that I had put *The Observations* and Noras journal back in her desk but could I remember if the key was in the lock, no I could not. I did not really want to pretend I had found it in her absence for she might worry that I had looked in the drawer and by flip I didn't want that.

'If you'll excuse me, marm,' I says, anxious to get up to her room before she did. 'I'll take your bags upstairs.'

I hurried out to the hall, expecting to find two portmanteaus however there was only one, the one that missus had taken. I glanced into the study but found it to be empty. The rest of the house was that silent you could have heard a spider fart. I went back to the kitchen. Missus was still at the table, admiring the likenesses. I stared at her for a moment.

Then I says, 'Did master James take his own bag up, marm?'

'Hmm?' she says. 'Oh no, I came back alone.'

She was bent over the photographs. I couldn't see her face.

'Why, marm? What happened?'

'Nothing *happened*,' she says. 'Why need something have happened? I just came back early.' She looked up and when she seen me, she laughed. 'Oh Bessy,' she says. 'I'd had quite enough of the town, thank you, once that dreadful dinner was done. And James didn't really need me any more.'

She gazed at me evenly. I wasn't sure whether I believed her or not. But before I had a chance to say anything further she says, 'Tell me, Bessy – what has been going on here in my absence?'

First Nora and then my mother appeared in my minds eye. I blinked them away. Then I thought of the tumble I had took down the bank, the speeding train rushing past, inches from my face.

I says, 'It's been very quiet, marm.'

'I see,' says missus. Perhaps it was her tone of voice or the way she looked at me I don't know but I was convinced she knew I was not telling the truth. She says, 'And you were not frightened to be here at night, all alone?'

'No marm.'

'Did you *see* anyone?'

'No marm,' I says. 'And please please *please* don't you be worrying yourself. Like we said before, there is no ghost here and there never ever was a one!'

Missus peered at me strangely and then she gave a little laugh. 'I only meant did you see Hector or any of the other farm servants.'

'Oh,' I says. 'Begging your pardon, marm. No, I – I did not. Well, I seen Hector for a minute but that was all.'

And then I hared off to take her bag upstairs.

The little brass key was in her desk and the drawer was locked. I pulled out the key and flung it under the bed, just in time too, for at that moment missus came bustling in and began to unpack. I stood beside her for a moment, making a point of frowning down at the floor this way and that and clucking like billy-o.

'Isn't it fearful dusty in here, marm?' I says.

Then I ran downstairs and returned with a broom. I began to sweep the floor. Moments later – quite by chance! – I discovered the key to her desk under the bed.

'Would you look at this, marm?!' I says, holding it up, astonished. 'Here's that key you lost! You must have kicked it under here by mistake.'

I was gratified to see her pounce on the key and stash it in her pocket. How pleased she looked as she turned away! Now she could open her drawer and write up her notes or *Observations* if she so desired. I hoped she *would* do it for I knew it made her happy.

That evening we took our meal together in the kitchen like the old days. While we ate she tellt me more about the trip to Edinburgh, the hotel with its stink of gas in the room, a visit to see a Fairy Fountain powered by Electricity and the stuffy dinner she'd had to sit through watching her husband lick the hairy ringpiece of Duncan Pollock MP, (except she put it more politely).

At one point, she took my hand and squeezed it. 'Dear Bessy,' she says. 'I know I haven't had as much time for you of late but all that will change. James should be going to Glasgow once this fountain is installed, perhaps for a fortnight. This time last year, he was gone for a whole month! So we will soon have plenty of time together.'

'Yes marm.'

'And I want to be more honest with you from now on,' she says. 'You see, there's something I haven't told you. It's a secret, Bessy. Nobody knows about it. But it was wrong of me to keep it from you.'

Funny what goes through our minds at times like these. Mine had went a little blank. I was looking at her skin and noticing how flawless it was. And that even her hair grew out her temples in what seemed a perfect way. How could anyone so lovely do anything wrong?

Missus stood up and took a few steps across the kitchen. After a moment of hesitation, she spoke.

'I am writing a book,' she says. 'A book about servants. Not a novel but a theoretical book about loyalty and obedience and so on. I am sure you must have guessed at something of the sort, because of certain things I may have asked you to do in the past.'

Here she paused as though expecting me to comment. But I couldn't think what to say so I just nodded. She went on.

'Now, this book is a secret. Not even my husband knows about it. If he knew I was writing this book – any book, in fact – he might tease me and then that would spoil it. I can't explain it any better than that. So he doesn't know about it. And I have taken a great risk in telling you because now you know something that you could use against me, if you chose to do so.'

Here, she paused again and gave me a searching look.

I says, 'Is that all, marm?'

'What do you mean?'

'Is that the only secret? That you're writing a book.'

She gave a little laugh. 'Why – yes. Is that not enough?'

'No marm. I mean yes marm. I just thought you might be going to tell me about some other secret thing, is all.'

In fact, I didn't really know what I meant. I was just wittering on like a great lilty.

Missus came and sat down beside me again. 'Isn't this lovely, Bessy?' she says. 'The two of us back together again, with the prospect of more time alone. I cannot tell you how much I've looked forward to it.'

What she said sounded happy. But there was a great sadness behind her eyes. Oh how I longed to blurt out everything I knew. To tell her that I had read her *Observations.* And that I'd done the very same walk that she'd sent Nora on. And that she was just wrong to go blaming herself for the stupid girls death. But, of course, I couldn't tell her any of that because I was feart to let her know that I'd been sniffing around amongst her things. Twice now I'd done it, wicked girl that I was. It would have to stop. I made a vow to myself. No more snooping. And I resolved to write an especially long entry in my little book (mostly made up, of course) in the hope that it might give her pleasure.

That night like the day that preceded it was cold and clear. My brain was buzzing with thoughts but I must have dropped off eventually because at some point I awoke and saw outside my window a brilliant sliver of moon suspended beneath a diamond star, both of them lit as though from within, pinned against the sky so they were, like earrings on dark velvet. Their combined light was so bright that at first I thought it had roused me – but then the silence was broke by a shrill guttural scream, a strange and wordless cry of terror that shook the house.

I sat bolt upright. The scream seemed to have come from the direction of missus room. It died away but I believe there must have been another just before it, because the sound was familiar, like an echo of something. Just as worrying was the stillness that followed in its wake. I sat there paralysed for a moment, my heart hammering raw in my chest. Then I leapt up and without pausing to dress or put anything on my feet I lashed downstairs to see was missus all right.

I had just reached the landing when her chamber door flew open and she came hurpling out towards me in her nightdress. Her hair was loose and in disarray, it seemed to stand upright around her face which was white and pinched. She fell upon me and pointed towards her room, her eyes wide with fear. She was shaking that hard she could not speak.

'What is it?' I whispered. 'What's the matter?'

'Shhh! – Shhhu! – Shhhu!' went missus at first I thought she was hushing me but then as she went on I realised she was only trying to say something.

'Shhu! – She! – She's there! She's there!'

I felt my oxters prickle and remembered the figure from a few nights before, hovered over the bed with that dreadful look on its face. Could missus have had the same dream as me? Or was it indeed an apparition? This time there was no doubt in my mind that I was wide awake. This time, I would be able to know for certain what it really was.

Missus clutched at my nightdress but despite her attempts to drag me back, I prised myself free and dashed across the threshold of her room.

Inside, I had expected to find all in darkness but was surprised to see a candle burning by the bed and the curtains drawn back to admit the moonlight. I looked at once to the place where Nora had 'appeared' to me, but saw nothing. And a glance around the rest of the chamber proved fruitless. There was nobody there.

Missus had crept in behind me and now she stood near the doorway, still trembling, as I took up the candle and searched behind the curtains and then in the press and under the bed. Nothing, nothing, nobody. I stood up.

'There's no-one here, marm,' I says. 'Nothing to worry about.'

Her eyes were wide and glassy. 'Are you sure, Bessy?'

'You were only dreaming, marm.'

She took a deep breath and then let it out again. 'Oh but you see,' she says. 'I wasn't asleep.'

I had just glanced away to set down the candle but on hearing *that* I turned back to look at her. She took a few steps and sat upon the bed. A book lay on the counterpane. She picked it up and showed it to me.

'I was reading,' she says. 'The moon was so bright, even though it's on the wane – did you notice? – and I had drawn back the curtains for more light. I couldn't sleep, you see. I must have read for an hour or so. And then all at once, as I turned a page, I became convinced that someone was watching me. I had this overwhelming sense of being under observation. It was not a pleasant feeling. Quite oppressive, in fact. I glanced up –'

Here, she looked towards the corner of the room, to a spot near the press. I followed her gaze. There was nothing there, just as before. Even so, I shivered.

'I glanced up – and there she was!'

Missus froze in her attitude of looking across the room, as though she still saw what had been there before. In the moonlight, her face seemed made up of nothing but shade and hollows. Staring eyes, open mouth, the dark holes of her nostrils, her sunken cheeks.

'Who, marm?' I says. 'Who was it?'

She turned towards me. 'Now don't be cross, Bessy,' she says, 'but I saw her as plain as you are standing there. It was Nora Hughes. Just as she was in life.'

The room seemed to tilt. There was an old tapestry stool beside me and I lowered myself onto it. Missus began to smooth down her hair, all the while gazing at me. After a moment, I was able to speak. I tried to make my voice light and undisturbed.

'Well, I am sure it was only a dream, marm,' I says. 'But what – what did she do?'

'Nothing at first,' says missus. 'She just stood there, looking at me.'

'Was she angry?'

'No – not angry. She looked rather sad than angry. Dreadfully sad.'

'Her lantern. Did she have it raised thus?' And I lifted my arm in the same threatening attitude Nora had adopted the night before.

Missus frowned. 'Lantern?' she says. 'She had no lantern.'

This flummoxed me since I had expected her dream to be the same in every detail as my own.

'Are you sure?'

'Quite certain,' she says. 'Because she did this.' Missus stopped smoothing her hair and reached out towards me in a beseeching gesture. She held the pose for a few seconds, then dropped it. 'And her hands were empty, do you see? I remember that most clearly.'

Every detail at odds with what I expected.

'Well – was she in night clothes?' I says, at last.

'No. She wore a print frock, in plaid. I believe it was the one that she may have been wearing – when she died.'

The candle guttered. Missus turned and stared into the flame.

'Did she approach the bed at any point?' I says.

Missus shook her head. 'No, she simply made that one gesture. And then – I think I may have covered my face with my hands for when I looked again, she had gone.'

'Is that when you screamed?'

'Did I scream?' Missus moved her hand to her throat. The fingers were trembling. 'I know I was frightened but I thought I'd been struck dumb. I had this suffocating feeling, do you see? I couldn't breathe. You saw me, on the landing. I couldn't speak.'

'But I heard a scream. It near took the roof off. Why d'you think I came running?'

'I don't know,' says missus. 'Perhaps it was *Nora* who screamed, do you think? Perhaps *she* wanted you to come.' She smiled at me. Her eyes glittered. It was a look that I recognised, a hint of the old fevered distraction.

'I think it was *you* that screamed, marm, but you just didn't know it, because you were fast asleep. You cried out while dreaming.'

Missus stood up abruptly. She glared at me. 'But I just told you, I was awake!'

'Marm,' I says, getting to my feet. 'Look around you. There is nobody here. There *was* nobody here. You *must* have been dreaming. We've all had dreams like that, at one time or another. I had one myself, just the other night.'

Missus had begun to pace the floor, in great agitation, but now she span around to face me. 'You did? What happened?'

'Nothing, marm. I was dreaming is all. Just like you were. You must have fell asleep while you were reading.'

'No,' she insisted. 'I was wide awake.'

It was hopeless, there was no reasoning with her. I felt the energy drain from me.

'Listen here to me,' I says. 'Our minds are filled with this nonsense about a ghost. And that's all it is, marm. Nonsense. We are imagining things because –' I bit my lip and held my breath, but found that there was nothing would stop the next words coming out.

They tumbled from me, one after the other, like so many buttons spilled from an overturned jar. 'It was *me*, marm, all the time. It wasn't a ghost. It was me made the noises in the attic and me that put gloves on your bed and *I* polished your shoes and all the other things that happened. Even the writing in the window. *I* did that. It was *me*. I stood up on tippy-toe to write it. D'you hear me? There never was a ghost. And so you didn't see one tonight.'

Once I had started, it was easy. And as the words came out relief flooded in to take their place. Missus seemed paralysed, she stood on the spot staring at me her mouth ½ open her arms at her sides. Only her fingers moved, softly clenching and unclenching like a sea creature I had once seen in a rock pool.

'You must believe me,' I says. 'I don't know why I did it, marm. It was just I thought you didn't like me any more and I – I wanted your attention. And you see, I must have done it well because I even scared myself. But there is no ghost marm. *I* am the ghost. And you can dismiss me now, if you wish. Only don't hold it against me. I would not hurt you for all the world and I'll never forgive myself for what I done. But it has to end here.'

Very slowly, missus reached up and took hold of her own nose as though she was about to plunge into water. She remained like that a moment. Thinking, frowning, her eyes still watching me darkly. Judging me. Hard to tell what was going through her mind. And then all at once she let go her nose and laughed out loud.

'I see what you are up to,' she says. 'I *almost* believed you there, just for a moment. You are a very sweet and clever girl, but I am afraid your little subterfuge – inventive though it is – doesn't work.'

'Marm, I –'

She held up a hand to silence me. 'Bessy, I know what I saw. She was there! Standing over there, as plain as I see you now. I *wasn't* asleep. You say you did all these things, the writing in the window and the gloves and so on. But are you going to tell me that you dug Nora up and dressed in her clothes and crept down here and appeared to me?'

'No, marm, of course I –'

'Of course not. Because you *didn't*. It wasn't you. It was Nora herself. And it always *has been* Nora.'

She was looking at me in a fond indulgent way, I had an urge to skelp her.

'Of course,' she says. 'I appreciate that you don't want me to be alarmed, Bessy. But you don't have to make up stories. I am not alarmed any more.'

'You're – you're not?'

'No,' she says. 'I've been thinking. There's no need to worry. It was that look on her face, do you see? I've realised now what I should have seen all along. She means us no harm. Of course not – she's Nora. She wouldn't hurt a fly. Come here, Bessy, look.'

She turned me so that we were both reflected in the looking glass. I seen missus, her smooth hair, the calm solid curves of her cheek and jaw, she seemed righteous and completely at ease. And then I noticed my own countenance, the colour drained from it the lips drawn back the eyes glaring and alert the hair in disarray.

'Do you see?' missus says. '*You* are the one that is disturbed, Bessy.'

Indeed, she was not mistaken. I looked absolutely horrified.

And then I gasped – for in the glass I had glimpsed a dark cloaked figure looming in the doorway. Missus dropped my hand and whirled round.

'What are you doing!' she snapped. 'Creeping about like a house-burglar! You gave us a fright.'

Master James (for it was he) pulled down the scarf that covered the lower part of his face. He gazed at us crossly and then glanced around the room, as though he expected to see somebody else lurking there. Upon finding that we were the sole occupants, he seemed to relax a little. When he spoke, he never once took his eyes off missus, even while he was addressing me.

'There was no cab and I was obliged to walk from the station,' he says. 'I approached the house on foot and came upstairs as silently as

I could in an attempt not to disturb you. I see now that my precautions were unnecessary. You were already awake. But I wonder what the two of you can be doing, burning candles at this time of night. Bessy, you are not in your own room. No doubt you have an explanation.'

'Yes sir,' I says, desperate to think of one that would protect missus, but all I could come up with was, 'I had a bad dream, sir.' And as soon as the words left my mouth, I knew they were a mistake.

'I see. A bad dream. And this dream caused you to get out of bed and walk down the stairs in your sleep and to waken your mistress. A strange sort of dream, I must say.'

'No sir,' I says. 'What happened was I was frightened and came down to check that all was well with missus. That's all.'

'An interesting story,' he says. 'No doubt you would corroborate it Arabella.'

All this while, he had not took his eyes off her and she had returned his gaze steadily. Now, she smiled.

'I am afraid I cannot,' she says. 'You see, Bessy is very sweetly attempting to prevent us from worrying. However the truth is James that there has been someone in my room this night.'

Master James breathed in sharply. 'Someone,' he says. His gaze flicked around the room. Then he turned back to missus. 'Be so good as to tell me what you mean, my dear.'

Missus spread her hands. 'I am not an expert,' she says. 'All I can say is that Nora was here tonight.'

'Nora,' repeated master James, slowly. Perhaps he couldn't remember who she was. This must have been how missus interpreted his response for she looked cross.

'The maid,' she told him. 'As was. Before Morag.'

'I am perfectly aware who you *mean*,' says master James. 'I am simply digesting the information.'

'It was definitely her,' missus continued. 'I looked up from my book and there she was, over there.' She pointed to the spot. 'I watched her for a moment. She made a pleading gesture, thus, and then she disappeared. I think she has come back, James. She does not rest easy and she has come back.' She clasped her hands and calmly awaited his response.

Master James nodded. 'Remarkable,' he says. 'Truly astonishing. And I do wish to hear all about it. But perhaps it can wait until morning. The hour is late and I am footsore and weary. Arabella, my dear, you must get some rest.' He flicked a glance in my direction. 'Bessy, you may go.'

You may go. Would to God I had a pound for every time somebody told me that, I could have put my mother on a flipping boat to Australia.

But I had to do as I was tellt. Reluctant though I was to leave missus, she was dutifully getting between the sheets and snuffing out her candle and so I had no choice but to leave the room. I hoped she would be all right. Poor love! I hated to think of her laying there all night alone, in case she took fright again. I would have walked a hundred mile on hot coals just to be able to watch over her.

16

I Get a Fright

Master James must have been up at the scrake of dawn so he must. When I took morning water to missus he was already there in her room, talking to her in a low voice. I tapped at the door and called out as usual, 'Good morning, marm!' but when I tried to go in he intercepted me by leaping to the threshold, bad cess on him. I was dreading this moment for I knew he was most likely furious about all this ghost business.

'Good morning, Bessy,' he says, that chilly it would have took your nose off.

He prised the water jug from my fingers and set it on the floor, then he fished a letter from his waistcoat pocket and pressed it into my hand.

'I need you to run down to Snatter,' he says. 'And deliver this.'

My blood went cold when I seen the addressee was MacGregor-Robertson. I tried to see beyond him into the room. 'The doctor, sir? Is missus all right?'

'Och yes,' he says. 'I simply feel that he should have a quick look at her. One can't be too careful. Our trip to Edinburgh may have been over-taxing.'

'Really sir?' I says. 'What's the matter with her? What happened in the night?'

'Nothing *happened*, Bessy,' he says. 'I simply need you to fetch the doctor.'

And then missus voice came from behind the door. 'I am quite fine, Bessy,' she says. 'No need to worry. Just do as your master says. And then hopefully we will be able to proceed with the day as usual.' She sounded tired and irritable but nothing worse than that.

'Very good then, marm,' I called out.

Master James gave me a tight smile. Then he shut the door and I ran downstairs and out the house and all the way to Snatter.

As it happened the doctor was not in so I left the letter with the bacon-faced girl that answered the door, her lights were dim but I think I impressed upon her that she should give it to him as soon as he returned. Then I hurried back up the road to Castle Haivers.

I was just crossing the hall on my way upstairs, when I glanced into the study and seen that master James was at his desk in the process of writing something. As I passed by, I noticed that he covered the page with his hands, as though he did not wish me to see what he was doing (though you would need eyes like a lynx to read what he had wrote from the threshold).

I hesitated at the doorway. 'Will there be anything else now, sir?'

'No. That will be all.'

'I'll take up a breakfast for missus then,' I says.

'That won't be necessary,' he says. 'She is asleep and shouldn't be disturbed.'

'But, sir, should she not have a cup of tea and something to eat?'

'She should,' says master James. 'And that is why, while you were gone from the house, I took her something myself. It may surprise you to know, Bessy, that in my days as a student it was not unheard of for me to make a cup of tea unaided. Complicated and challenging though the procedure may be, I found that it all came flooding back to me.'

And when I returned to the kitchen a few moments later, I found that there was indeed great evidence of tea-making and some flooding.

The doctor arrived within the hour and the two men conferred in the study for some time before going to see missus. I crept up after them and listened at the door but could hear nought except their voices murmuring in between periods of silence. I was on my way back to the kitchen when I noticed that master James had left the study door open. There on his desk was the piece of paper upon which he had been writing. Now normally I did not care a cocks wattles for what he might write. Only my curiosity was up because of how he had attempted to conceal the page. Perhaps he had been writing about missus, or what had happened in Edinburgh to bring her home early. And so I tiptoed into the room.

It turned out that master James was writing a letter to Duncan Pollock MP, it contained little of note but I read it just to make sure. He began by thanking the honourable member and said that he and missus enjoyed themselves prodigiously at the Assembly Rooms. Then he blabbed on about his blasted fountain for about ½ a century, and invited Pollock to the opening ceremony. He apologised for not having joined the MP and his wife on some walk that had been planned but explained that missus had come down with a sore head. He had now thoroughly settled it with his conscience (he said) that he should offer himself to the electors. In closing he expressed hope that expenses would not be prohibitive and enquired how much Pollock himself had laid out at the time of his own election.

All perfectly innocent. I wondered why he had attempted to hide the page. Perhaps he was not entirely proud of the fawning tone he had adopted.

I was about to replace the letter on the desk when I heard footsteps on the stairs. It seemed that master James and the doctor were descending with some haste. Indeed, they were almost at the hallway. Of a sudden I panicked and darted behind one of the faded old velvet curtains at the window, in the hope that master James would show the doctor straight out and then return upstairs to see his wife. Instead, to my dismay, I heard the two men enter the study and close the door firmly behind them.

I heard master James voice, gruff and low. 'Be my guest,' says he.

There was the creak of a chair as somebody settled into it and then various scraping, tapping and rubbing sounds that I could not at first identify but which soon enough with the strike and fizz of a match revealed themselves to be pipe-related. Some puffing and sucking of stems ensued. Another chair creaked and then, after a pause, master James spoke out, more clearly this time.

'Well then, sir,' he says. 'What do you make of it?'

His words startled me, largely because they constituted the first *true* question I had ever heard him utter. Perhaps he did not mind seeming uncertain in the private company of another man, who was (after all) his friend and a doctor besides.

I found that if I pressed my head against the casement recess I could peer through a small gap between curtain and wall. The two men were seated opposite each other beside the hearth, I could see both their faces although master James was more in profile. The doctor was leaning back, staring at the ceiling as he smoked and considered his response to master James question.

'This episode in Edinburgh,' he says, eventually. 'When did it happen, did you say – yesterday?'

'Aye,' says master James. 'We had planned to stay longer in town but – while I was talking to that fellow Knox she simply disappeared from the hotel and I found her back at home. Given what happened at the Register Office I would probably have insisted on our returning here in any case.'

'So it was only yesterday that she behaved so strangely,' says McGregor-Robertson. 'And yet she now refuses to speak of it or to acknowledge it in any way.'

Master James nodded. The two men paused a moment, puffing at their pipes, needless to say I was all agog.

Eventually master James says, 'You noticed, Douglas, even as I was going over what happened, she pretended not to hear me.'

'Yes – or shook her head and laughed as though it were *you* that were deluded! But perhaps she *has* no memory of it, James. Perhaps that is part of the problem.'

'I am not so sure. I think she remembers it all right. She is merely pretending that it never happened out of embarrassment or discomfort. No doubt she does not like to think of herself as being out of control or behaving abnormally.'

'These questions she was asking the girls – did you get to the bottom of what all that was about?'

Master James shook his head. 'No,' he says. 'I am not sure that Knox even knew. And if he did he didn't mention it. All we know is that they were of an intimate nature.'

'So,' says the doctor. 'On the one hand, we have a sequence of events in Edinburgh, verified by yourself and other persons of a reliable and respectable nature such as this Knox chappie, in which Arabella behaved in an indisputably bizarre fashion, inexplicable to the extreme and disturbing to those around her.'

'Indeed.'

'Events which today she either does not remember or is choosing not to acknowledge. And on the other hand we have the appearance of this supposed *spectre* in her room, something she not only remembers and acknowledges but moreover she absolutely insists upon the fact of its existence even in the face of rational explanation.'

'The spectre taking the form of Nora Hughes.'

'Aye,' says the doctor. There was a pause and then he says, 'Damn the girl – I would to God we had heard the last of *her*.'

This was such a strange and unexpected remark that for a moment I was quite taken aback. What the flip were they on about? I hoped one of them would say more. But to my frustration, master James fell to frowning and rubbing his chin whilst the doctor struck a match and spent the next few moments puffing up a head of steam.

Eventually, he spoke. 'To my mind, there are three possibilities to consider. Number one, the least likely, that this spectre is real.'

Master James snorted. 'Nonsense!' he says. 'In my opinion, sir, that is not even a possibility.'

The doctor held up his hand in protest. 'I agree with you James. However, we must consider every eventuality in order to dismiss those that do not apply in this case. We both doubt then – we strongly doubt – the existence of a ghost.'

'Correct.'

'Possibility number two, is that Arabella was dreaming.'

'Aye,' says master James.

They both fell to thinking and smoking.

After a moment, the doctor spoke again. 'She did seem very adamant that she was awake the whole time. When I tried to suggest otherwise she became heated, wouldn't you agree?'

Master James nodded. 'Aye,' he says. 'She was utterly convinced.'

'Do you believe her?'

'I think I do,' says master James. He nodded again (rather sadly I thought).

'We are prepared to allow, then,' says the doctor, 'that Arabella was awake when she saw this nocturnal visitation. That leaves us, therefore, with the third and final possibility, which is . . .?' He raised an eyebrow.

Master James stared at him, stony-faced, then says, 'Arabella has lost her wits.'

The doctor blinked in surprise. 'You are leaping ahead somewhat, James. I merely meant to say that, as a third and final possibility, Arabella conjured this spectral vision out of her imagination and did so with such a degree of success that she has convinced herself of its reality.'

'Yes,' says master James. Then he says, rather meekly, 'Does not that mean she has lost her wits?'

'Oh undoubtedly!' cried the doctor (with what to me seemed inappropriate good cheer, but he had been carried away by his own cleverness). 'The question is, how deep does the affliction run? Is it simply a temporary lapse? Or is it a permanent case of lunacy? I have books and papers about it. Something moves in the brain, there is a surge of blood perhaps, and a person is transformed, utterly. They see their own hand in front of their face and yet do not know what to call it. They become foul-mouthed and violent, whereas before they were timid. Or they conjure visions that can be seen by nobody but themselves. Lizards, toads or so-called unearthly spirits. Sometimes the episode lasts only days. Sometimes it can last a lifetime.'

Master James sat there, stricken, his face the colour of ash. His entire body was strained and rigid. I thought at one point that his fingers might crush the bowl of his pipe.

'I can scarce believe it,' he says, at last. 'But why has this happened now?'

The doctor stuck out his lower lip. 'All that blasted Nora business was last summer, was it not? There may be some delayed reaction. Although how what happened with the girls at the Register Office fits in, I don't quite know. Perhaps it is all just a coincidence.' He paused to suck at his pipe.

Once again, I was burning with curiosity. What Register Office? What girls? And what could he mean by 'all that blasted Nora business'? Why should it annoy the doctor that his friends servant had walked under a train?

MacGregor-Robertson stretched out his legs and sighed. 'As for whether this is a temporary phase or something more prolonged, we will simply have to wait and see.'

Master James was studying him, anxiously. After a moment, he says, 'You are not suggesting then, we take the step of – of an asylum?' (He seemed almost unable to bring himself to say the word.)

The doctor shook his head. 'Not in the first instance, no. That would be a wee bitty premature. For all we know, Arabella may wake up tomorrow morning, her memory intact, her hallucinations gone.'

'There is that possibility,' says master James. 'You're right, of course.'

He had been holding himself erect but now he sank back into his chair with relief. And no flipping wonder! In my own anxiety at the thought of missus in an asylum, I had caught hold of the worn green velvet and crushed a portion of it between my fingers.

'Besides,' says the doctor. 'The principles used in these places are straightforward enough. Containment, quiet, lack of stimulus. We can apply what we need of them over the next few days or weeks, and then we will see what's what. There are also a number of remedies we can try out.'

He stood up, glancing at his pocket watch. 'I have to go and take a look at old Sammy Sums over in Smoller,' he says. 'Apparently there is something growing on his head. Whether it is a set of horns or a boil has yet to be established. When I have finished with him, I shall collect those books I was talking about and bring them up here. We could take a look at them together, eh? They may throw some light on how we should proceed.'

'Excellent!' says master James, who had also risen hastily to his feet. To my great consternation, he reached out and tugged at the bell-pull. A faint tinkle could be heard from the distant kitchen. It was a very empty sound, followed by a great hollow silence. I shrank back into the shadows and lost my view of the men through the gap in the curtain.

Master James lowered his voice. 'I should say, Douglas, that I would be most grateful if you didn't mention any of this to our friend down at the manse. I am hoping for his brothers support when I come to stand. I fear it would do my cause no good if any of this were to get back to him. The old goat is always sticking his nose in and the less said about whats-her-face the better. We don't want to stir things up.'

'Fear not,' says the doctor. 'I had already thought of it.'

It was a strange way to refer to your wife, I thought. 'Whats-her-face'. Or had he meant Nora? But I did not have long to dwell on it for to my horror the bell rang a 2nd time. Again, the faint tinkle could be heard in the distance.

'Tsk! Drat the girl,' says master James. 'Where is she?'

I imagined stepping out from behind the curtain – ta-da! – and announcing my presence. The picture of it was so vivid in my head that I almost thought I had done it. Luckily, master James was impatient. I heard him open the study door, perhaps to peer out and see whether I was coming.

'God knows where she is,' he says, after a moment. 'I'll show you out myself, if you don't mind, Douglas?'

'Not at all,' says McGregor-Robertson. 'By the way, what did you make of Shorts Observatory?'

'Not much,' says master James. 'I believe its merits are overstated.'

I heard them cross the hall and exchange a few final words. Then the doctor left, promising to return later. I held my breath and waited to see what master James would do. At first, there was only silence and I supposed that he must be standing just inside the front door, collecting his thoughts. And then to my relief I heard his footsteps cross the hallway and head upstairs. Ere long I was able to slip out from my hiding place and scuttle back to the kitchen, most grateful that I had not been discovered for if I had it could surely have meant the end of my time at Castle Haivers with missus.

And I had a feeling that she might need me now more than ever.

Missus had behaved strangely in Edinburgh, that much was clear, something to do with girls and a Register Office. But what exactly had she done? And was it something to do with her *Observations*? I was extremely curious to know. As for what the men had said about Nora. Was there indeed a connection between her death and how missus was behaving? I certainly thought so, because of the walk. But I couldn't see how master James and the doctor would know about it, since missus kept her experiments secret. I had hoped that I might overhear something useful. But all in all what the two gentlemen had said left me betwattled.

My instructions were not to disturb missus and as a result I did not see her all morning. The doctor returned at about 11 o'clock bringing with him a leather satchel full of books. Master James tellt me to make a pot of coffee and then the two men set to reading and smoking in the study. I had hoped to get a few minutes alone with missus when I took her something to eat at midday but this was not to be. I snuck up quiet as a cat but barely had I knocked when McGregor-Robertson appeared at the threshold and lifted the tray out my hands. Then he thanked me and closed the door with his foot. I didn't even get a glance at missus.

The gentlemen ate a cold meal in the study. After they'd finished master James went out to have a word with the farm servants and returned a little later. I was summoned at about a ¼ past one, by a ring of the bell. As I reached the hallway master James emerged from the study to meet me.

'Bessy,' he says. 'I need you to go to Bathgate.'

'Sir?'

If I sounded surprised it was because this was indeed an unusual request as previously I had never been asked to go further than Snatter on my own. But master James may not have been aware of this, for the request was put quite casually.

'Yes, I need some things from the chemist,' he says. 'Biscuit Meek will give you a ride. He has to go to town and he'll bring you back when you're done. Here is a list of what is required.' He held up a folded piece of paper but did not yet place it in my hands. 'Now Bessy,' he says. 'Most importantly, I forbid you to speak about what has happened of late with your mistress. If anybody asks, you must say she's in good health but has been troubled recently by headaches and has been advised to rest.'

'Yes sir.'

'Don't talk to anyone about it, not to Biscuit Meek nor any other person. I take it you have been to the chemist before.'

'No sir.'

'You have not been to the chemist before,' he says. 'You surprise me. Well then. In that case, I presume the employees don't know who you are.'

'No sir, I doubt it. I have only been to Bathgate once.'

'That is all to the good. Now as far as I am aware we have an account at the chemist, but please don't charge the items to Castle Haivers or reveal who they are for.'

He patted at his pockets, frowning. Then he stepped back into the study and I heard him ask the doctor if he had any money on him. After a moment he reappeared with a handful of coins, these he gave to me along with the list.

'Make sure Biscuit Meek does *not* accompany you to the chemist,' he says. 'Get him to leave you at the hotel and then you run along to the shop on your own – it is just around the corner. If he expresses any curiosity about where you are going or what you are to buy, which I very much doubt, tell him your mistress urgently requires some – some –' He waved a hand in the air, unable to conjecture what order of thing missus might urgently require in Bathgate.

'Some braiding and silk thread?' I offered.

'Braiding and silk thread,' he says. 'Excellent suggestion. And when you return with your packages, make sure that everything is wrapped up and out of sight.'

'I will, sir.'

'I take it you have no question you wish to ask me.'

'No sir.'

'Then off you go. Biscuit is waiting patiently for you outside the stables.'

Biscuit was indeed outside the stables but he gave no hint that he might have been waiting for me, patiently or otherwise, he was not the kind of man to dance attendance on the likes of me, Oh no! He caught sight of me as I came around the corner of the house but did not look up or acknowledge me in any way, instead he finished tightening the horses girth and then without a word got up onto the cart. Thereafter he sat looking at the horses ears. When I bid him good afternoon he cast his eyes over me without interest – much as if I were an old log he'd briefly considered taking home for firewood before thinking better of it – and then he turned away and resumed his contemplation of the horse.

Believe you me, I would rather have sat on the cutty stool than share a narrow seat with Biscuit Meek but I had no real choice in the matter if I was to obey master James and so I clambered up beside him. During the course of the journey to Bathgate I did make one or two attempts at conversation but the only thing that emerged from Biscuit's mouth was fired out in liquid form at regular intervals and lay silently glistening on the road behind us. After a while I gave up trying to engage him and fell to examining the list master James had give me. Camphor, vinegar, senna and paragoric were common enough so they were but some items on the list were new to me such as gum ammoniac, vermifuge powder, ipecac, Rochel salt, flour of sulphur, I did not much like the sound of them. Presumably they were meant for missus. All I could say was they had better not do her any harm.

This vexed me all the way to Bathgate, to the coaching-yard behind the hotel. There Biscuit stopped the cart and descended in a slithering motion. He pointed fiercely at the ground and spoke two words the first of these being '4' and the 2nd being 'a'clock'. Thus having indicated the time he expected my return to that very spot he mooched off out the yard. I got down from the cart myself and wandered into the street just in time to see him disappear into a tavern across the way. Whether or not he went there on business for master James, I hadn't a notion but I cared not a flea turd for the doings of Biscuit Meek.

The apothecary himself was the only person in the shop. Remembering what master James had said and his pleas for discretion I kept conversation to a minimum by simply handing over the list. Thankfully, the man showed no interest in me whatsoever and made up the order with scarce a word or glance in my direction. A dram of this, an ounce of that, he tapped out powders and poured liquids from large bottles into smaller vials. Then, at my request, he wrapped each item separately and finally made them up into one large parcel. All in all it took only about ten minutes to complete the order.

Upon leaving the shop I returned to the hotel but there was no sign of Biscuit and almost an hour to wait until 4 o'clock. There was a few lads hanging about, playing chucky stones and throwing me glances. No doubt if I waited on the cart I would not be left in peace for long and so I decided to go for a walk. I left the yard and began making my way towards the main shopping streets where missus had led me the previous week.

My intention was to look in at shop windows but then I glimpsed the church bell tower above the chimneys and that started me thinking about the graveyard. I was never one for hanging around burial grounds for pleasure. Yet the more I gave it consideration, the more I thought it might be worth visiting Noras grave to have a word with her. Call it superstition. But both me and missus had seen something at Castle Haivers and if it was indeed a ghost (and not a dream or figment of our imaginations), then it might be worth speaking to Miss Perfect. I would lodge a complaint, if you like, at the source. I would raise objections at Headquarters.

Having decided this, it was only a matter of making my way to the church. The bell tower was visible now and then between the rooftops and I found the right street by heading towards it. A few market stalls had been set up outside the church and the place was hoaching with passers-by and carts and gigs. I went in at the church gate and up the steps. Last time I had been there, it was snowing and I'd been intent on following missus so had not paid much heed to the surroundings. Now, the snow was long gone and I was entirely on my own. Without its frosty coating, the graveyard took on a very different aspect. I seen that it was a driech place, the paths foul and mucky, the headstones be-slimed, many of them broken and everything choked with ivy.

I chose a path and began to pick my way through the quagmire towards the far corner where they put the RCs. Away from the road, the place grew silent. There were no visitors that day besides myself. Not a living thing stirred no bird sang and the only creatures you could imagine rustling in the undergrowth was rats.

Before too long I glimpsed Noras headstone, the white marble made it stand out amongst the other graves. As I approached, I was startled and not a little disturbed to see that the crocus missus had left at the foot of the grave had been overturned as if by some angry, violent hand. The pot was smashed and the earth (which was, I noticed, the colour of dried blood) lay scattered. The bulb and petals had been stamped into the ground. There was no telling who or what was responsible. Naughty boys could have knocked it over for no good reason, as they are wont. Or a fox could have done it, I had seen similar damage left by foxes in the vegetable garden. It might – just possibly – have been caused by the wind, or by accident. But the sight of this wanton destruction, in those surroundings, made my flesh creep. I glanced around anxious, but only the gravestones gazed back at me.

The crocus was beyond saving and so I just tidied up a little, picking up the shards of the pot and laying them neatly on the path and then kicking the dark red earth to mingle it with the grass. Afterwards I stood over the grave and tried to direct my thoughts into the ground. It was hard to imagine what lay under there. The coffin had been down there for months and I reckoned that it would probably still be fairly intact but I did not like to speculate what condition Noras body might be in. I tried to picture her whole and fresh, dressed all in white, with her eyes closed and hands clasped.

'Please leave missus alone,' I begged her. 'You don't belong in this world. I am sorry if I disturbed you or disrupted you but you must go now and leave missus. It's not her fault you're dead.'

These and other similar entreaties I sent into the grave, repeating them over and over. I tried to picture my words drilling through the earth and flooding into Noras ear like sea into in a shell. My girlish superstition may seem far-fetched or even ½ daft but I was desperate. I would have pulled out my own tonsils if it would have helped missus. And if there was a ghost then I wanted it laid to rest. I stood there for what seemed like donkeys years until twilight began to fall and my feet had went numb with the cold. Then I picked up my parcel and hurried back to the gate.

Horror of horrors, who was standing right at the entrance and handing out his blasted wee pamphlets but the Old Bollix. The market stalls had attracted a crowd and he had took advantage of it. His method was to amble up to people as if to greet them but at the last minute instead of shaking their hand he would slip them a tract and then shuffle off again. With most folk this seemed to work. Some of them thanked him and put the tracts directly in their pockets while others just stared at them, bewildered, before moving on.

I had no desire to be seen or accosted by him and so cast around for an escape route but the railings were too high to climb and the front gate seemed to be the only exit. Either I would have to retreat into the churchyard and wait, in the hope that he would go away, or I would have to try and slip past the old mundungus unnoticed. Since twilight was falling I had no desire to prolong my stay amongst the gravestones. And so I took a deep breath, clutched my parcel to my chest and moved towards the front steps, keeping one eye on Pollock all the while. At this point, he was bearing down on two builders in dusty duds who were stood talking in front of one of the stalls. They looked at the Reverend askance as he approached and when he tried to hand over a pamphlet, one man swore loudly and walked away.

People turned to stare. The 2nd man shouted. 'Oh boo! Boo! Away you go with your bloody tracts! We dinna want them! They'll not tell us anything we want to hear!' He made an exaggerated shooing motion, then stalked off to join his friend.

Pollock attempted to keep his dignity despite the fact that everybody was staring at him in his moment of rejection. He turned away, a fake smile fixed on his bake, and the first thing his eyes lit upon was me as I edged my way out the church gate. Like a drowning man might make for a raft he struck out for me, raising a hand and diving across the street. There was no escape. He came to a halt a few feet away, hauled up his breeks and regarded me with that self-satisfied flipping smile.

'Ah-haah!' he goes. 'Biddy, is it not?'

'Bessy, sir,' I says, through my teeth.

'Ah-haah!' His gaze flicked behind me to the churchyard and then he gave me one of his crafty looks. 'What can we do for you here in Bathgate?' he says. 'And in the churchyard too. I trust you are not come body snatching. Ah-haah!'

'No sir,' I says. 'I was on an errand for missus and – well – I thought I might take a short-cut but – you see – there is no way out at the other side and so I – yes – I had to come back out again.'

This awkward little speech annoyed me for I was loath to explain myself to him. But master James had swore me to secrecy not only that but I had heard him expressly ask the doctor *not* to mention anything about missus to the Reverend.

Meanwhile as I was speaking the old goat had been taking a long nosy look at the parcel in my hands, clearly trying to figure out what it might contain.

'Ah-haah!' he says. 'And how is your dear mistress?'

'Very well, sir, very well indeed.'

'I am glad to hear it. Ah-haah! I thought she looked a little pale last time I saw her. There is nothing the matter with her, I take it?'

'No, sir, she is quite well.'

'And your master? He is buying a public fountain from my brother is he not? I wonder do you know how that little project is progressing?'

'I am afraid I know nothing about it, sir.'

'Oh? Perhaps they don't discuss these things with you. Well James is a capable fellow, I am sure it will pass off without a hitch. Your master has done very well for himself, Bessy, with no help from anyone at all – apart, I understand, from a substantial legacy and various properties left to him by an uncle many years ago. Ah-haah! But you know all about that, I suppose.'

He studied me with his cold little eyes. I didn't say anything, and so he carried on.

'And of course, the latest good news, James has been asked to stand, I believe? As a member of parliament? What do you make of that, Bessy? Do you think that your master would make a good parliamentarian, hmm?' Again, he gave me a cunning look.

'I know nothing about politics, sir. And if you will excuse me I have to go now. I am being taken back at 4 o'clock.'

'Ah yes,' he says, peering once more at my parcel with his head on one side. He looked like a hen about to peck it. 'You have a lot of purchases there. Ah-haah! I hope your package isn't too heavy?'

'No, sir.'

'It's very unwieldy.' Clearly, he hoped that such comments would prompt me to reveal what it contained.

'I can manage, sir.'

He gave a mock frown and wagged a finger at me. 'Now I do hope you haven't been spending all your wages on fripperies,' he says. 'Hair clasps and cap ribbons and the like. Or have you been buying something for your mistress perhaps?'

Clearly he was not about to give up and I knew that my story about braid and thread would not fool him, the parcel being much too large.

'It's nothing, sir,' I says. 'Only some material and buttons.'

'Material and buttons, eh?' He shook his head and sighed through his nose. 'Silks and satins, no doubt. Well, let me see . . .' He pulled out his pamphlets and extracted one. 'Here we are,' he says, handing it to me. The thing was entitled 'The Eye Sore', and was an attack on any person that spent too long contemplating theirselves in the looking glass. 'Are you prone to vanity, Bessy, I suspect you are. Well, you may find this an enlightening read.'

I tried to give it back to him but would he take it, would he chook.

'No, no,' he says. 'Keep it. How did you fare with the last publications I gave you?'

'Oh,' I says. 'I haven't had time to read them yet.' (A lie. I had either thrown them away directly or wrote rude words in the margins and *then* thrown them out.)

He scrutinised me closely. 'Are you in fact *able* to read?' he says, as though to himself. 'I am beginning to suspect that perhaps you aren't.'

'I can read very well, sir,' I says, hot in the face. 'Now if you don't mind . . .'

But he detained me once again, this time by putting his hand on my arm.

'Wait a moment,' he says. 'This may come as a surprise to you, Bessy, but I can see potential in you. Ah-haah! You are quite different from other girls of your age and faith. I tell you what. If you like,

I will elucidate these texts for you and then you can ask me any questions. Also, I want to know more about your life before Castle Haivers. I know you were a housekeeper.'

I opened my mouth to protest, but he interrupted.

'No, no!' he says, throwing up his hands. 'Don't tell me anything, just yet.'

As if to flip I had been about to!

'It must wait until you come to the manse,' he says. 'What day would suit you?'

'I don't think I can call on you, sir.'

'You had time off to visit Mr Flemyng, I believe, over at Thrashburn. Did you not?'

'Yes, sir,' I says, feeling unaccountably embarrassed.

'Well then,' he says. 'If you can call on Flemyng then surely you can visit myself, especially when it is for the purpose of tract elucidation.'

'I'd have to ask for time off,' I says. 'And I don't know when I will get any. We are very busy just at the moment.'

'I tell you what,' he says. 'I am always at home on Thursday afternoons for visitors. Let us leave it at that. You can ask for a Thursday afternoon off. You need not even say that you're coming to see me. Come to think of it, let us not mention it to anyone. Just in case you change your mind.'

'Change my mind about what?'

He looked surprised. 'Why – about revoking your faith,' he says. 'Ah-haah!'

He beamed at me. I just stood there, speechless, for a moment and then I says, 'Goodbye, sir, I must go now.'

I made the merest shadow of a curtsey then walked away. When I glanced back, he had resumed distributing his pamphlets. As soon as I'd turned the corner I took 'The Eye Sore' and posted it through somebodys door.

Back at the house, master James and McGregor-Robertson were

holed up in the study in a fug of pipe smoke. Master James took the parcel of remedies from me and announced that the doctor would be staying for supper but that I was not to serve anything until ½ past 7, as they wanted to finish their reading and then go for a walk.

'We must stretch our legs,' he says. 'We've been cooped up in here all day.'

'Very good sir,' I says. 'What about missus?'

'She will remain indoors,' he says.

'No sir, I mean what about her food? Will she be eating with you downstairs?'

He and McGregor-Robertson exchanged a meaning look. I noticed, for the first time, that the doctor's eye was watering and that the skin around it seemed discoloured.

'Eh, no,' says the master, then he cleared his throat. 'Bessy, it's very important that my wife rests for a while.' He gestured to the many books that lay scattered around the room. 'All our reading on the matter confirms it. Unfortunately, your mistress doesn't yet appreciate that. You see, this afternoon while you were gone, she attempted several times to come downstairs. She became quite upset at one point.'

He glanced at the doctor for confirmation but McGregor-Robertson was once more absorbed in his book, with a fixed placid look on his face.

Master James turned back to me. 'In the end,' he says, 'for her own good, we were forced to lock the door of her room to make sure she didn't break out again.'

I must have looked startled because he put his hand on my shoulder.

'Now don't worry yourself,' he says. 'It is only for a short while. She needs to rest.'

'But sir she won't like being all cooped up, it'll only make her worse.'

'No, Bessy,' he says with a shake of his head. 'Believe you me it will make her better. Indeed, she has been much quieter since we locked the door. Now I want you to promise me that you won't let her out. She may try to persuade you, but you must be firm.'

I wasn't happy *at all*, but I had to promise all the same since I had to be seen to agree to do his bidding. Otherwise he might take it into his head to send me packing. And besides, maybe they were right. Perhaps she *did* need to rest. For it looked like she had give the doctor a black eye.

Right enough, I might have done the same, had he tried to lock *me* in a room.

Dinner preparations kept me in the kitchen for the next hour or so but I listened out in order to hear when they left the house for their walk. Eventually, I was rewarded with the sound of the front door banging shut. It was dark out and I knew that they would not stroll far from the house. Without delay, I hurried upstairs and pressed my ear to the missus door. All I could hear was the beating of my own heart. A lamp was lit somewhere inside the room for when I bent down I could see a glimmer of light through the keyhole. I spoke into the crack between door and frame.

'Marm? Are you there? Marm?'

For a moment there was only silence. Then I heard the creak of bedsprings and soft footsteps as somebody approached from the inside. A shadow passed across the keyhole and a little cold draft sent up by the movement of her skirts brushed my face.

'It's me, marm,' I says quietly. 'Are you all right?'

There was a pause, during which I thought I heard her murmur something to herself. Then I gave a start as she spoke suddenly, close to the door.

'It's locked, Bessy,' she says. 'Unless you have the key, you can't come in.'

'I know, marm. But it's only for a little while, I believe, so that you can rest properly. Are you resting? Is there something you need?' Though how I expected to give her anything, I haven't a baldy. I suppose I was just trying to reassure her.

'Oh I don't know,' she says, despondently. There was a brief silence. I squinted through the keyhole but now could see nothing but shadows and so assumed that she was standing just behind the door. After a moment, she says, very downhearted, 'I don't deserve anything. I am a bad person.'

'Nonsense, marm,' I says. 'Don't be like that.'

'A bad person, Bessy, and a guilty one.'

'Oh no, marm, not at all.'

There was no reply, except a hollow laugh from inside the room.

'You'll be all right, marm,' I told her and then, very briskly, I says, 'Do you know, I went for a walk today?'

'What?' she says, distracted.

'A walk, marm. I walked over the fields, to the north. I was just walking along, you know, looking about me, and then before I knew it, I fell down a slope. It took me quite by surprise, so it did.'

Missus sighed. 'What are you talking about, Bessy?'

'This walk I went on, marm. I am just telling you, I walked north over the fields and then I fell down a slope. And you'll never guess what I nearly landed on, marm?'

There was no reply, only a rustling sound from behind the door.

'Marm?'

'I am sorry – what did you say?'

'I says you'll never guess what I nearly landed on.'

'I hardly like to imagine,' says missus, very droll.

'Would you believe, now, it was a railway line?'

I waited for some reaction from her, but heard only silence.

'The railway line, marm. To the north of here. I near fell right onto it, quite by accident. I am telling you, it's easy done. I was just lucky there was no train. Why, if you fell and a train was coming, well, I don't know what might happen. It would be nobody's fault though. Nobody's fault at all but your own. Just an accident.'

Here, I stopped talking – not because there was no response from missus but because she had started muttering to herself. I leaned against the door to hear better.

'What was that, marm?'

Immediately, the muttering ceased. She called out. 'Carry on!' she goes. 'You were saying about this railway line.'

'Well, marm, like I said, it would be nobody's fault if you tripped up on that bank and went under a train. There ought to be a fence put up, it's the railway peoples fault –'

But I didn't continue further because, once again (this time in near-whispers), missus had begun talking to herself. I put my ear to the door. The murmur of the voice was distinct, though it was difficult to make out individual words. At one point I thought I heard my own name spoken, before the murmuring continued. She whispered, paused, whispered, then paused again. It was like listening to one side of a conversation, as though she was talking to another person in the room, a person whose words and responses could be heard by her alone.

At this insight, a prickling sensation crept across my shoulder blades. The corridor was freezing but my shivers were due to more than the cold. With great trepidation, for fear of what I might see, I knelt down quietly and put my eye to the keyhole. Once again, I seen the glimmer of the lamp and the outline of some furniture, which meant that missus had stepped away from the door. I peered this way and that but could not make out where she stood in the room. Yet the intermittent mutterings continued, apparently quite close at hand.

'Who's there, marm?' I called out. 'Who's in there with you?'

At once, the whispers ceased. There was a rushing, rustling sound and then a shadow passed once again across the keyhole. Another tiny cold draft blew a little puff of dust directly into my eye, which started to water. I flinched and drew back, to wipe it.

'What did you say, Bessy?'

'Why are you talking, marm? Who's in there with you?'

I heard a laugh. 'You are the one who is doing all the talking, Bessy,' she says. 'Tell me, did you hurt yourself when you fell down?'

'Eh – no, marm, not really.'

'Well that is a relief,' she says. 'I wouldn't want you to hurt yourself. But I don't see why you are making such a fuss about it. You tripped and fell and you saw a railway line. It is not really worthy of a Jeremiad. I am surprised at you. Normally your stories are more entertaining, Bessy, or have more point.'

This was not the response I had expected. It seemed that she had not yet made the connection between the walk I described and the one she had sent Nora on. I tried again.

'Marm?' I says. 'Do you know the path I mean, over the fields to the north?'

At this juncture, I thought I heard her move away from the door and then there was a faint creak, which I took to be mattress springs. To my mind, she had sat down on the bed. I peered in at the keyhole. At first I saw only shadowy furniture as before, illuminated by lamplight. Then of a sudden, as if from nowhere, an eye appeared, glaring back at me – a wild and cruel eye that seemed to stare right into my very soul.

I shrieked and leapt away from the door, I just about went arse over tip and landed on the other side of the corridor, banging my head on the wall. In the same moment, I heard the front door fly open. A freezing gust rushed up the stairwell and blew out the candle, causing me to shriek again. There was a bellowing roar from the hallway and footsteps came thundering upwards. Shadows careened back and forth on the ceiling and then master James and the doctor appeared at the head of the stairs, bearing lamps. They hesitated when they seen me sprawled in the passageway.

'What in Gods name is going on?' shouted master James.

In response, I pointed at the chamber door. Even in my state of shock, I was interested to note two things, that master James had once again been stunned into the interrogative form, and that my hand trembled most terribly, like that of an old woman.

'Sir!' I cried. 'I think there's someone in the room with missus!'

'What?' he goes. 'Who?' and 'How could that be?'

So many questions! But I had no answers for him, since I was too feart to mention what I thought, I just shook my head and trembled. With a snarl of exasperation he strode to the door and drew the key from his pocket. The doctor paused to help me to my feet then followed. Seconds later master James flung open the door and the two men burst in. I crept after them hardly daring to put one foot in front of the other.

Inside, the room appeared tranquil enough, apart from master James and the doctor who both stood panting in the middle of the floor, peering this way and that with scowls on their faces. Missus was sat in bed, with a shawl draped around her shoulders and some sewing in her lap. She had stopped her work and was gazing at the two men in mild astonishment. Apart from her and us, the room was empty.

'Gentlemen,' she says. 'Whatever seems to be the problem?'

17

Ominous News

Master James and the doctor went through the room like a dose of salts but they found nobody. Meanwhile, missus sat up in bed to all intents and purposes bemused by this feverish male intrusion. While they tore the place to ribbons I kept trying to catch her eye but she stubbornly refused to return my gaze until master James tellt me to go down and attend to dinner. Then, unnoticed by the men (who were stood with their backs to her), missus winked at me and touched a secret finger to her lips, a gesture of collusion that left me somewhat baffled.

Just before I served supper, the two gents visited me in the kitchen. They closed the door and proceeded to bombard me with questions. Who won the Derby in 46? What is the capital of Spain? If it takes six men three hours to dig a ditch, no not really. They wanted to know why I had thought there was someone in the room with missus. What had caused me to shriek and fall down? And what was I doing outside her door in the first place? I said I had went up to check that she was all right. And then I tellt them about the whispers I had heard. And about the eyeball that appeared. But I may as well have been talking out a hole in my head. They were having none of it. The whispers was just missus talking to herself, they says. And it was *her* eye that had appeared in the keyhole. Either that or I had conjured it up out the shadows.

I protested. 'But I heard her move away from the door and sit on the bed.'

'She returned,' the doctor says. 'Without your noticing. Or perhaps she didn't move very far away in the first place. She must simply have bent down to peer out at you.'

The both of them stared at me gloomily. I knew what I'd seen. But I didn't want to give them any more snash since it was clear they blamed me for the disturbance.

'I am sorry, sir,' I says. 'I must have made a mistake.'

Mistake my fat aunt!

Master James nodded. 'Very well, Bessy,' he says. 'But you must be careful from now on. This is exactly the kind of thing that is bound to upset your mistress. If she thinks that you can see this apparition it only adds credibility to her hallucinations. It would be for the best if your contact with her were severely limited for the time being. When you have made up her tray bring it to the study. One of us will carry it to her.'

I thought I might die, I was that upset at being kept from missus. But I had no choice. I made up a tray for her but it was her husband that took it up to her room. The two men threw some dinner into them then retired to the study but they weren't in there any time at all for whilst I was clearing the dining room I seen them head upstairs, carrying the various packets that I had brought from the chemist. They were off to give missus a dose. The thought of her locked away and drugged like a Chinaman was a knife turning in my liver, I was so busy staring in anguish after the two men that I tipped ½ the leftovers onto the tablecloth instead of a plate.

I was still trying to get the flipping stain out when they returned downstairs. They stood talking for a moment in the hall then the doctor left, saying that he would be back in the morning. I heard the front door close and master James drew the bolts. Now was the time, if I had the neck to do it. I dropped my cloth and hared out into the hall just as he was about to step into the study.

'Sir!' I goes.

He turned to face me, an eyebrow raised. Jesus Murphy my heart was up amongst my lungs. But I forced myself to continue.

'Sir, I am worried about missus. This locking her away and making her take remedies. I don't think it'll help her, sir. It seems a mite – extreme.'

He looked at me. 'A mite extreme,' he says. 'You think it a mite extreme.'

'Well – yes sir, I do.'

There was a glint in his eye as he considered me. Of a sudden, he was in a cold rage. 'I am very glad that you have brought this to my attention Bessy,' he says, but he was only being satirical. 'You think it extreme. Well girl I'll tell you something *extreme*.'

Oh dear. Calling me 'girl'. That was a bad sign.

'You would like to hear it, no doubt,' he says, glaring at me.

I wasn't sure I would, but I nodded anyway.

'I thought as much. Let me tell you, Bessy, a little story of our trip to Edinburgh.'

Despite my misgivings I was glad to hear him say that, since it meant I might learn what all this business was about with the Register Office.

'Yesterday afternoon passed off without event of much note,' he says. 'We visited a few of the sights, the gardens, the monument and so on, although we did not go to the top as the entrance fee is extortionate. Your mistress seemed in fair form, if a little distracted, and we did lose each other for a while in the crowds on Princes Street. One minute she was by my side and the next she was gone. When I found her again she was standing outside what turned out to be a Register Office for servants, looking as though she was on the point of entering the building. I asked her what she was doing, and she told me that her intention had been to go inside and request directions back to our hotel where she meant to await my own return. This seemed a fair explanation, I thought no more of it. The *Soiree* at the Assembly Rooms passed off well enough. Then yesterday morning when I arose Arabella was not to be found anywhere in our hotel. I waited two hours. At about eleven o'clock I was summoned to the foyer. There I was greeted by the sight of your mistress looking very shame-faced in the custody of a policeman and another gentleman, a Mr Knox. While the policeman escorted my wife to her room this Mr Knox and I retired to the lounge and he proceeded to tell me what my wife had done.'

Up until this point his story had not seemed that remarkable. But now boys oh dear I began to wonder. Why the polis?

'It seems that at about nine o'clock your mistress had presented herself at a Register Office for servants on Princes Street, the very one outside which I had found her the day before. Mr Knox informed me that he is the proprietor. At the reception desk, my wife apparently introduced herself to his assistant using a false name. She called herself Mrs Black of Corstorphine and said that she was there to have a look at some girls with a mind to engaging a parlourmaid.'

I must have looked alarmed for master James says, 'Do not worry yourself, Bessy. Your mistress does not wish to replace you, that doesn't seem to have been her purpose, as will become evident. Now, apparently Mr Knoxs assistant noticed that she had a box with her but thought nothing of it at the time, assuming that she had been shopping. She filled out a form and then was shown into a room where a number of girls were waiting to be looked at by ladies. There she picked out two or three girls and then retired to an interviewing room where the applicants were sent to her one by one. These first girls were not to her liking. The assistant recommended a few others and these were also sent in to be interviewed. Once again, none proved suitable. In the end she saw most of the girls, one after the other.' He sighed. 'Perhaps if every one of them had been shy or quiet, nothing would have come to light. However, it happened that one of the girls was bolder than the rest. When this girl emerged from the interview, she went straight to the reception and made a complaint. She claimed that your mistress had been asking her questions – questions that had no bearing on her suitability or otherwise for employment as a parlourmaid. She had also apparently asked the girl –'

Here he bit his lip and stared at the floor, before continuing.

'She asked her to – apparently within the box she had with her, there was a glass chamber pot and she then asked – she wanted the girl to – to void her bowels into it.'

I just looked at him. I do believe he was blushing. He went on.

'The girls complaint was at first not taken seriously and she might have been asked to leave the premises but when she persisted, another girl piped up saying that she too had been interrogated inappropriately. And then one by one all the girls who had been interviewed by your mistress confessed likewise. They all said that she'd asked improper questions and had requested of one or two that they utilise the chamber pot which, needless to say, they had refused to do. It was at this point that Mr Knox was summoned from his office. After a brief investigation, he asked my wife to leave. She refused. The assistant was called. A scuffle ensued. The glass pot was smashed. One or two of the maids pitched in. It became a general brawl and then somebody ran outside and hailed a passing policeman.'

Here he gave a short, bitter laugh. Then wiped his hand across his face and resumed. 'No charges are being brought. However the policeman did advise me to keep a more careful watch on my wife in future.'

The glint was back in his eye, he directed it at me.

'Now *that*, Bessy, is extreme. Extreme behaviour. Requiring extreme measures. I trust you would agree.'

Of course he wasn't to know about *The Observations*. I'd have laid good money that missus was only doing some experiment for her book. It was on the weird side right enough, asking parlourmaids to do their plops into glass pots. But surely she would have some good reason for it? I would have give my eye teeth to tell him what I thought, but missus had swore me to secrecy about her book and so I kept my trap shut.

'Believe you me,' he says. 'This extreme treatment, as you call it, is well merited.' And he give me the benefit of a fierce face for a moment or two, before continuing.

'When I had bid Mr Knox good day,' he says. 'I went to my wifes room only to find that she'd packed her bag and slipped out of the hotel. There was no doubt in my mind that she would have returned home, too ashamed to face me. I had one or two appointments that kept me in town and then I took the last train. When I got here, what did I find but yet *another* scene of madness.'

'Sir, you see what happened was–'

'Wheesht Bessy!' he says. 'Enough. Now, has your mistress . . . what I mean is . . . according to Knox, she claimed that she wanted to divine the girls characters from examination of their stools. Now tell the truth, Bessy – did she do this extraordinary thing when she employed you?'

I was glad to be able to reply without lying. 'No sir. Absolutely not. She never did and never has.'

Master James seemed relieved, just for a moment. Then he looked downcast.

'I still cannot imagine what she thought she was doing,' he says. 'Just think – if it had happened while I was with Duncan Pollock! Or if it became public knowledge!' He looked that miserable I couldn't help but feel sorry for him.

'Isn't there nothing I can do, sir?'

He shook his head slowly. Then he turned towards the study, took a few steps and of a sudden swivelled back. 'As a matter of fact,' he says. 'I'd appreciate a little distraction. It's a while since you read to me from the notices. I picked up a newspaper at the hotel.'

'Oh yes sir. Of course. Just let me finish clearing the table.'

When I returned a few minutes later, I found him seated at his desk in the study, writing another letter. He made no attempt to conceal this one, merely nodded at me and indicated that I should make myself comfortable. The newspaper lay ready on the little chair I usually sat on, near the lamp on his desk. I took my place, wondering if missus was already asleep upstairs, and what terrible concoction was it that the doctor had gave her. However, any thoughts of missus disappeared as soon as I unfolded the paper and seen the front page. My attention was drawn at once to the first notice in the left hand column not only because of its prominent position but also because it was longer than the others. What caught my eye was the first sentence. *STRAYED from her home on Wednesday the 2nd September last, DAISY O'TOOLE, also known as ROSEBUD or POD.*

How strange to see your own self published in a newspaper. DAISY, ROSEBUD or POD. At the sight of those familiar names I near cried out, so great was my shock. I glanced up, anxious that master James might have noticed. Lucky for me he was oblivious, his head bent over his correspondence. Having established that he'd noticed nothing untoward I began to read the item again but before I had time to scan more than a few words, he signed his letter and set it aside. Then he sat back and gave me a nod.

'Good girl, Bessy,' he says. 'You may begin.'

And so with a great effort at calming myself, I commenced reading aloud. Not with the first item on the page but with the one beneath, I believe it concerned a pair of missing spectacles. On a different day master James might have found this or the other notices amusing but he listened without a flicker of a smile and within ten minutes he'd had enough and sent me away. I asked if I could borrow the newspaper overnight and took it upstairs with me. There, heartsick, I spread it out on the bed and for the first time read the notice in full. Over subsequent days I reread it often enough to be able to reproduce it here word for word.

STRAYED from her home on Wednesday the 2nd September last, DAISY O'TOOLE, also known as ROSEBUD or POD. She is Irish, between 14 and 16 years of age and has brown hair, pale complexion, a moon-face. Her eyes are blue or green or grey and although she may seem a little wrong in the mind this is just the way with her. She is stubborn and not to be trusted. Had on yellow satin frock when last seen, too small for her, blue ribbons, no coat. Any person supplying information about her current whereabouts, believed to be in the SNATTER vicinity, would greatly oblige the devoted sister MISS BRIDGET O'TOOLE, by contacting her at 3 Saracen Lane, Glasgow, at their earliest convenience.

That this notice had been composed by my mother there could be no doubt. Even had she not put her own name to it I'd have guessed as much from the vague descriptions of my age and appearance and from some of the phrasing. Whether this was the first such advertisement she had placed or whether it was just the latest in a series, I hadn't a notion but the sight of it struck dread into my very marrow. How the flip had she tracked me down to Snatter?

My first impulse was to take French leave. Get as far away as I could, just in case she did manage to trace me to Castle Haivers. Mechanically, I began to gather my few things together in a bundle in preparation for setting out on the road. It so happened that one of the frocks missus had give me was hanging on the wall and when I tried to take it down I found that part of the lining had become fankled on the wall-peg. The more I attempted to disentangle it, the more fankled it became. I tugged the material this way and that, almost weeping with frustration. And in so doing I started to think of missus locked in her room downstairs doped to the gills and with nobody to look out for her except me. And just as the peg cleaved to my frock and would not release it, so my heart cleaved to missus. In that moment I realised that I simply could not desert her.

It may seem that my reaction to this possibility of being found by my mother was unwarranted. But I did not underestimate her wickedness.

At this point – although I have no great wish to do so – I am forced to confess what I have been avoiding. But perhaps, in order to tell about those events, I must delve back a little further in time. All this is not something that I wish to dwell upon. However, I must now out with it, it is no good sitting here digging my fingernails into my throat and cheeks which is what I have been doing for the past hour as I agonise over what I am now about to write.

Once upon a time there was a woman who made her money as many women before her had done, by giving men what they wanted. This woman – let us call her Bridget – saw no wrong in what she did. She liked life to be relatively easy. Let us be honest, she was a lazy woman and she scoffed at those who made their living in the factory or in service. Most of her work was done lying down and if it was done standing up it was over all the quicker, and so (as she said) she couldn't lose. What she enjoyed most was a good old raucous time, the kind that can only be had in drink. So she was not generally a sober woman and neither was she a kind woman. Or rather, let us say that her kindness was selective. It was not unknown for her to be moved to tears by some affecting sight, such as a basket of kittens or a lamb gambolling in a field. And she often claimed that her heart had been broken by various men. Therefore it follows that she cannot have been entirely heartless. But there was something in her nature that was cold. She lacked compassion. And, depending upon her mood and how much she had drunk, she could even be cruel.

This, then, was Bridget.

It is not recorded anywhere how she felt when she gave birth to a child, but it might be suspected that she saw this baby – a daughter – as little more than an inconvenience. The baby – let us call her Daisy – grew into a little girl and as she got older it suited Bridget to let it be known that Daisy was her sister, rather than her daughter, for this gave an impression of greater youthfulness, something that Bridget was keen to hang onto. And since they moved around a lot from town to town, such a deception was easy to maintain.

After some years had passed, they settled in Dublin. Bridget was by this point infatuated with a man. Let us call him Joe, and a bigger rascal never put an arm in a coat. When Joe skipped the country, Bridget wanted to follow but did not have enough money to buy passage for herself and little Daisy. And so she did what many might think an inconceivable thing. She sold her little girls innocence. There were plenty of men about that were partial to young girls and in no time at all Bridget had made enough money out of Daisy to follow Joe across the water.

Unfortunately, when they arrived in Glasgow town, there was no sign of Joe. Bridget began to search for him and meanwhile she and

Daisy made their money as before, with Bridget doing as little as possible and Daisy doing as she was told. As for Daisy, she knew no better. She was only a child. She knew no other way of life and thought that all families were the same. And, strange as it may seem, she loved this woman, her mother, and wanted nothing more than for Bridget to love her back. (Poor fool, she could not yet see that this would never happen.)

One evening, when Daisy was about 12 years old, Bridget brought a gentleman back to their lodgings. She sat him by the fire, gave him a drink and fussed over him a while. And then she took Daisy next door for a quiet word. Bridget paced about, dabbing scent of *Gardenias* at her throat. This gentleman, she said, did not want what was usually requested. Rather, he wanted something different and was willing to pay more than double for it. Indeed, if she and Daisy did what he asked, they would not have to work for the rest of the week.

Daisy was puzzled. What was this different thing? Bridget gave her a meaning look – a slow, exaggerated one, for she was in her cups. 'He doesn't know we are sisters,' she said, swaying about. (So pervasive was the deception of sisterhood that sometimes it seemed even Bridget herself believed it.) Daisy still did not understand. So Bridget winked and said, 'He thinks we are *friends*.'

But still Daisy did not follow her meaning. Exasperated, Bridget pulled out a chair. 'He will sit here and watch,' she says.

'But watch what?' said Daisy.

Bridget lost patience. 'Just you lie down on the bed,' she says. 'And do what I do and look as if you are enjoying it.'

And when Daisy began to protest – for she had suddenly realised what her mother meant – Bridget threatened to cut her in two.

I draw a veil over the rest of that evening.

Having just read over the last few pages, I realise that I have described what happened like a fairy story, one that happened to somebody else.

However, I have not quite finished. Suffice to say that word spread fast. Manys a discerning Glaswegian gentleman was prepared to pay extremely well for such a novelty. The little double-act that Daisy and Bridget performed that first night was oft repeated in subsequent weeks. The smidgeon of guilt that Bridget had felt (upon awakening on the morning after that first time) disappeared as soon as she took her first drink. And after a few weeks, she was even considering placing a notice in the catalogue to advertise the new service. Just as she was about to do so, an even better offer came along in the form of a Jewish gentleman Mr Levy who offered to pay a weekly sum for Daisy to live with him.

Excuse my mentioning all this if it seems to fall outwith the bounds of my narrative. It does have a place, as I hope will become clear.

To this day, scent of *Gardenias* makes me feel sick.

But enough. I did not like to dwell upon it in those days and have barely thought of it since. That is, not until I began to write this account.

Where was I? In my room at Castle Haivers, trying to disentangle the frock. Well, in the end I left it where it was and put away the other items I had gathered. Then I read the notice again, desperate for reassurance. I decided that a few things were in my favour. For starters anyone thereabouts knew me as 'Bessy' not Daisy, Rosebud or Pod. The yellow frock as mentioned I had not wore since I arrived. Also, there must have been hundreds of Irish girls like myself in the Snatter 'vicinity' with brown hair pale complexions and blue or green or grey eyes, all of us in service or in turnip fields or traipsing the country looking for work. My mothers description was just vague enough that nobody would make the connection. Her poor memory and lack of interest in anything except herself might work in my favour for once.

The newspaper was already a few days old. Thus far, I had not been found. It was quite possible (I tellt myself) that Bridgets plea would go entirely unobserved. And so on and so forth, in this way I convinced myself. Having done so, I stashed the paper under my bed. Then I returned to the kitchen to wash the dishes. If my mother was going to track me down then there was little I could do to stop her. For the time being I dealt with the problem in the only way I could, by putting it out my mind.

In the days that were to follow I had enough to deal with, forbye fretting about my mother.

18

A Startling Revelation

By Jove, McGregor-Robertson must have been bored to death with country life so he must, so fiercely did he attack the case of missus. He was a regular Zealot for her health and it seemed like almost every day he came up with a new remedy. It was her diet was at fault, he says. Meat must be eliminated. Then it was grain was the problem. Then potatoes. Then tea! In the end, after a week of footering about he settled on a regime of nuts, seeds and milk and wouldn't *hear* of her being give anything else. As for vittles I don't think missus could have cared less. But no cups of tea! You should have seen the face on her, it was long as a big hares back leg.

The doctors interest in what she ate was exceeded only by his fascination with what came out the other end. Since missus was confined to her room she no longer went outside to 'pluck a rose'. Thus her poe became something of a crystal ball for McGregor-Robertson, I often encountered him gazing into that vessel like a Prophet and then scribbling his conclusions in a notebook.

The doctors books decreed that confinement, quiet and rest were the best possible treatment for a patient such as missus. She was made to lie down for two hours after every meal. He increased the strength of her sleeping draughts. And henceforth anything that might engage her mind was banished from the chamber. Firstly her sewing was taken then after a few days her pen and ink and finally her novels and other books (although not, of course, *The Observations* which was hid in her desk as usual).

Shock almighty despite the removal of these distractions her condition continued to deteriorate! She had got most upset when she couldn't find her pen and ink (which had been whipped away while she slept) and she wept as though her heart might break when a few days later they carried away her novels.

She and I were not permitted to be alone together and I was also forbid from hanging around outside her door just in case we had an unfortunate repeat of what had happened last time. I was let into the chamber only to carry out necessary domestic tasks or to assist the doctor or master James. Whenever I went in, one or other or both of them were present. I tried to send missus reassuring smiles and glances behind their backs, but I wasn't sure these made any impression on her. Once or twice as I entered the room she glanced up with a look of anticipation on her face. I believe it was Nora she sought and perhaps just for a moment because I was wearing the girls old clothes it was Nora she saw. But soon as she realised it was only me her face would fall.

By the third week missus had grown listless and pale. At this point McGregor-Robertson – the bruise on his eye now faded – decided that clysters (what are sometimes called enemas) were necessary. For days on end he had me mixing up various combinations of milk, flour, whey, paragoric, green tea and linseed all of which he administered into her bowel with a syringe. And all to no avail. If anything she got worse. But the doctor would not be defeated. It transpired he planned to write a paper on his findings (I believe he was keen to prove some point to his cousin, who was Superintendent of an asylum). He continued to purge missus, telling master James that he was edging closer to a cure. She was suffering a form of Melancholia, he told master James. Or it was a Mania – he wasn't exactly sure.

Small wonder she was Melancholy, Jesus Murphy, locked up in her chamber with nought to do and no visitors and the only event of the day a jet of cold liquid up your fundament. I worried that if she was forced to inhabit the realm of her thoughts she could only dwell *more* on the guilt she felt about Nora and I had a suspicion that this would make her condition worse. In any case, if this regime continued much longer I feart it would be the end of her. I was desperate to talk to her alone, to make sure she was all right. If only I had the courage to tell her I had read Noras journal and *The Observations*, I might somehow persuade her to see that she was not responsible for the girls death.

Gaining access to the room would be easy as pissing the bed for a key was usually left on the ledge above the door. All I lacked was opportunity. During this time master James came and went from the house as usual, he had the estate to run moreover they were laying pipes in Snatter in readiness for the arrival of the fountain and he liked to keep an eye on things. Ordinarily I might have been able to get in to see missus while he was absent. However McGregor-Robertson had practically took up residence and though he slept at his own house he was always lurking about the place whenever master James was not at home. I did consider sneaking in to see missus in dead of night but her husbands room was just across the hall and in the end I decided it wasn't worth the risk. If he were to wake up and hear me I'd be out on my ear. The only solution was to bide my time and wait until both gentlemen were absent.

As luck would have it an opportunity arose sooner than I imagined. One afternoon I happened to be fetching water when I noticed Hector dashing in at the gate. Master James and his foreman Alasdair were over by the stables. Hector ran up to them and spoke a few words, I couldn't hear what he said but whatever it was caused master James to yelp with excitement. He talked to his men for a moment then came striding across the yard.

'It's here, Bessy!' he goes. 'My fountain!'

He disappeared into the house then moments later re-emerged. McGregor-Robertson stumbled out after him, pulling on his coat. The doctor strode across the yard towards the stables while master James paused to address me in passing.

'We're away to inspect the fountain. I presume you can take care of things here.'

'Yes sir,' I says.

He gave me a narrow look. 'Be sure not to upset or disturb your mistress.'

'I won't, sir.'

'And *don't* go near her room.'

I didn't answer that, only curtseyed so it wasn't really a lie. But master James did not seem to notice, he was already charging off in McGregor-Robertsons wake.

I lugged my buckets into the kitchen and as soon as I heard the horses ride away I hurried upstairs and put my ear to the door of the missus chamber. Inside, all was silent. Perhaps she was taking a nap. She dozed overmuch of late for the draughts the doctor gave her made her very sleepy.

I took the key from the ledge, unlocked the door and stepped inside.

Missus was sat in a wingback chair by the window, looking out. At the sound of the door opening she turned towards me. Would you look at her! Her skin was sallow and her eyes had a yolky bloodshot glow, she was worn out, poor dear. Nonetheless her demeanour was calm and she didn't seem surprised to see me.

'I thought it might be you,' she says. 'I heard horses. Where have they gone?'

'Snatter, marm. The fountain is arrived. They're away to see it.'

She gave a ghost of a smile. 'Dear James,' she says. 'He thinks this will win him votes. Well – perhaps it will.'

I noticed that her lips were dry and flaking. Of a sudden I wished I had brung her a cup of tea. But there was no time. I wasn't sure how long it would be before the gentlemen returned. They might be donkeys years. Or they might just take a quick skelly at the fountain and then ride back.

Missus made a sign that I should take the seat opposite her and I done as I was told.

'Marm,' I says. 'I need to talk to you. It's about Nora.'

She looked weary. 'I know,' she says. 'But we don't have much time. I think it would be better if you let me speak first. There are several things I must tell you.'

This response had me so stunned, I just sat there like a scone. Missus began to speak, gazing out at the sky as she did so as though the events she described were unfolding against the clouds.

'You already know that Nora worked here for several months, and that I was very pleased with her service. Well, when at first she disappeared some people said she had run away. I could not believe it, Bessy. I knew that she would never do such a thing. She was a good and loyal girl, like you are. Then they found the body on the railway line and a new story started to spread. They said that she had drunk too much at a celebration in one of the bothies and then, in the dark, missed her way and wandered onto the line in front of a train. Indeed she was noticed leaving the bothy by several people on the night she disappeared, and apparently that was the last anyone saw of her. That's what everyone *says*.'

At this point, I could not help but break in.

'But that must be what happened!' I says. 'She was drunk and it was dark! It was her own fault. You see – *your* walk had nothing to do with it. That's what I was trying to tell you the other day.'

She turned and frowned at me. 'What *are* you talking about?'

'The walk, marm! The one that you sent Nora on! You see, I have to tell you something. I have read your *Observations*. I know I shouldn't have and I am sorry I did. But it doesn't matter now because it's not your fault! It was just like everybody says, she was drunk and it was night. So you mustn't feel bad about the stupid walk at all.'

Missus screwed up her eyes and rubbed her forehead.

'Bessy,' she says. 'I don't know what you are talking about. You read my what? And what stupid walk?'

I opened my mouth to speak, but she held up her hand and interrupted me.

'Wait,' she says. 'I haven't finished. You see, all these theories about Nora are wrong in any case because as I was about to tell you –' Here she glanced at the door then turned and gazed at me very matter-of-fact. 'Nora isn't dead at all.'

'What?'

She'd lowered her voice, but I heard her all right. I just couldn't believe my ears.

'Nora is alive,' she says.

I looked at her. She was still gazing at me calmly, but there was a hint of pleasure behind her eyes at revealing her secret.

'I know it's hard to believe,' she says. 'But it's true. You see, as it turns out, she's been alive all this time. But she is in terrible, *terrible* trouble. And we have to help her, Bessy. I hope we can count on you. Will you help me to help Nora?'

I was so much betwattled at what she had said that I had not quite got beyond her first startling revelation.

'You mean, Nora isn't dead?'

'No!' says missus, her eyes shining. 'She is as alive as you or I!'

'But –' I gazed at her, astonished. 'If she isn't dead, then who is buried in the graveyard at Bathgate?'

Missus turned down the corners of her mouth. 'Who can say?' she says. 'Some other girl. But it certainly isn't Nora.'

'You visited the grave,' I says. 'You took a flower there, a crocus. You acted as though she was dead.'

A wrinkle appeared in her brow, then she nodded. 'That would have been subterfuge,' she says.

I gazed at her, without comprehension.

She waved a hand in the air. 'A stratagem. You see, nobody must know that she is alive. She's in hiding. Bessy, there are some people who are after her, some very dangerous people. And they will stop at nothing to get her. They are watching the house. You and I are not even safe.'

I shivered and glanced towards the door. She was scaring the mullacky out me. Right enough it was daylight but I was suddenly very aware that we were all alone in the house. The silence when neither of us spoke was eerie. You could have heard a flea speak.

'But who are these people?' I says. 'What do they want with Nora?'

Missus sighed. 'It's terrible, Bessy,' she says. 'I don't know if I should tell you.'

'Oh please, marm!' I says. 'You have to tell me, if I am to help.'

She gave me the beady eye for a moment.

'Very well,' she says. 'But you must understand that everything I say must remain secret. You mustn't breathe a word of it to anyone. And you must never *ever* let anyone know that Nora is alive. That is vital. You would be signing her death warrant.'

I nodded and dabbed my chest with my fingers. 'Hand on heart, marm, not a word.'

Missus smiled. 'Good girl. Nora told me that we could trust you.'

I gazed at her in amazement. 'You *spoke* to her?'

'Oh yes.' Missus gave me a shrewd look. 'But you must know I have seen her, Bessy? You heard me talking to her, did you not?'

My mind was in turmoil. 'I don't know, marm,' I says. 'When was this?'

'Why, just the other day. Remember? When you were listening at the door. You overheard me speak to someone. That was Nora,' missus says, triumphant. 'I thought you might have guessed it, but obviously you didn't. She was here, you see.'

I thought of the sudden appearance of that eye at the keyhole, and glanced about the place for some sign of a secret door or passageway – but could see none.

'I don't understand,' I says. 'When master James came in, there was nobody here.'

Missus laughed. 'Nora has visited me several times in the past few days and has done so without attracting any attention to herself. She comes and goes. But I can reveal no more than that. She's very clever, Bessy. She has to be, if she wants to avoid these people. You see,' she lowered her voice again, 'I did tell you what a marvellous servant she is, didn't I? What a sweet-natured and obliging person she is?'

I seemed to have lost the power of speech and so I just nodded.

'Well, these people – these terrible people – it is a man and a woman, by the way. She is the one who is in charge, the woman. He is simply her henchman – but don't be fooled, he is just as evil as his mistress and he is moreover a master of disguise. You see they run a Register Office for servants and it is very much in their interests to find out what makes a maid loyal and obedient. Well, somehow they have found out about Nora and how wonderful she is. And do you know what they want to do to her?'

'No,' I says faintly.

'It is a very sinister plan, Bessy. They want to cut her up! They want to cut her open and use pieces of her brain and intestines in an experiment to find out what constitutes the perfect maid! Isn't it awful?' She stared at me, wide-eyed.

I could not have said at what point exactly I had begun to be sceptical about what she was saying. Certainly, a seed of doubt was sown with her declaration that Nora had visited her, because I knew that nothing had been found when the room was searched (and I had recently even begun to wonder whether the eye at the keyhole might not indeed have belonged to missus herself). As for her mention of a 'master of disguise' this also set off a few alarm bells because it did sound vaguely like something out a storybook. But by the time she got to the sinister plan and pieces of brain and guts and Nora being cut up for an experiment by people who ran a Register Office, I had begun to feel very frightened indeed. You see, I *wanted* to believe what missus said. Desperately. But a growing part of me knew that she was talking nonsense. Dear God, it was gobaloon! That was the only word for it.

The godawfullness of it froze me to the spot. I just sat there appalled and distraught with my hand clamped over my mouth. Poor missus! My poor dear missus! She was gone moony. She really was gone mad! And I had done nought to stop it. Indeed, I had probably caused it! I had a sense of rising panic and simultaneous sinking despair. I thought I might faint. But missus didn't seem to notice that there was anything wrong.

'Nora came to me for help, you see,' she was saying. 'However, I didn't know it was her at first. The signs that she left were not specific enough. But then, do you remember, Bessy, the message in the attic window?'

Did I remember it. If only I had never *thought* of the scutting thing! It had caused more trouble! Arabella was looking at me for a response, I found I could tilt my head up and down in a sort of nod.

'At that stage,' she says, 'I have to admit, I was a little confused. I thought it was her *ghost*, you see, come back to haunt us. At first she only appeared before me and made that pleading gesture. Two or three times she came to me like that, though after the first time I did not mention it to you. I could see that she was trying to say something. Her lips would move but no sounds came out. And then one day she managed to speak.'

'What did she say?'

'That first time?' Missus reflected for a moment. 'It was "Help me, my lady." '

'I see,' I says and the word tasted like bitter ashes in my mouth.

'In our first conversation,' she went on, 'I questioned her about why she had come. She told me that she was not a ghost at all, that she was still alive. She was Nora, just as she always has been. And since then she has told me all about the trouble that she is in with these people. And I have offered her my protection as far as I am able.'

'So,' I says, trying to sound conversational. 'Where is she now, marm?' I glanced around the room. 'Is she here?'

'Don't be silly, Bessy,' says missus. 'She was here yesterday night. That was when she told me that we ought to bring you in on our secret, because you can help us. As you know, I am stuck in this room for the foreseeable future, and so I cannot be out and about, keeping an eye on things. We need somebody out in the world, because should these dreadful people come to the door then they have to be discouraged and sent away. You must be on the lookout for them, Bessy. Have you seen anyone lurking yet?'

I shook my head sadly.

She seemed surprised. 'Really?' she says. 'I have seen the woman herself several times, standing out there in the shrubbery, watching the house. Look out for her. They use assumed names. Currently she is known as Mrs Gilfillan and her henchman is McDonald.'

I did not know much about lunacy back then but to my untutored brain it seemed that the delusion must be fairly comprehensive if the Phantasy figures involved had names, assumed ones at that.

I says, 'Have you told any of this to master James?'

She scoffed at the very notion. 'Good gracious, no!' She leaned towards me so that her face was inches from mine. 'We're not entirely sure yet,' she says quietly. 'But we think it's possible that James might be on their side. McGregor-Robertson too. But we'll have to wait and see. I am keeping an eye on James and the doctor and that woman in the garden. Don't worry. I've got them all under observation.'

She peered wildly this way and that as though to demonstrate – and for the first time, I realised how much she looked like she had lost her wits. Seeing her this close it dawned on me that there could be no doubt. It had been *her* glaring, bloodshot eyeball that had appeared at the keyhole. Just then, she grabbed my wrist, I near had a heart attack.

'They think that they are observing *me*,' she says. 'But they don't know that they are the ones under scrutiny!'

A thought occurred to me. 'Was this anything to do with why you went to the Register Office in Edinburgh, marm? Were you looking for this Gilfillan woman?'

Missus gazed into the middle distance for a moment, frowning. 'Register Office in Edinburgh?' she says. Then she shook her head. 'I have no memory of it.'

'You interviewed girls, marm. You were asking them – things.'

She looked thoughtful. 'I imagine that if I was at a Register Office it must have been in connection with my research. I am writing a book you see, a book about servants and how to get the best out of them.'

'Yes, marm,' I says. 'You already told me about it.'

'Did I?' She looked puzzled. 'I do keep forgetting things these days.'

'*The Observations*, marm. Like I said, I have read them. Some of them, anyway.'

'Now, there you go again with these *Obligations*. What do you mean?'

'Your book, marm. It's called *The Observations*, is it not? Well, I went into your drawer there and read some of it.'

She looked at me, blankly. '*The Observations*? Is that what I called it? I must say, I began it so long ago, I can hardly remember the title. Wasn't it something about *Notes on the Domestic Class*? *Observations* you say? The important thing is, Gilfillan thinks she can get her hands on my research but she's mistaken. I cannot write anything at the moment, since James and the doctor have taken my pen and ink, supposedly to afford me more rest. However, Nora suspects – and I am inclined to believe her – that they don't want me to send her notes. Little do they know that she can come and go as she pleases.'

And so we were back to Nora again. How I had dreaded confessing that I'd read *The Observations* and built it up in my head until it was the size of China. And here it had gone almost unremarked!

'Are you – are you expecting Nora today, marm? I'd like to meet her.'

'Yes,' she says. 'You must meet her soon. She *may* come today, I am not quite sure. She has to be careful, you see, to avoid Gilfillan and McDonald. If they are lurking in the neighbourhood she will have to keep out of sight.'

'Of course,' I says. 'What do they look like, marm?'

'Why – I haven't seen McDonald but in any case he changes his appearance at will. He has been known to disguise himself variously as a sea captain, a chimney sweep and a Bishop. As for Mrs Gilfillan, she is unremarkable in appearance, brown haired, of middle years. I saw her not an hour ago, she was down there, peering out, hatless, from behind the beech tree wearing a brown dress and matching cape – no doubt trying to blend in with her surroundings.'

She sat back and smoothed out her skirts. I don't believe that I have ever in my life felt so sad for another person. Poor love! There she was, I could reach out and touch her. And yet she seemed to have slipped beyond my reach, as though she inhabited a different world from the one that was my own.

'Are you absolutely sure, marm, that all this is true? Could it not be that you are – well – mistaken about Mrs Gilfillan?'

'Oh no,' she says. 'I am afraid it is all too true, Bessy. You may not like to believe that such evil people exist in the world but they do.' She must have seen my expression change, for she added. 'But don't worry, dear. You will be quite safe. Nora and I are working on a plan to get rid of McDonald and Mrs Gilfillan permanently.'

'How would you do that, marm?'

She gave me a conspiratorial smile. 'You will just have to wait and see,' she says. 'But I am very confident that we shall have a positive result.'

I wished that I could have been so confident. To my distress I found that I was on the verge of tears. But I couldn't let her see me cry! She would wonder what was the matter. I leapt up from my seat.

'Horses, marm!' I says. 'That'll be master James and the doctor back from Snatter.' Keeping my face averted, I hurried to the door. Out the corner of my eye, I could see her peering out the window, startled. I took the chance to wipe my cheeks on my apron.

'Horses?' she says. 'I didn't hear anything. Do you think they've muffled the hooves in an attempt to surprise us?'

'No marm!' I says in despair for it seemed that everything I did or said thrust her towards more extremes of madness! 'It was just ordinary hooves I heard. Now I must go. But don't you worry, marm. I'll take care of everything.'

'I know you will, Bessy,' she says. 'Now if you see any strangers or if anyone comes to the door just let me know.'

Somewhere deep in her eyes, I thought I seen confusion and a vague hint of the old missus. It was as though a vestige of herself remained, present yet powerless, gazing out from behind her face.

Then she turned back to the window and peered out, looking for God knows what, strangers creeping about in the bushes or evidence of her husbands return on muffled hoofs. She appeared so frail that the wings of the chair seemed almost to swallow her up. I slipped from the room gazing back at her as anxiously and sorrowfully as if that was the final time I was ever to see her, keeping my eyes fixed on her until the last possible moment when the door closed between us.

My missus. My poor, dear missus!

½ an hour later, master James and the doctor returned. I had spent the preceding thirty minutes in my room, curled up on the bed, in an agony of sorrow, anxiety, guilt and rage. Sorrow, because it seemed like I had lost missus for good and the thought was too much to bear. Anxiety, because I didn't know what to do for the best. And guilt and rage, because I blamed myself. After all, it was in revenge for what she had wrote in her book that I'd begun the haunting. And it seemed that my false ghost had set her off on the route of madness. Moreover, I had failed to notice how much she had deteriorated, ever since the so-called apparition had appeared in her room. Right enough, I had barely seen her these past weeks since the doctor got involved. But to my mind, that was no excuse.

Of course, I knew now that there was no apparition. It was all in her head. And the Nora that I had seen at about the same time was just a dream, caused by my spooky thoughts. I had also been completely wrong about the walk. Far from feeling guilty about it, missus made no connection between Noras demise and that particular experiment. But then of course, missus no longer believed that Nora was dead.

I had made a right porridge of everything. With all my heart, I wished that I could go back to the beginning and start all over again at Castle Haivers. If only it could be so. Right from the very first, I would have behaved differently. For starters I wouldn't have dug around in the grate to look at that burnt book, which had turned out only to have belonged to Morag but which had set me off on a suspicious note in the house. I would never have gone into missus desk and read her *Observations*. And I certainly wouldn't have embarked upon my stupid path of revenge with the haunting.

So many things I would not have done. But it was too late. Missus was too far gone in her illness, beyond my powers to help her. And besides, I was scared of making things worse. Some other person had to take responsibility. Some person better educated and with a wiser brain and more common sense.

And so that is why, upon hearing master James and the doctor return, I went to the study and told them everything, right from the beginning and leaving nothing out.

I need not give a blow-by-blow account of what took place in that room. Suffice to say, I relayed all what missus had just tellt me and gave them my opinion – that she was gone mad and that it was my fault entirely. I confessed about the haunting I had inflicted on her and told them that I'd done it because of what I'd read in her book. I told them exactly what I thought. That because of her grieving for Nora, coupled with my interference and mischief, her mind had become confused and she had confounded her own experiments with a delusion about this imaginary figure Mrs Gilfillan. And when they wanted to know about *The Observations*, I explained what they were.

I'll say this much for the two gentlemen, they heard me out without really interrupting my testimony (for that is what it felt like I was giving). There was no exclamations or instant dismissals, no outraged behaviour, no storming about or throwing up of arms. Master James did chew his nails rather a lot whilst I was speaking and he looked quite surprised at a few of the things I revealed but the doctor, true to type, remained the least expressive of men, you could have set fire to his whiskers and he wouldn't have blinked an eyelid. When I had finished they turned to each other and exchanged a glance. The doctors gaze dropped back to the bowl of his pipe. Master James rose to his feet. He stepped to the fireplace then turned and looked me in the eye.

'That is quite a story, Bessy,' he says. 'I am not sure how much of it to believe, just at present, until we have had a chance to investigate further. You certainly give the appearance of speaking honestly, particularly since some of what you say, if true, is likely to result in your immediate dismissal from this house. Most specifically, I cannot see why on earth you would admit to pretending to be a ghost, unless you had indeed done so.' He glanced, perplexed, at the doctor as though expecting his intermission but McGregor-Robertson only continued to smoke placidly with downcast eyes and so master James addressed himself once more to me. 'As for the rest, for this story of sinister plots and an evil proprietress and of secret experiments and books being written by my wife when I am not at home – at the risk of understatement, might I say that it all sounds *a wee bit far-fetched*.'

'Believe me, sir,' I says. 'It is all true. I wish it weren't, but it is.'

He nodded. 'Perhaps you would leave us for a moment, Bessy. I would like to speak to the doctor alone. Don't stray too far, we may need you in a little while.'

I made them a curtsey and stepped outside. As soon as the door closed, they began talking in low voices but I did not eavesdrop as I might have done in the past. Instead I wandered about the hall touching the furniture, the hat-stand, letter table, banister, those things that I had dusted many times, I put my hands on their surfaces, it was as though I was saying goodbye to them all. For several minutes the voices in the study rose and fell. Then suddenly the door flew open and the two gentlemen strode out.

Master James approached me and with a glance upstairs spoke quietly. 'This book you mentioned. Suppose you tell me where it is kept.'

I hesitated, thinking of missus. Such a long time I had guarded her secret! But then I thought about the mad glint in her eye and all the guff she had come out with.

'It is in her desk, sir,' I says. 'But she keeps the drawer locked and the key is usually hid in her pocket.'

He had already swivelled on his heel and was making for the staircase with the doctor in pursuit. I waited a few moments and then – since they had not told me to do otherwise – followed. As I sped upstairs I heard them enter the missus chamber. There was a muffled exchange of words I couldn't quite make out and then a metallic clatter as though the fire irons had overturned in the hearth. Just as I reached the head of the stairs, I heard missus gasp and cry out.

'No!'

There was a scream, followed by sounds of a struggle and someone falling, then a repeated banging of metal on wood. Someone screamed again, louder this time. When I hurried into the room, I seen that master James was bent over the desk, wielding the poker as a lever and the doctor was grappling with missus on the floor. She kicked and thrashed as he pinned her down. When she caught sight of me, a look of wild and dreadful pleading came into her eyes. She was like a helpless animal, brought down by a predator.

'Stop him, Bessy! Stop him! They're with Gilfillan!! They'll take my results!!'

'It's all right, marm,' I tellt her. 'They're here to help you. Don't worry.'

But she only screamed and kicked harder.

Just then from the desk there was a groaning, wrenching sound and then a great snap! as the wood split. Master James staggered backwards. A broken section of the drawer clattered to the ground.

He reached inside and began pulling out the contents. First off, he produced *The Observations* itself and then, one after the other, out came the maids notebooks. There must have been dozens of them all told, for they littered the desktop. Ledger upon ledger, the diaries of many maids.

Missus went limp and began to weep softly. Realising that she had ceased to struggle, the doctor got to his feet and went to join master James at the desk. While missus continued to weep on the floor,

McGregor-Robertson picked up *The Observations* and began to read aloud from the first page.

'Had we an account of the nature, habits and training of the domestic class in my time and details of particular cases therein, no history could be more entertaining or useful.'

He cast a glance at missus, then continued reading, this time silently.

I crouched down beside her and tried to stroke her head but she flinched and looked at me suspiciously. 'Do not pretend to be my friend,' she says, tears in her eyes.

'But I *am* your friend, marm,' I says. 'Your very best friend.'

She glared at me for a moment and then it appeared she decided to trust me, for our eyes locked and she lowered her voice to a near-whisper. 'What about Nora?' she croaked. 'Is she safe?'

I opened my mouth to speak, though I wasn't sure what to say but master James saved me the effort. He turned from the desk and addressed his wife harshly.

'Arabella! As you are well aware, that girl Nora is *dead*!'

At these words, missus looked stricken. Her eyes grew huge with panic and her hand flew to her throat. 'Dead?' she says. 'Really dead? Dead really and truly?'

'Aye,' he says. 'For God sake, you must remember. It was on the railway line.'

She cocked her head to one side. 'The railway line? Yes, yes, I remember now.' She turned to me. 'But what about the little one?' she says. 'What about her little one?'

I just looked at her. 'What?' I says and was about to add 'What little one?' when the two gentlemen descended on us and the words were wrenched from me, as master James hauled me to my feet while the doctor knelt down in front of missus, shielding her from my view. Master James steered me in the direction of the door.

'Now, Bessy,' he says. 'We are all a little overheated and your mistress is not herself, as you well know. She is not making sense. I think it would be a good idea if you left us alone with her. We need to speak to her to find out if what you claim is true. In any case, I want you to run down to Snatter and bring back some – some –'

'Ale,' says McGregor-Roberston, looking up coolly from his position on the floor. 'For pitys sake let it be ale, for I would certainly like a drink this night after all that has taken place.'

Master James looked relieved. 'Yes, ale!' he says. 'I'd like some myself.' He began patting his pockets. 'Er – Douglas, have you a few coins on you?' The doctor reached into his pocket and handed him some money, which master James pushed into my hand as he manoeuvred me onto the landing. Once there, he looked at me sternly. 'Now not a word about this to anyone,' he says.

'No sir.'

'I have no desire to see you drunk but similarly I do not wish to see you back here for the next hour or so. Buy yourself a drink and make it last. The doctor and I will see if we can get any sense out of your mistress. As for you –' he looked at me sternly. 'I haven't yet decided what course of action I will take. I shall think about it overnight. Until I have come to a decision, Bessy, you may continue in my employ – but only on a strict warning.'

He went back inside the chamber and closed the door with a thud and then I heard the key turn in the lock.

19

I Lose Hope

Down at Janets the porch was empty but the hatch was open. There was a smell of burning fat in the air. I peered through into the taproom and seen with dismay that Hector was sat there with his feet up on the table. Janet was stood at the stove, I supposed she was cooking for some customer that had lodged upstairs. Neither one of them noticed me which was just as well for of a sudden I realised that I couldn't face anybody. I stepped behind the door and pressed myself into a dark corner where it smelled of dust and spilt beer, old wood and piss and mould. I kept on seeing the broken desk, *The Observations* exposed and missus laying on the floor of her room, gazing up at me all helpless, with that trusting look in her eyes. Trusting me still, when I had done the dirty on her, and more than once!

I pressed myself harder into the corner, the wooden slats of the wall was uneven and split, I pushed my back against them. The sharp end of a nail jabbed into me and I dragged my shoulder across it on purpose, it ripped my frock and sliced into my skin. Just then, two men stepped in, they looked like miners from the village. I froze, ready to make some excuse for why I was hid behind the door but they went straight to the hatch and stood with their backs to me. Janet filled their bottles then returned to the stove, her eyes never once strayed in my direction and the two men left the porch without seeing me. Perhaps that should be my fate, I thought. To stand forevermore in a cold clatty corner, invisible to them that came and went, clutching empty bottles to my chest and cutting my back open on an old nail. For flip sake, that was *better* than I deserved.

Just then, Janet turned and set a dinner plate of chops and potatoes beside Hector. 'Nip up the stair with that, would ye?' she says.

Hector, who had been cleaning his fingernails with a knife, came over all offended at the request. He considered the plate with some disdain then *slowly* got to his feet. He stretched and yawned, he scratched his head, he took note of a hole in the front of his waistcoat, he examined it, picked at it, stuck his finger through it. Finally, as if it was an afterthought, he lifted the plate and carried it upstairs, whistling 'Anything for a Crust'.

Since I was in no mood for Hector this was as good a chance as any to be served. I stepped up to the hatch, thinking Janet would notice me but she turned away, it seemed I really was invisible. I had to cough to announce my presence and then she span around.

'Och flip me!' she says. 'I didnae hear you come in there.'

She wasn't to know I'd been there near 20 minutes already! I sank the glass she poured me while she filled the bottles. Then I asked for another.

'I've no seen you in a wee while,' she says. 'They keeping you busy?'

'I suppose.'

She threw me a glance. 'Whit's wrang, ma honey? Yer face is tripping ye. Are they no treating you right? Huv they no give ye your wages yet?'

'I am quite well,' I says shortly and paid her. Janet went back to the stove and began wiping it down. I thought about leaving but then something occurred to me.

'Remember last time I was here,' I says. 'You were talking about that girl Nora.'

'Oh aye,' says Janet, looking interested.

Just then Hector came skyting downstairs with the plateful of chops and spuds in his hand. My heart sank as he caught sight of me and grinned. He gave the plate back to Janet.

'Happarently this is hall ferry fwhell,' he says. 'But fwhat habout the gravy?'

Janet clucked her tongue. 'Gravy?' she says. 'Forflipsake!'

She began banging pots around on the range, adding a drop of water to the scrapings in the frying pan. Hector put his hand in his pocket and sauntered towards me. As he leaned through the hatch, giving me a slow wink, I thought how easy it would be to take the head off his shoulders. He was only young and a pest, but for some reason at that moment I hated him more than anything in the world.

'Chust tell me this, Bessy,' he says. 'Fwhy fwould you be following me?'

'I am not,' I says then wait till you hear, I pretended to be frightened. 'But there is something after me!' I goes, all panic-struck. 'It's white and it – it follows me everywhere!'

Hector looked anxious and peered out into the darkness beyond me. 'What is it?' he says.

'My arse,' I replied.

It was an old trick we used to play down the Gallowgate. I derived no humour from it that night, just bitter satisfaction at the sight of Hectors face when he seen it was a cod.

Just then, Janet appeared behind him with the plate. 'Gravy,' she goes.

Hector tellt me I was ferry funny and then disappeared upstairs with the food. It was still too early to go back to Castle Haivers so I asked Janet for more ale. She filled my glass. 'So whit dae ye want tae know aboot Nora?' she says.

Good question. I thought about it for a moment. Then says, 'Did you ever see her with a child?'

'A *child*?' Janet shook her head. 'She came in here fae time to time. And I seen her roond aboot the village. But I never saw her wi' a wean.'

Hector slid down the bannister, carrying a bottle.

Janet turned to him. 'Did ye ever see that Nora Hughes with a wean?' she says.

He shook his head and tossed her the bottle, lucky enough she caught it. 'More ale fwanted,' he says.

Janet rolled her eyes heavenward. 'Will ah never hae a minutes peace?'

While she went to fill the bottle Hector took her place at the hatch. He folded his arms gravely and looked me up and down, shaking his head.

'Fwhite and follows you heverywhere. Ferry good.' And then he peered at me. 'Har you hallright, Bessy?'

I was about to give him two in the head when Janet reappeared and handed him the bottle. 'Take that up fur me, would ye?' she says. 'I am scunnered. Thon bell hasnae stopped ringing all day.'

Hector turned and ran upstairs, calling out to me, 'Don't go awhay now!'

I looked at Janet. 'When did he start working here?'

'He doesnae,' says she. 'He just hings aboot. So what's all this aboot Nora?'

'Well, I don't know,' I says. 'Were you here when she died? You says something before about it, that I should ask my missus what happened.'

'Did I say that?' She laughed and shook her head. 'I must huv bin drunk.'

I shrugged. 'Well – she says it was an accident.'

'Aye, so they say. The day of the Free Gardeners Parade it was. There was a randan going on up in one of the bothies, all the farm servants were there and the temporary workers and them. Supposedly Nora had too much tae drink and wandered aff in the dark, fell in front of a train. That's what they say.'

'But what do *you* think?'

She thought for a moment, then shook her head. 'Ach, I don't know, honey. I just think that one's a right queer fish, your missus Reid. Locking girls up in cupboards and God knows what, working them like slaves. Just wouldnae surprise me if she didnae *drive* that girl tae it.'

'You mean – to kill herself?'

Janet widened her eyes and turned her mouth down at the corners. 'Mebbe,' she says.

Balderdash!

'Not missus,' says I. 'She wouldn't hurt a fly.'

Hector came charging downstairs, this time he was holding dirty cutlery and the plate, now scraped clean of chops and gravy. Clatter bang! he tossed the lot onto the table. 'Your customer fwhants to know, fwould you be having henny cheese?'

Janets jaw dropped. She looked at me, astounded. 'Cheese!?' she says. 'Cheese now is it!?'

She strode over to a cupboard and took from it a plate of something green and furry, this she gave to Hector. 'There's cheese,' she says.

He went upstairs with it. Janet came back to the hatch.

I says, 'About the time Nora died, did you notice anything?'

'How d'ye mean?'

'Just – did she look any different? Was she – any fatter?'

Janet frowned. 'Fatter? No, she wasnae fatter,' she says. 'If anything, she had lost a wee bit weight.'

'And you're sure you never seen her with a child?'

'Never did,' says Janet.

At the sound of Hector thundering downstairs once more Janet turned and glared, as though defying him to make yet another request on behalf of the demanding customer. He came clattering to the foot of the steps then strolled across to the table. He sat down, took out his knife and resumed cleaning his nails. A moment passed. He looked up and realised that Janet was staring at him.

'What?' he says.

And then the upstairs bell began to tinkle.

Janet shook her fist at the rafters. 'Right that's it!' she says. 'I'll see what it is this time!' And she bustled across the room and up the stairs, the face on her like a bag of hammers.

It was quiet once she was gone. Hector gazed across the table at me and moved his eyebrows up and down. 'Chust you and me then, Bessy,' he says.

What did he think he was, a flipping prince? I glared at him, hating him. But hating myself more. Something rose up in me, like blind rage. 'Come on then,' I says.

He blinked at me, astonished. 'What?'

'Come on,' I says. 'While she's upstairs. We'll go round the back.' And without another word I picked up my bottles and stepped outside.

The air out there was damp but mild. My face was numb, but I felt safe behind it. Here and there, I could see lights burning in windows, a few cottages only a stones throw away across a hedge. Peoples homes. They meant nothing to me. Folk I had never met and didn't care about. Come to think of it, I didn't care about them or myself or about anything.

The darkest spot was behind the porch and so I made my way towards it. There was all this broken glass crunching underfoot, I stepped in against the wall and put down my bottles to wait. A door creaked somewhere at the back of the inn then Hector came around the corner. He felt his way along the wall, his breath all quick and excited. I suppose he could scarce believe his luck.

'Bessy?' he says.

I grabbed his arm and dragged him back into the shadows.

And there, I will say no more. Not only for the sake of decency but because I am so very ashamed of all that I have done in my life.

Dear me, how strange that after all these years the retelling of such an event has the power to upset a person. But there you go, I make no excuses for what I done except to say that I believe I had lost all respect for myself. At any rate, no point getting miserable about it now! I must press on with my account. The gentlemen who asked me for it may not be expecting all these diversions, when really it is missus who is of more interest.

Let me move on to some little while later when I found myself back at Castle Haivers. Master James had commanded me not to return until late but I had nowhere else to go and so I crept unseen up to my room, intending to hide there until I might emerge without upsetting him. Whilst I waited, I took the opportunity to tidy myself and as I washed and put myself in order I overheard a certain amount of activity from the floors below, doors opening and closing, footsteps on the stairs, all this. Presumably (I thought), master James and the doctor were still attending to missus.

I was desperate to see her so as soon as *nearly* enough time had elapsed, I made my way down and presented myself at her room to learn what master James might require of me. I knocked – and was astounded when the door was unlocked and opened by none other than Curdle Features. There she stood like a gaoler at the threshold, beef to the heels, a fat grin on her phiz and the arms all akimbow.

'What's the go here!?' I says.

'You're no tae come in,' she says. 'Master James does not indorse it. He tellt me I am to keep you *oot*.' And she gave me another nasty smirk.

For flip sake! *Indorse* it indeed. I had a good mind to indorse her face with my fist. That this mopsie should be allowed access to missus instead of me! Although whether it meant I was fired or not, I wasn't sure.

I tried to see past her, into the room. 'Is missus all right?'

Muriel shrugged. 'She's sound asleep.'

'And where's the master?'

'How'm a supposed tae know?' she says, off-hand.

To stop myself punching the lard out her, I turned my back and scoured off downstairs. There were voices coming from the study and so I went to the kitchen and put the ale from Janets on a tray along with two glasses. I wished to gob I'd never clapped eyes on those there bottles for the sight of them near made my stomach turn over with the memory of what I had let happen with Hector. But I put it from my mind and went back to the hall. The study door was ½ open, I could see master James slumped in a chair with his head in his hand, whilst the doctor was stood by the fire, scribbling in his notebook. *The Observations* and all the maids journals had been piled up on the table behind them. I was scarce across the threshold before the doctor fell upon the tray and began pouring ale. He handed a glass to master James, who took it mechanically, without even raising his eyes.

I made a curtsey. 'Sir,' I says. 'Excuse me, is missus going to be all right now?'

But master James did not look at me. Instead, the doctor piped up. He turned his face to me and closed his eyelids so they fluttered. 'She has calmed down for now, Bessy,' he says. 'I gave her something to help her sleep. Before that, we questioned her and ascertained that she is indeed, as you said, suffering from various delusions. It is most intriguing, I've never quite come across anything like it.' He opened his eyes and leafed through his notebook. 'She believes that there is a woman spying on her and that your master and I are somehow involved and that this girl Nora –'

Of a sudden, master James cleared his throat loudly. McGregor-Robertson fell silent.

'She did think Nora was alive,' I says quickly. 'Earlier on. But then when you tellt her Nora was dead she started talking about a baby. She never mentioned that before. She never talked about a baby. But I think there's something wrong, sir. She's in her delusions sir but I think what she said up there was real. Something *did* happen to that girl Nora.'

Master James shifted in his chair. His gaze slid away from me towards the fire.

The doctor closed his notebook with a snap. 'Dearie me!' he says. 'I wouldn't set any store by what your mistress comes out with at the moment. She may well talk about babies. There are any number of delusions infecting her brain!'

'Bessy,' says master James, sounding stern but weary. I turned to him and he gave me a warning look. 'Bear in mind that your position here is extremely precarious. I still have not decided what to do with you – but believe me when I say that you are within a hairs breadth of losing your place here.' He sighed. 'Indeed, if it were not for the difficulty of replacing you I would probably have shown you the door already.'

I curtseyed, very low. 'Yes sir, I am aware of that, sir. But I would do anything sir, to be able to stay on and help missus get better.

Whatever is necessary, sir. Because I feel it is my fault, sir, and I want to –'

'Wheesht wheesht!' says master James, waving his hand in the air. 'You have said all that. However, although there is no doubt that you've done wrong, I wouldn't blame yourself as much as you do. This little haunting you carried out was a piece of mischief, of that there is no doubt. But I must impress upon you this fact – that it is very likely your mistress would have fallen ill in any case. Your little pranks are – quite frankly – not *that* important in the matter. We are almost certain that she would have been taken with delusions of some sort, whether you acted as you did or not. Is that not so, doctor?'

'Indeed,' says McGregor-Robertson. 'You should not feel so responsible.' His eyes sealed over as he regarded me, his lips lengthened. I realised he was attempting a smile. It was like watching bacon curl.

I didn't agree with what they were saying, but I had no wish to contradict them, given that I was out of favour. And so I held my tongue and stared at the floor as master James continued.

'You see, in her present state Arabella is likely to misinterpret what all of us say and do, in order to make it fit with her delusions.' He paused. 'Look at me, Bessy.'

I raised my head and met his gaze. There were shadows like bruises under his eyes, I had never noticed them before.

'For the moment,' he says, 'I have put Muriel in charge of looking after your mistress. Muriel is a less – suggestible – personality and is not so involved with my wife as you are. The doctor feels this will be better for her health. If she is exposed to too much *emotion*, it could be aggravating. For the time being you may continue with your duties but they *stop* at the threshold of your mistress room. Muriel will see to her most intimate needs, with the doctor in supervision. In return, you may have to take over some of Muriels duties. Have a word with Jessie about it, she may need you, she may not. But as for you – I am putting you on trial, Bessy. You will be under close scrutiny and should you fail to meet the standards I require or should you misbehave just once more, you will be instantly dismissed. Make no mistake about it.'

I could not bear to have him look at me any longer. My gaze dropped to the carpet. There was a lump in my throat, like a solid object rising up. I swallowed it down.

'You should dismiss me, sir,' I says.

He sniffed. 'And I may yet do so,' he says, and gestured towards the door.

My cue to leave, and I did so like a trueborn lackey, walking backwards and bobbing and scraping, it is quite an art to exit a room like that but I would have done it on my marrow bones if I had to, I was that sorry and grateful.

For the next few days, the heart in me leapt any time the bell rang or if ever master James hove into view. I felt myself to be on the brink of disaster, like an egg balanced on the edge of a table, set to topple at any moment. I truly expected to be dismissed and indeed felt it would have been no more than I deserved. Hector I avoided at all costs for the sight of him was a reminder of what a thoroughly rotten person I was. He came to the kitchen window one time and gazed in at me with cow eyes no doubt hoping for another stroll down Cock Lane but I chucked water over him and the next time he showed his face I threw a tray at his head and slammed the door on his fingers, he is lucky it was not his flipping nutmegs. After that, he left me alone.

Poor dear missus remained in a stable condition, according to the doctor. Thank gob, we were done with the milk and seeds and the clysters, he put the boots on all that. Instead she was to have normal food. Her reading books was restored to her room, as was pen, ink and writing paper and in a complete arsey-varsey of procedure, McGregor-Robertson now proclaimed that her brain must be kept active – since this would leave less room for bad thoughts and hallucinations to accumulate and fester.

A number of times when I took bachelor fare into the study I would find him there, making notes. He was most intrigued by her case and had begun composing another medical paper. It was not progressing well, he confessed. The problem was that since missus suspected him of being part of the conspiracy, she refused to answer any questions.

'Has she said any more about the baby?' I asked him once.

He shook his head. 'Certainly not!' he says. 'Mark my words – when she spoke of that, the woman was quite delirious.'

I could not help but wonder what he and master James were trying to hide. My first thoughts, that Nora had borne a child, or was carrying a child, seemed disproved by what Janet had tellt me, but I could not be sure. For one thing, not all women grow fat in the first months, my own mother being an example. I was the only child she had ever brought to term right enough, but there had been other unlucky mistakes, they never lasted more than a few months and when they came loose, they weren't exactly falls of soot, as she used to jest but they weren't far off it. At any rate, always without exception Bridget had grown not fat but thin from all the sickness. So Nora could have been with child and been thinner, if she was just a few months gone.

Missus might be able to tell me what was behind it all, if only I could get a minute alone with her. However. I suspect that Curdle Features was not much of a nurse but by Jove she would have made a good Yeoman Warder, for there was no getting past her. In the hopes of catching a glimpse of missus or sending her an encouraging word, I often found excuses to knock at the chamber door but alas! Muriel would always emerge to block the threshold. You could never be sure that she would pass on a message and she was as broad-hipped and impassable as one of her blasted cows. She slept in the chamber and only left it to visit the dunegan, and even then she locked the door and took the key. Once or twice, while she was outside whistling away on the throne, I did consider tearing upstairs to talk to missus through the keyhole. But I was not sure how much sense I'd get out her with door between us. And were I caught it could mean marching orders. I decided not to take risks and to wait until the right moment presented itself.

As it turned out I did not have to help with the milking. Jessie claimed she had no need of assistance. Her aunt – a retired dairymaid – had come to visit and apparently was happy to take on Muriels duties, without payment. Clearly Jessie preferred to work with somebody who knew what they were doing. And who could blame her. I tellt master James what had happened, in case he should think I was mitching, but I gathered he wasn't fussed who did the work so long as he didn't have to pay extra.

Day upon day, the books that they had found in the missus desk sat on the table in the study, Noras journal among them and all within a hands reach of master James and the doctor. Jesus Murphy, if either one of them cracked open *The Observations* and seen what she had wrote about my past, Mr Levy, all this, flip the scutting trial period, my feet would not touch the ground. But so far, apart from the first day when they glanced through some of the books, the gentlemen had exhibited little or no interest in what missus had wrote. Master James seemed to think that *The Observations* was partly to blame for her getting into such a state of nervosity in the first place. Scribblings, he called them and I heard him tell the doctor that it would be for the best for missus if she never wrote in her book again.

It so happened that one morning, while I was filling the coalscuttles, I found the study empty and noticed that *The Observations* and journals had gone from their place on the table and were nowhere to be seen. And when I returned to the kitchen I happened to glance out the window and caught a glimpse of smoke rising from the vegetable garden.

The Observations and journals gone. A fire in the garden. I could not help but think that these two facts might be related. And so I dropped what I was doing and hared outside. Sure enough, over by the broken-down glasshouse, I found a bonfire burning merrily. Somebody had used old branches from a fallen apple tree to form the base and the journals and *Observations* were piled on top. A few of the books were no more than ashes but by some miracle it looked as though *The Observations* had been thrown on last of all. Only a few flames were licking at it. I took a stick and dragged it out the fire. The front and back covers was charred but most of the pages inside were intact.

I poked around with my stick among the embers, in the hope of finding Noras journal, but I fear it was burnt. This was a blow, as I would have liked to read over her last entries once again. Now that I'd heard missus talk of a baby it was hard not to view what Nora had wrote in a new light. If I remembered correctly, she had been overly concerned with the subject of newborn animals. And I also seemed to recall that she had mentioned being 'reflective' of late. In the old days, I was acquainted with a few girls that had 'sprained their ankles' (which was what we used to say when a girl was in the family way) and some of them had got very reflective. That was how it took some people, my mother used to say.

Now that Noras journal was gone, I wondered again about those missing pages. They might have been destroyed – burnt or torn to shreds – and I might never know what they had contained. And yet something tellt me that they were still in one piece somewhere. If Nora had snipped out the pages herself, I got to speculating where she might have hid them. After all, her domain would have been the same as mine – the kitchen, the pantry, the washhouse, the little bedroom in the attic.

I stuffed *The Observations* up my apron and skulked back to the house. Luckily, I did not encounter a soul. Upstairs, I hid the book under my mattress. And later that morning I scoured every place I could think of for those missing pages, but found nothing except 3 buttons, a bawbee and a dead mouse.

Then I remembered Noras box. Right enough, I had nosed around in there before but it occurred to me that I might easy have overlooked a few old scraps of paper.

It was no more trouble than a fleabite to get up to the attic unnoticed. Although master James had *said* he'd be keeping an eye on me, in actual fact he was far too busy with the installation of his fountain to watch over me every minute, and McGregor-Robertson did not skulk about the place so much now that there were no clysters to administer. On that particular day, the doctor wasn't expected until late afternoon and master James had went down to the village after breakfast.

Here's what I did. At midday I delivered a tray to the missus chamber and waited a while until I knew that Muriel would have the nosebag on. Then I took a lamp and slinked up to the attic, silent as an eel in a barrel of tripe for (God forbid!) I didn't want missus to hear me and get the wrong idea, not again.

Last time I had went up there was to wipe the message off the skylight. Now, I avoided even glancing upwards, for the sight of that little window made me feel like ending myself. I kept my head down and my mind on the trunk. For starters I emptied it and peered into every corner but as far as I could tell there was no false bottom and nothing hid behind the lining paper. Then I examined each of Noras belongings. I flicked through the flimsy pages of her Bible and emptied out her workbox. I pulled off her dolls cap and poked around under the skirts. Now I came to think of it, was the doll Noras at all? Or had it perhaps been bought for a baby? Whatever the case, it concealed no visible scraps of paper. And so I started on the tracts, a dozen of them there was in total, some of them with scribbles in the margins, not rude words like you might expect but little comments and questions about what was printed there. By Jove, that Nora was a Holy Mary right enough! I flapped every single one of those blasted pamphlets in the air to see if a scrap of paper might come floating out, but I might as well have tried to get milk out a pigeon. The last thing I done was (ever so gently) to lift the trunk and look underneath, but I found nothing. Either those pages were stashed good and proper or somebody had made them disappear forever.

By this time, it was early March. That week, I remember, ½ the farm servants had come down with the influenza. The weather turned filthy again, we were plunged back into the depths of winter. Rain and hail lashed down for two days, the kind of weather nobody goes out in unless he must. Then, on the afternoon of the 2nd day, the rain stopped and it turned bitter cold. Despite this, master James threw on his coat and boots and went down to Snatter. The fountain ceremony was to take place on the following day and he was anxious to see how much the weather had held up the last stages of work. It was his intention, he informed me, to dine at the doctors house and so he would not be back until late.

Missus had been quite calm for the past few days but an hour or so after the rain stopped she became agitated and Muriel tellt me she had gave her some remedy to quiet her down. By the time I took up their supper – a light meal of egg and toast – Arabella was fast asleep. There was no gentlemans dinner to prepare but I was banjaxed and so after I had collected the tray from Muriel I brought my arse to anchor in the kitchen and sat there bringing my little book up to date, in case I should ever get a chance to show it to missus.

I had been there 5 minutes or so, when I heard a pattering at the window. Rain, I thought, and did not even glance up. There was silence for a while then came another patter, this time louder, as of a fresh and heavier burst of raindrops. Once again, I did not lift my eyes from the page. A minute later, however, I was startled by a loud rattle at the glass which made me look up, believing that the rain must have turned to hail. And then, as I watched, a handful of muck and grit spattered against the windowpane, making the same sound.

It was Hector, playing some trick on me. That is what I thought for just a second. I set aside my journal and hurried over to the window. But then I remembered that Hector had took the influenza and been ordered to bed after fainting like a big Miss Molly in the byre. Perhaps it was the 2nd sight, but of a sudden I imagined that there was something nasty in the way the dirt and stones had struck the glass. My heart began to thud – for by dint of superstition or imagination, the next culprit my mind settled upon was Nora.

The lamp and firelight reflected on the glass, making it hard to see out and so I opened the back door and stepped into the yard. The cat ran out behind me and disappeared with a yowl into the shadows. Through the window I could see the chair I had just vacated, and realised that anybody could have stood outside watching me. The very thought made my flesh creep. I whirled round and peered into the night. At first, I could make out only the pump and beyond that the dark shapes of the trees thrusting their branches this way and that in the wind. And then I seen her. A figure emerging from the darkness, her pale gloved hands raised towards me, coming at me quickly, like something out a nightmare. I knew her at once and yet wished to gob I didn't know her. I seen her and wished I had never seen her. As she approached, the wind grabbed her hat veil so that it streamed upwards, to crack and ripple like a long thin flag.

Raising a finger to her lips, she stepped into the pool of light that fell from the window, and whispered. 'It's me dear, your mother. No need to be frightened.'

I must have staggered back a few paces for my ankle hit something hard and then I stumbled and sat smack down on the cold step.

Bridget (for it was she!) chuckled quietly. 'Woops!' she whispered. 'Watch where you put your feet, love.'

It felt as though all the air had been knocked out me, I couldn't move a muscle, as on she came a further step or two. She wore dark clothes, a jacket fitted over her frock, the veiled hat. She bent down. Her hands gripped my arms. I smelled her scent, the same old *Gardenias*. She helped me to my feet but as soon as I was standing I recoiled from her, back up the steps.

'What do you want?' I asked her.

'Want?' she repeated in a whisper, and then she smiled. 'I don't want anything, dear. I just wanted to see you, to know that you are all right. You gave me quite a scare, going off and disappearing like that.'

She was nervous, I could tell by the way her fingers rubbed against her thumbs. She gazed beyond me into the kitchen then tipped back her head and looked up at the house. 'Don't you think we should go inside, dear?' she says, in a soft wheedling voice. 'Somebody might hear us if we stand around chatting on the step.'

'Chatting' was the last thing in the world I wanted to do, and I resented her nerve. I believe she sensed my lack of willing, for she gave a little laugh. 'I am not exactly a gentleman caller, now am I?'

I said nothing to that. But part of me had to admit that she was right. Any noise in the yard could be heard from the upstairs rooms on that side of the house. God forbid Muriel would come down and stick her big neb in. And if my missus woke up I didn't want her hearing a strange voice that might send her airy. At least if I took Bridget into the kitchen, nobody would hear us. And so with some reluctance I led the way inside.

By the light of the lamp, I could see her more clearly. The hem of her frock was damp and muddied. She looked foundered. I wondered how far she had walked that night, how long she had stood outside, waiting. She wore no crinoline, which might have been her one concession to country manners. The fingers of her gloves were dirty, probably from the handfuls of muck she had thrown at the window. She was pinning her veil to her hat, looking about her with a glassy smile. I had a feeling that she wanted to mock the surroundings, but was holding her tongue.

'This is the kitchen, is it dear?' she says. 'Where you work?'

'What do you want?'

She gave me an injured look. 'Now then,' she says. 'No need to be like that. All the trouble I've had to find you! My own daughter! My very own daughter!'

How strange to hear her claim me as offspring! when she had denied it so frequently in the past. I almost laughed in her face. Then for dear sake what did she do but pull my chair closer to the fire and sit down at it, unbuttoning her jacket and spreading out her skirts to dry! I could have knocked the bark off her.

'How *did* you find me?' I says.

'Well!' she says. 'I'll tell you this, it was not easy. If I put one thing in the flipping papers, I must have put a dozen. Did you not see any of them? I was up and down those newspaper offices for *weeks*.' She glanced around, as if to see whether I had any newspapers lying about.

I said not a word, did not want to give her even the nod of my head.

'What *happened* to you, dear?' she was saying. 'One minute you were there. The next, you just walked out. I thought you were coming back. That's what you said anyway. I says to Joe, she'll be back in a minute, I says, wait till you see her. Three hours later, still no sign. And then days passed, no word. I was worried sick.'

She gave me a pained look as if to prove it and then resumed glancing with great interest at all the things in the kitchen. I stared at her in sullen shock, the blood still pounding in my veins.

'That was a terrible shame about old Levy,' she says, after a minute. Then she clucked her tongue. 'And he didn't leave you a penny piece? Miserable old bastard.'

I made no response to that. She was watching me carefully. No doubt, she would have sniffed out all the details of his will as soon as she heard he was dead. She probably knew I had come in for nothing, but wanted to be sure. I decided to change the subject.

'So who was it seen your notice in the paper?'

She cackled. 'Well, you'd never guess,' she says. 'It was an aul' Blueskin. Imagine that! He wrote me a letter! Dear Miss O'Toole, all this. I was maist interestet tae read your annooncement, ni-hoot ni-hoot ni-hoo! I just about wet myself when I seen his name at the bottom. Yours sincerely, Reverend Mr Archibald Somebody.'

'Pollock,' I says, and it was like spitting.

'That's him! D'you know him?'

I shook my head.

'Well, that's peculiar. He seems to know you very well. *Very* well. Wrote me all about you, so he did, how you'd settled into your job, all this, how much you were enjoying it, how much Mrs Reid was pleased with you.'

'He's a busybody,' I tellt her. 'An old goat of a busybody.'

Would you credit it, she started poking at the loaf on the table, picking off bits of bread and stuffing them in her mouth as she spoke.

'So he writes to me, what he says is he doesn't want the reward, it would suffice for him to know that he had helped out a fellow human being.'

'Huh,' I says. 'What else?'

'Well, he said there was a person answering the description and that she works in a house called Castle Haivers, near where he lives, but that he wasn't sure it was the same girl because *this* girl went by a *different* name from the ones I'd mentioned in the paper. Well, right away I thought to myself, that could be my girl, given herself a new name. My wee girl.' She smiled at me all sentimental, all this.

I thought about pushing her into the fire. And could have done it too. I don't know why I did not.

'Then he just wrote a lot of nosy questions,' she says. 'About who you were and what did your father do, all this.'

I looked at her, alarmed. 'Did you write back to him?'

'Of course not!' she says, and stuffed another lump of bread in her mouth. 'What do you think I am? Anyway, his was the only reply I got. So I just came down here to see for myself if it was you. And here you are, fine rightly! Why don't you sit down, love? Are you worried about your Mr Reid coming back?'

It did not escape my attention that she knew master James was not at home. Which implied that she must have been waiting outside for a while, since before dark.

'You might find it easier to talk,' I says. 'If you finished what was in your mouth before speaking.'

She peered at me, chewing open-mouthed all the while. 'Eh?' she says. 'What are you on about?'

Missus might have taught me table manners but it should have been no surprise that my mother was probably not interested to learn them. Besides, that was the least of my worries.

'Anyway,' I says. 'What is it you want?'

'You keep *asking* that!' she says, her voice for the first time reaching the high-pitched indignant notes I remembered so well. 'I told you I don't want anything!' She paused a moment, then gave a little smile. 'Although there is *one* thing, dear.'

'Oh aye,' says I.

'You may well look at me like that,' she says. 'But it's something I have to tell you and you'll thank me when you hear it.' She paused and looked about her, smacking her lips. 'Have you anything to drink here, love, have you?' she says. 'I've a powerful thirst on me.'

I indicated the jug. 'There's milk.'

She raised her hands in horror, I may as well have suggested she drink a spittoon.

'Milk!' she says. 'Is that what *you* drink?'

I shrugged, impatiently. 'Look, if you've got something to tell me, get on with it.'

'Disgusting!' she says, of the milk jug. Then she looked pleased and patted the swell of her bosom. 'Well, I have something here,' she says, gloating. 'Something would interest you.'

I just looked at her. She flashed her eyes at me. Then she reached down the front of her frock and after some rummaging and re-arranging, she produced a folded piece of something so crumpled and well-fingered and damp that it was soft and sheeny and seemed more like cloth than paper, but paper it was. She laid it on her lap to smooth out the worst of the creases and then she offered it to me. I didn't take it, but could see by the firelight that it was a ballad sheet. Across the top was the song title 'Ailsa Craig' and beside that the words 'By David Flemyng'.

I snatched the page from her and looked it all over. But nowhere did my name appear. Bridget was watching me closely.

'You see?' she says. 'They've been singing this on every street corner from the Gallowgate to the Byres Road. Not so much of late, but a couple of weeks ago it was all the rage.' She stabbed her finger at Flemyngs name. '*This* man, whoever he is, has stole your song! My wee girls song! I couldn't believe it the first time I heard it. Of course, I recognised it right away when I heard it in the street, for did you not used to drive me mad singing it all the time. I says to Joe – we were down by the Trongate so we were – I says to him that's our Daisys song she made up! And I went up to the aul' buck that was singing it and took the sheet off him to look for your name.' Bridget slapped her leg and made an astonished face, to show me how shocked she had been.

'Well! No flipping name on it except *this* bastard. So I asks the aul' fella, where is she? I says to him. Where's Daisy? What have you done with her? Turned out he knew flip all about it. He was just the song seller. You have to go to the publisher if you want to know anything. Mr Lochhead is the publisher, the aul' buck says. So that's what I did, went all the way to the office in Jamaica Street. But then that old scut Lochhead wouldn't tell me anything either! He just said he didn't know who you were, and he swore blind you couldn't have wrote it! Only just lucky for me he happened to mention that your man thingumbob lived out Snatter way. And that was how I knew you must be out here somewhere, for him to have heard your song and all. I even put his name in a couple of the notices, but he never wrote to me, and I am not surprised for my guess is he doesn't want to be caught. No doubt he's plucked you and then filched your song. Probably made a flipping fortune out of you.'

A little breathless after this tirade, she sat back in her seat and gazed at me, obviously very pleased with herself. I knew what she wanted now. It was straightforward enough, a question of profits. But I had far more important things on my mind than a few bob and putting my name to a song. I did not even bother denying the rest of what she had suggested.

'He can have the money if he wants it,' I says. 'I don't care two turds.'

'Oh!' says my mother. 'Well, I just thought you might be interested is all.'

She shrugged offhandedly and put the songsheet on the table. Then she glanced about her once again, scratching her neck. I was surprised to see how easily she had let the matter drop. She turned to me brightly.

'Where is it you sleep?' she says. 'Have you a wee garret to yourself upstairs?'

At once my surprise turned to alarm. 'You can't stay here! You wouldn't be allowed. Somebody would find out!'

She chortled. 'I've no *intention* of staying here,' she says. 'I've got a room of my own, thank you very much.'

This also took me by surprise. It had not even occurred to me that she might have arrived earlier and set herself up with some kind of lodgings.

'Where?' I says, warily.

She shook her head. 'Jesus Murphy,' she says. 'That woman should *never* have put herself in the tavern trade.'

'What woman?'

'I never met *anybody* worse suited to serving the public. And her inn's a dump.'

'What inn? What's it called?'

'The Gushet,' says Bridget. 'But for dear sake you can't even ask for a spot of gravy or cheese or a pudding without she bites your head off.'

The Gushet! Janets place. The very thought of Janet and my mother knowing each other was bad enough. But something else was vexing me. For a moment, I couldn't work out what it was. And then I remembered.

Gravy. Cheese. Hector running up and down the stairs. I looked at Bridget, aghast.

'How long have you been here?'

She glanced up at the ceiling. 'Not long,' she says vaguely. 'A week or so.'

'A *week*?'

'I am on holiday!' she says, irritably. Of a sudden, she reached out and grabbed hold of my skirts, coming over all apologetic. 'Look, dear. Sweetheart. I am sorry. I was all set to come and speak to you a couple of days ago. But then the weather turned bad and I hardly dared set foot outside until this afternoon. And then I came up and your man went out and there you were in the kitchen. It seemed like too good a chance to miss. I just wanted to see were you all right, dear. But listen here to me, I don't know why you're doing this.'

'Doing what?'

'This! Feeding hens and running about like a slave up and down the stairs and in my ladys chamber and – cleaning out the pigsty, for flip sake!'

I turned and stared out the window. Beyond the glass, I could see only blackness. It was a fortnight since I'd cleaned out the pigsty. Something was beginning to dawn on me.

'You've been here,' I says. 'You've been spying on me.'

'Not *spying* exactly,' she says. 'Just *looking*. I wanted to see you. And I had to bide my time, dear, find a way to talk to you, when there was nobody about. I don't know what you've told them, you see. But what are you doing, love? Haring about like a lackey while that bracket-faced one with the big arse sits up there doing nothing. Does she get paid for that? And your woman with the big eyes, Mrs Reid if that's her name, what's the matter with *her*? All she does is stare out the window and read books.'

'Have you been standing in the bushes out there?'

'I might have been,' she says, coyly. 'Not just in the bushes. There's a few spots you get a good view of the house. You know me.' She winked. 'In and out of the shadows.'

The truth of the situation struck me, it was like a fist grabbing my insides. There was scarcely a breath left in my body.

'God almighty,' I says. 'You're Gilfillan!'

My mother curled her lip. 'I am what?'

I couldn't answer, since I was struggling to breathe and to laugh at the same time. So missus *had* witnessed somebody lurking outside the house. But it wasn't a delusion after all. *It was my mother!*

She was grinning at me now, wanting in on the joke. 'What?' she goes. 'What is it?'

'Never mind,' I says and the laugh died in my throat. Just for a moment there I had thought that missus might not be demented after all. But the truth of it was, even if her sightings of Mrs Gilfillan could be explained by Bridgets presence, there was too much else about her behaviour that was mad, the nonsense she talked about Nora appearing in her room, the cutting up of brains, the henchman &c. Although, regarding him, a thought occurred to me.

'Where's Joe?' I says.

The smile froze on my mothers face. 'Joe dear?' she says. 'Joe Dimpsey?'

'Did he not come with you?'

'Och he couldn't come,' she says. 'He was too busy. Yes, so he was. Too busy.'

There was something odd about that response, but before I could say more she'd clapped her hands together and sprang to her feet.

'Here's me dying of thirst,' she goes. 'What do you say we go down the road and have a drink, the two of us, to celebrate? I'll tell you all the crack.'

I had no intention of going for a drink. But a thought had just struck me. 'You haven't told Janet Murray or anybody that you – I mean – you haven't told them who you are?'

Bridget raised an eyebrow and gave me a look that would have scalded a cat.

'That I am your *mother*?' she says. 'No, dear.'

'Or my – my sister?'

She scowled. 'I haven't told nobody nothing,' she says. 'D'you think I am stupid?'

'Yes.'

She wasn't stupid. She just had a bad streak in her. But I wanted to annoy her.

'For your information,' she says, putting on the voice she used when she wanted to sound more high class. 'I am a widow. Mrs Kirk. Mrs Kirk has never heard of you. She is come to the country to take the air for a few weeks. She is looking about her. She may settle down here. She may not.'

'But not really,' I says, for her words had struck me cold with dread.

Bridget smiled slowly. 'Mrs Kirk doesn't know yet,' she says in a sing-song voice. 'She hasn't made up her Kirky mind.'

She turned and took a stroll around the kitchen, looking at every item – the clock, the scales, the big tureen – as if weighing up its value. There was a bread-knife on the table. The impulse to grab it and plunge it into her back, right between the shoulder blades, was overpowering. My fingers reached out and closed around the handle. I snatched up the knife, then jerked open a drawer and threw it inside. After that, I slammed the drawer shut.

Bridget had come to a halt at the door that led to the rest of the house. She stared at it a moment, then looked at me a bit sentimental again.

'What did you tell them about yourself, dear?' she says, gently. 'Did you not need a character to get your job?'

I shook my head. 'They think I was a housekeeper before. I didn't need a character.' I paused, then I says, weakly, 'I have liked it here, you know.'

My mother blinked and looked hurt. 'So I see,' she says.

She took another stroll around the kitchen, I had the feeling she was working herself up to something. Then she approached me with something like concern on her face.

'Would you look at your hands?' she says.

She took hold of my fingers and rubbed them. I let her do it, and didn't move away.

'You'll end up like a washerwoman,' she says. 'Look, I've money left from what Levy was giving me. I am not really going to stay here, don't be daft. Sure why would I stay here? I've got myself a nice new place all set up back in Glasgow, in King Street. Remember King Street? Two lovely rooms I've took, all furnished so they are.'

'Good for you,' I says.

She put her head to one side and considered me, a bit wistful. 'My wee girl, all grown up.' Then her eyes twinkled. 'Jesus, you've got the curse now and everything, by God!'

I blushed hotly, wondering how she could know such a thing just by looking at me (for it was true). But then she says, 'Or don't tell me – you wash and hang out the rags for her upstairs?'

I shook my head in shame. To hide my face, I turned and began to poke the fire. My mother sighed. Out the corner of my eye, I seen her glance again at the clock.

'Grand rooms in King Street,' she says. 'You'd like them, so you would.'

Fearful of where the conversation was heading, I began shovelling coal for all I was worth. 'Does Joe like them?' I says.

She didn't speak for a minute, because of the noise of the coal. Then when I put down the scuttle, she says, 'That's what I was going to tell you.'

I turned to face her.

She smiled at me, a bit shame-faced. 'What I said before, dear. It wasn't quite true. Well you see, what it is, Joe's gone. He's away to America. To New York. He went a few weeks ago.'

'America?!'

'I know!' she says, mistaking my surprise for concern. 'Isn't it awful? With there's that terrible war on there and everything. He might get hurt.'

I was reasonably confident that the war was not actually taking place in New York and I said as much.

My mother looked puzzled. 'Really?' she says. 'I thought New York was in America.'

'It is.'

'Well then!' she says.

I might have found her amusing were I not related to her and were it not for a few other reasons. As it was, she always managed to get up my nose.

'What's he doing in New York anyway?' I says.

'Ah now, you see, he had to go at short notice. It was the polis were after him. All a mistake, of course. He didn't do it. Anyway lucky he got a tip-off and they were too late. He'll come back when it all dies down. But until then – I am –'

Of a sudden, and quite unexpectedly, her lip trembled and she began to weep. I felt an impulse to back away from her but that would have meant stepping into the fire, so I moved to one side. She pulled a snoot-cloot from her sleeve and dabbed at her eyes. I patted her on the shoulder, it was as much as I could bring myself to do. She wept on for a few minutes. Eventually, she sniffed a few times and dried her cheeks.

'Listen dear,' she says. 'Would you ever think about coming home with me? The two of us together. Just like the grand old days.'

What grand old days she was on about, I haven't a baldy. But at last, here was what she wanted. It wasn't money she was after at all. It was me. She wanted *me* back. Without Joe, without somebody, she was nothing. She wanted company. Oh, she might well have some money left, but when it ran out she'd have me out on the streets faster than fart. I'd start taking a budge before I went, just to be able to face the night. And it would be a short slip from there back to other things, terrible things that I did not want even to consider.

I must have looked most awful troubled for at once she shrugged and started to make light of her suggestion. 'It was only a thought,' she says, unpinning her veil. 'For when you get tired of it here. Or if you get the chuck.'

Her tone was light – but had she meant to imply something by that last remark? I was only too aware of how my fate now lay in her hands. It would take just a few words in the right ear, I'd be exposed to master James as a fraud and then given the rogues march.

She was smiling at me, holding up her veil. 'Are you coming for a drink or what?' she says.

I shook my head.

'Suit yourself,' she says. She let the veil fall. There was a moment when I thought she might try to hug me. But then she just reached out and squeezed my arm. 'Well, the offer's there,' she says.

Without hardly knowing how I did it, I managed to get her out the house. I watched her pick her way across the yard and even when she was swallowed by the night I still expected her to come rushing back out the darkness towards me. And so I quickly closed and bolted the door. Then I went back to sit on the floor by the fire with the lamp turned out this time so that nobody could watch me from outside, and there I sat, as dull and waxen and stupid as a stump of candle, almost too frightened to think.

All this while I had imagined myself safe. Even when I'd seen that notice in the paper, I thought she wouldn't find me. But now I realised that no matter where I went, she would track me down. Joe wasn't coming back and I think she knew it. She'd never let me be. It was only a matter of time before she got me fired. And then where would I go, with no character and no money? She'd only come after me again and even if I found another job, she'd spoil it for me by telling them what I was.

Of course, my missus didn't care about all that. Dear lovely missus! She didn't mind what I'd been. Poor missus, who had kept me on, even though she'd found out all about me! But master James was of a different kidney. He wouldn't want tongues clacking, to harm his election prospects. The fact of the matter was, his wifes word counted for nothing. Even if she wasn't ½ mad, it didn't matter whether she wanted me or not.

She would have stood up for me though, I knew she would have. That is, if she'd been in her right mind. But of course, she wasn't in her right mind. And there was a strong chance she might never, ever recover.

And whose fault was that?

As I stared into the dying embers of the fire, I kept on seeing a vision, like a picture of the future. There was me, down the Gallowgate, laying drunk in the filthy gutter and some brute in dirty clothes and big boots stomping on me. And as he kicks me over onto my back, my face just visible behind the tangle of my hair, you can see that I am smiling. Smiling. Because I know that such treatment is no more than I deserve.

PART FIVE

20

I Am Made Captive

I never went to bed at all that night, only sat by the kitchen hearth until the dawn broke, chill and grey and thick with fog. By that time, I had made up my mind what I was going to do. First I took paper and pen and wrote a note addressed to my mother at The Gushet. I tellt her that I had thought over her proposal and was agreeable to it, I would go back with her to Glasgow and take up our old life there. I said that before I left I had a few things to do, but asked her to meet me at 3 o'clock in the Railway Tavern, from which place we could easy buy tickets and take a late afternoon train.

After that, I wrote to master James. This letter was a flipsight more difficult. All through the darkest hours of the night I had agonised over whether to work a notice of a month, as I knew that was the done thing and I didn't want to let him or missus down. But now that my mind was made up to go, I wanted to be away as soon as possible. Rushing towards my fate was how it felt, and the grubbier and more squalid it was and the quicker I embarked upon it, the better. Besides which my mother had the patience of a flea. If I waited a month she'd get restless. Better to go now than risk her blabbing her trap off all over the place. I felt pig-sick leaving master James in the lurch but I knew it would be for the best. He'd find a girl to replace me soon enough. And for dear sake whoever she was, she could not make a worse fist of it than I had.

The letter to master James ended up very stiff and formal.

Dear mister Reid, Forgive me but circumstances have arose and I have to leave Castle Haivers at once, there is something of my past has caught up with me and it is better that I go now before any damage is done to your name or to missus. I apologise for the inconvenience caused but have no choice. I have enjoyed working for missus I cannot tell you how much, it has been an honour and a pleasure to serve her.

I hope with all my heart she recovers from whatever it is that ails her.

Yours truly
Bessy Buckley

PS Please take good care of her make sure she has all she needs and is comfortable and you know fresh air can do her no harm.

Of course it was not my place to say such things, but it no longer mattered. I was hardly risking my job. And by the time he read it, I would be long gone.

The unveiling of the fountain was to take place that afternoon down at the Cross. Most of the farm servants would be there, and the doctor, the Reverend and probably ½ the flipping village besides. I knew from overhearing discussions of the plans that the ceremony was due to begin at one o'clock. After the speeches and all this the invited guests would head over to the dining room above the Swan Inn which master James had hired for the purpose. He had says I could go to the unveiling if I wanted, but I had declined. I knew there would be nobody near the house all afternoon and not another opportunity like it to say goodbye to missus. Of course, Curdle Features would be left behind and I'd need some ruse to get past her but I wasn't too worried. If all else failed, I'd give her the truth. Surely even *she* could not refuse me a few minutes alone with my missus for a last farewell.

Ordinarily I would have sent Hector down the village with the note for my mother but I was avoiding him and so I loitered about the gate until the postman came by and got him to deliver it instead. The letter for master James I kept hid in the pocket of my apron, intending to leave it in the study for him to find upon his return that evening. As well as the usual chores, the morning was took up with running around like a lilty after the master – sewing a button onto his coat, locating a lost cufflink, smoothing once again a shirt that had somehow got creased on the hanger, sponging an egg-stain off his waistcoat. He himself was in a panic because the temperature had dropped overnight and the water that fed the fountain had froze. He spent ½ the morning at the Cross, trying to get the men to thaw the pipes. Then he had to race back and change his clothes before his guests arrived to meet him at the Swan. He charged about the place, up and down the stairs, from study to chamber and back again. The house was in a state of chassis. And then abruptly towards midday he was gone again, leaving behind a silence and stillness that would have been welcome, except it left me alone with my thoughts.

I scrubbed the kitchen, until every surface gleamed. Then I went upstairs and put all my things in a bundle. Except Noras frocks which I hung on the wall to leave behind, for they did not belong to me and I did not want to be accused of thieving. For going away (how strange to put it like that, as though it were to be a happy ending with a marriage, when really nothing could be further from the truth!), let me say then for *leaving*, I put on what I had been wearing when I arrived, the yellow satin with its lace and bows. That frock was once a favourite of mine but now it seemed gaudy and desperate uncomfortable. My old stays I shoved in the bundle, I hadn't wore them for donkeys years at least not since soon after I had arrived. Perhaps I would grow used to them again when I was back in Glasgow, but for the moment I needed to breathe.

That left *The Observations*. I did not want to leave them behind in case master James destroyed them. Perhaps in the future missus would get well, and I could send them to her. But in the meantime I folded the ledger in old newspaper and stuffed it into my bundle along with my clothes. Then I cleaned my room from top to bottom. At least when I was gone they would not be able to say I was a slattern.

Last of all I went down and placed my letter to master James on his desk and at ½ past 12 exactly, I knocked at the door of missus room. Only four little raps of my knuckles on wood, that was all, yet how significant they seemed for I knew I should not be knocking on that door again, not ever. The key turned in the lock. Then the door swung open. There stood C. Features, slack-jawed and chewing, one hand in the pocket of her skirt while in the other she held an apple. As usual she kept her foot planted behind the door, as though I might push past her into the room. She said nothing at first. There was a look she was using on me of late, ever since she'd been put in charge of missus. It was calculated to express equal amounts of amusement and pity. She was using it on me now, the skyte, as she took in what I was wearing. She must have practised in the mirror, it was indeed most irritating.

I had planned to come straight to the point, to tell her I was leaving and ask if I could have a few minutes alone with missus. But just as I was about to speak, missus herself appeared, strolling into view behind Muriel. Even now I remember that she seemed remarkably in control of her faculties. Her hair was dressed neat as ninepence and she wore a dark blue frock. She had a glance to see who was at the door then stepped out of sight once again, making no sound and giving no sign that she'd recognised me.

Of a sudden I could not bear to tell Muriel that I was leaving, just as a cod to get into the room. No doubt, missus would hear me and it felt wrong to be giving C. Features that information first. Although missus may have lost her senses somewhat, she still deserved to be treated with respect. I decided that *she* should be the first one to hear of my plans.

As you can see, what I have outlined above – Muriel at the door, missus floating in and out of view, me changing my mind – requires some little while to describe on paper, whereas in reality it all happened within a matter of moments. And what took place next was also fast. So flipping fast that it was over practically before I knew it had begun.

'Well?' says Muriel, her lips slobbery with apple juice. 'Whit dae ye want now?'

'Do you need any coal?' I says, which was me stalling for time (having abandoned my first strategy, I had yet to come up with another).

In the event, I didn't have to think of one because – with no warning whatsoever – missus dashed out the room, turning to shove me as she went, so that I went arse over tip. I knocked Muriel down like a skittle and landed on top of her, my forehead cracking her on the chin. She yelped, as a gust of air (caused by the door slamming behind us) blew up my skirts. The apple rolled away across the floor. There was the unmistakable sound of a key turning in the lock and then footsteps hurrying away down the stairs.

A second passed during which Muriel and I stared, dumfounded – and at rather close quarters – into each others eyes. Then I rolled off her, we scrambled to our feet and tried to open the door. But it was too late. We were locked in. And there we were to remain for the rest of the afternoon – whilst down in Snatter and unbeknown to us, mayhem unfolded.

Events in the village, I will return to ere long. But for the time being, it was just myself and C. Features locked in the bedroom. Muriel booted the door a few times then gave me such a look I feared she might inflict the same punishment upon my person.

'This is aw your fault,' she says. 'I better no get the blame.'

Were this another kind of story, being trapped together might prove to be a transforming experience, at the end of which we would forget our differences and emerge from the chamber arm in arm, chuckling away about all those times in the past that we had took objection to each other, when all along we were meant to be the best of chums. But this is not *The Bathgate Monthly Visitor* and not that kind of story, although perhaps it is just that neither Muriel nor I were that kind of person. At any rate, after she had growled at me, she went to the window, threw up the sash and screamed at the top of her lungs.

'Help!! Help!'

Everything was muffled by the fog. Her cries echoed back into the room as though she had been shouting at a brick wall rather than out into open country.

'Help! Over here! He-elp!'

Cold mist began to seep in through the open window. The fog was that thick you couldn't even see to the far side of the yard. After a few more shouts Muriel fell silent and we listened for a reply. But there was nothing, only a stupid dog barking in the distance. Muriel resumed shouting and I went over to tend the fire, which gave me a moment for reflection.

Had missus planned this escape for a while or had she just seen an opportunity and took it? She must have waited until C. Features was talking to me and then crept up behind the door and slipped the key out the lock. It was a risk, for Muriel might have heard her, or either one of us could have grabbed her as she passed. But she had two things on her side, one was the element of surprise and the other was sheer desperation. That shove she gave me sent me flying, she was strong as 6 men, so she was. Which was remarkable, given her frail appearance.

I did feel rather slighted that she'd deemed it necessary to make *me* a prisoner for it aligned me with Muriel, this clodhopper, in a way I didn't appreciate. Missus ought to know by now that I was on *her* side. Just for a moment, I felt thrilled at the thought of her, free and at large. 3 cheers for missus! She had broke out!

But in no time at all, I began to worry. Where would she go in this weather? And in her state of mind? How could she expect to live, with no money and no husband? She would perish of the cold, or come to harm. Somebody might find her wandering and take advantage of her. The very thought made me shudder. It was then that I realised she was smarter than I thought because – much as I was on her side – I would never have let her run away, for her own safety. So she'd been wise to make me a prisoner after all.

C. Features had turned away from the window and was staring at me. 'Ye might well look worried,' she says. 'But naebody can blame *me* she goat oot.'

The fire was burning brightly now, so I got to my feet and sat in the armchair. Muriel turned back to the window and shouted a few more times but clearly there was nobody within earshot. She lowered the sash and came to warm her hands at the grate.

'I just hope missus'll be all right,' I says.

Muriel didn't seem very interested in missus or her welfare. 'Naebody can blame me,' she says again. 'It wasnae ma fault.'

'D'you think she'll try to get back to Wimbledon?'

'Where?'

'Wimbledon. Where she's from. It's a village, down in England.'

'Oh is it now?' says Muriel, rolling her eyes, to show how much she cared for Wimbledon, England and all *that*. 'She can go up the Clyde oan a clootie dumpling, if she wants.'

At this mention of the river, I suddenly thought of my mother. It seemed unlikely now that I would get to the Railway Tavern by 3 o'clock. If I didn't put in an appearance Bridget might walk to Castle Haivers to see what had become of me. But no. Most likely she would just sit there drinking into the evening, into her altitudes. She'd forget all about me, until she woke up somewhere with a sore head in the morning. Perhaps only then she'd come and find me. But by that time, I thought, master James would have returned and we'd be set free. And then I remembered the letter on his desk. I had planned to get away without any fuss, without having to face him. But that was also beginning to look extremely unlikely.

'This is a right old curfuffle, eh?' says Muriel. 'Telling you, I better not get intae trouble with Mr Reid.'

I was sick fed up to the back teeth of her harping on the one subject. 'What are you?' I says. 'Scared of him?'

She looked scornful. 'Am not,' she says. 'I can tell ye whit I think of that man in one word.'

'Go on then,' I says.

'He's a miser.'

That was 3 words. I could have pointed it out but I didn't. Instead I says, 'What do you think of missus then?'

Muriel scoffed. 'One word? She's a gowk.'

Gob strike me blind, it was an effort not to leap on her and give her a basting. But it would not do to get into a fight, what with the door locked and dear only knows how long to wait before we got out. Instead, I decided to pursue this little game to pass the time. And also it occurred to me that this might be a way to find out more about Nora. For all I knew, C. Features might have been there the night she died. Nonetheless, I did not want her to know that I was curious about Nora in particular, so I asked about a few other people first.

'What about me?' I says. 'Describe me in one word.'

Muriel glanced away. 'Irish,' she says. She might as well have said 'gowk', it was as much of an insult from her lips. But I didn't care a lousebag for what she thought of me.

'What about Hector?' I says.

'W. H. T.,' says Muriel and when I didn't understand, she elaborated. 'Wandering Hand Trouble.' She gave me a meaning look and my face grew hot. For one awful moment, I thought she knew about the other night and was teasing me, perhaps he'd blabbed it all around the farm. And then I realised that, of course, she was talking about her own experience of Hector. He probably tried his luck with everybody, even an old fussock like her. Still, I wished I hadn't asked about him. I passed on quickly.

'What about Janet, down The Gushet?'

Muriel thought for a second. Then she says, 'Nosy. Always wants tae know if a person got their wages or their day aff, when it's nane of her business.'

Just a few more, and I would ask about Nora. 'McGregor-Robertson?'

'Snob,' goes Muriel, without hesitation.

'Reverend Pollock?'

She rolled her eyes again. 'W. H. T.'

Interesting, because I'd have said 'busybody' but I wasn't about to quibble.

'Nora Hughes?'

Muriel shrugged and looked gloomy. 'Irish,' she says.

I shook my head. 'You said that about me. Say something else.'

There was a pause and then she says, 'Gone to Kingdom Come.' I was about to ask her more but of a sudden she stood up and crossed the room. 'What would you no give for a bed like this,' she says, and without any further hesitation she climbed between the covers and pulled them over her head.

'Muriel,' I says. 'Were you here the night Nora died?'

But there was no answer. She only grunted and within moments she was breathing deeply, leaving me to sit by the fire, alone with my thoughts.

Well that had been a grand waste of time. She had tellt me little more than nothing. And yet, *something* in what she had said was troubling me, but I couldn't work out what. Perhaps I'd ask her more when she woke up. Whenever that might be. How long were we to be stuck in this room? And where was missus gone?

Dear Arabella. For some reason, I imagined her seated on a train, whizzing along, headed for some different and better place. In my vision she was alone in the carriage and gazing out the window at the passing landscape of green fields and trees. And then, to my great surprise, I found myself sliding open the door and sitting opposite her. For dear sake, I was only dreaming! Missus smiled at me and took my hand. We both gazed out the window and I seen that this must be some train, for it had left the fields and was now passing across the sea! Sunlight dappled the green waves. Ailsa Craig floated by like a rotten tooth.

'We're going back home,' I tellt missus. 'We're going across the water.'

She frowned as she peered out the window. 'Not to my home, Bessy,' she says, smoothing down her hair. A handful of it came out as she stroked and I seen that it was not hair exactly, but seaweed in flat green ribbons. She pulled out another hank and another, leaving bloody patches on her scalp, the skin hanging off, she was making herself bald and I could not stop her, so help me God . . .

Of a sudden I jolted awake, sweating, and gazed about me. Muriel was still dozing in the bed and the house was silent. I went over and tried the door but it was still locked. There was nothing to do except wait. I returned to my seat. There I laid down my head and closed my eyes and this time I slept without dreaming.

A while later, I awoke to the sound of footsteps on the stairs. I glanced at my watch and was flabbergasted to see that almost two hours had passed. Muriel was still fast asleep. I ran over and gave her a shoogle.

'Somebody's coming.'

She grunted and peered at me groggily. The footsteps came thudding to a halt outside the chamber and the door rattled as somebody tried to open it. Muriel stretched and yawned. 'Hurry up!' I says and went to stand next the fire. I knew it couldn't be missus returning alone. The footsteps was too heavy. And the voices I could hear muttering outside the door was male. Perhaps they had found her and fetched her back. There was a cry, as though someone had made a discovery and then a moment later, a key slid into the lock.

That was it for Muriel, she scrambled out the bed like a tic with a scorched arse. And not a moment too soon. The door flew open and in strode master James looking angry and upset. His face was flushed and he was breathing heavy, as though he had been running. Behind him, on the landing, I caught a glimpse of Hector peering in, all agog.

Muriel and I kept our traps shut, we just hung our heads and waited. The sight of us stood there, shame-faced, seemed to fill master James with further anguish.

He motioned abruptly for Hector to move back. 'Wait there!' he commanded. 'At the top of the stairs. Let no-one pass!'

As Hector shrank out of sight, master James began to pace the room, keeping one eye on me and Muriel all the while. He tugged back the curtains and glanced behind them, as though he expected somebody to be hiding there. Then he knelt down and peered under the bed. Finally he got to his feet and addressed us coldly.

'Where is my wife?'

Muriel made a curtsey. She could not have known, but the pillow had left red crumpled marks on her cheek.

'Sir,' she says. 'I am awfy sorry, sir. But she ran past us, sir. There was nae stopping her. And she locked us in. There was nothing we could dae, sir. She pushed Bessy in and locked the door on us, sir!'

This news appeared to distress master James even more. His eyes glazed over like he was staring at eternity, and it wasn't a good one.

'When was this?' he says.

Muriel glanced at me in a panic, I expect she was confused by sleep and had not noticed the time. I stepped forward.

'About ½ past 12, sir,' I says. 'Perhaps two hours ago.'

His shoulders slumped and he stood there, bereft. Presently, his gaze fell upon the bed. Muriel had left the covers in disarray. Master James frowned and reached out, plunging his hand between the sheets. His face cleared as he raised his head to look at us.

'Still warm,' he says. 'So she cannot have been gone that long.'

He glanced around, suddenly hopeful, as if we might be concealing her somewhere. Muriel stared at the floor, chewing her lip, her face burning a deep red.

'Sir,' I says. 'It was not missus in the bed, sir.'

His head whipped round. 'What the Devil do you mean?'

Muriel was scowling at me now, her eyes full of resentment. I thought of the letter down in the study and of being gone from there. It didn't matter what I told him.

'While we were waiting,' I says. 'I lay in the bed, sir, and fell asleep.'

He yanked his arm out the bedclothes and glared at me. I did not look at Muriel but could feel her eyes upon me.

'I am sorry, sir,' I says.

He let out a great sigh, shaking his head in exasperation. I waited for him to dismiss me on the spot. But then his mind seemed to wander. He appeared to forget about me altogether and was overcome by other graver thoughts. His face grew haggard. He put his hands to his head and clutched at his hair. He moaned.

'Sir, if you don't mind my asking,' I says. 'What has happened? Did you find missus, sir? Did she go to the village? Has somebody seen her?'

He gazed at me dead-eyed as if he had never seen me before. And then instead of answering, he turned on his heel and walked from the room. I heard him cross the hall and enter his own chamber. The door shut and then there was silence.

Muriel and I looked at each other.

'What did you say that fur?' she says. 'You're for it now.'

'It doesn't matter. I am leaving here anyway.'

'Are ye?'

At that moment, one of the landing floorboards creaked and Hector poked his snitch in at the door. He didn't look at Muriel, only me.

'You'll neffer kess fwhat hess happened!' he says.

21

Pandemonium

Well, I was not present for most of the events I am about to describe but the tongues were clacking like castanets afterwards and the story has been much repeated down the years. There was articles in two newspapers and since those days I have spoke to a number of people who were involved or who seen what happened. From this and with a little imagination, I have pieced together an account.

To begin then, at the very beginning. It seems that having locked Muriel and I in her own chamber missus set the door-key on the linen chest where it was later discovered by master James and Hector. She could easy have slipped it in her own pocket or chucked it away but I like to think she didn't want us to be imprisoned for too long and thus put the means of our release in plain view.

Thereafter she ran downstairs (as overheard by myself and Muriel) and went to the kitchen, where she must have found the old coat that she had give me, and the ancient bonnet I sometimes wore when it was cold. In years to come, when people talked about having seen her that day, they describe the old coat and granny bonnet. Why did she choose these garments, as opposed to any of her own? Well I'll tell you. I think she wanted to disguise herself. In a shabby coat and battered hat, nobody would recognise her and that suited her purpose.

Dressed in these duds, she left the house and made her way through the fog to the village. Most people were by that time gathered at the Cross, for the fountain ceremony. At any rate, the first sighting of missus was some way up the road at around one o'clock, just outside the Swan, which was the larger inn and as such the one that housed most lodgers.

There was a driver sat on the step of his cab, he noticed a woman in an old-fashioned bonnet at the doorway of the taproom. She seemed reluctant to go in. He seen her step back, look up and down the street and then waylay a small ragged boy who was hurrying along towards her. She spoke to this boy, apparently asking him something. But he shook his head and scuttled by without pausing. The woman then approached the cab driver himself. By his account, she kept turning her head this way and that, using the wings of the bonnet to shield herself from his view. She seemed nervous and requested that he go into the Swan but before he could find out why, a gentleman passenger stepped up to the cab in haste and the driver had to accept the fare. He apologised to the woman in the bonnet and told her she would have to find someone else to help. The last he seen of her, she was stood in the street outside the tavern, looking a little lost.

Some time later, presumably having failed to find anyone else to go in on her behalf, missus entered the taproom herself and approached the proprietor, who was it but AP Henderson the bastard grocer, he had newly expanded his business and took over the Swan. If you believe a word he says, missus seemed ill at ease being in a public house. She did not stay long and kept her face in shadow all the while. Her eyes seemed drawn towards the stairs that led to the 2nd floor. She asked him if there was a Mrs Gilfillan in residence. When he told her that there was not, she described the lady she had in mind, but nobody answering that description was lodged there and he tellt her as much. Upon hearing this, she thanked him and left. Henderson thought no more about the incident until much later, as he was particularly busy with preparations for the dinner that was to be held that evening to celebrate the unveiling of the fountain.

Some minutes then elapsed before missus was next seen, this time at the other end of the village. Here, in The Gushet, Janet Murray was redding up the place in the hope that those not among the dozen worthies invited to the dinner at the Swan might instead celebrate at her premises. Apparently, she glanced up from wiping a glass to see a woman in the doorway. At first, Janet did not recognise her because of what she wore. But she knew missus well enough, had often seen her about the district over the years and she soon realised who was at the threshold. Never a great enthusiast for the gentry, Janet did not encourage her to come in. Besides, missus seemed agitated. She made no pleasantries just asked whether there was a Mrs Gilfillan in residence.

When Janet failed to recognise that name, missus gave a description that sounded to Janet the very glass and image of her only guest, the demanding Mrs Kirk, an Irish widow (ho-ho!) who had been lodging at The Gushet for the past few weeks. Mrs Kirk would be leaving Snatter that very afternoon, Janet told missus. But, for the moment, she was not on the premises. As far as Janet knew, she was away up the road to the Cross along with everybody else to see the fountain. Janet expressed surprise that missus Reid was not up there herself, seeing as how it was her husband that was behind it all. But missus apparently ignored that remark and asked whether Mrs Kirk had been accompanied by a man, who perhaps went by the name MacDonald. Janet knew nothing of any such person and said as much. Upon which, missus turned on her heel and left, barely pausing to thank Janet, who would later say that such was the way with these folk, they would not give you the steam off their porridge, or words to that effect.

Meanwhile the fountain ceremony was well advanced. Despite the fog and cold, quite a crowd had gathered at the Cross, mostly Snatter and Smoller residents but since this was the Edinburgh road, a number of strangers and passers-by had also stopped to see what was the go. The fountain was shrouded in green canvas. Beside it, a little platform had been erected, upon which stood the various dignitaries, master James, the Reverend Mr Pollock and his brother Mr Duncan Pollock (*Member of Parliament!*), Mrs Duncan Pollock, Mr Calvert the engineer from the foundry, and other honoured guests. Due to the small dimensions of the platform they were all rather huddled together at the back, 'closer than a shirt tail and a shitty arse', as one onlooker remarked.

Master James had begun the proceedings promptly by ringing a wee bell to command attention. Thereafter he produced a huge sheaf of paper upon which he claimed (rather bashfully) to have wrote his speech. This was thought to be a great joke and was greeted by much laughter until the crowd realised their mistake – the reams of paper did in fact constitute a lengthy oration. Perhaps master James was keen to flex his parliamentary muscle. At any rate, his speech dragged on and on. Several folk drifted away and more might have joined them had not a few bystanders with watches taken it upon themselves to *time* master James with the result that a hasty sweepstake was got up, which revitalised proceedings no end and ensured that everyone present hung onto his every word, both those who had made a bet and those who were just tickled to see who would win.

As the inexplicable restlessness among the crowd turned to what seemed like rapt attention, master James grew in confidence. He poked fun at the old wells in the village, saying that the supply of water drawn from there had two advantages, that it was a tea saver (since the colour was light brown) and that because it swarmed with animalcule it could be said to be both food and drink. These were familiar jests, but politely received nonetheless. Much encouraged, he went on. He had great plans for Snatter, he tellt them. This fountain was just the beginning. It would be gas in pipes next, he said, to light the street and perhaps even gas candelabras in every household. Again, there was laughter from the crowd and some wag called out, 'Aye, and refrigeration machines,' which caused much hilarity. Undeterred, master James pressed on. He thanked his honoured guests at length, in particular Mr Duncan Pollock (Member). And so it went on. And on and on.

Once the 30 minute mark had been reached, most estimates of how long the speech would last had been surpassed and the majority of those who had placed bets had been forced to drop out. Only two men were left in the contest, Biscuit Meek and Willie Aitken, the old Tollman. Willie had estimated 35 minutes and Biscuit had gone for 46. Perhaps Biscuit could be expected to know his master better, but as it turned out the speech lasted just over 37 minutes, making Willies estimate the closer and him the victor. Since Willie was a well-liked man and Biscuit was no such thing, the outcome of the sweepstake caused great jubilation among the crowd. As master James made his closing remarks and retired to the back of the platform, hats were thrown into the air and there was general cheering and hurrahs all round. Master James, mistaking this happy clamour for the reception to his address, looked most gratified.

After that, and with only a few small technical delays, the canopy was removed from the fountain, which prompted many whistles and cries of 'Oooh!' and 'Aaahh!' not all of which were satirical. Master James invited the honoured guests to taste the water, which was pronounced cold but delicious and while the nabobs were busy with their spouts and cups, many of the general assembly took advantage of the pause to settle their debts. A few arguments broke out and small boys ran hither and thither with money and flasks that had been recharged over at the Swan. Presently, the little bell was rung to bring everyone to order for it was now the turn of the Reverend Mr Archibald Pollock to address the people.

The Reverend spoke without notes and held up both his hands to prove it, before sticking two fingers in his waistcoat pocket, the better to stride about the stage. He began by congratulating master James on his excellent address, saying that by comparison his own offering would be a mere Pygmey. With a smile of the utmost modesty, Reverend Pollock confessed himself to be no Mr Dickens. He would not be orating at any length, he said, nor pausing to roll up his shirt-sleeves, nor mopping his fevered brow with a kerchief, nor indeed staggering, spent, from the stage. During these remarks he gazed at the crowd with his beady eye, looking neither right nor left and certainly not behind him at the previous speaker, but it was generally felt that his comments were somehow directed at master James.

The Reverend then turned to gaze upon the fountain, good-natured appreciation writ large across his features. He was reminded, he said, of William of Orange.

Master James, who had until this point been staring at the platform, looked up, apparently startled. Aye, says the Reverend, William the Third who – it was too little realised – had not only been a great soldier and politician but an accomplished gardener as well, with a great fondness for extravagant waterworks and, yes, fountains not unlike this one. Reverend Pollock confessed that he had not had the good fortune to see the great Kings famous gardens at Het Loo but that he had on two occasions visited Hampton Court and there seen many a wonderful fountain, most of them perhaps a little more extravagant than this one – but then (he said) Mr Reid was well known locally for his superlative fiscal ability.

Here, the Reverend paused a moment, to smile into the crowd. Behind him, master James was scowling and looking this way and that, as though he had smelled something bad. The Reverend approached the front of the platform and in a stage whisper confided that although it might not yet be common knowledge, Mr Reid wished to emulate his own good brother, Mr Duncan Pollock, by pursuing a career in politics. Some people, he said, might be of the opinion that benevolent acts, such as providing public fountains, were a means of buying popular support. The Reverend shook his head and wagged his finger. He was not one of those people. And to prove it he sketched a low bow towards master James and wished him every good fortune. In closing, he expressed his fervent hope that – one day – Mr Reid would turn out to be as successful and popular as his mentor Mr Duncan Pollock. The minister then retreated to thc back of the platform, from where he graciously acknowledged the applause with a wave of his hand.

Master James gave a stiff little bow and thanked the Reverend for his kind remarks. Then he invited the good people of Snatter to approach the fountain in an orderly manner to sample its water. A near-riot ensued as folk pushed to get to the front of the queue.

Master James put his foreman Alasdair in charge of controlling the crowd whilst he buttonholed Duncan Pollock and wife, drawing them to safety, away from the general stramash on the other side of the Cross.

It was at about this time that missus was seen talking to Reverend Pollock. Previously, during his speech, one or two folk claim to have noticed a woman stood on the fringes of the crowd, staring at the Reverend with a certain cold intensity from behind the wings of her bonnet. She was said to have been muttering to herself and one man seen her call out an oath and shake her fist in the direction of the platform, but this behaviour did not seem *too* unusual for spirits were high. In any case, her cry went unheard amid the general racket.

It seems that she must have been careful to avoid being noticed by those who knew her, for nobody of her acquaintance recalls seeing her at the ceremony. That is, except the Reverend Pollock. He was now standing alone next to the platform, beaming upon the populace as they drank from the fountain with a fond indulgent smile on his face, almost as if (as one person commented) he had passed the water himself.

According to his own account, the Reverend did not at first recognise Mrs Reid. Bear in mind, she had grown even thinner since his last visit and she was wearing shabby outer garments that he would not have associated with her. Moreover he was not expecting to see her that day, having been told (along with everyone else) that she was suffering from a headache and would not be in attendance. Her appearance, therefore, took him by surprise. He claims that she spoke to him 'quiet as a mouse in cheese' so that he had to lean towards her to hear what she said. He gathered, after a moment, that she wanted to show him something and requested that he follow her. Somewhat bemused but unsuspecting, the Reverend complied, thinking that perhaps she wished to give him a peek at some secret present she had bought for her husband as a way of marking this important day.

To his surprise, missus led him into the alley at the side of AP Hendersons shop. There they were seen by a Mrs Annie Bell, a miners wife, who was at her first floor window. This window overlooked not only the alley but also the Cross and it was from here that Mrs Bell, recently moved to the area from Leadhills, had chose to watch the unveiling of the fountain, because it was cold and she had a dose of 'the snuffles'. She said that the woman in the bonnet led the minister to the grocery yard just below her window and there they stopped, apparently to converse. The yard was rather more cluttered than usual, having been used as a temporary storage place by workmen involved in the installation of the fountain and it was stacked with lengths of pipe, stone slabs, tools and other such materials.

Heretofore, according to the Reverend, missus had been quite charming, almost solicitous. However, once in the yard, out of public view, she became irate and began interrogating him about some woman he had never heard of. When asked later, he could not remember the womans name, but thought it might have been something like Whelan, Finnegan or Gilligan. Missus began to berate him as a liar and charlatan and even accused him of *masquerading* as a man of the cloth! It quickly became clear to the Reverend that her wits were disordered. He decided to extricate himself from her company and alert her poor husband to the problem. Informing her that his presence would be required over at the fountain, he turned to leave, with the intention of hurrying back to the Cross.

At this point, Mrs Bell lost interest. She had been watching the scene below with mild curiosity, since there was evidently some kind of argument going on, but it now seemed that the pair were about to quit the yard. However, as she turned from the window she heard the sound of a loud blow. Looking out, she seen that the Reverend was kneeling on the ground with blood coming from his head. The woman was standing over him with a spade in her hands, which she must have grabbed from the tools that had been left against the wall. Mrs Bell remembered that the blood was a very bright red colour against the ministers skin.

So shocked was she, that she froze momentarily. Thus she witnessed what happened in the next few seconds. The woman lifted the spade and continued to rain down further blows on the Reverends head and shoulders. He dropped forwards onto his hands and knees and tried to crawl away, calling out for help, but in a small voice that did not carry. The woman followed him, beating him with the spade, shouting things and calling him terrible names (about which Mrs Bell would not be specific except to say that they involved the letter 'F').

The Reverend Mr Pollock, for his part, does not remember much after being hit on the head. He has a dim memory of further blows to his person as he crawled across the gravel, but cannot remember anything that was said to him.

Luckily, within moments, Annie Bell came to her senses and was able to scream for help. As her cries rang out, the woman in the bonnet turned abruptly with the spade in her hands and stared up at the window. For the first time, her features were revealed. Mrs Bell, being new to the area, did not recognise her. But she would never forget the look that the woman gave her. It was, she said, 'a look of cold death'. Fearing for her own self, she screamed again. The woman seemed to scrutinise her, as though to determine who she was. And then, apparently, she lost interest. She dropped the spade to the ground and set off across the yard, away from the alley.

By this time, Mrs Bells screams had attracted attention and several people were hurrying over from the gathering at the fountain. At the sound of their footsteps in the alleyway, the woman picked up her skirts and ran off. When help arrived in the yard, Mrs Bell pointed out the direction in which she had gone and a number of men and boys gave chase. But they returned not long afterwards. It seemed that the woman who had attacked the Reverend had disappeared into the mist – or at least into the woods that began behind the Free Gardeners Lodge.

The minister was carried to the fountain, where his head was washed and where the doctor examined and bound his wounds. At this stage, Reverend Pollock was not capable of speech. He was badly shaken and could only open and shut his mouth like a fish, making a gulping sound in the back of his throat. Because of this, he was unable to identify his attacker and although he kept pointing at master James, nobody was able to understand what he meant since master James had been in full view of everyone all afternoon and it could not possibly have been his fault.

The miners wife, Mrs Bell, was brought down to the Cross. She described what she had seen from her window but at that stage nobody gave much credibility to her story. She was a newcomer, after all. And it was hard to believe that such violence could have been carried out by a woman. Certainly, nobody connected her tale of a shabbily dressed woman in a bonnet with Mrs Arabella Reid (not even master James, who was at that time fairly sure that his wife was locked up safely in her chamber at Castle Haivers).

Talk was rife amongst the crowd, who could have done this thing, and why? In public everyone expressed shock that such an assault could have happened. However, the Reverend (whilst *seeming* to be a genial sort of fellow), had in fact managed to get up many noses over the years and there was more than one person would have liked to give him a good kicking. Privately, there were those who were surprised – not so much that someone had *attacked* him – but that nobody had done so years ago and many times over.

Meanwhile, where was Bridget (or Mrs Kirk, as Janet Murray thought of her)? Janet had tellt Arabella that Mrs Kirk had gone along with everybody else to have a look at the unveiling of the fountain. And indeed, she had been present for the start of proceedings, but was one of those for whom the opening speech proved too much. While master James was droning on and the sweepstake was getting underway, a few folk in Bridgets vicinity consulted quietly amongst themselves and decided to retire in advance to the taproom of the Swan. The seats would need warming up, they said. The ale should be tested! Bridget invited herself along and it was there, in seclusion with her newfound friends (mostly rapscallions), that she spent the rest of the afternoon. She had already settled her bill with Janet Murray and craftily avoided a further trip out into the cold by paying a boy tuppence to fetch her bag from The Gushet.

AP Henderson was in and out the taproom all afternoon but his attention was focused on preparations in the kitchen and in the dining room upstairs. He did notice the group of folk sitting in the corner and the Irish woman who was with them, but did not connect her with the woman that he'd been asked about earlier in the day.

At about two o'clock, the company in the taproom were startled when a ferret-faced local man burst in, demanding a pot of brandy for medicinal purposes and saying that Reverend Pollocks head had been split open by a gang of Taigs. (This was the current best theory, since nobody wanted to believe Mrs Bell and a culprit was yet to be apprehended.)

The patrons of the Swan hurried outside. Some folk – possibly Catholics – disappeared into the mist, fearing retribution. Others accompanied the wee weaver, to see what all the fuss was about. Bridget (no doubt keeping her trap shut about her own lapsed faith) went with them. The throng at the Cross had swelled, since word had spread and a violent assault is infinitely more appealing than a few snobs giving speeches. People at the back had to strain to see what was going on and Bridget was soon lost among the crowd.

In the centre of it all, a group of gentlemen (including Duncan Pollock, McGregor-Robertson, Mr Flemyng and master James) stood over the minister, keeping the masses at bay. The Reverend had been propped up against the base of the fountain. He looked frail and defenceless. His head was wrapped in a temporary bandage. Someone had covered him with a blanket. The brandy was passed to the doctor, who crouched down and held the pot to the ministers lips.

After a few slugs, Reverend Pollock spluttered and coughed. 'Whoof! Sheesh!' he says, the first almost coherent sounds he had made.

McGregor-Robertson leaned closer. 'Who did this, Archie? Who was it?'

The Reverend raised his eyes slowly. He gazed beyond the doctor and seemed with a sense of wonderment to take in the crowd and then the other gentlemen. As soon as he clapped eyes on master James, he gave a start then let out a shuddering breath. Some folk said he looked bewildered and frightened. Others that he looked stunned. Whilst a few others thought that, despite his injuries, he seemed to be making a meal of it, and taking some pleasure at being the centre of an unfolding drama.

'Dearie me,' he says. 'I – I – don't know – oh!'

He was staring at master James all the while. Then he closed his eyes and let out another great shuddering sigh, as if it was all too much to bear. 'Ah-haaah!' he goes. 'Oh-ho!'

The doctor put a reassuring hand on his shoulder.

'You're going to be all right, Archie,' he says. 'You are hurt but it will heal. Now tell us, who did this to you? What did they look like?'

The ministers eyes snapped open and once again his gaze fixed on master James, who was beginning to look a little uncomfortable. Reverend Pollock gulped and swallowed. His mouth worked. Then he licked his lips and whispered. 'It was – it was –'

The crowd strained forwards to hear. He raised his arm and pointed at the group of gentlemen. His finger wavered dramatically to and fro before it became apparent that he was indicating master James. And then he spoke out in precise, ringing tones. Indeed, if he had been in a theatre, his voice would have reached the back of the stalls.

'I was attacked – by Arabella Reid!'

22

An Unexpected Loss

Like I says, the most of this I learned about or put together much later. That day, on the landing, all we had from Hector was the bare minimum of information, a few words on the subject rolled together in a sentence along with something else that was on his mind.

'Missus Reid hit the Refferent Pollock on the head wit a shoffel and ran afwhay fwhould you be fwhanting to go for a walk wit me Bessy, hon your day hoff?'

'Eh?' says Muriel. 'A shovel?'

But before I had time to take in the first part of what Hector had said, master James re-emerged from his room and came skyting past us, the coat-tails on him all a-flurry.

'Come along, Hector,' he says. It seemed that a few moments alone were all that he needed to recover. Hector trotted off in his wake. I stood there in a dwam a second and then I hared after them.

'Sir, sir! Are you going to look for missus?'

'Of course!' he says crossly, without glancing back.

I took a deep breath. 'Could I come with you, sir? Could I help?'

He paused at the top of the stairs, one hand on the banister, and looked at me. I noticed that he had torn off his stiff collar and changed his shiny shoes for old boots. He gave me a mocking smile.

'A very gracious offer,' he says. 'But I was assuming you'd be going back to bed to continue your nap.'

'No sir,' I says. 'I want to help.'

He stuck out his chin. 'Somebody will need to stay here,' he says sternly. 'In case she returns. And I will be wanting to speak to you later.'

A voice came from behind me. 'I'll stay here, sir.'

I glanced round to see that Muriel had stepped forward. For dear sake! She wouldn't catch my eye, but went on, 'Ah don't mind waiting, sir, if Bessy wants tae go.'

Master James sighed. 'Very well,' he says, and continued down the stairs, he had more important things on his mind than the doings of maids so he did.

Well I turned to thank Muriel but she was having none of it, she brushed past me saying, 'Don't!' Most likely she would never thank me for getting her out of trouble but she had returned my favour swiftly and that was, in her opinion, an end to it.

Master James and Hector were already heading out the front door. I flew downstairs, overtaking Muriel, and ran into the kitchen, to the back door. It was then I discovered my coat was missing. I must have cried out in frustration, for Muriel came in and asked me what was the go. When I tellt her, she didn't say a word, just lifted her own coat off the peg and dropped it in my arms. Then (I suspect taken aback by her own generosity), she headed out towards the dunegan, a 'whatever-next' expression on her phiz, with her gob tucked up at one corner, as though somebody had put a stitch in her cheek.

Hector and Master James had gone in the direction of the stables, so I struck out on my own down the lane. If I stirred my stumps I might even get to Snatter before they did. The ground was rutted and froze, so I could not run too fast for fear of going tip over arse. But I trotted along quick as I could, my breath exploding as smoke in front of my face then whipping off to mingle with the mist in my wake.

Try as I might I could not fathom what had happened. I knew missus didn't really like the Reverend but it was incredible that she would have belted him with a shovel, even in her present state of mind. My only thought was that perhaps he had tried to stop her running away and she had attacked him as a way of escaping.

Just as I got to the edge of the village, a horse came scuddering out the mist behind me and overtook me at a gallop. It was master James, with Hector mounted behind him. As they sped on towards the Cross, Hector turned and blew me a kiss. I made a point of ignoring him and hurried on, arriving at the fountain a few moments later.

The place was heaving, with people standing about in various groups. Master James had just dismounted. He left Hector to tie up the horse while he went to speak to Alasdair who was stood on the platform, organising folk into search parties. It would not be dark for a few hours yet but a number of villagers were running back and forth, bringing lamps from their cottages. Somebody was handing out bread and AP Henderson the old nip-cheese had not missed a trick, he had set up a barrel on a table and was selling ale to them that wanted refreshment. Of the Old Bollix no sign. Presumably by this time he had been took home to rest. I noticed that master James and the doctor were now talking to a woman I didn't recognise, a toaty wee woman in a blue shawl.

Flemyng was hovering in the background. I caught his eye and just for badness gave him a saucy wink and a wave. A look of alarm crossed his face and he leaned in towards master James and the doctor, and pretended to be engrossed in their conversations. Sicken him.

I had hoped to get a message somehow to my mother but it looked as though the search parties were ready to move off any minute. There was a small boy just in front of me about 7 years old. He had a pencil in his hand and was running about to no purpose as small boys are wont to do, sometimes aiming his pencil at people as though it were a musket and at other times arguing with himself in badgering voices as though he were an entire company of soldiers.

I called him over and showed him a farthing that I took from my pocket. 'Do you know the Railway Tavern?' I says to him.

He nodded, the eyes on him never once leaving the coin in my hand. I tellt him he would get the farthing – and another on top – if he went to the Railway Tavern and gave a message to a lady by the name of Mrs Kirk. Then I took the pencil off him and used it to write a message on the handkerchief master James had give me for Christmas. It was difficult to make marks on the cloth and my mother was no great shakes at the reading so I kept the note short.

Am delayed. Sorry. We can go tomorrw. Yrs Daisy.

How strange to be writing my own name, the first time in months I had used it, but I supposed I should get used to it once more. I tucked the snoot-cloot into the boys pocket and gave him his pencil and the farthing, telling him that he would get the other when he had delivered the message and found me again. He lit off at full tilt and once I'd checked that he was heading up the Station road sure enough, I began to make my way towards the fountain to be told what to do.

I had not took but two steps when who accosted me but Hector. Into my path he jumped and began to dance at me, trotting this way and that like a pony with the head staggers. Over his shoulder I noticed master James on the platform, still talking to the wee woman in the blue shawl.

'Whell now,' says Hector. 'Hif it's not Miss Hoity-Toity.'

'Flip away off,' I says, trying to elbow past him. 'Or I'll ottomise you.'

Hector grabbed my shoulder and held me at arms length. He looked offended.

'Now fwhat's the matter fwhith you?' he says. 'Come on now! I greased the way in there hallready. Fwhun minute your thingumbob is biting your arse for it, the next you fwhant to be left halone.'

(And you can be sure he did not say 'thingumbob').

He pinched my waist and tried to get his arms round me. But I twisted out his grasp and turned to face him.

'All right, mundungus,' I says, as if I didn't care. 'But you have to pay for it.'

'I beg your pardon?' says Hector.

'And it's 5 shillings.'

At this, he looked as though his hat might blow off with astonishment.

'*Fife shillings!*'

'That's right,' I says. And while he was still chewing on that morsel, I jerked my thumb towards the platform. 'Who's your wee woman talking to master James?'

'Eh?' He glanced over, his mouth hanging open. 'Och that's

Missus Bell,' he says. 'She's the fwhun that seen Missus Reid hit the minister. Fife shillings? Are you haffing a choke fwhith me?'

'That's what it costs,' I says. 'From now on. So think about it. You better start saving up so. Either that or away and fetch mettle.'

And I left him scratching his head and staring after me, betwattled.

I was in one of the last search parties to be formed so I was and thank God Hector was put in another. We were about twelve of us in our group and our task was to walk in line around the perimeter of the trees, beginning at the Free Gardeners Lodge and then heading east and then south and so on, clockwise through the fields and around the woods until we returned to the village. It was thought that missus had been hiding somewhere in the trees but that the noise of the search parties crashing about in the undergrowth might have flushed her out like a gamebird. We took a few lamps and torches against the fog. Alasdair had tellt us to keep at an even distance from each other, with the stretch of two arms or thereabouts between each pair. The party was mostly made up of weavers and some wives and a couple of mopsqueezes like myself. The only folk I recognised were the two miners that I'd seen in The Gushet but since they had never noticed me hiding behind the door I kept my trap shut.

The women on either side of me lived right by the Cross and by Jove they could talk to beat Banagher, so they could. They were more than happy to tell me about all what I had missed during the day. I was very curious about what Mrs Bell had seen from her window. Apparently she'd heard missus getting on at the minister. This was the part I was interested in. Getting on at him about what? I wanted to know, but even though they both had tongue enough for two sets of teeth neither of the women could tell me. They were most impressed to hear that I worked at Castle Haivers but I didn't want them asking too many questions so I tellt them I was a farm servant and had never seen Mrs Reid except at a distance. If only they knew!

After a while the talk died out and we paced the fields in watchful silence. Sometimes in places where the fog was thinner, the odd light became visible, flickering among the mist and trees, where other search parties were looking. Sometimes we heard a voice call out, or a sudden burst of laughter. And once, my heart went sideways when a shadow bolted across our path, but it was only a deer, with a skitter of hooves and her white tail bobbing until it was swallowed by the mist. I wondered what would have happened had it been missus. Would somebody have given chase and brought her crashing to the ground? I didn't like to think of her being hunted down like an animal. But neither did I want her to freeze to death under a bush. I imagined her huddled somewhere, or perhaps fleeing ahead of her pursuers, darting wild-eyed from tree to tree. The thought of her in distress made me want to boke.

It took about an hour and a ½ to walk the circuit of the woods. By the time we straggled back to the Cross, it was getting on for twilight. A great bonfire had been lit at the side of the road and somebody had strung up lanterns on the fountain. A few of the search parties had already returned and were taking a break before being sent out again in another direction. Some people were drifting off towards their homes, I wasn't sure they would be back. It was a cold day, after all, to be traipsing the countryside. Those that were left had congregated around the fire.

A group of old women were doling out tea from a big pot that they had brought from one of the houses. I wasn't thirsty but I took a jar to warm my hands. Then I went over to the bonfire. Alasdair was stood a little way off, by the fountain, talking to Hector and Biscuit Meek. There was no sign of master James at first but as I peered about me this way and that, I seen his horse emerge from the direction of the trees. He cantered up to his men and jumped down to talk to them. Presumably he'd been riding between search parties to see if anything had been found.

Just then, I near leapt out my skin as an armful of wood landed with a clatter on the flames beside me. I glanced round and seen that it had been thrown by the wee woman in the blue shawl that I'd noticed earlier talking to master James. Dear sake, she was that small if you put a pigeon on her shoulder it could have picked a pea out her arse.

'Mrs Bell?' I says.

She smiled up at me. Her face was plump like a belter of a scone, with her eyes dark and small as currants.

I says, 'It was my missus you seen earlier, with the minister.'

'Oh dear,' she says and gave me a look like she felt sorry for me. It made me want to defend missus.

'Normally she wouldn't hurt a fly,' I explained. 'Not in the usual way of things. Only she's not been well of late, with her nerves.'

Mrs Bell nodded and patted my arm.

I went on, encouraged. 'Somebody says she was shouting at the minister. Did you hear what she said?'

Mrs Bell frowned. 'Well aye,' she says. 'Afore she hit him she wanted to know where somebody was. Some woman. *Where is she?* she kept saying. *Where is she?*'

Now by this did missus mean Nora, I wondered? Or the imaginary Mrs Gilfillan? And did it mean that she had mistook Reverend Pollock for the henchman MacDonald or whatever his name was, the supposed master of disguise?

Mrs Bell went on. 'And then she started warning him to keep his hands aff somebody. *You can't have her*, she kept saying. *You can't have her*. She was demented, poor dear.'

'What else did she say?'

'It was mostly calling him names. Did she huv a temper, your missus?'

'Not really.'

'She kept saying something was all his fault. He should never have done it, she says. She wasnae in her right senses, dear. It was getting a bit confused by that point. And all his wee leaflets had fell oot his pocket, poor man, and they were lying scattered aboot the place. He looked like he was trying to pick them up.'

Him and his scutting tracts. Only a fool would be taken in by all that nonsense. I thought of Nora, her box and the many tracts in there. I could just see her all prim and proper, sat in her room, reading them by candlelight. And then in a flash, I remembered the day I had bumped into the Old Bollix in Bathgate and the invitation he made me, to visit him. For – what had he called it – tract elucidation? The old sly boots, he did not fool me for a second. But he might have fooled Nora. All those notes in the margins of her tracts – what was that but elucidation?

Of a sudden, I was convinced that she must have got the tracts from Pollock and had been to visit him – more than once, given the amount of tracts in her box. And then I thought back to what Muriel had said about the Reverend and 'Wandering Hand Trouble'. He was such an arsepiece the very thought of it turned my stomach. But right enough, he was a handsome man for his age. And those tub-thumpers can be persuasive. If he had got Nora alone in a room, over the course of a few weeks, who could say what might not have happened? The poor girl. She might even have been stupid enough to fall in love with him.

All at once, I thought I knew the secret behind Noras death. Everything made sense now, why missus had attacked Reverend Pollock, even why she had went mad with grief.

I glanced around to see if master James was still there. I wanted to tell him what I thought right away, for if the truth came out it might help missus get better. To my relief, I seen that he was still standing with Alasdair beside the fountain.

I was about to head over and speak to him when a man came running down Main Street, from the Glasgow direction. A young man he was, dressed in working clothes, in a jacket but no overcoat. He clutched his hat in his hand, perhaps because it would have fell off his head as he ran. A few folk looked at him as he passed but nobody paid much heed at first because any news about missus was expected to come from the woods.

When he seen master James he started yelling. 'Mr Reid! Mr Reid! They've found her!'

And then everybody turned to watch him, as he ran up to the

group of men by the fountain and blurted out a few more words, pointing over the rooftops of the village, not to where he had come from exactly, but more towards the north-west.

Mrs Bell touched my arm. 'What's he saying?' she asked me.

'Shh!' I tellt her. 'I can't hear.'

But something was wrong. Master James was stood stock-still, his face turning pale and stricken as he listened to the man. I seen Alasdair put a hand on his shoulder, as if to give him courage. Then of a sudden a few of the men in the group began pelting down West Main Street. Another leapt up on a cart and grabbed the reins. The doctor jumped up on his trap. Panic had broke out. People started running, mostly in the same direction, down the Great Road. A few others headed up towards the Station. Master James stood in the centre of it all, like a statue. It was only when McGregor-Robertson leaned down and spoke to him that he seemed to will himself into action. He swung up beside the doctor and then the trap sped away up Station road.

I shouted to one of the men as he raced past us. 'What's happened? Where is she?'

The man stopped running and turned back. 'They found her body up on the railway line! She was hit by a train!'

So help me God, I believe I may have laughed out loud. But it was a short laugh, and one that came from shock. I know that now, having since seen the same thing happen a few times. The laughter died on my lips, and still I could not make sense of his words. They echoed inside my head but they had no meaning. Train. Railway line. Body. This last, in particular, confused me. Mr Levy, curled up on the Turkey carpet, cold and still. *That* was a body. Or Nora, lying in her eternity box. Body.

It was not a word I could associate with missus.

Hail Mary Holy Mary save me.

The man was looking at me askance, he had mistook my laugh for a hardness of heart. 'It's not funny,' he says, turning away. 'The woman's dead.'

And then he broke into a run and sped away from us, until the fog and darkness closed around him.

As I sit here now writing this account, I am trying to remember what I was thinking in the seconds and minutes that followed. But there was no thought. Only absence of thought and a bedlam of activity all around me. Everybody was going somewhere at speed. Those that had horses were jumping on them and riding off towards the railway line, taking either the Station road or heading down Main Street. Those that didn't were running in the same directions. A few people had grabbed whatever vehicles were available and everywhere you looked were carts and traps over-laden with passengers.

The moving figures and horses became a blur. I thought I might pass out and then I realised that Mrs Bell was holding me up. It was my one small piece of good fortune that I had her beside me. She had not been offended by my outburst of laughter, having seen that it came from shock. Now, she was supporting me. I tried to concentrate on her grasp, I got it into my head that it might stop me swooning if I fixed my thoughts on some physical feeling. So hard did I concentrate that the rest of me seemed to disappear. All that was left was the band of flesh midway up my arm, encircled by Mrs Bells fingers. The rest of my body was gone. I became aware that she was taking this band of flesh across the street towards the Swan. There was a dogcart emerging from the yard, driven by old AP Bastard himself. Mrs Bell spoke to him and then she took the band of flesh and handed it up onto the bench after which she climbed up herself.

As soon as the dogcart jolted into motion, I was jerked back into my body, for the rattle and shake of the vehicle went through my arse-bones and up my spine into my skull where it made my teeth chatter. It felt as though the springs of the cart were shot, although I don't believe they were, it was just that in the absence of thought I seemed to be experiencing every sensation more intensively. As we turned up the Station road and picked up speed, the vibrations grew worse, I was bounced around like a footmans diddle until every part of my body quivered and trembled. I could practically feel my bones separating from my flesh. The flesh falling off, like cold silk ribbons. I was being shaken apart, I was dissolving, I was melting in fact, my mouth filling up with saliva. I was becoming vapour, my breath shooting out in steamy gasps as though I had been running. And yet I was seated, or at least seated as much as the jumping and slithering of the rig across the frozen mud would allow. The air smelled of smoke and soot. Cold, ragged curtains of fog whipped towards us as Henderson drove the horses harder, flailing the whip, and urging them on with yells, and as we approached the slope up to the railway bridge it felt to me as though we were rattling towards the very gates of Hell.

Here at the bridge Henderson slowed the horses for there was a line of vehicles waiting to turn. The road carried on to the north. Down to the right lay the station. To the left was a rough lane that ran in more or less the same direction as the railway track for about two miles before it ended at another road bridge – from where, if you turned south and carried on across country you would eventually reach Castle Haivers. Every vehicle was heading down this lane and we followed. Once the horses got around the turn they picked up speed and on we went, past various people that were racing along on foot. To one side of us lay the railway track, sometimes gleaming, close enough to touch. At other times, the ground sloped away sharply as the line went through a cutting.

A little way ahead, a few carts and traps had pulled up on the grass beside the lane. There were horses tethered to the trees and a group of folk stood at the edge of a steep cutting, while others were leaving their gigs and carts and running to join them. A moment later, we reached the same spot. Henderson brought the horses to a stop. I helped Mrs Bell to the ground and then hurried over towards where the crowd had gathered.

From the edge of the slope you could see down onto the railway line. A group of four men in working clothes were stood beside the track. They didn't look very happy. On the ground next to them lay a shape or form, it had been covered by empty potato sacks. Another similar form, also covered by sacks, lay a few yards distant, further along the track. Sammy Sums stood a little way off, counting the sack-covered forms, pointing at one then the other. One, two, he went. One, two. One, two.

Master James and the doctor were beetling down the grassy bank and when they reached the bottom, they went over to the men. A few words were spoken. Mrs Bell appeared beside me and took hold of my arm but before I knew it I found myself breaking free from her and scrabbling downhill.

Just as I reached level ground, one of the labourers bent down and raised a corner of the sacks. Master James, his face full of trepidation, leaned down to see what lay beneath. A moment later, the trepidation changed to amazement. After which I heard him say, 'That is not her. That is not my wife.'

Relief shot through me, it was like a knock of gin on an empty gut. I stepped closer, to look for myself, just to be sure, and saw that master James was exactly right. For the person laying dead by the tracks was not missus. It was Bridget. It was my mother.

She was on her back, her eyes closed. She looked tiny, like a child. There appeared to be not a mark on her. Her hair, her face, the little that I could see of her clothes – everything perfect. It was as if she would open her eyes at any moment and stretch her arms and start talking. Only, there was something not quite right. At first, I couldn't work out what it was. The doctor was crouching down to have a closer look at her while master James had turned away. Beyond him lay the other pile of sacks. They had definitely been used to cover something up. Two corpses! Could this other be missus? Sammy Sums was still counting. One, two. One, two. For a moment, I could not make sense of what I was seeing. Why did they not show master James the *other* corpse? And then, with a sickening jolt, I realised my mistake and why my mother had looked so small. It was not a 2nd body that lay beneath the other sacks. Not a 2nd body at all.

I doubled over and boked and carried on boking until I boked only air. And as I knelt there, heaving into the dirt and stones at the side of the tracks, the mens voices came to me as if from a great distance.

'We were jist walking home alang this way,' says one of the labourers. 'And we seen her lying there. And then – we found the rest ae her, over there.'

I lifted my head and saw him pointing to the other pile of sacks.

'Cut right in two,' says the doctor. 'Dear God.'

'Aye, she was probably walking along the line, like we were. Except she couldn't have seen the train because ae the fog. And she was drunk. You can smell drink on her.'

'She might have fallen off that bridge back there,' says the doctor. 'Or been carried along by the train that hit her. That's not uncommon.'

More words were spoken but I don't remember anything because the next thing I knew, master James had noticed me and was walking towards me. 'Bessy, Bessy,' he was saying, not unkindly. 'What the Devil are you doing down here?'

I gazed at him and then beyond him at the thing that lay under the sacks and then up at the folk gathered on the top of the grassy slope, peering down. My head felt like it might explode. Master James was waiting for me to say something but I couldn't speak for fear I was about to burst. The sweat was pouring off me. I wanted to leap at him and batter the lard out him with my fists. That was the solution, by Jove! To have a square-go, wigs on the green! That was what I had to do. Why had I not thought of it before? I almost did it too, I had my fists bunched up but just at the last moment I changed my mind. *Motion* was what I needed, I suddenly realised. Motion and distance. And with no more thought than that I took to my heels and began running as fast as my legs would carry me, along the side of the track, with somebody calling out after me, the name 'Bessy' echoing in my ears.

There was no plan to my flight. To be blunt, I did not know where the Hell I was going. I simply kept running alongside the track. Despite the clamour in my brain, it was good to be running. I got quite a rhythm going. I was the running girl, so I was. After some time, it might have been a few minutes or it might have been many, I came to a station. There must have been a train due because people were stood on the platform looking down at me running along the track. There they were, waiting on a train and instead what comes puffing along but a girl. I found that enormously funny for some reason. All these people staring at me, some of them with GREAT disapproval, you could just see it on their phizogs. Would you look at that girl there, running along? Trespassing on railway property so she is, causing a nuisance, acting in an unseemly fashion! I was guilty of it all, but I didn't give a tuppenny damn. I just scrambled up onto one of the platforms and glared back at them all until they looked away. And then I stood there like a great lilty not knowing what the flip to do. If a train had arrived I might probably have jumped onto it, but nothing came immediately and I had no patience, I needed motion again. So after about 5 seconds I started to run once more.

Out the station I went and up towards the main road. There was a man coming downhill towards the ticket office. He opened his mouth as if he was about to yell at me but instead he just yawned and then he kept yawning as he walked along, it was the biggest yawn I'd ever seen. He was still at it as he went past me. How strange to be able to yawn with such contentment! I did not think I would ever be doing that again.

Up at the road I looked about me but hadn't a clue where I was. To the right, I seen a row of big houses with wooden gates and archways of privet in their gardens and beyond them glasshouses in a field and so I ran up there and ducked through a gap in the hedge and after that I kept running across country. It was open marshland there, with no trees and in the distance only tall chimneys and squat bings. At one point I splashed through a stinking black bog that sucked the shoes off my feet and soaked me to the wishbone. It was agony to run in bare feet but I kept going. After a while, the lie of the land rose and the marsh became heath, with dark earth and knee-deep rusty heather, going through it was like wading through waves and my legs grew heavy. I struck out for a scribble of trees I seen in the distance but when I got there found it was not the edge of a forest, only a thin strip of woods. At the other side was a narrow unmetalled road and so I turned and began to follow where it led. On I went, sometimes crossing little bridges butted by clumps of trees, sometimes passing the ruins of old works, with tumbledown heaps of bricks, and beams exposed to the sky like a ribcage. The light began to fade just as I came to the outskirts of a village. Last thing I wanted was to encounter another human and so I struck off the road across more fields until I came to a place that was all fenced in. I peered through a gap in the fence and seen a few ramshackle sheds and a greystone bothy. Next to them was some kind of tank and the entrance to a tunnel but not a living thing in sight. It was a coal pit, all shut down for the night, though I didn't realise it at the time.

By now the twilight was almost gone. I found a hole in the fence and slipped through, with the intention of resting in one of the shacks. As it turned out, the bothy itself wasn't locked. I went inside, there was only one room, it must have been the office though there was nothing much in it except an old desk and chair and a blackened fireplace. No curtain or piece of cloth or cushion but at least it was a fraction warmer than outside and it was dry. I wrapped my shawl and Muriels coat around me and crouched in the corner with my back to the wall, hugging my knees and shivering because the sweat had gone cold on me now that I was no longer in motion. As yet I had not stopped to think. I had only run and walked, hurrying onward, filled with misery and dread. On reflection, I perceived that I felt strange and terrible. I was trembling all over and my head was splitting. No food had passed my lips since the day before. I believe I must have lost my senses. At one point, I started to have a daydream about how if I cleaned out the bothy and got curtains and a table and chair and a little mattress I could live there instead of going back to Glasgow. It was a daft idea, I know, but I kept thinking about it anyway. The only way it would work, I decided, was if nobody knew I was there. I'd have to forage for food at night. And then I started to think that if I could make myself cry it might help me get rid of the terrible anguish I was feeling. But no tears would come. I said out loud the words, 'My mammy,' to see what would happen, but nothing did. And so I said it again, 'My mammy.' But still I did not cry. And then I just started saying it over and over again. 'My mammy, my mammy, my mammy, my mammy.' And then it just turned into, 'Mammy, mammy, mammy.'

And then the tears came. Like a stubborn cork, they had stuck in my throat. But when they slipped out, unexpectedly and with great force, they took me by surprise. I wept like I was delirious and then sank into sleep like a dead person.

23

Desolation

Let me go on. When once again I became aware of what was around about me, the bothy was filled with silvery light. It must have been not long after dawn. How much time had passed or what I was doing in that hut in the middle of nowhere I hadn't a notion but when I opened my eyes there was a rough, begrimed hand on my shoulder. I looked up and saw before me a man in working clothes, peering down. His face was weathered and cut with deep lines and he had on him a wild untrimmed beard and whiskers that gave him the look of a startled owl. Beyond him were several other men, younger than he, but dressed the same in baggy trousers and loose jackets. Some of them wore caps. They were crowding in at the entrance to the bothy, all staring at me, practically clambering over each other to get a better view. In my delirious state, I thought they meant me harm. I cried out and tried to get to my feet but my body was too heavy, it was as though I had become part of the floor. I sank back. Whiskers said something I couldn't make out. And then a circle of blackness closed in and claimed me once more.

In the next interval I was dimly aware of some sensations. Hands lifted me, pulling at my clothes. I moaned and struggled but I was not molested, it was simply that they were trying to hold me upright. Then the world fell away from my feet and tilted sharply as I was borne aloft. 'You go there!' a man called out and – thinking that he had spoke to me – I tried to rouse myself and move my legs but found that the hands only gripped me tighter. 'Get her, Charlie!' the voice says. 'Mind that arm, that's it! Watch her now!' My ankles were gripped, my spine stretched, my head was cushioned against a pillow of corduroy that smelt of tobacco and soap (I realised later it was probably a waist-coated chest). I heard grunts and throat-clearings. 'Right here we go!' says the man. And then everything jolted into motion. I turned my head and seen the earth flow beneath me like a river, mud-caked floorboards giving way to hard-packed earth and then after some time, a rutted lane. It was as if I was trapped in a moving machine that gripped me and sped me along. I did not know its purpose but I had a feeling it was an old machine for the further we travelled the more it began to wheeze and pant like an old mare fit for the knacker, and sometimes it spat off into the grass and now and then it made a comment to itself and once, to my surprise, part of it chuckled at something another part had said.

In time, the swaying movement lulled me and I slipped once more into oblivion. My next sensation was of being set down with a slight jolt. I was in a bed recess and close at hand there was a commotion of leave-taking, whispers and low voices and many pairs of boots shuffling out, it could have been the end of Mass. A door closed. Silence fell. A womans hands settled a blanket over me and gave me milk to drink. And then she pulled the curtains to block out the light. My eyes closed over and I felt as sealed away from the world as though I had been shut forever in a tomb.

So would you believe that I remained in that bed recess for about four days and nights. Jesus Murphy there was not an ounce of strength in my limbs, I had as much command over them as I would have had over molten lead. I drifted in and out of sleep and was sometimes aware of movement and hushed voices in the room beyond the curtain. There were times when I heard a child crying. At other times, smells of cooking seeped into my little coffin. The woman that had give me milk brought me food at intervals, mostly stirabout and broth, and she fed me the few spoonfuls that I was able to swallow. I soon gathered that she was a miners wife and that her husband was the owl-faced man I had first seen in the bothy. He looked in on me each day when he came home from the pit, the whiskers on him still wet from his wash. His name was Chick and his wife was Helen, this I knew from hearing them call to one another in the next room. (What I didn't at first appreciate was that this was only a two-room cottage and that the bed I lay in was their own which they had give up to me, while they slept on a tick next door.)

Helen and Chick were not the worlds greatest talkers but sometimes, in what I took to be evening, I overheard them whispering about me. Once I heard him say to her, 'Has she said anything yet?' Helen made no reply, but must have shook her head, for I hadn't uttered a peep since I arrived. Another time she says to him, 'D'you think she's a gowk?' and he replied, 'Mebbe.'

What was it about me that people were always taking me for a simpleton?

Mostly the drapes kept out the light so I was hardly aware what hour it was. But one day, I awoke to see the curtains part and in the gap appeared one fair tousled head and then another. Two wee girls were peering in at me, one about three years old, the other perhaps six. These, I gathered, must be the children of Helen and Chick. They stared at me in silence with sombre faces and eyes as round as pennies until their mother noticed them and chased them away.

On the fourth day, when Helen brought me some stirabout I had just enough energy to whisper my thanks and she near dropped the bowl in shock. 'Hooch!' she goes, 'Man girl! You've no says a word in days. We thocht you were a dummy!'

At the sound of their mothers voice, the two children came scuttling into the room. They darted behind her skirts and peered out at me with great suspicion, the eyebrows on them drawn down. Helen took my hand.

'Poor bairn,' she says. 'You were just starved and exhaustit. But you're looking better now. D'you want a message sending to anybody?'

For a second, I wanted to tell her everything, but just as quickly realised that I did not have the strength. And so I just shook my head.

She squeezed my hand. 'Well then,' she says. 'You just eat this porridge and hae another wee sleep.' Then she left me the bowl and steered her girls out the room.

The following morning I was well enough to sit up. And the morning after that, I got out of bed, though my legs trembled as if somebody had whacked me on the head.

It was the first really fine day of the year and Helen placed a chair for me by the front door where I sat wrapped in a blanket, the sunlight warming my face. She had mended my stockings as best she could and brushed the dirt off my clothes and Muriels coat. She had even give me her other pair of shoes. They were her best shoes, made of highly polished leather and hardly ever worn. I knew by now that the row of cottages where I found myself was part of Stoneydyke, a pit village some ten miles to the north east of Snatter. Neither Helen nor Chick had pressed me for information about myself. I kept putting off telling them how I had ended up there, saying to myself, 'I'll tell them this afternoon. Tonight. Tomorrow. When I feel stronger.' But in the end, somehow, I couldn't bear to talk about what had happened and so I tellt them only that I'd got lost on my way to Edinburgh and had sought shelter in the pit bothy. They seemed happy enough with that explanation. I could have wished they weren't quite so taciturn, however, since I'd heard no news of Snatter since I arrived.

About 11 o'clock that morning, Helen joined me outside the front door and I helped her to scrape potatoes for the dinner. This seemed as good a chance as any to find out what she knew. I began cautiously enough.

'There was a place I went through the other day,' I says. 'They had a big crowd there, all gathered round a fountain so they were, and a man making a speech.'

'Oh aye,' says Helen, without looking up from her scraping.

I tried again. 'What would the name of that place be now? It was on the Great Road. There was an inn, the Swan I think it was called. And The Gushet.'

'Snatter,' says Helen.

'That's it,' I says. 'There was a man making a speech when I went by, a minister.'

Helens mouth turned down at the corners. 'Him that was attacked,' she says.

I made a surprised face. 'Attacked?'

She nodded, but infuriatingly just went on with her scraping.

'Well – what happened?' I says.

She shrugged. 'Some lady attacked him. Then she ran away. English lady, I think. Completely mad. Hit him wi' a shovel.'

'Oh – oh dear,' I says. 'Did they – did they find her at all?'

'I am no sure,' she says. 'I don't think so. They did find somebody though. The very same day, some poor soul fell affy a bridge and was killed by a train. Irish woman. Tragic. They want to make they bridge walls higher.' Of a sudden she peered at me, concerned. 'Are you all right, dear? You've went aw pale again. Should you lie down?'

'I am fine, thank you.' After a while I says, 'So it was – definitely an accident then, the woman on the railway line? Was it?'

'Oh aye,' says Helen. 'By all accounts, she'd spent the day in the Swan and the Railway Tavern. Then she weaved oot, might have been a call of nature, you know. And it was foggy. Probably lost her footing.' There was a pause then she says, 'Are you defeated?'

For a moment there, I thought she was talking about my life in general. How did she know that things were so bad? But when I looked up I realised she'd only meant my pile of potatoes. She made to take them off my hands.

'No,' I says. 'Let me finish them. You've done so much for me. And eh – I have to be going, this afternoon.'

She looked at me askance. 'Are you sure that's wise?'

'I have to. You need your bed back. And I am feeling so much better.'

To be honest, I had no more strength than a wet wasp. But even a wet wasp will creep towards jam – and so it was with me, I was drawn back to Castle Haivers and to missus.

I will pass swiftly over my departure from Stoneydyke. Suffice to say that as well as the thanks I offered to Helen and a promise to return her shoes as soon as I had my own boots, I silently vowed to repay her and Chick for the kindness they had done me. However, the flipping shoes were that stiff they might as well have been made of metal. By the time I had walked the first mile my feet were cut to ribbons. Also I was worn out. I doubt I'd have got within a hounds howl of Castle Haivers but thank God I was took up by a rag and bone man and so could rest a while on his cart. He dropped me at Smoller, from where I hobbled the last mile or two, taking the back route up Cowburnhill since I didn't really feel like showing my face in Snatter. I might bump into gob knows who, even the Old Bollix, if his head had mended. And I don't know what I might have done had I seen him.

The sun was setting as I approached the side gate of the house. It felt strange to be coming back like this, just as if I was returning from the shops or what have you. The place had a deserted look. No smoke rose from any of the chimneys. Nothing stirred in the vegetable garden. The bonfire out of which I'd plucked *The Observations* was now just a heap of cold ash and charred remains. As I neared the yard, I noticed a sharp, rotting smell that hung in the air, like something had took a watery shite and died. Fearing for the animals, I hared round to their pens. But to my surprise, I seen that both the sty and the hen run lay empty. No pig, no chickens. And no sign of the cat.

I glanced over at the house. The last of the suns rays lit up the windows. They were gold and dazzling, yet it was not pretty but somehow blank and foreboding. Just then something pecked at my shin, I just about lit 6 foot in the air but it was only a single stray hen, a bit bedraggled looking. I shooed her away and approached the house. At first I considered going round the outside and peering in from room to room to see who was there but then I changed my mind, telling myself it was in case anybody got a fright at me spying in at windows. But really I think it was because *I* was feart of what I might see.

The best thing to do, I decided, was to go inside and find out what was the go. The back door lay open. I poked my head round and seen that the kitchen was empty so I went in and closed the door behind me, for it was cold now that the sun was setting. First thing I did was prise off Helens shoes. Then I peeled off my stockings and blew on my blistered feet. After that I looked around, trying to work out if anything had changed since last I'd been there. Now, the fire was out and cold. A drop of milk left in a jug had turned sour. The bread had been stale before I left and now it was furred with green mould. And there was a rank smell rising from the swill bucket. I stood quite still and listened, but the house was silent. The passage to the hall lay empty and quiet, dust motes hung almost motionless in the last rays of sun. I glided silently through, making the dust swirl and dance. After the cold stone of the kitchen, the floorboards felt warmer to my bare feet. Beneath the posting slit lay a small pile of letters. Did that mean there was nobody here? It occurred to me that master James might have went looking for missus somewhere. And then I seen my old coat and the granny bonnet, draped over the newel post. Exactly what missus had been wearing when she had gone missing. She had returned home then.

With my heart up between my ears, I padded across to the parlour and peeked in. There was the chair where she always used to sit. I imagined her sat there now, glancing up from her sewing and smiling at me as I stepped into the room. 'Bessy!' she might say. 'Where have you been?' Or – 'Bessy! What are you thinking of?'

But she wasn't there. And the cushion that usually sat on her chair was on the floor at the other side of the room as though it had been flung there in a temper. Next to it, a candlestick lay overturned. There was also broken glass in the hearth. It occurred to me that if the place had been deserted for a few days then perhaps some intruder – or intruders – might have come in by the back door. Perhaps they were still here now.

No sooner had this thought crossed my mind than I heard something. It sounded very much like the creak of a chair and it had come from the study. My breath caught in my throat. I turned and stepped across the hall, my bare legs trembling. I tried to be silent but the floorboards were sticky and with each step the skin on the soles of my feet peeled away with a rasp that anybody could have heard. The study door was ½ shut. I placed my hand against it and pushed. It swung open slowly and without a sound. There on the wall was the local map I had consulted to see where the railways ran. And there, on the desk, my letter to master James – opened, beside an empty bottle of whisky. And there, sprawled on the sofa on his back, with one arm flung across his face, the man himself. He wore no shoes. The stocking feet on him were filthy and the rest of his clothes dishevelled. There was a glass of whisky on the floor next him and another bottle, this one nearly full. The place was a shambles with dirty plates and glasses on the floor and clothes discarded here and there.

As I gazed at him he sighed and drew his arm away from his face but his eyes remained shut for a moment as he continued to look inwards at his thoughts. They cannot have been pleasant ones, for the expression he wore was pained. His hand fumbled blindly for the whisky glass and failed to find it. Then he opened his eyes. Because of where I stood he was looking straight at me.

'Oh Bessy, do come in,' he says and it touched my heart for he was obviously in the depths of misery but had tried to sound welcoming. He gave me a weak smile as I stepped forwards.

'Sir,' I says. 'Are you all right? Where is missus?'

He took in a great breath as though to answer me but it made something catch in his throat and he fell into a paroxysm of coughing. Jesus Murphy that was some cough he had. He sat up and took a few gulps of whisky, which seemed to help. Meanwhile, he indicated a chair by the hearth. I sat down and waited. Eventually, the coughing fit came to an end. He drew his trembling fingers away from his mouth and leaned his elbow on his knee.

'As you can see,' he says. 'I have been in better health. As for your mistress –' He pursed his lips. 'It is nobodys fault – except perhaps my own.' He put his head in his hand and gave another cough.

His words had done nought but fill me with alarm. 'What is it sir? What's happened? Did you find her?'

'Aye,' he says. 'We found her. As a matter of fact, she was here. She must have come back to the house after –' The pained look crept across his face again. He peered at me. 'She attacked the Reverend Pollock, you know.'

'Yes sir, I was here when you came back with Hector. And then I helped look for her, down at the woods.'

'Oh aye, that's right,' he says. 'So you did. Well, she must have come back here after what – happened – with the Reverend. Meanwhile, they thought they'd found her body up at the railway line but it wasn't her, it was just some woman, a stranger.' He looked at me, his face cleared. 'Ah – you were there too, I remember now.'

'Yes sir.'

'At any rate, Arabella came back here at some point. I don't know how long she was here for but she had gone back up to her room. Nobody saw her return. But Muriel found her upstairs when she went up later, around 6 o'clock. She was on the bed.'

He stopped speaking and seemed to drift off for a second. I had a godawful dread in the pit of my stomach.

'Dead, sir?' I whispered.

He turned to look at me in surprise. 'Not dead. She was quite calmly turning the pages of a book. She's fine, Bessy. At any rate, I mean, she is alive. But we have had to –' He paused and put his hand to his head. 'She has been placed in an asylum.'

The words went through me like a knife. I kept on staring at him. I could not seem to look away. Could not blink. Could not move or speak.

He says, 'It seems that Reverend Pollock contacted the Procurator Fiscal and – well, in brief, McGregor-Robertsons cousin has kindly provided accommodation for her at his establishment. I suppose, frankly, I should have taken steps before now. But I kept hoping that we might be able to make her better here. I was wrong about that.'

My missus! My poor missus – in an asylum!

'I was wrong about it, as I have been wrong about so many things.' He looked at me levelly. 'I neglected your mistress, Bessy. When I should have been here with her, I was off – God knows where –' He gave a hollow laugh, which almost immediately became another coughing fit.

My missus in an asylum – with loonies!

His cough receded. 'It was Arabella that should have been the politician,' he says. 'She is much better with people than I am. It was always her that they liked, that they warmed to. My interest in people has always been – an effort. Insincere.' He stared in misery at the floor. 'We should have lived in Glasgow,' he says. 'She would have fared much better there. But I had my eye on this seat, you see, and I thought it was better to be here, on the spot.' He glanced up and caught my gaze. His eyes were watery, the look in them angry and bitter. But he was angry with himself, not me.

He says, 'I hardly need tell you, it is fairly certain that any chance I might have had of being asked to stand for election has now vanished. The Reverend Pollock will see to that.' His lip curled. 'Never has a man with such extensive head injuries been quite so pleased with himself.' Here he broke off, seeming to remember that I was there and that I was only a maid. 'I don't know if you are interested in this, Bessy. Forgive me.'

'Go on, sir.'

He thought for a moment. 'People like to be associated with success. But as soon as misery comes in the door, society flies out the window. Not a word have I heard from Duncan Pollock, *Member of Parliament*' (this was the first time I'd heard him say it in such mocking tones). 'Not a single word. Even though he cannot fail to know my situation. He fled back to Edinburgh as soon as he could decently extricate himself from his brothers household, probably thanking the Lord that he had not ingratiated himself with us any more than he had already. I believe he'd conceived quite a fancy for Arabella – only to find out that she is not in command of her wits. He must feel duped. As for everybody else –' He made a helpless gesture, by which I understood that people had not exactly been falling over themselves to offer support or condolences.

'Have you had no servant, sir?'

It was not a difficult question but he looked at me blankly, wiping his hand back and forth across his jaw.

'To look after you, sir, I mean. What's happened to the farm servants?'

'Oh,' he says. 'They're here. Muriel or Hector come in a few times a day to get me food, if I want it. I have not had much appetite.' He gazed at the few dirty plates on the floor and then at the whisky bottle. 'Muriels sister Jessie is threatening to leave the estate and take Alasdair with her. Doesn't like the scandal. Doesn't want to be associated with such people as the Reids.' He gave a short, sardonic laugh and I realised for the first time that he was quite drunk. 'I thought you had gone, Bessy,' he says. 'I read your letter.' And then, as if it had just occurred to him, 'You have not yet told me where you have been.'

'I – I got sick, sir, and was taken in by some people for a few days. But I wanted to come back and see was missus all right. Did you know the animals are gone, sir?'

'Animals? Ah yes!' he says. 'That pig and what have you.'

'Hens. And the cat.'

'Aye, they took them back to the farm. I am at a loss to know why they were here in the first place. You don't keep a pig so near the house. I told Arabella that, I don't know how many times.'

'I think missus liked to have them here, sir, so she could watch her girls feed them and clean them out. It wasn't an experiment exactly but she did like to see us working outside. It was all part of her *Observations*.'

'Aye,' he says, darkly. 'Her *Observations*.' He pulled at his lip, looking at me. 'I suspect you are very fond of your mistress, Bessy.'

'That I am, sir.'

He sat back and then drifted off again, staring mournfully after his thoughts like they were a boat floating out to sea. Then something inside him seemed to crumple. After a moment, with his voice hoarse and broken, he says, 'I should have done what she wanted.'

I waited a moment but he didn't elaborate. 'What was that, sir?'

He sighed. 'Arabella is very fond of you,' he says, in an apparent change of subject. 'You must know that, Bessy. Understand that. But I fear she will never get over that other girl.' He looked directly at me now, the anger and bitterness returned to his eyes. 'That's what has really sent her mad. Noras death.' He gritted his teeth. 'And that was my fault.'

I looked at him. '*Your* fault, sir?'

But again, he had fell silent. I waited. Then I says, 'I know that Nora had got herself in bother, sir.'

He frowned at me, his eyes hooded. Was he confused? Or wary?

'Sir, that she was expecting a baby when she died.'

He drew his head back, without changing his expression. 'I presume you would not mind telling me where you heard such a thing.'

'Oh, I didn't hear it, sir, I worked it out. From things missus said and from your reactions, sir, yours and the doctors. And from the way Nora wrote in her journal.'

Master James had been watching me while I spoke. Now he let out a huge shuddering breath that was ½ sigh and ½ yawn. He was not bored, just exhausted. I wondered when was the last time he'd slept. The shadows under his eyes were dark grey. His jacket and collar had gathered up around his neck. It made him appear hunched and defenceless. When he spoke, it was almost a whisper.

'Nora went to her for help, you see. The girl didn't know what to do. She couldn't go to – to the father. That was out of the question. So she appealed to my wife.' He paused. 'I believe Arabella was rather shocked at first. She had thought of the girl as being perfect, unspoiled. Unspoilable. But, as it turned out, there was some coercion involved. I gather that Nora was not altogether a voluntary participant in what happened.'

'I don't expect so, sir,' I says. But he didn't seem to hear me.

He went on, almost mechanically. 'And then Arabella came to me with the news. She had it all worked out. She wanted me to agree to adopt the child so that she and Nora could bring it up here. She was

– excited about it. Of course,' he laughed, bitterly, 'I told her it was out of the question. I – couldn't countenance any threat of scandal. What Arabella was suggesting – it was – a lunatic idea. And so I told her that she would simply have to dismiss the girl.' He gazed off into space. There was a long pause. Then he says, 'I believe it broke both their hearts.'

'Reverend Pollock – he refused to help her then, sir?'

Master James gave a start and blinked at me, astonished. 'How the Devil do you know it was him?'

'Just a guess, sir. Nora had all these tracts, you see. And I heard tell he is prone to making advances at girls. I know missus was in her delusions, sir. But I think part of her knew what she was doing. She blamed him for what had happened to Nora.'

He was still looking at me, surprised. I had suspected all these things for a while but now it was confirmed I suddenly felt like my head might burst, I was that raging.

'So he turned his back on her, did he?' I says. 'The poor girl. Dropped her cold!'

Master James gazed up at the ceiling, biting at his lower lip, plucking at his cheeks with his fingers, as though he wanted to damage himself.

'No,' he says, after a time. 'That would be convenient, would it not? Then he could be the true villain of the piece.'

'I don't understand, sir.'

'He doesn't know.'

'What?'

'Reverend Pollock doesn't know anything. Nobody told him.'

'He doesn't know . . .?'

'That the girl was expecting a baby when she died. Nora didn't ever tell him about her condition, didn't want to go near him after it happened. I believe she was a little frightened of him. As for him, he thinks he got away with it. Had his way with her and then, oh dear! A few months later, she falls under a train. Boo hoo.' He coughed and looked like he might go into another paroxysm, but then it subsided so he went on. 'And you see, nobody else told him. McGregor-Robertson knows everything because he examined the girls body after it was found and saw that she was carrying a child. But he agreed with me that no purpose would be served in telling Pollock.'

'What about missus?'

'No. I forbid her from speaking to Pollock about it. I didn't want to upset him. I didn't want him to have any regretful associations with this household. I wanted to curry his favour, not make accusations. Besides, what would she have said to him? How could she even have brought it into the conversation?' He paused and sighed. Then he went on. 'Arabella hated me for covering it up. She thought he should be made to face up to what he'd done, to carry some of the guilt. She hated him anyway and hated that she was forced to continue accepting his visits at the house. But of course Pollock was oblivious. He thought that Nora had just died in an accident.'

'But her being hit by the train – it wasn't an accident, sir. Was it?'

He said nothing for a time, just stared into the empty hearth as though it were an abyss. Eventually he spoke. 'She left a note. For my wife. Saying goodbye and telling Arabella not to blame herself.' He lifted his head and looked at me, almost indignantly. 'You see, right to the last, that girl was thinking of others.' He took a long swallow from the bottle.

'Would it be possible to see the note, sir?'

He shook his head. 'I insisted that Arabella destroy it,' he says. 'The general opinion and verdict was that Nora had wandered onto the line by accident. And that's the way it has stayed. The only people who know the truth about what happened are myself, McGregor-Robertson, Arabella – and now you. Had you asked me about all this a few days ago I would have denied every word, and probably dismissed you. I'd have been worried that you might gossip and that the minister might get to hear about it. But now . . .' He gestured around him at the shambles, the whisky bottle. 'It's over. And I don't give two flips about Reverend Pollock. In fact, I would happily take a shovel to him myself.'

We sat there for a moment in silence, master James staring into space, biting at his nails, though there was nothing left to bite and his fingertips were raw and bleeding.

Of a sudden he froze and took his hand away from his mouth. 'What day is it, Bessy?'

'I don't know, sir. It might be Tuesday? Or Wednesday?'

'Ah good,' he says. 'Not Saturday, then. I am to visit Arabella on Saturday. They said that I must not go too often to see her at present, not more than once a week. They are concerned that my presence might upset her.' He said this as though it amused him – although it was perfectly clear that he was distraught. Then he looked at me, hopefully. 'Would you visit her, Bessy? I'll give you money for a carriage. I have plenty of money – here, look.'

He delved into his pockets and began pulling out handfuls of coins. They spilled onto his lap and across the couch. He began gathering them up, holding them out towards me. The coins dropped from between his fingers. Leaning forwards, I began to retrieve them for him. Master James whimpered and when I glanced up, I seen that he had thrown himself on his face onto the sofa.

'Oh, Arabella! What have I done?' he cried. And then he began to sob. His shoulders heaved. I left the coins where they lay and knelt down, reaching out to comfort him by putting a hand on his arm. By the force of his weeping, I thought it might go on for some time.

PART SIX

24

A New Preoccupation

I stayed that night in my old room at Castle Haivers. Master James was in the study when I left him and he was there still when I rose in the morning. He may have got some sleep on the hard little sofa. That is, if he slept at all. I know I didn't get much rest. First thing, I took him a breakfast of porridge, which he washed down with whisky. He seemed a little more cheerful than he had the previous night. He was thinking of selling the estate, he said. Mr Rankin, the neighbour that had come to dinner, had already expressed an interest in buying most of the land in order to sink pits. Master James hadn't decided yet whether to hang on to the house and grounds. He might sell everything and move to town, he says. He was even considering going back to the Law.

'But you are welcome to stay on here, Bessy,' he says. 'Until such time as I do dispose of the land. These things can take months to complete.'

'Thank you, sir. That is kind. But I might head back to Glasgow, try my luck there.'

Or go on somewhere else. Tell the truth, I didn't know what the flip I was going to do. But I knew one thing for certain and that was that I didn't want to stay on at Castle Haivers without missus. Before I did anything, however, I planned to go and see her. There were a few things I wanted to ask – that is if I was able to get any sense out her. Apparently, she had not been very happy at first to find herself in an asylum. Master James and McGregor-Robertson had took her there in a carriage. According to master James, she'd been quite content on the journey, even a little excited, but only because the doctor had lied and tellt her that she was going to visit Nora. However, once they had arrived at the asylum she began to realise that she'd been duped. He and the doctor had to sneak away.

It was upsetting, master James said. It had broke his heart to leave her.

Since then, according to McGregor-Robertsons cousin, the Superintendent, she had suffered from terrible mood swings. Initially, she was distraught and angry and had even attempted to escape over the wall. But just in the last day or so, she had calmed down and begun to seem almost at ease in her new surroundings.

Apparently the asylum was about twenty miles distant. It was a private institution, situated back in the direction of Glasgow but quite a way south of the Great Road, on the outskirts of a village I will call Foulburn, several miles to the southeast of the city. There was no railway station nearby and so master James offered me use of the carriage and when I refused that (since I had no desire to be driven by Biscuit Meek) he repeated his offer to pay for the hire of a coach out the Swan. This I accepted, only because I was still weak and my feet too cut up to walk far. In addition, he promised me a good character should I need one. I only had to write to him, he says, and he would send it by return of post. And he gave me the wages I was owed with ½ as much again, saying that I merited the extra because of my courage and loyalty. He said it would also contribute to my lodgings at Foulburn, since I'd be doing him a favour by going to see his wife at a time when he was not allowed access to her.

He seen me out himself. I believe it was only the 2nd occasion I had walked through that front door. It was still early morning. The dew was running on the slates and the sky was pink. Master James skulked inside the hall in his stocking feet, squinting out at the daylight, while he hugged himself, his cuffs loose and flapping, his waistcoat wrongly buttoned, his hair awry, if anybody looked like they should be in an asylum it was him.

He handed me a letter. 'Be so good as to give that to Arabella. Tell her I'll see her on Saturday. Tell her not to worry.'

I tucked the letter into my bundle, which had been sitting all this time in my room, already packed. 'I will, sir.'

'Goodbye, Bessy,' he says. 'I do hope you will not think too badly of us.'

'No sir, I won't.'

He left off hugging himself for a moment, just long enough to stretch out and take my hand. It was the first time I had ever shook hands with a gent and for some reason it made me blush to my toe nails. Which seems funny now, when you think about what all else I'd done with men in my short life.

'Goodbye, sir,' I says. And then I turned and hobbled all the way down to Snatter, not once looking back.

By mid-morning the sun had burned away the pink clouds, leaving behind a sky that was clear and blue. Only a week ago, we had been in the depths of winter, now it was as hot as a summer day, too warm even to wear my coat which I had took from the newel post. The hired carriage rolled through villages and wherever I looked out the window people were enjoying the sun. Everybody seemed to be on tremendous form. Instead of huddling into their coats and hurrying on their way, people stopped to talk to each other. All the men were in shirtsleeves. I seen a man selling hokey-pokeys from a barrow. I seen a boy with no shirt on at all rolling a hoop right into a bakers shop and the woman at the counter didn't shout at him, she just smiled.

On the Great Road, the going was good enough and the carriage made decent time but once we had turned onto the byways our progress slowed and in the end it took almost two hours to reach Foulburn. The asylum was situated outside the village, off the main road and along a lane that wound upwards and was banked by tall trees. After a few minutes, the carriage drew up at an iron gate between stone gateposts. I pulled down the window and peered out. Beyond the gate I could see yew and fir trees, an area of grass, a short drive and then the main building itself. I got a queer shock when I seen it for I'd been expecting something huge, dark and foreboding like the Glasgow asylum which was visible from the top floor at Mr Levys and a right sombre looking place it was too. But this had the appearance of a private mansion house, more like Castle Haivers, though much larger in scale.

An old man opened the gate and waved us through. He was in shirtsleeves and an old cloth bunnet and looked to me more like a gardener than a warder. I heard the gates clang shut behind us, the clink-clank of a chain as they were locked. The carriage came to a halt in front of the steps. I took the letter master James had gave me from my bundle and slipped it into my pocket. Leaving my bundle on the seat, I stepped down and told the driver to wait and while he trotted off to turn the carriage, I looked up at the building.

It was of red sandstone, two storeys high and with a porch and white colonnades on each side. Wide shallow steps led up to the front entrance. The place had a pleasant enough aspect and I got the impression that the grounds extended much further to the side and back of the house than was at first apparent. I had expected bars at the windows, there were none. The windows were tall and wide, the kind that let in a good deal of light. I had expected to see loonies shuffling about like ghosts and men pulling on their jacks and muttering filth. But there was nobody of that sort, only ½ a dozen men playing cricket on the grass, and about the same number of plain-dressed women watching. I supposed they must be the off-duty warders.

As I stood there taking all this in, a stout woman appeared at the open door of the house and came down the steps to meet me. She wore a dark stuff frock and an apron. I thought she looked like some kind of housekeeper. We exchanged good mornings and I tellt her I was there to see Mrs Arabella Reid, and she said at once, 'Of course' (although why that should have been so evident I don't know) and, 'I am Mrs Robertson. Do follow me.' Turning on her heel, she led me inside the house.

By Jove I had never before seen such a grand place. The hall was about as big as a ballroom with a polished floor and central staircase.

There was several wide doorways off to either side and a smaller door at the back, beyond the stairs, to the kitchens. To my surprise, the stout woman ushered me into a drawing room on the right where a maid was arranging a bowl of daffodils on a table at the far end. I had expected to be taken to some kind of ward and realised that I'd forgot to identify myself. Here I was in my satin frock and it occurred to me that because I'd arrived in a carriage this Mrs Robertson had mistook me for a lady. I hesitated at the threshold wondering what to do. Was it too late to say something? But perhaps the housekeeper had just come in to speak to the maid for she had approached her and was saying a few words in her ear. The maid turned.

And as she did so the heart in me just about leapt across the room for I seen at once that it was not a maid at all but missus! She was smiling, walking towards me. Jesus Murphy! I had not even recognised her. She wore a short navy frock that exposed her ankles, a cream apron, thick stockings and sturdy shoes. Her hair was dressed different and she had a little cap pinned to the back of her head.

'Bessy!' She opened her arms and I stepped into them without a word and nestled against her. 'Look at you!' says missus, stroking my hair. 'Have you been in the wars?'

'No, marm.' I wanted to cry but didn't wish to upset her. I almost felt like we should dance. For the sake of saying something, anything, I asked her, 'Have they made you into a maid or what?'

She stepped back and turned, dipping, from side to side as though to let me admire her image. 'Do you like it?' she says, and laughed. 'I am quite the fashion card am I not? I have another the same, in pink.'

I must have looked shocked for she laughed again and took my hand. 'No, no, Bessy,' she says. 'It is the philosophy here that everyone takes part in the running of the place. This morning I have been downstairs dusting and tidying and arranging flowers. Yesterday I was making beds.' She turned and called to the stout woman who was adjusting the hang of the curtains. 'Mrs Robertson, would it be acceptable to take Bessy for a walk in the gardens?'

The woman glanced over. 'On you go, Mrs Reid,' she says. 'We're finished here in any case. Would your guest like to stay for luncheon?'

Missus looked at me enquiringly. I hesitated, still thinking that I had been mistook for a lady. Everything was a shock. Missus in her new clothes. Walks in the gardens. Luncheon, for flip sake!

'Oh, you must stay!' says missus. And then in an undertone, 'The food is dull but by no means inedible.' She turned back to the stout woman and called out. 'Mrs Robertson, this is Bessy, the dear and faithful maid I was telling you about.'

The woman smiled and looked at me. 'So will you be wanting to stay for luncheon, miss?' she says. Miss, she called me. Even though she knew I was a maid!

Missus squeezed my hand and said my name. I realised I was just standing there like a scone, with my mouth open.

'Oh, yes. Please,' I says.

'Very good, I'll let them know in the kitchen,' says the woman and she turned back to tugging at the curtains, while missus drew me by the hand through the hall and onto the front steps. There, she paused and gazed at me with great affection.

'I knew you would come to see me,' she says. 'I've been waiting for you, Bessy.'

Her eyes were gleaming, brighter than I remembered, the green of them so pure in the sunlight that it was almost startling. Boys oh dear, she was a sight for sore eyes.

And then I remembered the letter. I took it from my pocket and handed it to her. 'From master James.'

Without even looking at it, she put it in her apron. 'Poor James,' she says, and with a sigh, she turned to look at the group on the grass, playing cricket. Her eyes narrowed. After a moment, she says, 'Do you know, Bessy, that this is the most fascinating place I have ever been in my entire life?'

I followed her gaze, wondering what was so fascinating. All I could see was the men with bat and ball and a few groups of women seated on the grass, watching them and occasionally applauding a good catch.

'Are they the warders, marm?' I says.

She turned to look at me. 'Warders?' she says. 'Good gracious no! And in any case we don't call them that. We say "attendants". Mrs Robertson, the lady you just met, is an attendant. Well, she is the chief attendant, the Matron. Those ladies and gentlemen that you see over there' – she turned back to the cricket match – 'are patients.'

And then I noticed that the women were all wearing the same kind of gown as missus, in different colours. So these were patients! Some of them looked quite ordinary. Right enough, one or two were on the thin side and a few others looked quite pale. But for the most part, they looked like you and me.

Missus was smiling. 'Let's take a walk, Bessy,' she says.

We went down the steps and wandered along the drive in the direction of the group on the grass. I was worried that we might go right up amongst them and God forbid have to talk to them but missus steered me past, keeping us at a little distance. A few of the ladies smiled over at her and nodded and she returned their greeting. One or two of the men doffed their hats. We turned off the drive into a rose garden at the side of the house. Missus led me along the shingle paths between the rose bushes, which were pruned and ready for their spring growth. The cricket match was still visible, but the participants were out of earshot.

Now that we were in private, I felt we could talk more freely. 'How are you, marm?' I says. 'Are you being treated all right?'

'Oh yes,' she says. 'I have to tell you Bessy that this place is not at all what I thought it might be at first. I admit that I was rather upset when I realised where James had brought me. I should have known that something was wrong as soon as McGregor-Robertson told me he was taking me to see Nora. Of course I knew that was a trick to get me into the carriage. But I was curious to know what they were up to. So I went along with them. And when we arrived here I was not too suspicious to begin with. Then I was talking to someone, a very nice gentleman who I have now established is McGregor-Robertsons cousin, Doctor Lawrence – he runs the place you know. I was talking to him and when I turned around I noticed that James and McGregor-Robertson had gone. And then I was shown to my room and suddenly I realised what was going on. However, since then I have come to realise that being here for a while might not be such a bad thing.'

We had reached the centre of the rose garden where the path opened out, there was a bench in front of a sundial. Missus took a seat and I joined her. Straight down the path in front of us lay the lawn and the cricket match. This was a sheltered spot. It was getting on for noon. There was a smell of cooking from somewhere and it felt like the temperature had risen yet again, I had never known such a summery day in March.

Missus tilted her head back and closed her eyes, letting the sun warm her face. 'Do you see that man there with the cricket bat?' she says, confidentially and without opening her eyes.

I looked down the path and seen a short stocky gent, clean-shaven, thin-lipped and with limp dark hair. He had clenched his knees together and was swinging the bat smartly to and fro in warlike fashion, while a tall man strolled away from him.

'Yes,' I says.

'He thinks that he is Napoleon Bonaparte,' says missus quietly. She opened her eyes and surveyed the group on the lawn. 'Do you see the man walking away from him?'

'Yes,' I says.

'He thinks that he is the Lord,' says missus. She looked at me, with wide eyes. 'Not the *laird*, mark you. What I mean is, he thinks that he is Jesus Christ our Lord and Saviour. Isn't that remarkable?'

I gazed at the tall man once again. He looked an ordinary enough cove to me, if a bit on the stringy side. I had barely enough time to think about it before missus had addressed me again, out the corner of her mouth.

'That lady over there,' she says. 'I have no wish to point but she is in a grey dress, seated in a group of four ladies, under the Scots Pine tree.'

'Oh yes,' I says.

'She believes that there are little people living on her shoulders. Yesterday afternoon, somebody bumped into her by accident. You've never seen such a fuss. All the little people were knocked to the floor, don't you know. We had to help her pick them up! Of course there was nothing there. But we humoured the poor dear. We put them back on her shoulders. She was in tears. Those are the most interesting patients, Bessy, those who believe outlandish things. Most of them, bless them, are just rather melancholy or have strange fears of things that are not at all frightening, like corners for example. There is one man who is afraid of corners.'

I looked at missus. She seemed excited, almost thrilled. Careful to keep my voice conversational, I says, 'And have you seen Nora since you got here?'

'Oh no,' she says. 'Nora is gone.'

She glanced over her shoulder to make sure that there was nobody close at hand. The old man that had opened the gate was clipping a hedge at the far end of the rose garden, but he was too far away to overhear us.

'That is what I wanted to talk to you about,' says missus. She clutched my hands. 'I am so glad you've come, Bessy! You see, Nora and I – well, you know that we planned to get rid of Mrs Gilfillan and her henchman, so that Nora could be free?'

Not knowing what else to do, I nodded.

Missus shook her head and rolled her eyes. 'There are some strange things that I have to tell you, Bessy,' she says. 'First of all, you should know that I met with the woman herself. Believe it or not, I met Gilfillan! I knew her right away, as soon as I saw her. It was quite a stroke of luck. I had been looking for her everywhere – even though it was difficult to achieve as I myself had certain reasons to keep out of sight. I happened to have found my way to the Station road and was in a garden there, peering out from behind a hedge to see if the coast was clear when all at once there she was, just up the road, emerging from the Railway Tavern! The very same person that I had seen lurking at Castle Haivers, the one who had been watching us all that time. It was her, to the life!'

I felt sick with dread, ½ desperate to know what missus might say next and ½ horrified of what she might reveal.

'What happened?' I says.

'Well,' says missus. 'I could not let this opportunity pass me by. And so I stepped out of the hedge and hurried after her. She had disappeared around the side of the Tavern and I caught up with her just as she stepped out from behind a stack of barrels. I promptly introduced myself and engaged her in some light conversation, about the terrible weather. She seemed suspicious of me at first but after we had spoken for a few moments she appeared to let down her guard somewhat. I asked her to accompany me, saying that I had something of interest to show her. And as we walked we had a very interesting conversation. We did not go far, only to the bridge – where I drew her attention to the low wall there. I don't want to say too much about it. But let's just say that with the application of a little pressure, I persuaded her to reconsider her position.'

She gave me a mysterious smile. I thought of my mothers severed body, lying beside the railway tracks, not ½ a mile from the bridge. It was true then. What I had suspected was true!

Missus squeezed my hands. 'But Bessy, you must know, the most incredible thing about it, I still have to tell you. You won't believe it.'

'What?' I says faintly.

'You see, it wasn't *Nora* that the woman wanted after all.'

'No?'

Missus shook her head. 'No, dear,' she says. 'It was you! She was going to take *you* to Glasgow. Why – she pretended not to have heard of Nora! But when I mentioned your name, and said what a wonderful maid you had proved to be, she became very animated. And then we had a disagreement. Horrible woman! She really was a monster! And then – well, I have said enough. I persuaded her to leave you alone. Just rest assured, dear, she won't be bothering you. You are quite safe now.'

She stroked my cheek and looked into my eyes. 'Dear Bessy,' she says. 'What are you thinking of?'

I shook my head, blinking away my tears. 'Nothing, marm,' I says. 'Nothing.'

She smiled. 'Do you know, dear, I have come to a conclusion about you. And Nora agrees with me. I consulted her and she told me that I was quite right.'

'What – what conclusion is that, marm?'

'That you really are the most loyal, courageous and true friend a person could ever wish for. I am blessed to have found you.'

And with that, she turned back to watch the cricket match. There was a pause in play. Napoleon was berating another member of his team. Meanwhile, Jesus performed a cartwheel and was applauded by the ladies. They all looked blurry to me.

After a while, missus spoke again. 'This place is most intriguing, don't you think?' she says. 'I have spoken to Doctor Lawrence about it and he agrees with me. I don't know how long I am going to be here, Bessy, but while I am, I intend to make good use of the time. All that work I did on servants and obedience! Now that I am out in the world, I see that there are far more interesting subjects. The lunatic! What could be more pertinent than that for our age? It is my new preoccupation. They have given me pen and paper. I am not making a public announcement about it at this stage. But just between you and me, I have begun to write another book.'

She turned to me. 'You shall have to help me think of a title,' she says. 'What was it you called my other book?'

'*The Observations*, marm.'

She sat back with a smile. 'That's right,' she says. '*The Observations*. Well, if you don't mind me saying, Bessy, it's not a very good title is it? No, we shall have to think of something better this time.'

*

I was going to start a fresh chapter, telling all about what has happened since then. But I don't like goodbyes and from hereon in, it is only goodbye that I would be saying. So I will keep it short and sweet.

It had been my intention to stay in Foulburn for a while, so that I could visit missus more than once. That afternoon, I took a lodging at the village inn and later I went back to the asylum for tea. It was quite strange to see how properly everything was run, with all the patients four to a table and the lady patients doling out scones and slices of bread and butter. I even met Jesus and Napoleon. Jesus was all right but Napoleon was frosty-faced. And the man who had a fear of corners kept cringing at all the little triangles of bread.

In the evening, I returned to my lodging and it was upon undoing my bundle to unpack that I came across *The Observations*, wrapped up in my clothes. I had forgot all about putting them in there, it seemed like a lifetime ago. I wondered whether Dr Lawrence would have any objection to me returning the book to missus. It didn't look or smell too pretty, now it was burned. I flipped open the cover and seen that the scorching had reached inside. The corner of the black and white label EX~BIBLIOTHEC~CASTEL~HAIVERS had burned away and the lady and her maid had lost their slippered feet.

And then I noticed that something was poking out from behind the label. Another sheet of paper. I drew it out and seen that it was not one piece but a few pages, folded together. A note. I opened it up and recognised at once the neat copperplate hand as belonging to Nora. One edge of all the sheets were uneven, as if they had been cut. Here, at last, were the missing pages.

In fact, it was the letter that Nora had wrote to missus, the one master James had tellt missus to destroy. Nora must have cut the pages out her journal herself, lacking notepaper. And missus had disobeyed her husband and hid them under the label in her book.

It was a private letter so I will not quote from it here at any length. Suffice to say, its main purpose was to exempt missus from all blame. In the final paragraph, Nora wrote,

My dear lady, I know how difficult it was for you to dismiss me but I also know that it was not really your doing. Please do not despair! We had the best of times together, did we not? My life from now on would not be worth living, given what has happened. Only misery awaits me were I to go on. I am sorry to put you through this but do not be sad. Pray for me instead, for who is there to do so but your own sweet self? Be happy for me. I am setting out on a grand new adventure. Fear not, you and I shall meet again one day.

I pray the Lord my soul to take. Amen

That Nora was a bit Holy, it has to be said.

But in the end, I think I might have got to like her. She was more similar to myself than I had ever cared to admit. And dear missus! I hated to think of the grief and dread that must have overcame her when she came across this note. So help me God, she may not always have been in command of her wits but one thing was for sure, she did care about us. All us girls blown like chaff across the water. We settle here, we settle there. We pass through. And when we quit this earth for good we leave little or no trace, nothing to say where we have been. But missus had hung onto that last note from Nora and she'd made sure she had a headstone. Above all, she had kept us in her heart.

I folded up the pages and slid them back underneath the label. It was a provoking thing that note, that book. I worried that it could be too upsetting for missus. I didn't know whether it would be better to give it to her or not. And so I decided that before I left Foulburn, I would hand *The Observations* over to Doctor Lawrence, so that he could be the one to decide what should be done with them.

The following morning, I happened to be on my way up to visit missus when I passed the shop in Foulburn. It was one of those places where they kept notices in the window and I saw one that was headed up 'URGENT, Kitchen Maid Wanted'. Of course, it attracted my attention since at the time it was on my mind that I would have to get on me and find work sooner or later. When I looked closer, however, I was even more intrigued to see that the position to be filled was at none other establishment than the asylum! Now here was a turn up for the books! Over the next few days, I gave the matter some private consideration and then I raised it with missus. How would she feel about me taking such a post? Well, she could think of no better idea! For then we could see each other every day, for as long as she was there. I was worried that being acquainted with one of the patients might go against me, but as it turned out that didn't matter at all. Mrs Robertson was the person to be applied to and she practically got on her knees and begged me to take the job. I soon realised that – pleasant though conditions were at the asylum – it is difficult to find staff to work in such places. Nobody likes the thought of loonies. But to be honest I have found great solace in it and satisfaction, and a fair few laughs as well.

I began that very week in the kitchens and within a few months was promoted to attendant, which post I have now fulfilled for over three years. It was Doctor Lawrence himself that did ask me to write this history of missus and how we met and all that, for he thought it would be an interesting and useful document for him and his colleagues to read since they are still intrigued by her case. I began writing the first chapter not long after I came here but my hours of leisure are scarce and it has took me all these years to reach the end. I do believe my style may have improved as the months went by but I am aware that there are still some mistakes for unless I keep my wits about me I tend to write as I speak.

Missus has been here all this time, and with every day that passes, is more fascinated by her fellow patients. Always she is watching, watching, watching them and asking questions of them, just as she used to of me when I was her servant and she was writing her *Observations*. Now, her great work is on the subject of insanity. I asked her last week when it would be finished. She just looked at me and says, 'Bessy it is barely begun.'

As for *The Observations*. Well I should say that the manuscript is in my possession and a very good read it is too. I have been trying for some while to find a suitable publisher. No success as yet but it can only be a matter of time as there has already over the past few years been a good deal of interest. Indeed, with the exception of some early refusals *The Observations* has met with tremendous approval everywhere it has been sent.

For instance, upon receipt of my introductory letter, Mr R— of the eminent publishing house William R— and Sons did ask *immediately* to see the book and the very next week – although he had decided that the content was 'not quite' to his taste – he did not hesitate to suggest that it be sent elsewhere – and does this prompt and helpful response not surely prove that the work has merit? Beyond a shadow of a doubt it does.

Very encouraged, I sent it off to Mr W— of Harold W— and Co. Now here was a different response. This Mr W kept the manuscript for so long that I eventually became convinced that he intended to steal it and sneak it out to great acclaim under a different title without telling me. But in the end, after many months and several letters requesting a response, he returned the work saying that although it was 'quite well done' his firm wouldn't be publishing any books that year which seemed to me a strange way to run a business and I wrote and told him as much. Since his lack of enthusiasm was due only to his companys peculiarities (and in the end, they must have took my advice because to my certain knowledge they did in fact bring out several books in that year!), I was not daunted in the least and sent the manuscript off forthwith to Mr G of G—, B— and T—.

After a brief interval he wrote back, *absolutely delighted*, saying that he had never come across anything quite like it. This was a surprise to me as I had already sent him the manuscript the previous year under its original title 'Observations of the Habits and Nature of the Domestic Class in My Time' by 'A Lady' but on that occasion he had returned it, unread, with a brief, one-word note which said simply 'Never'.

However, he must have liked the new title because this time he sent a very conversational and friendly letter in which he complimented the manuscripts 'satirical' style and begged to know the true identity of 'the mysterious Arabella R'. Apparently it is rare to encounter such an original and refreshing book in a business that is full of, as he put it 'nothing but corner boys and sharks'. As a for instance Mr G went on to complain at length about the man he had just had lunch with, another publisher who, it seemed, was a terrible fellow that had, in the past, stole one of Mr Gs books. Mr G was very bitter about it and he became quite abusive at points in his recriminations to this man. However, towards the end of the letter, about the 9th page, he seemed to regain something of his former good humour. He apologised for the stain (where some fool in his office had knocked over a glass of wine) and invited me to take lunch with him, saying that he was curious to know the full story behind this 'highly entertaining' manuscript and calling me a 'capital fellow'. To be perfectly honest, some aspects of his response gave me the impression that he had perhaps not read the manuscript all the way through. For one thing, I think he had confused me with Arabella and misunderstood her book altogether, that was two things. Not only that (here's a third), he seemed to think that we were a man, *pretending* to be a woman!

I replied immediately, assuring him that *The Observations* was an important work of research written in all seriousness, *and* by a lady, and that I would be delighted to meet him and discuss its publication. However, he seems to have took offence at something I said because I have heard nothing from him since. Perhaps he does no longer be working at G—, B— and T—s. (He did mention some jealousies among colleagues that had put him in mind to hand in his resignation.)

These then are but a few examples of how well *The Observations* has been received and if the response so far is anything to go by then ½ the country wants to see this manuscript and publish it! But be advised once again that prior application must be made to myself and I will see what I can do.

*

What other news? Master James did visit missus quite a lot to begin with in those early months but as time went on, he appeared less and less and for the past year he has come not at all. As far as I know, he now lives in Manchester and is a Bigwig at the courts there.

I still have Mr Levys last act in my possession. Unfortunately it did dry out over time and last year it met with a small accident and is now only a pinch of dust in the velvet bag. But I am keeping it nonetheless, to remind me of that dear man.

Talking of constipation, it seems Davy Flemyng is 'blocked', leastwise there is no sign yet of his Masterwork and I do believe he has moved to Corstorphine in search of his Muse.

And what else? Well now it may interest you to know that Reverend Pollock was a passenger on the ill-fated SS *London* bound for Australia when that ship foundered in the Bay of Biscay in the year '66. He was one of those many souls that perished, a horrible death by all accounts, sucked beneath the waves they were, whilst singing 'Rock of Ages'. The Bay of Biscay is north of Spain. Which reminds me, I have always imagined Spain to be a wonderful country, though I have never visited there of course.

Three cheers for Spain!

And three cheers for missus!

She is very popular here and still pretty as a rose. We have a lot of country dances at the asylum and she is never lacking a partner. Dancing and exercise and association are great cures for all ails, that is what Doctor Lawrence says and I have to agree with him for I believe that missus is happier here than she ever was at Castle Haivers.

Gentlemen, please forgive the many shortcomings of this document. In the main, I mean, where I describe too much of my own part in things. Also please excuse where I have wrote down oaths and their approximations, and where I have described squalid or unpleasant matters. It is only because I was asked to relay the story 'warts and all'. I have been assured that no matter what I reveal here, no action will be taken against any person as a result and I trust in Doctor

Lawrence to fulfil that promise. He has shown me the locked cupboard where the manuscript is to be kept. He is a good and honest man and only wishes to examine the case of missus, in the hope of being more help to her.

But here we go now. It is high time I put the boots on all this. I am not sure what there is to be learned from these pages, except perhaps that happiness can be found in the strangest of places, even amongst those poor souls whose minds have become, for whatever reason, unhinged. Now that I am finished, Doctor Lawrence wants to know what I think of what I have wrote. All I can say is that it will be strange to be no longer doing it. I may have to think of another story to write to fill up those few hours between completing work and laying my head upon the pillow. But this time, instead of just recounting what has happened, it will have to be a story that I make up out my own head, because more or less all that I have ever known or done or seen or heard or felt in my life has been included in this account. And there is nothing more left over to tell.

So there you go. Farewell. *Au revoir*. Or, as they say where I come from, safe home.

Acknowledgements

Thanks to Noeleen Collins, Sheila Dundee, Kate and George Mulvagh, Lucy Mulvagh, and Tom Shankland. Thanks to Anna Andresen and Ali Reid. Thanks to Vivien Green, Stephen Mulrine and Rose Tremain.

I am also indebted to Hannah Griffiths and all at Faber and Faber, Emma Parry, Jon Riley, Molly Stern, Euan Thorneycroft, Jonny Geller and all at Curtis Brown.

Of research materials the following indispensable publications deserve mention: *The Diaries of Hannah Cullwick, Victorian Maidservant*, ed. Liz Stanley, Virago, 1984. *Farm Servants and Labour in Lowland Scotland 1770–1914*, ed. T. M. Devine, John Donald Publishers Ltd, 1984. *Shadow's Midnight Scenes and Social Photographs, Glasgow 1858*, republished UGP, 1976. *Some Observations of the Change of Manners in My Own Time, 1700–1790*, by Elizabeth Mure, published in *Scottish Diaries and Memoirs*, ed. J. G. Fyfe, Stirling, 1942. *Armadale Past and Present*, by R. Hyde-Brown, F. Johnstone and Co., 1906. *Slanguage*, by Bernard Share, Gill and Macmillan Ltd, 2003.